THE

Italians

LUCA, MARCO & ALESSANDRO

THE

Italians

COLLECTION

August 2015

September 2015

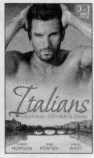
October 2015

November 2015

December 2015

January 2016

THE
Italians

Luca, Marco & Alessandro

NATALIE ANDERSON
KATHERINE GARBERA
AMY ANDREWS

Published in Great Britain 2015
by Mills & Boon, an imprint of Harlequin (UK) Limited,
Eton House, 18-24 Paradise Road, Richmond, Surrey, TW9 1SR

THE ITALIANS: LUCA, MARCO & ALESSANDRO
© 2015 Harlequin Books S.A.

Between the Italian's Sheets © 2009 Natalie Anderson
The Moretti Heir © 2009 Katherine Garbera
Alessandro and the Cheery Nanny © 2010 Amy Andrews

ISBN: 978-0-263-91572-3

026-1115

Harlequin (UK) Limited's policy is to use papers that are natural, renewable and recyclable products and made from wood grown in sustainable forests. The logging and manufacturing processes conform to the legal environmental regulations of the country of origin.

Printed and bound in Spain
by CPI, Barcelona

BETWEEN THE ITALIAN'S SHEETS

NATALIE ANDERSON

For Rosie and Simon.
You two have the most incredible generosity, kindness and sheer zest for life. Our holiday in London at Casa King-Currie was amazing—every moment fun and relaxing and memorable. Luca and Emily's story would never have come out into the light if it hadn't been for the break you enabled us to have, and for that I really, really thank you.

Natalie Anderson adores a happy ending, which is why she always reads the back of a book first. Just to be sure. So you can be sure you've got a happy ending in your hands right now—because she promises nothing less. Along with happy endings, she loves peppermint-filled dark chocolate, pineapple juice and extremely long showers. Not to mention spending hours teasing her imaginary friends with dating dilemmas. She tends to torment them before eventually relenting and offering—you guessed it—a happy ending. She lives in Christchurch, New Zealand, with her gorgeous husband and four fabulous children.

If, like her, you love a happy ending, be sure to come and say hi on Facebook, www.facebook.com/authornataliea, and on Twitter, @authornataliea or her website/blog, www.natalie-anderson.com.

CHAPTER ONE

ARROGANCE personified. Emily stared at him, her temper going from sizzling to spitting hot. He stood right in front of her, with the height of a basketball star, and shoulders the breadth of a rugby prop. A man mountain, a mighty example of the male in physical prime. Totally obscuring her view. Totally commanding attention.

Typical.

Worse than that, he had one of those fancy phone gadgets that did everything—not merely phone calls, but music, web connection, camera—the works. And every time he pushed the buttons they beeped. Loudly. The overture was about to begin, Emily found the rapid succession of beeps incredibly annoying.

Pointedly, she cleared her throat.

She had not spent the last year working crazy hours, scrimping and saving every last cent to get her sister and herself all the way to Italy and to this fabulous opera only for the moment to be ruined by some selfish jerk who thought his social life was more important than the live performance about to unfold. More important than showing some respect to the other people there who wanted to appreciate the evening.

She cleared her throat again.

Fractionally he turned, threw a quick glance her way, but the beeping didn't stop. Rather it was the cacophony of trills and fragments of well-known phrases that ceased as under the direction of the lead violinist the orchestra stilled. Then came the lone note from the oboe to which the other instruments would tune. But did that stop him? No. The purity of the sound was shattered by the relentless beeping.

Any minute now the conductor would walk out and applause would greet him. Beeps didn't constitute applause. Beeps were annoying. And she couldn't *see* through him.

She glared at his back now as well as clearing her throat once more. A tailored jacket hung from those doorframe-wide shoulders, one hand on his hip pulling the jacket back, emphasising the narrowing of his torso to a slim waist and hips. She knew there were serious muscles under the white shirt and dark trousers. She'd watched as he'd walked up from the super-expensive seats. He was hard not to notice, taller than almost all the people there. From the front she'd seen the way his shirt neatly tucked into his trousers with not an ounce of anything unnecessary—like fat—rippling the smooth, straight stretch of white cotton. Well dressed, good-looking, so sophisticated and cool in this hot and crowded space. She figured he'd come up so as not to disturb those in his own elite strata—no, he'd conduct his business and bother the plebs up in the cheap seats.

One of the waiters came past, singing his way through the crowd for one final time before he'd quieten for the spectacle, tormenting her with his cry.

'Bebite! Acqua! Cola! Vino bianca! Vino rosso! Bebite...'

She'd go for all those drinks right now. She was hot. She was thirsty. She was irritated.

This time she coughed.

Where on earth was Kate? What was taking her so long? Only her little sister could need the bathroom right as the opera was about to start. And as far as Emily could tell, the toilets in the ancient arena were few and far between and had queues centuries long. Meanwhile her mouth was dry and she wanted the six-foot-plus pillar blocking her view of centre stage to move. And then he did, turning right round as he held the gadget up in front of him. The flash of his grin was more blinding than the sudden flash of bright light.

'What—' she asked tartly '—you're taking photos now?'

'Sì.' He nodded, smiling like the Cheshire cat. 'I need a new wallpaper photo for my phone. And this is such a spectacular view, don't you think?'

'I think the "view" is *behind* you. You know, the stage, the set, the orchestra.'

'Oh, no, you're wrong. The beauty of the night is right in front of me.' As he put the phone thing in his pocket he held her gaze with a long, lazy, unmistakably challenging stare that she felt from the top of her head to her fingertips and all the way to her toes. And in all the secret spaces in between she burned. Spitting hot became unbearable— she was melting, literally melting at his feet. And stupidly she wished she were wearing something a little more glam than her cheap cotton skirt and tee combo. Why couldn't she have a gorgeous black gown, some serious bling and ice-queen sophistication to set it off?

She choked for real then—half giggling, half spluttering on a speck of something in her throat.

Eyes watering, she heard his call to the passing waiter. He spoke rapidly in Italian. She didn't catch a word of it. Only glimpsed the smile pass between the two men and then the money. He took the step separating where he stood and she sat, and handed her the bottle of water he'd just bought.

'For your throat.' Dry amusement was all obvious and all aggravating. 'Please.' He held the bottle a little closer, right in her face, and she knew he wasn't going to remove it.

What could she do? Act the totally irritated diva? She couldn't, not when the opera hadn't actually started, and he'd put the phone away and was suddenly smiling. It was some smile.

'Thank you,' she said, mentally blaming the breathiness of her reply on the awkward angle of her neck as she craned it right back to look at him.

He sat in the gap next to her. 'You're looking forward to the opera?'

'Yes.' Where was Kate? Where was the conductor? But time was playing tricks and the tiniest of moments became eons.

He nodded. 'It is a good one. They perform it every year here.'

'I know.' She'd read it in the tourist books she'd devoured from the library. Right now her eyes were devouring something else. Up close he wasn't just good-looking, he was incredible-looking. While his physical presence had been noticeable from a distance, nearer it was his expression that arrested her attention.

He was tall, he was dark, he was handsome. So far, so cliché. Like almost every man she'd seen in this city he was immaculately groomed. But there was so much more. There was the strong, angled jaw and the faint shadow of stubble. And in the heart of that was his mouth—wide and full—contrasting with the steep planes of his cheekbones. That mouth raised questions that Emily wanted to answer—was it as smooth as it looked? Warm or cool? It was certainly infinitely touchable. Utterly inviting.

Vying for first place with his lips were his eyes. Deep chocolate-brown, they were set off by the requisite thick, long lashes. But the chocolate didn't have the dull, matte quality of a solid block. It was warm and glossy and liquid, the dark variety—there was no diluting milky sweetness. And at the very centre there was a hardness—a 'don't go there' dangerous quality that totally aroused the curiosity of Pandora in Emily. It was like the bitterness at the bottom of a strong coffee or the darkest of dark chocolate that her taste buds both desired and recoiled from.

'Aren't you going to have your drink?' He didn't seem fazed by her scrutiny, instead seemed quite content to sit and study her right back. Closely.

She remembered the bottle and marvelled that steam wasn't rising from it. Surely the water should be boiling from the red-hot elements that were her hands?

'I think you should,' he spoke easily. 'You seem thirsty.'

That smile had broken the arrogant set to his features once more. A wide, sensual slash, his lips were surprisingly soft-looking, and framed white, straight, strong teeth. Oh, he had it all, didn't he? The height and body of a champion athlete, and the full features of a sensuous lover.

He glanced at the cheap cloth bag beside her, so obviously empty. 'You have no picnic? No lover to share the music and the magic of the night with you?' He gestured around them where many in the audience were snacking on treats stored in small baskets. Most were paired off, couples sitting close, the scent of romance heavy in the atmosphere.

'I'm here with my sister. She's just gone to get something.' Emily's defence mounted.

'Ah, your sister.' He nodded, tone cryptic.

For want of something, anything to stop her staring at him, she flipped the lid on the water bottle.

'Where are you from?'

It was obvious to him that she was foreign. He'd spoken in English to her from the off. She figured it was the travel garb, the ancient clothes that had left that budget chain store many seasons ago and hadn't ever seen an iron. She was no fabulous Italian fashionista.

'New Zealand.' She tossed her head, scraping for some pride.

A hint of surprise lifted his expression. 'You've come a long way. No wonder you're looking forward to the music.'

'Yes. I've wanted to come here for years.' It had been her fantasy escape. Now she wanted to know if Italy was as warm and flavoursome a country as she'd always imagined. The opera had been the way to convince Kate to stop here en route to London.

If Emily had both the choice and the money, she'd travel on to Venice, Florence, Rome…everywhere. Countless times she'd watched every Italian movie they had at the DVD store where she'd worked. She even had a few phrases to try out on friendly looking faces. She looked down at the stage, where the lights were gleaming and the orchestra was now waiting quietly. It was the realisation of a dream.

Her irritation melted away and she drank from the water bottle—a long, deep swig that ended with an unstoppable sigh of satisfaction.

Light, cool, strong fingers took her chin, and he turned her face back towards his. Stunned, she let him, silently absorbing the intensity of his expression, feeling it draw her even closer to him. And then it was only his index finger touching her, carefully sliding with gentle but firm pressure along her lower lip, rubbing the droplets of water into her dry lips.

'*Very* thirsty,' he said softly.

As his fingers caressed sensations surged within her— the sparks of bliss in her nerve endings, the devilish desire to flick out her tongue and taste him.

The audience of thousands was silent with expectation but it was nothing compared to the anticipation enthralling her. She didn't want him to break the delightful contact. Rather the wish for more rocketed. This was crazy. She couldn't want a complete stranger to kiss her, could she? To touch his lips to the spot where his finger now stroked?

But yes. Emily, who had never been one for flings, let

alone one-night stands, was almost overcome by the urge to lie back and let him do as he pleased—right here, right now, in an amphitheatre filled to capacity. The water bottle slid from her weak grasp to the stone seat beside her as she mumbled, 'You realise it's about to start?'

His gaze lowered, lids almost closing right over his eyes, hiding the sharpening gleam in the even darker chocolate. 'What makes you think it hasn't started already?'

Oh, my. His fingers left her mouth but brushed her thigh as he picked up the small candle that she'd completely forgotten. Instinctively every deep internal muscle within her tensed, wanted to squirm. The onward rush of sensation was heady and new and delightful. His eyes flipped back to hers, and she knew he was aware of the waves that were crashing over her, drowning her in unaccustomed, unexpected desire.

'Let's light this, *sì*?' He pulled a lighter from his pocket. There was a metallic click and the flicker sent a warm glow into his face. She couldn't look away—she was fascinated by the tension in his jaw, the firm curve of his mouth, the brilliance in his dark eyes. Inside and out, she adored his searing attention.

Luca made himself break free of her mesmerising stare and concentrated stupidly hard on lighting the candle. But when he held it out for her she didn't move and he just had to look close again. Like a statue she sat, still gazing at him with those sky-wide, sea-green eyes. He couldn't help grinning as he transferred the candle to his other hand, using his nearest to capture hers. God, she was gorgeous.

Honey-coloured hair and a softly curved figure in a pale green tee that brought out the depths in those eyes. He'd noticed her on his way up to get better reception for his phone and then he'd been entertained by her less than subtle methods of showing her displeasure at where he was standing. He'd strung out sending his text just to feel her reaction. And then he'd had to capture it—the sultry glare, the long legs bent beneath her.

Irresistible.

He felt her quiver, tightened his own fingers instinctively, and made her take the burning candle. For a nanosecond that felt like for ever, they held the flame together, his fist encompassing hers. He liked the feel of her in his hand. He'd like to feel more of her in his hand.

'You should have a lover to sit with at the opera.' If it were him he'd slide his arm around her and pull her in snug against his chest.

'So should you.' Her gaze was direct.

'True. Unfortunately I have other guests to entertain.' Helplessly he shrugged. 'But in a parallel universe I'd be here with you.'

'A total stranger?' Coy mockery flavoured her tone and her glance.

'We wouldn't be strangers for long.'

The green in her eyes deepened again and her mouth parted with the faintest of gasps. Yes, he did mean exactly that—they would be close and physical and fulfilled. And, yes, it was crazy. Since when did he sit holding the hand of a strange woman and fantasise about holding her in his arms? Since when did he think he could ever be fulfilled?

Not like that—not by connecting with another person. People—*relationships*—were beyond him. It was only from work that he sought satisfaction now.

Her colour steadily rose but still she held his gaze. 'What a shame there's no such thing as parallel universes.'

'Yes.' This fantasy was the strongest temptation—and he searched for a way to sustain it, just for a moment more. 'But there's always tomorrow.'

She smiled at that. 'Tomorrow.'

The burst of applause was deafening. He blinked and the bubble was burst. A quick glance down showed the conductor at the podium, his baton raised. He'd better get back to his seat—he did have guests to entertain. Damn. But he sent her a smile as he let go of her hand and stood. *'Ciao, bella.'*

CHAPTER TWO

EMILY spent the next moment of eternity trying to remember how to breathe. Then she shook her head and laughed weakly—puffing away the lingering intensity with a self-prescribed dose of sarcasm. What a flirt. He'd transformed her heat of anger into the heat of attraction, totally overcoming her annoyance and leaving her practically panting.

She watched as he descended the steps and re-entered the exclusive zone. He didn't look back. He'd already forgotten her. He must do it all the time—gaze at an unsuspecting female with his deep brown, dangerous eyes; lay a single finger on her person—of course she'd say yes in a heartbeat. No wonder he wore that mantle of lazy arrogance. He was the kind of guy for whom everything came easy—especially women.

But the surprising fact was, Emily would quite happily have been one of his women.

Irresistible.

As the opening chords of the overture began Kate flung into the cavernous space beside her.

'Great, you got some water,' she said, picking the bottle

up from beside Emily and half draining it. 'Just in time for the show.'

Emily pressed her finger on her needy lips—retracing the path his had taken. As far as she was concerned, the main event was already over.

But the Arena di Verona did not disappoint. Over two hours later as the applause thundered and cries of *encore* and *bravo* rang out, pleasure and relief rippled through Emily. It had been *so* worth it. The warmth, the atmosphere, the music, the spectacle—everything had been as wonderful as she could have wished. Well, almost everything. Somehow that fleeting encounter with a gorgeous stranger had made her miss something she hadn't had time to want until now—touch, pleasure, a sense of her own desirability. It had been a long time coming. She'd been too busy to date, and the one attempt at a boyfriend really hadn't been worth it. But suddenly, with one touch from him, that closed door to the sensual part of herself had been swung wide open. And now she was left wondering, wanting to walk through it.

She and Kate moved among the mass of bubbling, happy people, finding their way out of the amphitheatre and into the piazza where the crowd spilled and milled. Emily didn't want the night to end. She lingered, still feeling the vibrations from the sound of orchestra and voice, but most of all still feeling the touch of a finger on her lips…wanting *more*.

'Did you think the soprano was a bit off in that last duet?'

Emily knew Kate was about to dissect the performance note by note, but honestly she hadn't been listening too close in that one. She'd hadn't been able to stop her gaze from travelling down to a certain spot in the rich seats where a dark head was slightly elevated above the others. The music had become the soundtrack to the kind of fantasy that she didn't usually have time to indulge in.

'Umm, which bit?' Warmth pervaded her entire body and she smiled, reliving the secret pleasure of that chance meeting. Then she glanced at her sister, saw her mouth open and the deep breath. Her smile disappeared altogether as Kate launched full tilt into the final refrain of the biggest 'hit' of the night.

'Kate!' Emily whispered—mentally screaming. How embarrassing. But her sister just threw her a naughty glance and kept on going. As people turned to look a moat of space appeared around them and Emily longed for a lifeboat to take her back into the crowd. She scanned it, discomfort prickling as more and more turned their way. Then she saw the group of well-dressed men. He stood in the centre, half a head taller. Striking, and staring right in their direction. There was a woman there too. Of course there was. Standing right beside him—beautiful and elegant, obviously an Italian fashionista and obviously interested in him. A lover to sit with at the opera?

A stupidly strong sense of loss washed through her. They'd only shared a few words on the steps, but it had felt as if a myriad of possibilities had been unveiled. But she wasn't anything like the woman he was with, so there was no 'possibility' after all, and her disappointment was bitter.

The second Kate paused for breath Emily grasped her arm, propelling her forwards. 'Are you done?'

'No.' Kate threw a smile in the direction of anyone still looking their way and fell into step. 'I've had a great idea.'

Emily didn't want to listen. Emily just wanted to get away. But, unlike him, Emily had to look back. She turned her head over her shoulder for one final glimpse. He was staring right at her, smile curling upwards, and as she met his gaze he winked. She didn't smile, but she kept looking, needing to capture his image in her mind for one final moment before turning away.

They rounded the corner into one of the busy side streets and Kate lurched to a halt. 'I am not just having bread for the next two days. We're in Italy. I want pasta, I want pizza. I want a restaurant.'

'Kate.' Emily was close to exasperation point. Why couldn't she understand that they just didn't have the funds for that?

'I'm going to get us some more money.'

'How?'

'Busking.'

'Kate.' Emily's heart sank. She knew what her sister was like—the attention she'd got would only have whetted her appetite.

'Come on, Em, you saw the crowd that gathered just then. Three songs and we'll have enough for the most fabulous meal tomorrow—one of those long, lazy lunches at one of those tables outside, with millions of courses and lots of wine.'

Admittedly Emily's mouth was watering at the idea but she tried to ignore it. 'You're probably supposed to have permits to perform.'

Kate yawned big and fake. 'Rules, Em?'

'One of us has to be responsible.' And she always had been—as a matter of necessity. She'd had sole responsibility for the two of them for years. Mother, father, sister, friend, breadwinner, cook, cleaner, chauffeur—all rolled into one.

'It's a shame there's no piano for you to accompany me. Unless you want to do that duet?'

'Not on your life.' Kate could have the limelight. Emily was happy to accompany but centre stage was too bright for her.

'I'll only be ten minutes. No one will mind.'

Emily sighed and stepped to the side, watching as Kate shook out her hair from under her straw hat. Her sister was impetuous, impulsive and impossible to say no to and, as she'd predicted, she had a crowd around her within minutes. Emily wasn't surprised. With her long red locks and slender figure, Kate turned heads even before she opened her mouth. And when she started singing? The angelic, pure tones made anything with ears stop and listen. As the crowd of people thickened Kate flung her a triumphant glance and truly got into her stride. Emily stood to the side and looked around, anxiously keeping an eye for sight of a *carabiniere*, not wanting to get into trouble.

'Your sister is talented.'

She jumped. He was right behind her. She turned a fraction, and yes, really, he was there—looming large. Her body went hypersensitive. Her brain threatened to shut down altogether. 'Yes.'

'And so are you.'

Umm, how did he figure that? She shook her head. 'Not quite in the same way.'

'No,' he agreed before his voice dropped, the alien lilt becoming more audible. 'Your sister is still a child. Whereas you, I think, have the talents of a woman.'

Emily drew a sharp breath and turned to face him full on. 'You've got to be kidding.'

'No.' His dark eyes held hers, amused and challenging. 'You send me a look like that over your shoulder? What choice did I have but to follow?'

The gauntlet had been thrown. Silver fire raced through her veins. She had the talents of a woman? If only she did—why, then she'd have him on his knees before her, with all his arrogance and experience rendered useless. Wanting her beyond reason and willing to grant her anything—the crazy idea sent a thrill through her. Since when was she any kind of sex goddess? When was it that she'd last *had* sex?

She forgot about Kate warbling in the background, forgot about the woman she'd seen near him, only heard the humour in his voice, only saw the sexy smile... To be talking suggestively like this was so foreign, but so much fun. She wanted it to continue.

She tried an almost saucy reply. 'If that's the case, then perhaps you should be careful.'

His smile went wicked. 'Definitely.' He held out his hand. 'Luca Bianchi.'

She glanced to his hand and then back to his face, letting her own smile go sinful. 'You're not afraid I might bite?'

'I'm half hoping you will.'

She lifted her hand. 'Emily Dodds.' The frisson raced up her arm as contact was made.

'Emily.' The way he said it made her toes and everything inside her curl up tight. His hand gripped hers firmly. 'Did you enjoy the opera?'

'I loved it.'

He nodded. 'It was a good performance.'

'And a lovely atmosphere.'

'My company could have been a little better. How about yours?'

'It wasn't bad.'

'But it could have been better.'

'Perhaps.' Faux demurely, she looked down. 'Are you going to give me my hand back?'

'I was thinking I might keep it and take it home with me.'

'Not tonight.' She refused, but she couldn't hold back her smile. Pleasure thrilled through her—to be so overtly admired, courted, frankly *chased*…by a man as attractive as this was heady stuff.

'No? What a shame.' His mouth curved too. 'But there's always tomorrow.'

For a long moment she stared into his melting chocolate eyes, a million 'if onlys' circulating in her head. His fingers tightened.

'See, I told you!' Kate bubbled up, shaking her upturned hat in front of her. 'Enough for a five-course feast in a fancy restaurant.'

Emily tugged her hand and after a gentle squeeze he let it slip from his.

'Singing for your supper?' he asked dryly.

'Lunch tomorrow!' Kate answered. 'Hi, I'm Kate.'

'Hello, Kate. I'm Luca. I'm a friend of your sister's.'

Emily glanced at him. *Friend?* There was a tease in his eyes directed totally at her. 'Let me get you two a drink. You must be thirsty after performing in the heat like this.'

'Oh, we—' The sensible side of Emily thought she should refuse. But there was a whisker of a wink again. It was enough to tip her over. She was in Italy—her dream holiday destination—and she was flirting with the dreamiest guy imaginable. Little Miss Sassy elbowed Little Miss Sensible out of the way for good. 'Thanks.'

Luca tried and failed to remember when he'd ever done anything as crazy as this. It had been so long, yet all of a sudden he was chasing hard for something that could only be momentary. But, hell, it would be fun. And wasn't he due for a little fun? While the waiter fetched the wine, Luca tried to remind himself that in reality one-night stands were never as good as you thought they were going to be, but gave up after half a thought. Fact was, he hadn't wanted a woman quite like this, quite in this way, ever. An instant, visceral demand—his whole body was tight with anticipation.

It was going to happen; he'd make certain of it. Therefore he didn't need to be staring at her like some starving dog. However, controlling that urge was something of a problem when she looked at him like that—green eyes glittering with both challenge and caution.

'What brings you to Verona?' He made small but necessary talk.

'We're on our way to London,' the sister answered. 'I want to sing there.'

He spared a quick glance for the pretty young redhead and her pale blue eyes. She could do it if she wanted. 'You have the talent to sing anywhere. But do you have the determination?'

'Absolutely.'

His gaze was drawn back to the other direction—Emily. Scattered across her nose were a few freckles that he'd like to kiss and beneath that a mouth that he wanted to kiss even more. She didn't have the girlish skinny physique of her sister. She'd still be considered trim but with more curves and length. Hips to cushion his, legs to wrap around his waist, hair to wind round his wrist and tug on so he could access her neck and kiss his way down to her full breasts.

As Kate babbled on about her career plans he sipped his wine and watched the faint dusky pink blush spread over Emily's face. The more he watched, the more it spread and the deeper the colour grew. His own temperature began to lift.

'You want a wonderful lunch, Kate?' He finally interrupted the incessant flow. 'I know just the place. You and Emily meet me outside here tomorrow at one and I'll take you.'

'Really?' Kate's desire was too easy to please. He had the suspicion her sister might be more of a challenge—but a very welcome one.

'Absolutely. It would be my pleasure.' He directed that last word right to Emily, allowing in the faint provocation. All the pleasure would be in seeing her.

She lifted her gaze from her seemingly minute contemplation of her empty glass. Her eyes were such a deep green—thoughtful, assessing, seeking. He met them squarely. If they were alone it would be so easy. But they weren't alone—not yet—and he had to hold back from moving the way he wanted. So for the first time in his life he found himself almost begging. 'It'll be the best you've ever had.'

'Tomorrow?' It was the kid sister all excited.

'Yes.' He refused to break the bond with Emily, only vaguely satisfied when he saw the faint upward tweak of her lips. 'Tomorrow.'

When Emily walked to the piazza with Kate, they found Luca waiting, as promised, in front of the Arena. But he was not alone. On either side of him stood a beautiful woman. A cold, hard ball grew in Emily, freezing her throat, her chest, her tummy. What was he doing—building a harem? And yet as she walked towards him his eyes seemed to be eating her up. When his long, intense stare finally made it up to her face she was all hot again. Desire, curiosity, a wanting for a kind of wickedness—and above all vexation about those two other women. What made it worse was that she knew he'd read her expression, and right now he looked totally smug.

When they got within earshot it was to Kate that he turned. 'Kate, meet Maria and Anne—both singers with the opera of the Arena di Verona. How would you like to spend the afternoon touring backstage and join in a rehearsal?'

Kate's eyes were shining. 'Really?'

Luca laughed, indulgence audible. 'Yes, really. But wait, there's more.' His tone was full of irony. He handed her an envelope. 'I have a contact that you might find useful in London. Here are the details. Be sure to get in touch because he's expecting to hear from you.'

'Really?' Kate's shriek was right up there at the top of her vocal range.

'Maria and Anne will ensure you get some lunch. Perhaps not five courses in a fancy restaurant, but something.'

'Oh, it doesn't matter. I'm not that hungry anyway.'

'Fine, so run along, then. These two will take care of you.'

And she was just like a child, thrilled to have had her most prized wish granted. Not even sparing Emily a second glance.

'Kate, will you be—?' Emily didn't get the 'OK' out.

'Em, don't be a nag. I'm nearly nineteen, remember? Back home I can drink, drive and vote.'

'Yeah, but not all in the same afternoon.' Officially she might be all grown up but Emily couldn't seem to shake the responsibility just yet. Kate was all she had.

But her sister was practically skipping, already asking question after question of the two professional singers.

'Don't worry, Kate,' Luca drawled after her. 'I'll take care of Emily.'

Kate didn't turn, simply sang back, 'I know.'

Emily watched them depart, not trusting herself to meet his gaze too soon. He'd take care of her? At twenty-four she didn't need taking care of, but she had the feeling he didn't mean in the protective parental sense.

After a long silent moment he spoke—quietly but, oh, so clearly. 'So, Emily, it's just you and me.'

She inclined her head, silently applauding him. This

was a man who would get what he wanted—every time. And in that moment she knew that if she was what he wanted, she was what he would get.

She was free. Her sister—her responsibility—was gone for the afternoon, she was on holiday in the most beautiful city and she wanted to explore *everything*.

'I said I'd show you the best of Verona. Are you willing?'

She looked at him then. Raised a single eyebrow so they both knew she was. His broad smile made one of its appearances—boyish and fun and infectious. 'Then let's walk.'

She couldn't hold back the answering smile, nor could she quell the shiver as he took her hand. His grip tightened and he flashed a whisker of a wink, before leading them towards a side street.

'Where are you taking me?'

'On a brief tour of some of the city's highlights and then to lunch. Sound OK?'

'Sounds fine.'

He stopped. 'Don't swamp me with your enthusiasm, Emily.'

'No, that sounds great.'

'Have you seen Casa de Giulietta?'

'Yes.' Supposedly Juliet's balcony from Romeo and Juliet—aside from the fact that that story was fiction.

'Of course you have. Did you leave a message?'

'No.' People left love notes and prayers on the wall.

'No lover to leave a message for?'

How many times was he going to ask her that one? 'Actually I'm not a fan of graffiti.' She sidestepped with a grin and then narrowed her gaze at him. 'Have you ever left a message there?'

'I'm not romantic. What about Castelvecchio and San Zeno—been to those?'

'Yes.'

'Duomo?'

'Yes.'

He frowned and stopped walking. 'How long have you been in Verona?'

'This is our fifth day. For the first two I took Kate on a route march around the city. I think I've seen most of the essentials.'

'So that wasn't your first opera at the Arena? They perform every other night.'

'I know, but it was. We couldn't afford to go twice. I just wanted to spend some time in Italy.'

'Did you manage a day trip to Venice?'

'Yes.' She beamed. 'It was wonderful.'

'Right.' He pulled on her hand and started walking quickly in the opposite direction from which they'd started.

'Where are we going now?'

'Straight to lunch.'

Excellent. Emily's feeling of freedom grew as he led her across a bridge to the other side of the river and along a little farther until they reached some gates. Turning to her, his eyes sparkling with irresistibly sinful promise, he invited, 'Come into the Giardino with me, Emily.'

CHAPTER THREE

GIARDINO GIUSTI. The beautiful Renaissance gardens had been designed centuries ago and were magnificent. The green upon green of the trees was a pleasant contrast to the grey and stone of the buildings in the centre of town. They wound their way through the formal topiary section. And although it was quieter and should have been cooler, all Emily felt was hotter and more attuned to the tiniest of sounds—the trickle of water, the hum of a bee, the shortness of her own breath…and the nearness of him.

He led her along a path, to where it seemed to be a little wilder, more shade, taller trees and a moist grotto not far in the distance. She looked at a shaded grassy bank.

'Oh, look, someone's having a picnic.'

'Yes.' He smiled that boyish smile. 'We are.'

He walked up to the dark-suited man standing beside the spread. They spoke briefly and then the man walked away, down the path to the exit.

Luca gestured for her to come closer. 'You're hungry?'

As she stared she felt her insides light up. 'And you say

you're not romantic, Luca?' she gently mocked to cover the thrill.

'It's a simple picnic.'

There was nothing simple about it. A large, ruby-red blanket was spread, and scattered on top of it were round cushions in heavy, gilt fabric—deeper reds, threaded with gold. Another rug was folded on one corner—what, should they need more room or was it for them to hide beneath? Oh, Emily was tickled…and so tempted.

Beside the space upon which they were so clearly meant to recline stood a large basket. Luca had knelt beside it already and pulled out wine. As he poured into the crystal glasses Emily decided she'd entered paradise.

Unhesitatingly she sat on the rug, accepted the glass he gave her and looked across the view of the impeccably maintained garden, needing a moment to recapture her sanity before she tossed all caution aside.

'This is incredible.'

'The best of Italy.' He smiled, as if he knew she'd already lost it. 'Here for you.'

'The basket doesn't look big enough.'

'I wasn't referring to the basket.'

'Very sure of your own worth, aren't you?'

'Down to the last euro, yes. But we're not talking money now.'

'No?'

'We're talking pleasure. And you can't put a price on absolute pleasure.'

* * *

Luca couldn't look away from her. Her expression of delight was so genuine, so pleased, it made him feel guilty. 'I didn't pick all this, or lay it out.'

She laughed. 'I know. But it was your idea.'

It was. And now he felt even more guilty—he wanted to wine, dine and woo her. For one night only. And for all her fiery eyes and flirting she was more sweet than sophisticated. Really, he had no right to mess with her, not unless she wanted it too. Not unless she understood the rules. A one-off, holiday fling. 'The hotel prepared the food.'

'So I get the five-course feast.'

'You do.'

'How come you have connections at the opera?'

'My company is a corporate sponsor.'

'Your company?'

'*Mine.*' It was all his and it was all his life. He had spent almost the entire decade dedicated to it. Getting his education, the experience and growing the private finance firm into the extreme success it was. He had taken no help from his father. He didn't need his uninterested parent throwing him nothing but pretty patterned paper. He could make his own money, prove his own worth. 'I often take valued clients and their wives.'

'Their wives?'

'*Sì.*' He suppressed a smile. So she'd wondered about the woman with them last night. Yes, she was the wife of a client and, no, he wasn't interested. He sent her a meaningful look, but saw she was checking out his left hand. He tensed. He'd worn a ring on that finger once. He'd kept it on for some time after—using it like a talisman to ward off

women. But every time he'd looked at it he'd been reminded. Nikki hadn't had the strength to push it on and
he'd had to do it himself. And despite its tiny circumfer-
ence, the ring he'd given her had hung loose, threatening
to slide over her bony knuckle. There hadn't been an engagement ring. There hadn't been time.

Eventually he'd taken his ring off and allowed the sun
to brown the pale mark. But even so he couldn't forget.
Even now, when he was plotting a moment of madness, the
memory clung to him, reminding him of what not to do:
don't ever get attached.

'What does your company do?'

'Hedge funds.' Good, when painful thoughts impinged
he turned back to work—that was the way Luca liked it.

'Hedges?' Her nose wrinkled. 'So it's like gardens?'

He hesitated, unwilling to launch into a detailed explanation of the complex transactions he managed, so he
fudged it instead. 'I like making things grow.'

'Money trees.' Her eyes were sparkling with amusement.

He laughed—her naiveté had been a ploy and she was
teasing him. 'Right.'

'And you like the opera?'

Why did she think that was a surprise? 'I'm Italian, of
course I like the opera.'

'You don't sound all that Italian.'

'The curse of my education—boarding school in
England from the age of seven. Over a decade 'til I
emerged from the system. But I guess I inherited my ap-
preciation of the opera from my mother.' But more painful
memories lurked with the mention of her so he moved the

conversation back to Emily. 'Do you like Italy?' He didn't need to hear her answer, already had it as her face lit up and it was his turn to tease. 'Your first visit, right? Is it everything you hoped it would be?'

'Actually it's better.'

There was that genuine, warm enthusiasm again. Her anger had risen from that last night—based on the desire to enjoy herself, to make the most of the moment she'd obviously been waiting a while for. The freshness was tantalising. 'Are you enjoying the food?'

She nodded.

'Have you tried some of the local specialities?'

She looked vague so perhaps not. Of course, budget was an issue. He could help out with that today. 'Italian cuisine isn't just buffalo mozzarella and sun-dried tomatoes, you know.'

'No?' She pouted. 'But I love buffalo mozzarella and sun-dried tomatoes.'

He chuckled. 'Come on, try some more with me now.'

He delved deeper into the basket. The hotel had done a fabulous job, filling it with many small containers, each holding samples of this and that. Some were simple, just a few olives, other were complex miniatures of great dishes.

He lifted them out and explained them to her, where each came from, made her say the Italian name for them and then watched as she tried each, waiting for her reaction before tasting them himself. And all the while, his appetite grew.

Emily licked the sweet oil from her lips. Yes, she loved sun-dried tomatoes but, my goodness, the nibbles in those containers were out of this world. By now, eating as much as she had, under the shade of the trees, in this warmth, she would ordinarily have been overcome with laziness. But his presence, so close, precluded that. He was stretched out, propped up on one elbow, his long, athletic length stretching from one end of the blankets to the other. Relaxed.

Emily ached to touch him now—one appetite filled, another starving. Instead she took a breadstick from the box, needing something to fiddle with.

'Tell me about your life.' He looked across the small gap between them now littered with lids and containers, to where she sat up, legs curled beneath her.

She wrinkled her nose. 'There's really not that much to tell.' There really wasn't, certainly nothing glamorous or exciting.

'Where are your parents?'

As she broke the grissini in two the shadow on her heart must have crossed her face.

'I'm sorry,' he said quietly. 'Will you tell me what happened?'

'Of course.' She smiled the moment away. 'It was a long time ago.' She broke one half of the grissini into quarters and gave him the potted summary. 'Mum died in a car crash when I was fifteen. After the accident Dad went into a decline. He drank a lot. Smoked. Stopped eating.' She rubbed the crumbs between her fingers and looked down at the trees. 'I think with her gone he lost the will to live.'

'Even though he had two beautiful daughters to look after?'

She could understand the question, perceived the faint

judgment. Hadn't she thought the same in those moments of anger that had sometimes come in the wee small hours? But she also knew the whole story; things never were black and white—shades of grey all the way. And so she shared a part of it.

'He was driving the car, Luca. He never got over the guilt.' She flicked away the final crumb, sat back on her hands and stared down the gentle slope to the row of cypresses. 'He died two years after her.'

Two years of trying to get him through it. But the depression had pulled him so far down and the drinking had gone from problem to illness and the damage to his mind and body had become irreparable. He couldn't climb out of it and he didn't want to. He simply shut down. Emily had taken over everything.

'What happened then?'

'I was eighteen. Kate was nearly thirteen. They let her stay with me. I left school and got a job.'

Emily had been thinking of studying piano at university but instead she'd worked and they'd put all they had into Kate's singing. Her younger sister had the looks, the talent and the drive. Now, nearly nineteen, she was determined to come overseas and make her break before, as she put it, she got 'over the hill'. Emily was her accompanist—both in terms of playing the piano for her to sing, and in terms of support.

'So you looked after Kate.'

Emily shrugged. 'We looked after each other.' There was no one else.

The silence was long and finally she looked at him. The

darkness in his eyes reflected the dark days. Somehow he knew. He understood the struggle and the loneliness. And for a second there she thought she saw pity. Well, she didn't want that—not today, not from him. She'd lived through it, she'd survived and so had Kate. Now they were off, heading towards that new horizon. Life was moving forward. And she was totally trying to ignore the fear thumping in the pit of her stomach. For the last six years she'd worked two jobs plus done all the household chores. She'd created stability, routine…now nothing was stable, there was no routine and she couldn't foresee the future. All she knew was that she wanted more than what her life had been back home. A more satisfying job, a more satis-fying social life… And sitting with this gorgeous man in this beautiful garden, it felt as if the chance to open up a new part of her life was being offered right now.

'What about you?' she asked, lightening her tone. 'Where's your family?'

His face tightened and she knew the shadow was a match for her own. 'Really?'

'Cancer killed my mother when I was seven.' He spoke bluntly but it was clear the pain was still sharp.

'And your father?'

He shrugged. 'I went to boarding school straight after. We're not close.' The bare recitation spoke volumes.

She sat back, shocked. He'd been sent away? To a whole other country where they didn't even speak his first lan-guage?

The slight smile in his eyes was all cynical. 'I take after my mother. I think I was too painful a reminder.'

So in a way they'd both been rejected by their surviving parent. Luca had been sent away, and Emily's father had gone away himself—in mind and spirit anyway—leaving Emily to shoulder the burden of caring for his fading shell.

'Where's your dad now?'

'He remarried. They live just outside Rome.'

Their eyes met. Was that part of what had drawn them together? That somehow they'd recognised that they had shadows in common?

She barely had the chance to process that when he sat up. 'Enough gloom. The day is too short.' He reached into the apparently bottomless basket. 'Let's try dessert.'

Perhaps their pasts had nothing to do with the attraction. Perhaps it all came down to the fact that he was the most physically dynamic man she'd ever seen. And he was right. They didn't need to share more in the way of gloom. Today was about holidays and sun.

The dessert was some creamy confection. He held the spoon, his laughter a soft rumble as he made her lean closer to taste it.

Oh, my. It was the taste of pure decadence.

'Good, isn't it?' He had a spoonful and then offered her another.

'Mmm-hmm.'

She stretched out and lay back on the pillow then, giving herself over to the utter indulgence. Closing her eyes, letting her mind savour the flavour and soak up the heat. She wanted more of the sweet, wanted much more of him.

'So all this time you've been looking after your sister,'

he spoke softly. 'Now you need someone to satisfy *your* needs.'

She turned her head and opened her eyes. His head was close, resting on the cushion right by hers. 'What makes you think I haven't got someone already?'

'If you did, you wouldn't be looking at me with those hungry eyes.'

She lifted her head, a little on her dignity. 'You don't need to lay it on with a trowel, Luca. I'm not completely inexperienced.'

'Only *relatively*, *sì*?' He laughed. 'What was he? Some young fool who wouldn't know how to give pleasure to a woman even if she gave him step by step instructions and a map showing the way?'

She felt the blush covering her cheeks and neck and she shut her eyes again to pretend it wasn't happening. Her ex had been exactly like that.

'Emily. I can offer you nothing but a memory.' His voice was a little strained. 'But I think it would be some memory.'

She reopened her eyes then—drawn by the power behind his words.

'When did you last do something *you* wanted to do?' he asked. 'Not something for someone else, or something you *had* to do. But something you wanted, just for you?'

She couldn't remember. And she knew he knew. 'Is that what you're offering? How generous of you, Luca,' she mocked gently. 'As if there's nothing in it for you.'

'There's everything in it for me. I admit it.' He shrugged. 'I'm selfish. Be selfish with me.' He raised himself back up on one elbow, rolling onto his side to face her. 'We have more in common than you might think. I've been working hard too and you've worked hard for so long. Don't you deserve a treat?'

'Is that what you are?'

He leaned closer. 'You tell me.' He reached across and took her hand, lifted it and pressed it to his chest. 'Feel it? Accelerating?'

The solid thump in his chest was strong and regular and hypnotic and her fingers wanted the fabric to disappear so she could feel his skin direct.

'Is it like this for you, when we touch? When our arms brush as we walk side by side, does your body want more? Mine does.' He still spoke quietly but she felt the force of his underlying feeling pierce through to her marrow. 'What if I did that to you, Emily—would your heart start to race?'

It already was—faster and faster with every word and the spiralling anticipation.

'I think we should find out.' He let her hand go and reached across to her, his fingers drawing along the line of her collarbone.

'Luca…' She shook her head but couldn't deny the fire his touch ignited.

His hand slid down, pressed against her tee shirt, pulling it close to her skin, so that her breast was displayed, and he looked at her tight, peaking nipple. He smiled as it jutted out for him; he didn't need to feel her heart to know his effect on her.

He looked back into her face, intensely determined. 'Just one kiss.'

One afternoon. One absolute temptation.

He didn't need to coax her mouth open. She met him halfway, already wet and pliant and seeking. She closed her eyes, able to focus on nothing but him. And there was nothing but his kiss. His mouth moved over hers, his tongue probing, tasting. Rapidly it became more insistent—plundering, taking. She raised her hands, sliding them into his hair. Surrendering and then beginning to make her own demands—opening wider, seeking deeper, harder.

It was bliss. She wanted it to last, wanted to savour each stage. But too soon she wanted more. The need to move closer grew, she wanted him to roll right above her, wanted to feel his weight, to be pressed down into the soft rugs by his hard hips, wanted to explore his...

He drew back. 'Emily.'

She opened her eyes, hating the interruption.

'I am going to take you back to my hotel and kiss you like that all over your body. Is that OK with you?'

'Is your hotel far?'

He laughed, an uncontrolled shout of genuine amusement.

'I'm serious. Can't we just do this some more here?' She didn't want to wait. She wanted it all, right now.

He smiled, that wonderful warm, relaxed smile, and leaned over her again. The kiss was right back at hot. And then he was kissing her jaw, her throat, his hand was at her breast and she learnt him too, learning the boundaries with her touch—learning that with Luca there *were* no boundaries. The kisses and caresses were so intense and satisfying yet awakening such an appetite that she knew there would be no saying no. No tomorrow and no regrets. There was only now and a need so great it was overwhelming.

Through heavy eyes she saw the blue of the sky and the green of the branches above them, felt the heat of summer, and all her senses appreciated this paradise. And there was more to come; he promised so much more with every kiss. She shifted on the rug, restless. She'd never known how desire could be a sort of suffering, hadn't felt this depth of longing for physical fulfilment. The pain of it and the way the body could absolutely overrule reason.

He groaned, as if he too were in pain, and as if he'd read her mind and knew how willing she was, how much she wanted. 'I'd love to see you naked under these trees, but the Giardino is public. Unless spending the night with the *carabinieri* is on your list of tourist activities, then we need to leave. Now.'

She almost, almost didn't care, caught between not wanting this moment to end and wanting to get to the end as fast as possible—to completion.

'OK.' She forced the answer; it was like dragging herself out of the warmest, sweetest water. And all she wanted to do was disappear into the depths again. Had he drugged her with that food? But, no, it was his body, and his touch, that were the opiate.

He rose to his feet and held out his hand. 'Then come.'

Their eyes met for a pregnant moment. And then she smiled.

'What about this?' She gestured to the rumpled rug and scattered cushions and containers, not wanting to have to think about them, but years of taking responsibility insisted on it.

He shook his head. 'It's taken care of. Don't worry.'

He took her hand and led her down the sloping gardens. Waiting at the gates was a sleek grey car. Luca held the door open for her and she slid in. He climbed in the back with her. The driver pulled away. It was only minutes to the centre of Verona and his hotel, but all of them were occupied as with light fingers he turned her head towards him and kissed her. She didn't want to stop. She didn't want him ever to stop.

CHAPTER FOUR

SURFACING from the car into a hazy reality, Emily walked beside Luca into the hotel. When she finally focused on her surroundings she almost stumbled. Opulence wasn't the word. And suddenly she feared she had no place here in her crumpled skirt and camping tee shirt. It was the early afternoon and they were walking into his hotel for an erotic indulgence. She was so turned on, she could hardly walk for the way she'd gone weak at the knees, and she had the horrible feeling that everyone must know. It was so strong to her that surely it must be obvious to everyone else? She longed to return to the quiet solitude they'd had in the warm gardens. This was sophisticated and exclusive and so not her.

He seemed to sense her discomfort, taking her arm and shielding her from the eyes of those in Reception. Smoothly he guided her through the lobby to the lift. It wasn't a possessive touch, he didn't put his arm around her and haul her close, it was merely a light hand at her elbow, and the simplicity and the politeness made the doubts wane. There was respect in his manner and she knew he had every intention of taking care of her. Suddenly nothing else mattered.

He didn't maul her in the lift either, stood beside her quietly, keeping his hand still light on her arm as he escorted her onto his floor. He swiped the key card and opened the door. She walked in, relieved to be alone with him again but still knocked sideways. He didn't just have a room, he had a suite. She'd guessed he had money, understood he was a financier of some sort. But she hadn't realised it was quite like this.

She turned to study him, reassessing. All Italians dressed nicely, didn't they?

'Second thoughts?' He was watching her just as keenly. 'It's OK to say no.'

Concentrating on him made the intimidating surroundings disappear. She melted all over again.

'No,' she said, then smiled naughtily at the flash in his eyes. 'I don't want to say no,' she elaborated firmly.

She watched, quite pleased as with obvious effort he unclenched his jaw. 'Good.'

'It will be the best, won't it, Luca?' She searched for final reassurance. Having had a sample of what could only be heaven, she didn't want disappointment. She'd had that before. 'I want the best.' And she did. To be lost from herself for just a few magic moments. One afternoon where she could forget the past and ignore the future. Let go of worries and responsibilities and be free to feel pleasure. It would be the first time and she'd been waiting for ever.

He closed the gap between them with slow, sure steps.

His finger traced her lower lip as it had the night at the opera. 'Don't doubt it.'

Her eyelids lowered slowly as the crazy lethargy returned. It was as if her senses were tuning out everything except him—his touch, his voice, his scent and his determination. There would be no saying no. It wasn't even an option, not for her.

This magic, this mysterious man—she wanted to know no more, except of his body. It had been there, from the first glance, the blink and reassessment that had happened in the quickest instance—one body's recognition of the other.

She didn't believe in love at first sight. But now she most certainly believed in lust at first sight. Her body programmed to seek his as her mate. It had never happened to her before. The few dates she'd been on, that past boyfriend—she'd felt nothing. But this, this was as if she'd been branded with a white-hot iron—*his*.

She hadn't been able to take her eyes off him. She still couldn't. Through her half-closed lids she watched him concentrate as slowly, so slowly, the tips of his fingers moved from her lips, brushing down her jaw, her neck and down the slope of her chest. She went taut with anticipation but his path diverted, going around her nipples rather than directly over them. She hissed out her breath, wanting him to touch her there.

But his fingers skimmed down her sides, and then took the hem of her tee shirt. Carefully he raised it, automatically she lifted her arms to help. In a second he had it off her, and tossed it to the side.

She stared at him, unashamed about the way her full breasts were trying to burst out of her bra, at the way her nipples were pressing hard against the fabric—begging him the only way they could. She just wanted him to *touch*.

His jaw was clenched hard again. His hands lifted. The light, gentle fingertips went back to her waist, slipping around her skirt to find the zip.

She wriggled her hips to help it slide down. And then she was standing before him, for a second stupidly hoping that it didn't matter that her bra and briefs didn't match.

He curved his arms right around her, fingers at work once more, unclasping the hooks. The straps loosened. He tweaked them at her shoulder and the shells of her bra slipped from her breasts.

For a moment there was nothing, only his fierce attention as he looked, colour rising in his face. She was almost about to plead when his hands lifted, cupping her breasts the way her bra had, only pushing them a little higher and then closer together. His thumbs rubbed gently over her peaking nipples as his hands explored their soft weight.

Her mouth opened, unconsciously doing what she wanted him to do—to open up and taste her.

His gaze lifted to meet hers, reading her expression, revealing his own hot desire. And then his mouth caught hers in a kiss that was deep and carnal and demanding, his tongue driving in and claiming. She met him, stroke for stroke, thrusting her hands into his hair and holding him. But he moved his kiss. Following the path his fingers had taken from her mouth, her jaw, her neck until finally, thankfully he was kissing her chest, up the slopes to where his hands held her breasts, pushing them together so his tongue could assault both her nipples with strong licks, and then he sucked her into his mouth.

She swayed towards him, the heat turning mass and muscle to liquid. But at her unbridled moan he lifted away, his thumbs instantly working to soothe the yearning in her breasts.

'Do you want me to take my shirt off, or do you want to do it yourself?' His breathlessness heightened her longing.

She too was breathing hard but she couldn't pass on the challenge or the pleasure. 'Let me.'

She fumbled with the first button but got the knack of them after the next. Drinking in the sight of his chest as it was slowly revealed. She reached out a hand, touched the hard heat of it, feeling the roughness where hair dappled it, finally placing her hand back over his heart. To where he'd placed it in the garden but this time on bare skin, feeling the life force beating, feeling the rhythm. And then she scraped his nipple with the tip of her thumb, watched the definition of his abs go even sharper. She pushed the shirt off his broad shoulders, stretching her arms wide to reach down his arms. All rock-hard, barely restrained muscle.

At that she didn't hesitate to go lower and pull out the loop of his belt. His trousers dropped to the floor. Then she was confronted with his boxers—and their package.

She blew out the breath she'd seemed to be holding for ever. Feeling the heat suffuse her cheeks, she tried to stretch the fabric over his large erection. Until, hands shaking, feeling both embarrassed and excited, she mumbled, 'I think you better do…that bit.'

He caught her wrists and pulled her close, laughter rumbling in his chest. 'But shouldn't that be the best bit?'

She nodded. 'I'm sure it is, but I might need a moment to get used to it.'

He kissed her again, long and deep, and then without warning pushed her back onto the bed, coming down hard on top. She wriggled, unbelievably happy to have the weight of him on her at last.

He held his head from hers, teasing. 'I think we should take things very, very slow.'

If this was taking things slow, then heaven help her if he decided to speed them up.

But then he did go slow. Kisses trailed and fingers toyed as he did as he'd promised and kissed her all over her body. As he peeled off her panties and made his way back to the tops of her thighs she couldn't hold back the squirm—overly aware of what was going to happen.

'Don't be shy,' he said calmly.

She breathed in deep. He was right. Why be shy? This was her afternoon, after all. She reached out a hand, felt the strength of his thigh. Rubbed her fingers through the masculine hair, felt the muscles working underneath it. And found her appetite to explore more was ravenous. How good he felt beneath her fingers—how much better might he feel beneath her lips? So she tried exactly that. Never had she had such a body to explore before—to taste, to delight in. Now she understood why humans sought beauty, marvelled in it, celebrated it.

Perfection.

Silently he let her play, she could feel him watching her,

feel the tension mounting until he suddenly jerked away from her, pulling open the drawer in the table beside the bed so hard the whole thing fell out. No matter, he had what he wanted, was out of the boxers, had rolled the condom on and she watched and smiled, knowing that soon, soon, soon, she would have all that *she* wanted.

He took the lead again, pinning her down with his heavy, strong body. And she poised, waiting for him to move, wanting him to thrust into her.

But still he didn't. He smiled, that cheeky, boyish smile, and moved down her body. Doing once more as he'd promised, kissing her with wet, deep kisses all over her body. Only this time he did go *all* over. Until then he was kissing her there and only there—the most intimate of places. His fingers joining in too until she was rocking and pleading and about to burst. She thrashed, arms raking the sheets, not wanting it to end yet, wanting *all* of him but unable to hold herself back.

'Don't fight it,' he commanded.

And she couldn't any more. She gave in to the insistence of his mouth and fingers, lost control completely with a harsh cry. Every limb stretched long, her body arched and taut and then suddenly buckling, writhing as the tension snapped and pleasure pulsed through every cell.

Even as she was still shuddering he was moving back up her length. Kissing her stomach as it spasmed, then her screaming tight nipples were anointed by his tongue again.

He was above her now, his hand gently stroking down her jaw. She opened her eyes to find him watching her closely. She could hide nothing from him.

'You were right,' she panted. 'That was the best.'

There was no answering smile. 'No.' His eyes bored into hers, intense, serious and incredibly focused. 'That was just the beginning.'

The force of it was almost a threat. Half dizzy, she shook her head. 'I'm not sure I can...'

She felt him then, hard and thick, probing in her wetness. With a whoosh the fire inside raged back. The tiny moment of calm obliterated as the storm broke.

His hands cupped her bottom, moving her to accept him, making her mould and melt for him. She cried out at his devastating, overpowering demand.

'You can do it,' his voice encouraged gently, while his body wielded its mastery.

What she couldn't do was hold back any longer. She bent her knees, instinctively opening up more for him. She'd thought she'd been unleashed before but she'd been dreaming. Now she was beyond boundaries. There was nothing left—no thought, no shyness, no self-consciousness, no self-control as she shuddered beneath him, finally absorbing every last inch.

The rough moan that passed her lips as she arched her back was the result of raw bliss. She sighed, louder, lifting to meet him once more, unable to believe how fantastic he felt. She stroked her hand down the hard strength of his back, kissed the skin nearest to her—up and down the column of his throat, tasting the salt in the hollow of his shoulder, delighting in the way his beautiful, big body locked so completely into hers. She pressed her hips in time to meet his—again and then again, following the rhythm he set, faster and faster until finally they were moving together with a pace that was frantic, the feral sounds from her throat matched by the hoarse grunts from his. Sweat slicked them. Temperatures and sensations spiked so high that in the heat and light and speed of it all there was nothing but brilliance. Her fingers curled into claws, scouring across his skin, making him pummel so hard and so deep and so deliciously that she screamed her way to the stars and beyond.

'Open your eyes.'

She automatically obeyed. The ceiling was above her. So the world still existed. She hadn't been sure until then.

'Look at me.'

She couldn't ignore the imperative.

He had slid down the bed a bit, so his body was no longer crushing hers. Dazed, she studied the difference in their colouring. She had come from a cold winter so her skin was pale, whereas his olive complexion had been enhanced in the height of the European summer. Between her legs she could feel his strength, his heart thudding intimately against her thigh.

He was staring at her, his expression unreadable. Then a sort of smile twisted his lips. 'You're very beautiful, Emily.'

She almost smiled too but couldn't quite manage it in the tumbling emotional aftermath. 'Is it always like that for you?'

'No.'

Of course he would say that. She knew now what a gentleman he was.

His gaze dropped from hers and he pressed a kiss to her hip. 'It is never like that.'

As he spoke the words faint colour stained his cheeks and she was suddenly certain he was speaking the truth. She closed her eyes again, desperately needing to rest, to recover from the sensory overload and to deny the fleeting feeling of regret that there would be no more than this moment. He moved to lie beside her, drawing the sheet up to cover their cooling skin, bringing her head onto his chest and sliding his strong arms around her, giving her trembling body the comfort of a sure embrace.

She didn't know how long she slept. It couldn't have been that long as the sun was still high in the sky. He was awake, watching her with eyes so dark and deep they were almost all black. She didn't know *what* to say to him. How could she possibly express the intensity she'd felt?

But he shook his head slightly as if he knew. There shouldn't be words; they couldn't do it justice.

'Shower with me.' He stood from the bed and as she stared at his magnificent form the urge inside flared once more.

Her hunger must have been obvious because he smiled. 'I want to see you come again, Emily.'

She rose onto all fours, feeling the thrill of power as his eyes widened at the sight of her. 'Well, I guess that's up to you.'

The shower had never been such an exotic, erotic experience. He carried her, still connected to her, back to the bed so he could continue to manipulate her body, making her respond in a way that was fierce and passionate and almost frightening but all incredible.

For a while they lay, half-dozing, half-wrapped in towels, and through the window she watched the blue of the sky intensify. Finally she stirred, achingly stunned but also content.

'I'd better get back to the hostel.'

He didn't argue. In almost companionable silence they dressed. She drifted her way downstairs, uncaring of anyone's opinion now. None of that mattered—not in the face of this moment of bliss.

It was only when they were leaving the hotel that he spoke. 'You fly to London tomorrow?'

'Yes.' She chose not to look in his face, or at the impending reality. It was what it was, it had been shockingly wonderful, and there was nothing else to say.

Luca escorted her through the streets and fought to regain mastery over his emotions. She'd just torn every shred of self-control and reservation from him. He'd expected sweet, simple enthusiasm and he'd got a vehement passion that had rocked him to the core.

He wanted more. Oh, my God, he wanted. It was good she was going. Because despite that deep response, she was young and inexperienced and he'd be a heel to take advantage any more than he already had. The very occasional affairs he had were ultra short and he only had them with women well used to that sort of game. That wasn't Emily.

Yet the glow that had enveloped her as she lay cushioning him was like a soft, flattering light—it was how she was meant to look. Utterly beautiful and the most sensual person he'd known—and the most dangerous. Because if she could rip him open in one afternoon, what would she threaten if he saw her again? Luca had spent the best part of a decade sealing away his emotions, had zero tolerance for that kind of risk. He'd held and lost too much before and he wasn't taking the chance on it ever happening again.

Maybe he should feel guilty already but he couldn't. He'd seen the completion in her eyes—that he'd given her. It had made him feel mightier than anything. And she'd asked him for it, accepted it—understanding without asking why that this afternoon was all there could be. But, ironically, that got to him. Why didn't she want more?

She turned to him across the street from the hostel. It hung on her now, the last vestiges of satisfaction. She smiled, a serene smile that he wanted to capture and keep in his memory for ever. 'Thank you, Luca. It was the best, wasn't it?'

He nodded, unable to speak. He tilted her chin towards him with a finger, brushed her lips with his. He intended only a light kiss, a sweet goodbye to an even sweeter afternoon. But her mouth opened to him and he couldn't stop going further. And the fingers that he'd lightly rested under her chin slipped further to cup the back of her neck and pull her that little bit closer. He stroked the soft heat of her mouth with his tongue. The tiny moan in the back of her throat almost tipped him into madness.

Tearing his mouth from hers, he looked into those luminous green eyes that one last time and choked, *'Ciao, bella.'*

He turned his back to the hostel, to her, and walked. Instinctive reluctance tried to drag him back. He resisted with the determination that had seen him climb to the top of his ultra-competitive market. Yet even as he pushed his feet away he pulled out his PDA. He might not be going to see her again, but he couldn't beat the desire to ensure her arrival in London was secure—couldn't beat the need to know she was safe.

CHAPTER FIVE

THE LIGHTS of London seemed to stretch on and on. It felt as if they'd been flying over the city for hours—would they ever land? Nerves quickened Emily's pulse—part excitement, part anxiety. For the first time in her life, she had no idea what she was going to do next.

Luca dominated her thoughts. Her stiff, sore body reminded her with every tiny movement how passionate they'd been together. But she had no regrets. There was no shame or embarrassment. How could there be when it had been so natural, so right? But there was that soft romantic part of her that wished it could have lasted—could have been more. That kiss by the hostel had only refuelled her desire. She couldn't imagine having a response so absolute to anyone other than Luca.

Damn. Because Luca was in Italy and she was in England. And they would never meet again.

She forced her focus onto Kate. She was here to help her sister succeed, and succeed Kate would because she had that rare drive—there was nothing more important to her. And Emily was glad to be able to help—she'd play at her auditions, help her practise... All her adult life she'd been putting someone else first; it was easier that way. But she knew she had to sort her own problems soon, when she'd had the chance to settle Kate in. Because her life would change now; it was A.L.—*After Luca*. She smiled as the wheels of the plane touched down. For Emily, *After Luca* meant nothing would ever be the same.

As they exited the walkway from the plane Kate noticed the man holding the sign that had both their names scrawled on it. Emily approached him, heart drumming loud in her ears, wondering what on earth the message could be.

He greeted them with almost a bow and a broad smile. 'I'm under instruction to take you wherever you wish to go.'

Wherever? He was Italian. Emily's breath hitched. Could he take them back to Italy? Oh, yes, please! 'Whose instruction?' She dared not dream of the answer.

'Luca Bianchi.'

The bubble of excitement blossomed. '*Grazie,*' she replied shyly, smiling back at him. Luca had arranged this? How?

The driver's smile just went wider. He lifted their bags and led the way. Kate was giggling. It was no ordinary taxi—not a taxi at all, in fact. It was a sleek, powerful, private machine that was even bigger than the one she'd ridden in with Luca in Verona.

Emily felt a fraud pulling up outside the budget hostel in such flash wheels.

As they unloaded she didn't know whether they were supposed to tip the driver, reached for her wallet to be on the safe side.

He saw and shook his head. 'Please, Luca is a good employer but he would fire me on the spot if I took money from you.'

He lifted their packs and put them in Reception for them. Anticipation, shameless hope curled high in Emily from her toes right up to her slightly spinning head. Where was Luca? What did he want?

But there was no message, no note, no comment, *niente*—nothing. And then he was gone. The silent, smiling chauffeur, her last link to Luca, disappeared out of the door and drove away.

By the time Emily slogged up the stairs, Kate had already nabbed the top bunk and was hauling out a piece of paper. One Emily had seen too many times for comfort.

'Do you think it's too late to give this guy a call?'

'What do you think?' Emily answered, unable to hide irritation as she gestured to the window and the darkness of the night sky.

But Kate didn't even notice. 'I think it's all going to happen.' She read the note aloud for the millionth time, then asked, 'How fortunate were we to meet him?'

Emily was no longer sure. She looked at Luca's strong, bold handwriting—listing details of a very senior executive at an international recording label. She smarted inside over the way he seemed happy to pull strings for Kate and yet had made no attempt to retain contact with Emily at all. Indeed the note he'd given to Kate had been written on hotel stationery—no address or email or anything that would allow her to contact him again. He'd told her it could only be a memory—and while in her head that was fine…it wasn't fine in her heart. She couldn't stop herself from wondering…why had he sent his driver? And why then hadn't he left a message?

Being human, she found the little hurt wouldn't ease, and nor would the hope die.

'Get some sleep, Kate,' she shushed and flopped onto the bottom bunk. Trying not to talk or even think about him any more, wishing she could just put him in a box and appreciate him as that 'memory'—failing at two out of three.

Three weeks later Emily ambled along the footpath towards the hostel. She was no further ahead than when she'd first landed. By rights she should have walked into a job quickly. She'd been the one working for years— sure, it was 'only' in retail but she'd worked her way up to a managerial position and had fabulous references emphasizing her reliability. Instead it was Kate who had scored a job working in a specialist music store, found a room to rent in an apartment and she'd phoned Luca's contact—wheels were starting to turn. He'd been expecting her call, had invited her in for an audition and she'd impressed them.

So much had happened for her sister, yet for Emily herself nothing much at all. But that had been her decision. After what had happened in Italy—that taste of pleasure, the discovery of an identity away from Kate, the revelation of what she'd been missing out on—she'd realised the last thing she wanted was to recreate the life she'd had back at home. She wanted to live her own life and as part of that she didn't want to work in retail any more. All she had to do now was figure out what job she did want—not so easy. But she'd saved hard, could live frugally and so could take more time to think.

She wandered through the sights and streets, just chilling and absorbing the scene. She knew she didn't want to return to New Zealand, but she wasn't sure she'd stay in London either. So she explored the city while she could.

It was a strange feeling—the lack of responsibility. For the first time she had no one to have to cook for or care for or chase after. No hours to meet and obligations to fulfil. No real, necessary demands on her. Hadn't she been dreaming of this for so long? Finally free to observe and do nothing.

Yet alone, a little lonely, it wasn't quite as much fun as it should have been.

She heard the slam of the door nearby and turned her head. She recognised the grey car. Had to think to keep her feet walking in a straight line, then gave up, not walking at all, just watching as with deliberate steps he crossed to the footpath in front of her.

'Emily.'

That magic foreign tinge was more audible than the first time he'd spoken to her. Emily bit the inside of her cheek to stop herself moving towards him, to stop herself saying how pleased she was to see him, because she wasn't sure why he was here—was he really here?

He took another step forward and reached for her hand.

Luca. Real and vital and in a suit so sharp she had to close her eyes for a moment as his fingers curled firmly around hers.

'What are you doing here?' Were those soft words hers?

'I wanted to see how you were getting on.' His answer

came unevenly and he took in a deep breath. 'You're still living in a youth hostel.'

'Yes.'

'And yet Kate's in a flat. How did that happen?'

That was Luca, cutting straight to the chase. She could hear the condemnation in his question. He must know it all from his music business mate.

'She's young.' Emily shook her head. 'She's enjoying the freedom of adult life. Don't judge her.'

But he was. She could see the disapproval narrowing his eyes.

'What about your freedom? What were you doing when you were eighteen?'

'It was different for me. I'm pleased Kate doesn't have to deal with what I had to.' Kate had found some friends, fallen in with them so quickly, and was working hard and having fun. And why shouldn't she?

'Perhaps. But she shows not even the littlest amount of loyalty.'

'I told her to go.' Emily had never wanted to hold Kate back. Her whole aim had been to see her fly. She just hadn't realised it would happen so soon.

'She still shouldn't have. Her family should mean more to her.'

That tiny hurt part of Emily agreed with him but she couldn't voice it, couldn't admit to Kate's faults—*her* sense of loyalty wouldn't let her. The realisation that her kid sister was all grown up and no longer needed her had cut Emily to the quick. Kate had landed on her feet in this town, scored a job, settled into a flat just like that. It was

Emily who hadn't seen it coming. Emily who was still figuring out where she wanted to go and what she wanted to do…and right now she didn't need him highlighting the point. What was he doing here anyway?

'I've been in Milan.' Luca abruptly changed the subject as he saw the shadows in her eyes darken. He hadn't meant to hurt her, just wanted to know what the hell was going on. 'I returned to London late last night.' He didn't add that he'd brought forward his return by almost a week because he couldn't wait any longer to see her again. And now that he had, he could hardly wait to hold her again. Every fibre in him wanted to pull her close. He wanted to see fire in her eyes—not the tinge of pain he could see there now.

But she'd frozen up. Maybe he shouldn't have mentioned Kate yet but he'd been stunned to hear about her moving in with some other wannabe musos and leaving Emily high and dry. He'd sent his driver to the airport so she'd get to her hostel safely, right? But really it had been so he'd find out where she was staying. All along, deep inside, he'd known he had to see her again.

'Returned to London? Right,' she said with bite. 'I thought you lived in Italy.'

He hadn't even told her that. A prickle of remorse roughened his answer. 'I mostly live in London but spend a lot of time in Milan—I go to Verona from there.'

She nodded, but he wasn't sure she'd heard him all that well. 'Why didn't you tell me that before?'

'There wasn't really time.' It was a pathetic excuse and he knew she knew it as well as he.

'Why didn't you try to contact me? You didn't even ask for an email address or a phone number or anything.' Mottled pink colour was slowly sweeping across her skin.

'I wanted it to be over.' His blood was pumping faster too and his senses were more acute—he couldn't tear his gaze from her.

'So why are you here now?' She was trembling; he could feel the tremors through her fingers.

'Because I missed you.' Every muscle in him tensed at the admission—at the desire. He knew her body moulded perfectly to his and he had to fight to stop himself pulling her close.

'And?' Was it anger or passion stirring her eyes to that emerald-green?

He couldn't resist her, couldn't stop the words tearing from him, low and harsh. 'Because I wanted to see you again.'

'You're seeing me now.'

'You know what I mean.'

'What, you want to have your wicked way with me again?' She tossed her head to glare at him, all spirit and spark.

'*Wicked?*' He challenged her right back.

She closed her eyes at that. 'Wild.'

It had been one wild, wonderful afternoon. He denied any wickedness—they had both wanted it. They both still did—he just had to get her to admit that too. Another tumble with her was all he wanted. As much as he hated to admit it, once hadn't been enough. 'Say yes, Emily, and we could do that again.'

* * *

Emily battled the satisfaction thrilling through her. He still wanted her. He'd come after her for that very purpose.

Unrelenting need.

Hadn't she been aching with it for days now? But she tried to let rational thought have a moment of supremacy over that most basic instinct governing her. This was different. This might lead to a mess. As it was she'd been feeling below par. It had to be different this time—there had to be more.

She breathed deep, spoke carefully. 'That afternoon was so complete. So perfect. Should we run the risk of ruining the memory of it?'

'Yes.' Decisive. Emphatic. No hesitation in his reply.

'Why?'

He stepped even closer. 'Because it wasn't complete. It wasn't perfect.' His head lowered towards hers. 'We were left wanting.'

Her lips tingled, his were so very near and the rush of memories was mixing with the present. It felt so natural and right for her to tilt that little bit further forward.

Her mouth touched his, clung to the warmth. Would have parted further and let him in if he'd made the move. But he lifted away, just a fraction, and she barely controlled the moan of disappointment, failed to suppress the sigh. *Frustration.*

His smile was slight, and his eyes were dark with determination. 'See?'

There were commuters rushing all around them. Staring straight ahead, pacing along the footpath, keen to get home, to after-work assignations, to the gym, to whatever it was that they were looking forward to after a long day at the office. But in their tiny patch of the universe, less than a metre square, there was stillness, save their slow breathing.

'Let's get dinner.' His mouth hardly moved as he spoke.

'I'm not really dressed for dinner.' She didn't want to be dressed at all. His gaze frisked her. She knew he'd caught her thought and she also knew his reply. He'd be happy to eat there and then and she was the dish of the day.

'Dinner. Tonight. Now.' He seemed to have lost the ability to form whole sentences.

'OK.' Just as she had lost the ability to think at all.

As she stared out of the window Emily's whole body quivered, tightening with the thrill of remembered ecstasy. She could only hear the rush of her pulse, not the reason of her mind. A tiny part of her was tense with warning, but the rest tense with longing. He was staring ahead at the road, his face shadowed by a frown, concentrating harder than the slow-moving traffic warranted.

'Have you been busy with work?' Oh, it was inane, but she had to break the taut silence somehow.

'Very,' came the brief reply. Then he too seemed to make the effort. 'It's always pretty busy. But things have been really hectic the last couple of weeks.' He glanced at her. 'What about you? Have you found a job?'

'I haven't really been looking. I'm still deciding what I want to do so I've just been cruising.'

'Are you enjoying not working?'

'Well, I don't miss being on my feet all day.' She laughed. 'It's weird not having to be anywhere at a prescribed hour.'

Or having anyone to talk to. She'd easily spent more than one day not talking to anyone in this city of millions.

'How have you been filling your days?'

'Just walking. Sightseeing. There are lots of sights in London.'

'So you are still on your feet all day,' he teased.

'It's a little different.' She grinned.

She watched him drive, his sure, calm control of the machine. It wasn't long before they were back in the heart of the city. He pulled into a parking space, escorted her with his innate politeness to the door. Unlocking it, he swung the heavy wood wide, before pressing a security keypad on the inside wall. She stepped forward into the surprisingly light foyer and looked at the calm colours, the polished wooden floor. Spacious, with high ceilings, wide doorways, and a long staircase, his house was beautiful. He didn't stop to give her the tour, led her straight to the airy kitchen at the back of the ground floor, where he fiddled with buttons on the oven. Then he reached into a cupboard, drawing out a bottle of red with one hand and tossing her a box of grissini with the other. And she watched—every sure movement of his strong body. His large, confident hands worked the cork out of the bottle, the glass fitted snugly into his palm as he poured generously. He had beautiful hands. He had beautiful everything.

She kept watching as he pulled out a tray from the oven—smothered in vegetables, roasted to perfection and a joint of meat resting in the middle. Her mouth was watering but it wasn't because of the food.

'Just a little something you prepared earlier?' she asked, amazed.

A half-smile twinkled. 'I have a housekeeper—Micaela. She works every weekday. On weekends when necessary.'

Of course he had hired help. That was OK. It had still been his idea—like the picnic in Verona. Memories haunted her muscles. Emily fiddled with the box of grissini—anything to keep her hands from fiddling with him. The ache inside was becoming a pain now. He was here, he was so close and she *wanted*.

'You hungry?' he asked, watching the tray as he lifted it to the bench.

'Mmm-hmm.' She couldn't trust herself to speak. Her voice already felt rusty, desire corroding it.

He turned, lanced her with his all-seeing eyes and spoke dryly. 'Don't hold back, Emily.'

She broke free of his piercing gaze, ripped at the box and grabbed a breadstick as others spilled across the bench.

He took the two steps to get right into her space. She couldn't not look at him then. He knew. She knew he understood the depth of her need. And as if to prove it his fingers lightly danced down her throat, sliding down her chest until his palm moved to cup her swollen breast, thumb tormenting her taut nipple as it had those few weeks ago.

The breadstick snapped between her fingers.

His face lit up with that smile. His other hand slid up her leg then, under her skirt all the way up to her knickers. They were no barrier and she gasped in pleasure as his fingers slipped under the elastic, testing and instantly moving to tease as he felt the full extent of her appetite.

'Luca…'

'If you're hungry, Emily,' he instructed solemnly, 'you should *never* hold back.'

So she didn't—couldn't. Her insides were like lava. Her deeply hidden core that she'd always thought firm and cool, rational and sensible, was now molten, blistering hot and bending her towards him. Driving her. Rocking her pelvis into his hand, she met his mouth with hers open and needy, her hands moving, fighting to touch him—going straight for the kill.

He groaned as his fingers stroked deep. 'I've been wanting this again since the moment I left you in Verona.'

'So what took you so long?'

'I'm stubborn.'

'Why do you want to fight it?' Panting, she unzipped his trousers with a rough jerk. Got her hands on him the way he had his on her—intimate and demanding.

Everything was unleashed. The kiss was hard and passionate and their hands provoked even more until they were both shaking. Teeth scraped and tongues thrust and yet for her they were nowhere near close enough or fast enough or *anything* enough. She growled as he tore his lips from hers.

'This isn't how…' He looked into her eyes and the fire arced between them—incandescent and unstoppable.

With a smile she hooked an arm around his neck and pulled him to meet her open, hungry mouth. Moments, minutes, hours lost in another kiss so passionate it almost hurt.

He whipped his hands from her body and she rolled onto

her toes, only just keeping her balance. His hands came back—hard on her arms. 'No. We should talk first. And before we do that we should eat.'

'I'm not in imminent danger of fading away—let's talk now.' Frustration made her snappy.

He stared hard at her. 'This can only be a fling, Emily. That's all I can offer.'

'Why?' Why put limits on this before it had really begun—why not just see where it went?

Silence.

She watched the darkness grow in his eyes. 'Did someone hurt you, Luca?'

His hands tightened on her arms. 'Badly.'

'I won't hurt you.' She liked him. She'd like to get to know him more.

'I know.' A blunt response. 'Because I won't let you.' His grip loosened, fingers skimmed down to her wrists. 'But I don't want to hurt you either.'

'Who says you will?' She placed the palms of her hands on his chest. His arrogant assumption that he might annoyed her. Defensive pride reared its head. 'Maybe all I want from you is *just* this—no-holds-barred sex and nothing else.'

He glared back, the frown drowning in a glower of epic proportions. 'OK,' he said. 'Seeing we're being honest, let me put it plain. I don't do relationships. I don't do commitment. I've been married once before and I will *never* do it again.'

She tightened her muscles, absorbing the shock, but his brutal honesty continued.

'No commitment, Emily. No strings. Do you still want this, knowing that?'

She stared hard into the darkness of his eyes, let hers roam over his features, his olive skin, the angled jaw that right now was shadowed with stubble, the full mouth.

Just a few nights of mind-bending passion?

It was already too late.

'Didn't I just say that? No-holds-barred sex and nothing else? Let's say I think of you as my holiday fling.'

'You're sure?'

'Yes.'

'Then that's it.' He vanquished all possibility of any further thought with a few words and a lot of action. His hands intimately invaded her body, his mouth pressed bruisingly hard on hers blocking everything but sensation.

Passion, born of pent-up need and sudden anger, had her go straight for the zenith too—hands back hard on the thing she wanted right inside her. Pulling him closer, firmer, faster.

A breathless second apart as he pulled a condom from his pocket, tearing the foil open and forcing the rubber on. And almost fully clothed, their dinner waiting, they surged together. Frantic, fast—both desperately fighting for that fix of pleasure.

It was mere seconds in coming—their bodies clenched together like vices, racked with violent shudders.

After the echo of her screams passed, it was their breathing—short, sharp, harsh—that filled her ears.

She opened her eyes, looked straight into his—where a

flicker of rue nestled. 'Wow,' he muttered. 'I'm thinking that was the appetiser.'

She took a deep breath, stepped back, rested her weight on her hands on the bench behind her and tried to act completely cool—as if this sort of meltdown were nothing out of the ordinary. 'I'm looking forward to the main course.'

His brows lifted. 'While I'm looking forward to dessert.'

She flushed—she hadn't meant… He caught her eye and winked. Her colour still burning, she turned away and adjusted her clothing. When she'd summoned the courage and calm to turn back, he'd done the same.

He concentrated on serving—quick and efficient. She just focused on breathing and standing upright. He looked across at her. 'Are you OK?'

She nodded. 'I think so.'

He shook his head. 'Let's eat, OK?'

The dinner was divine, the meat melt-in-the-mouth tender, the vegetables tangy with some sort of marinade, but her mind was spinning too fast for her to truly enjoy it.

He held his fork with his left hand, using his right to cover hers—curling his fingers around hers. It wasn't a possessive grip, nor demanding in a sexual way. It was simple contact. Almost comfort. And she appreciated it, needing the connection. While there was to be nothing long-lasting between them, she needed to know there was some sort of caring.

'Have you got a mobile?'

'I picked up a prepay last week.' To field calls from employment agencies she'd yet to sign up with. To stay in contact with her sister who was too busy to bother.

'I'll give you my number.' He stood, pushed the plates away and pulled her into his arms. 'I'm not settling for a morsel this time. I'm having the whole banquet.'

Drugging kisses led to all-consuming passion, he carried her up the stairs to a room that was light and fresh and utterly impersonal.

She glanced, vision blurry. 'This isn't your room?'

'My room's a mess. I couldn't let you see it with all my stuff all over the floor.' And then he kissed her more, all over, confusing her thoughts, until she no longer cared about anything but having him inside her.

But after, as she lay loose-limbed and replete, she started to wonder what was going to happen next. She decided to test the waters. 'I should get back to the hostel.'

He lay beside her, said nothing.

'All my things are there,' she couldn't stop adding.

'I'll take you.'

She shouldn't feel the thump of disappointment when she'd been prepared. But it walloped her in the stomach all the same. He didn't want her to stay—not even the rest of the night. It really was just the fulfilment of an urge—scratching the itch and all that.

He left to change and she quickly pulled on her clothes, refusing to let emptiness eat away her satisfaction. Finding her way back down to the living area, she hardened her heart. This was her treat, remember? This was her chance to have and take what *she* wanted—and she had wanted. And she *still* wanted.

He was already waiting for her. In jeans and tee—she'd never seen him in jeans and, oh, yes, he was still her treat.

They drove back to the hostel in silence. Pulling up outside, he unclicked his seat belt.

'Don't come in,' she said hurriedly, not wanting awkwardness to swallow the last remnants of pleasure.

He didn't kiss her this time, just looked at her with shadowed, burning eyes that seemed to touch her skin just as if they were his lips anyway. 'I'll be in touch.'

CHAPTER SIX

THE more Luca thought about it, the more he didn't like it. And he spent all day thinking about it. Emily couldn't stay there, but the solution was no more tolerable—either way he was confronted with a situation he wasn't comfortable with. But inevitably, as it had once already, desire won. He strode into the hostel common room wearing jeans and a shirt and a scowl. 'Get your bag.'

'Pardon?' She was sitting cross-legged on a sofa, eating toast and reading the paper—at nine-thirty at night.

'You shouldn't be staying here. It's not safe.'

'Not safe?'

'No,' he asserted, feeling all the more grumpy. 'Not safe. Full of transients and people you don't know. I wouldn't let my sister stay in a place like this on her own.'

'Do you have a sister?'

'No, but if I did, I wouldn't let her stay here.'

'You wouldn't *let* her?'

He ignored the emphasis. 'Come on, get your bag. You're coming home with me.'

'Do you have a brother?'

'No. But again, if I did, I wouldn't want him staying here. Not if I could convince him otherwise. It's not right for a lone woman to stay here.' He paced in a circle. 'When you were with your sister it was different—just. But not now.'

She stepped in front of him, blocking his path. 'And you don't think moving in with some stranger is more risky?'

A flash of surprise checked him. 'I'm not a stranger. And you know you have nothing to fear from me.'

He watched her think about it. Watched her sleepy, luminescent eyes widen.

'Save your money and stay with me.' He knew he almost had it won. He added some frills. 'I'm your holiday fling, right? Why not let me provide the whole package—room, food and entertainment? Take your time to decide on a job and a flat. I don't mind.'

'Why, how generous you are, Luca,' she drawled. 'And what do you get out of it?'

'What we're both counting on.' His house was his sanctuary. Quiet, relaxing—his and his alone. But for a few days he'd have to adjust. His body's need was too strong—breaking through the boundaries he'd established years ago. And he couldn't rest knowing she was alone in this hostel. Privacy and isolation could be restored—after.

'You know I can't say no.'

'I was counting on that too.'

Did she really have nothing to fear? A little doubt niggled in the back of Emily's brain. No strings, no commitment—wouldn't living together make it harder to keep that distance? But she couldn't resist his offer—and it *was* generous. Even though she was a with-it woman living in the twenty-first century and totally capable of safely staying in the hostel all by herself, she couldn't help her instinctive, pleased response to his display of macho protectiveness. And while it might not be that risky, it was certainly reckless. Reckless was something Emily hadn't ever been until that day in Verona. That hedonism, the holiday mood enveloped her now—bringing back the warmth of the Italian sun, the taste of bliss in his arms... Why couldn't she extend that holiday, just for a little while longer? Didn't, as he'd once said, she deserve it?

'Your room, ma'am.'

He put her pack inside the door of the bedroom they'd lain in last night. The guest bedroom. So boundaries would be maintained—she wouldn't actually be sleeping in *his* bed. She crossed the room and looked out of the window— last night she hadn't been lucid enough to notice the view over the private gated gardens.

'I'll show you where the key is. You can go and read the morning paper in the sun. It's very nice.' He took her hand. 'Let me show you the rest of the facilities. You've seen the kitchen and you have your own bathroom off your bedroom, so let's move on to entertainment.'

'I thought you were my entertainment.'

'I'll entertain you again and again. But this is for while I'm at work.'

And, if last night was anything to go by, it would be her recovery time. She followed him into the big, light room. A large sofa stretched in front of her and opposite was a wall of bookcases.

'Take your pick, but if you don't fancy reading…' He pushed a couple of buttons on a remote and with a click and a whir half the bookcases seemed to disappear and a giant flat-screen TV was revealed.

'Oh, that's clever.'

'Very Batman, don't you think?' he joked. 'The DVDs are in this cabinet. I have a reasonable collection, but if you want to watch something else just let me know and I can get it delivered.'

A reasonable collection? There were masses of DVDs— enough to rival the entire stock of the DVD store where she'd worked. Although they were a little on the action/thriller side. Not too many romcom chick flicks— maybe his ex took them when they split up? She felt burningly curious about that part of his life—what had gone wrong? She'd ask some time, but was cautious about prying too much too soon. There had been real pain in his eyes when he'd admitted to being hurt and she didn't want to spoil the lightness of the mood now. Not when she sensed this was a little out of the ordinary for him. It was way out of the ordinary for her too.

'I take them out of the cases. It makes it easier to store more.'

'And are they filed alphabetically, by genre, or director or something?'

'No.' He grinned. 'In order of purchase. By all means sort them if you want, though. Watch any, watch all.'

'You expect me to figure out all these remote controls? The stereo, the TV, the DVD player, the *curtains*…'

He laughed and gestured towards the bi-folding doors

along the back wall. 'Through there is a formal lounge I don't tend to use unless I have some sort of gathering. Now follow. I've saved the best 'til last.'

His room? She was *very* curious about that. But while he led her to the stairs it wasn't up but down that he went. At the very bottom they were confronted with a closed door. He pushed buttons on the keypad on the wall beside them. 'I'll give you the number.'

'I'm going to need a two-hundred-page manual to re-member how to work this place.'

'It won't take you that long.'

'Why the security?'

'My housekeeper has a young son. I don't want him in here without supervision.'

'Supervision?' What on earth was in there? 'And you said I had nothing to fear? Let me guess, it's a soundproof room and filled with electric guitars and drum kit 'cos you're really a metal head.'

He shook his head.

'Wine cellar?'

He grinned. 'I have a couple of cabinets upstairs but the bulk of my collection is stored offsite.'

He was serious about that?

'Believe it or not this is much more fun.' He opened the door.

She blinked as he switched on the lights. Oh, wow. She would never have expected this.

The expanse of blue was lit underneath—the light was subtle and it was warm and cast pretty patterns on the gleaming white walls.

'Oh.' The water was about two lanes wide and went the length of the room.

'There's a small gym down there and a bathroom through there.' He walked down the last step onto the small paved area at the head of the pool. 'Nice, huh?' He whipped off his tee shirt, and kicked away his shoes. His hands went to his belt.

'Very nice.' Her smile broadened as he pulled his jeans down and stepped out of them. His boxers followed. 'Really, very nice.'

He winked back, then turned, dived straight in, his arms moving in a perfect arc. He surfaced several feet out in the pool, droplets of water flew as he shook his head. 'Aren't you coming in?'

She stood at the edge and thought of the lamest excuse she could. 'I don't have my swimsuit with me.'

'Emily, this is hardly the public pools. You don't need a swimsuit.'

Time for honesty, then. 'Actually, I'm not the most confident swimmer.'

'You come from an island nation. I thought you were all born swimming.'

'I can swim. I'm just not that confident. I don't like it when my feet can't touch the bottom. It looks really deep there.'

'It is really deep. But I can make it shallower for you.'

'How?'

'It has an adjustable floor. I can't do it right now, but will do later if you want.'

Adjustable floor? 'Why do you have it so deep?'

'I like diving.'

'As in somersaults and flips and stuff?'

'No, as in scuba- and free diving. I practise down here. Have you ever gone scuba diving? Underwater gardens are as beautiful as the trees and flowers sort.'

'I don't think that's for me.' She shook her head. 'I'd be afraid of being swallowed whole and never finding my way to the surface.'

'It's easy. Come on, come in. It's really shallow this end. Think of it as a giant bath.'

It was too beautiful to resist. Just like him.

'I'm not going in that deep end.' She tried not to feel self-conscious as she stripped, felt better as he swam closer, looking more wicked the more naked she became.

She stepped down the ladder. It *was* a giant bath—but tepid, neither too cold nor too warm.

'You're not a risk-taker?' He reached out for her.

'I haven't been in a position to be able to take risks.' She let him pull her through the water.

'But you're in a position to now.'

Yes. And she already was taking a huge risk.

The floor of the pool suddenly dropped away.

'Hold onto me.' He put her arms around his neck. Their bodies bumped, warm and wet, and she wound her legs round his waist. His legs worked, keeping them both afloat, moving them through the water.

'Does nothing scare you?' she asked. He seemed so strong, so sure of himself.

'The things that scare me are the things that happen outside of my control but that impact on my life.'

'What—like hurricanes?' She felt his puff of laughter.

'Hurricanes of the human kind.'

'Like losing your mum?'

'Yeah, I guess.' No laughter this time.

'What was boarding school like?' She still couldn't get over that one—how isolated he must have been.

'Actually it wasn't that bad. It wasn't an archetypal horror. I had good teachers, stability—year in, year out, same place, same people. My father provided the money for a first-class education and all the extras I could want. Swimming, skiing, scuba. I studied hard but I had a good time too. More of a good time than you probably did. Was there no one else for you and Kate?'

'Mum had a brother but he lived hours away and wasn't able to help. We were OK. I had Kate.' She looked down into the blue; it really was very deep beneath them. 'You like going down there?'

'I like the quiet. The weightlessness. Free of encumbrances.'

'You've got an encumbrance now.'

'You weigh nothing in the water, Emily.' He grinned. 'I'll help you go below and then find the surface again. You'll be swimming like a mermaid in no time.'

They were heading back towards the end of the pool and she swam away from him to the edge.

'I might be a mermaid who plays in the shallows.' She climbed up the ladder, chanced a look at him over her shoulder and burst out laughing.

He stood, the water lapping at his hips, his erection thrusting from the water like some sort of missile, and his face bore the expression of a satyr.

'I'm thinking you're more of a siren than a mermaid.' He didn't bother with the ladder, simply vaulted over the side and lunged for her. 'You're going to like the shower down here.'

Emily slept for longer than she'd ever slept in her life. When conscious at last, she lay quietly listening for sounds of movement, but he must have gone to work hours ago. She showered in the spacious en suite, standing for a long time under the hot, heavy jet of water, washing away the faint aches from Luca's all-physical passion. Slowly she dressed, unsure of what she wanted to do today. She hadn't had a holiday since she was a kid. And now she had the time to consider her options—to work out what her options even were. Stomach rumbling, she headed straight to the kitchen.

As she entered the room she could suddenly hear a noise nearby. The door to the walk-in pantry was shut, but the door beside it was open. Emily went through and looked at the stranger in the middle of the small room she'd hadn't even known was there. She was a petite woman who looked as if she'd swallowed a beach ball—pregnant as anything.

'You must be Emily.' She spoke, a pretty Italian accent colouring her words. 'I'm Micaela.'

The tiny brunette was drowning in sheets. Some complex ironing contraption in front of her and a wall of high thread count all round.

Emily nodded. Amazed at the scene, she took in the sound of the washing machine and the dryer beside it.

'I can make my bed,' Emily said hurriedly as she looked at the sheet mountain. 'Please.'

Micaela smiled. 'You are staying in—'

'The room with that incredible view over the gardens.' She wondered if the view from the floor above would be even more spectacular... Luca's own personal space... what was it like?

Emily looked at the housekeeper again, worried. She was tiny and pregnant and shouldn't be scrubbing the floors, or wrestling with the ironing or anything much, surely.

'Can I help you with those?' She automatically stepped in, taking one end of the sheet and helping to fold the smooth linen.

'Don't worry,' Micaela assured her as they stacked the folded sheet on top of the others. 'My husband usually helps and he does any heavy work. You've met him already. Ricardo. He drove you from the airport.'

Oh. That was her husband? So they both worked for Luca. And Micaela knew about the airport ride. Emily wondered what she made of it—wondered if it was normal for Luca to pick up strange women when overseas.

'Luca thinks I should stop working altogether, but I like to keep busy. So—' Micaela stepped out from behind the mass of white and led the way back to the kitchen '—what can I get you for lunch?'

'Oh. Nothing.' Emily was embarrassed on several levels—she wasn't used to someone preparing food for her, and was it really lunchtime already? 'I'll make myself a sandwich later. And I promise I'll clean up after.'

Micaela's smile was almost friendly. 'Well, if you need anything, please just let me know.'

'Thank you,' Emily murmured awkwardly. She drifted

through a door and found herself in the formal lounge that Luca had gestured to last night. A gleaming black baby grand piano stood showcased in the corner. She was instantly drawn to it. Happiness flooded her—she hadn't played properly in weeks. She ran a finger along the edge—not a speck of dust. She doubted that Luca played—it didn't seem to fit his image somehow. But owning one that was so magnificent didn't surprise her. Luca had nothing but the best.

Gingerly she sat at the piano seat, a little in awe, and experimented with a key here and there, then a chord. It was perfectly tuned. But she sensed this instrument hadn't been played properly in a long time. She stretched her fingers out, feeling the pressure of the piano resisting her. She pushed harder on the keys and then softer to get the right tone. Her foot tentatively touched the pedals.

The sound she wanted started to come. And then she forgot her surroundings—simply sat and played as she hadn't in years. Not the accompaniment to one of Kate's songs—beautiful as they were—but a solo piece, just for her own pleasure.

A step sounded right behind her. Emily spun on the seat. Nearly fell off it as she saw the small boy only a nose away watching her. So much for thinking she had any sort of sixth sense. How long had he been standing there?

'Hi,' she said. He must be the housekeeper's son and rather gorgeous he was too.

He said nothing in reply. His eyes darted to the piano behind her.

'Want to hear some more?'

He didn't answer, but he looked like a yes. Emily smiled. He was cute.

'Come on, then.' She turned back to the keyboard, not wanting to make him more self-conscious and run away. She launched straight into another piece—one that he might recognise. A few minutes later she felt his restlessness at her side. She glanced at him—was he over it already? Had enough? Itching to get away? But no, he was watching her fingers on the keys and she realised the restlessness was his own little fingers moving.

'You want to have a go?'

There was a smile then.

At first she had palpitations over some kid's sticky fingers bashing the keys. But it was built to be played—to be used, to be loved. And she could tell by the roundness of his eyes that this was something he'd wanted for a while.

Her smile grew as wide as his as she guided his fingers and they tapped out 'Twinkle Twinkle'. He giggled. She understood exactly how he felt.

'Marco.'

He jumped. So did Emily.

'It's OK.' Emily turned quickly to speak to Micaela. She didn't want him to get in trouble. But then she saw the indulgence in his mother's eyes and knew there was no way this boy could ever do anything bad as far as she was concerned. She said something softly to him in Italian that had him running out of the room.

'Thank you,' Micaela said.

'It's nice to have someone who likes to listen,' Emily said simply. 'How old is he?'

'Almost five. He'll be starting school in a couple of weeks.'

Emily nodded. 'He's lovely.' She felt braver now, able to talk. 'When are you due?'

'December.' Micaela's smile was different this time, full and unreserved. 'Our own little Christmas miracle.'

By the time Luca got home—late—Emily's need, like a fever, had her hot and jumpy. Passion was the only cure for the madness bubbling her blood—unfortunately, it was also the cause. She met him at the door and the look in his eye mirrored hers—ravenous. Melting against him, she savagely ran her fingers through his hair. They dropped to the floor, keeping the contact of the kiss as much as they could. Unashamedly she stretched out, spreading her legs, arching up as he pressed down on her, his hands forcing fabric aside. He thrust deep as she was still undoing the top button on his shirt, only just getting him naked enough for her to curl her nails into his skin as the spasms hit and she came.

'Not enough,' he growled, rocking harder into her. 'I want it to last…' But instead he groaned as she clamped tight around him, flexing her feminine muscles to trap and release him hard and fast and revelling as he finally collapsed.

Lying beneath him, she forced herself to ignore the burgeoning feelings that now followed so fast after the physical relief. She had to remember what they'd agreed. She had to keep it carefree.

'So, honey—' she put on a cooing tone '—did you have a good day?'

CHAPTER SEVEN

'PLAY the elephant one again.'

'OK,' Emily laughed. 'But you have to do the singing.'

She and Marco were having a fine time at the piano. Giggling over Emily's deliberately wrong notes and the game of starting over again.

'What's going on?' Luca didn't sound anywhere near as amused as they were.

Marco leapt off the seat but Emily refused to jump to attention. She slowly turned. What was he doing home in the middle of the day?

'We're playing the piano.' Coolly she answered with the obvious.

'Marco.' Micaela was at the doorway in a blink and her son scarpered from the room. Emily saw the anxious glance the housekeeper sent Luca. She didn't blame her. There was something in his silent appraisal that had her feeling uncomfortable too. But she wasn't going to let it show. Luca might be the boss of Micaela, but he wasn't the boss of her. She was his guest—wasn't she? Not an employee to be told off for insubordination or overstepping the mark.

Micaela said something in Italian. He gave only a brief reply, a flash of teeth and then the woman stepped back. She sent a small smile in Emily's direction, but Emily barely saw it, too busy trying to read the unreadable mask that was Luca's face and growing all the more irritated with her failure.

Luca heard the door click and knew Micaela had headed to the kitchen. He stepped further into the lounge, unable to take his eyes off Emily, unable to stop the churning feeling inside.

For the forty-six thousandth time he asked himself what he was doing. Jerked his shoulders because he had no idea and it irritated him. He couldn't have left her at that hostel, he'd been right to bring her here—a week or so, she'd get sorted and they'd burn themselves out. But he hadn't had enough of her. If anything his desire was growing. Only two days into it and here he was at home in the middle of the day because he wanted to *see* her, wanted to talk to her, wanted to spend time with her.

With wary movements she turned a little to the side and gestured. 'It's a beautiful piano. I hope you don't mind.'

'No.' She looked disconcerted at his bald reply and he forced himself to elaborate. 'I used to sit by my mother when she played.' It was one of the few happy memories he had of her before the sickness had struck.

'Was this hers?'

'No. My father got rid of it not long after her death. This is the one she should have had.'

'Is that why you have it?'

'I needed something to fill the space.' He shrugged. 'I didn't know you played.'

'I've accompanied Kate for years.'

Of course she had—literally, emotionally. Only now Kate no longer needed her. 'Will you play for me?' He wanted to sit where Marco had.

'Maybe later.' She closed the lid.

He was going to take her out to lunch. This was her first trip to London and so far she hadn't exactly had the best tour of it. It wasn't so much fun seeing the sights on your own. He didn't bother when he travelled for work, just focused on the job. But he felt a whim to see Emily enjoy London; he wanted to see how beautiful she was as she explored it. Only now that idea went right out the window as he stared at her, sitting at his piano.

'You were wearing that tee shirt at the Arena.' Her eyes were that bright green. His mouth went dry, senses homed in on one thing only—her. The need was stronger than ever. He stepped closer, watching her reaction—he could see her breathing accelerate, see her breasts tighten and her mouth part.

Sì.

He took her face in both hands, caressed her high, smooth cheekbones with his thumbs before bending close. Sliding his fingers into her hair, he looked into her flushed features, at her gleaming, dilated eyes, and raw satisfaction kicked as she leant back towards him—seeking.

This was what he wanted. He scooped her up and carried her straight up to her room, hooking her door shut behind him with his foot.

As he set her down she mumbled beneath his mouth, 'Micaela…Marco.'

'They won't hear us.' And he made sure of it by simply placing his lips back over hers and keeping them there. Kissing and connecting deep. And all the while he refused to think, refused to analyse why it was that when he was sealed together with her like this, his very soul seemed to soar. He just wanted to fly.

Emily drew the sheet over her and watched as he stepped into the en suite bathroom and showered briefly before dressing. He looked a different man from the dark angel who had appeared before. Now his expression was lighter; he was smiling as he pulled his trousers back on.

'Is that what you came home for?'

'Actually, no.' He grinned. 'But there's always tomorrow. And—' a quick kiss on her lips '—I'll be back tonight.' He was out of the door before she had the chance to ask more.

Moments later she heard him speaking in Italian, heard the higher-pitched tones as Micaela answered. Emily winced. He'd still been doing up his belt as he'd left her room. It couldn't have been more obvious that they'd had a tryst. That he was a satisfied man. And for the first time in their affair, a trickle of embarrassment crept in.

What had that been all about if not purely for a lunchtime quickie? Never mind that she'd revelled in it—loving the sense of closeness that had come with all the kissing. But it wasn't real, was it, that closeness? That had just been to stop them shouting and making even more of an awkward situation with Micaela and her son in the rooms below. All it was to Luca was the sex. There was no hint of involvement with his life—no dates, no suggestion of going out to dinner, no plans to see or do anything…

Wasn't she good enough for even a little romance? Couldn't he at least play at it as he had that day in Verona— with his posh picnic and fine wine and saucy sweet talk? Or did he think he didn't need to bother any more? That he knew she'd put out for him the minute he so much as looked at her?

And it was true. Damn it. She would. Because nothing on earth had ever felt as good as having Luca in her bed, in her arms and in her body.

She waited in her room until she was sure Micaela and Marco would have left for the day. Then she walked—for hours along the river, trying to figure out how to fix the crack that was appearing in the holiday fling. She didn't want it to end but she might have to reset the rules.

Luca got home as soon as he could without officially declaring it a holiday. Who was he kidding? His brain had gone AWOL days ago. And after leaving her earlier, he had taken a detour. Another whim, another moment of madness. He'd wanted to find something for her. In his mind's eye he'd seen her playing the piano, in that old worn shirt and thin skirt, her bare arms and naked fingers making such music. He'd never felt jealous of a four-year-old boy before but he'd have given anything to sit where Marco had been sitting and be the beneficiary of that beautiful smile and all that attention.

He had the even stronger desire to take a few days off and take her on a jaunt—truly make it a holiday. But as that idea teased he clenched his teeth hard together; mentally he inked the line and underlined it again. Too damn dangerous. Already he was in a position he'd vowed never to let happen—he had a lover who'd lasted more than a few dates and, worse, she was staying in his own home. And while he was trying to maintain much of his usual distance, every day it was eroding and the desire to keep distant was eroding fast with it.

He had to fight harder. He had to finish this sooner rather than later because the one thing he refused to risk again was getting close to anyone. Because he always lost out, didn't he? Those he loved never stuck around. Losing Nikki had been the worst thing that had ever happened to him. In no way was he up for anything like a repeat. He wanted some fun now, he'd earned it with all the years of nothing but work, but fun was all it could be.

But when he walked in and found Emily was out, disappointment hit him heavy in the chest. He sat at the kitchen counter and opened another box of the grissini he'd got Micaela to find especially for her. Gnawing on the bread-stick, he appreciated it for the displacement activity it was.

He glanced at his watch and then out at the sky. Not long now and the darkness would fall completely. Maybe she'd gone to see Kate. Maybe she'd left him? At that thought he went to her room and felt relief gush as he saw her pack still there, small items still scattered on the table.

And then irritation mopped all the good feeling up. Well, where was she, then? And what was he doing even worrying about it? *This* was what he didn't want. He didn't want to be so concerned about someone else; he was comfort-eating breadsticks while he waited for her. He didn't want to wait for anybody. He didn't want to be sitting around letting someone else mess with his emotions.

He poured wine, drank it, decided to give her 'til nine and then he'd start walking the neighbourhood.

Ten minutes later the key scraped against the door and he raced to jerk it open.

'Where have you been?' he positively barked, and then had to take a breath and remind himself to chill out.

'Walking.' She looked surprised. 'I didn't think you'd be home this early.'

'Oh.' Ordinarily he wasn't. But ordinarily his ultimate temptation wasn't waiting for him on his sofa.

Except she hadn't been. She'd been out somewhere and now she looked knackered. 'Come and eat. You look done in.'

She sat at the counter and helped herself to the grissini as he poured a large glass of red. He let her sip and munch while he pulled a salad from the fridge, tossed some onto a plate for her, and broke some bread to put alongside it. 'Where did you go?'

She shrugged. 'For a walk down by the river.' She crunched for another moment. 'It's a lovely night. Lots of people spilling out of pubs.'

'You didn't go in?'

'Not on my own, no.'

He hadn't been down that way in ages. She was right, he wasn't usually home by now—still working, watching the US markets, and then when they closed those in Asia were almost due to open again… He glanced out of the window. It was a warm night—a drink by the river would be nice.

Then he remembered his mild panic when she hadn't been home—not nice—and so he held back the whim. He'd succumbed to two of those already today. He set down a platter of cheese and meat for her to pick at as well as the salad.

'Have you spoken to Kate at all?' She should go out with her sister. Then he wouldn't have either this niggle of guilt or this leap of temptation.

'No.' She kept her eyes on the plates. 'She's busy.'

Busy being self-absorbed.

But he didn't go there, he let her eat, told her some lame scuba story. When she'd finished he whisked away her plate. 'Come on, let's go somewhere comfortable.'

She did look tired. He wanted to make her smile—he hoped he had just the thing. He led her to the lounge and nudged her onto the sofa and went to the stereo to choose some music.

Emily sighed as she found the page in her book and tried to concentrate, wondering whether she really did have the guts to mention the rules, let alone reset them. He sat beside her but had no book tonight, seemed content to lie down, using her thighs as his pillow. She stroked his hair with her fingers, unable to resist touching. He turned his face towards her. She felt his warmth through her shirt. Maybe he wasn't so content because she could feel his fingers, feel his breath, feel his…lips.

He batted her book with his hand, knocking it to the floor. She shifted back a fraction and looked down.

'You weren't reading it anyway,' he defended, eyes dancing.

She leant forward this time, so her sensitive nipple brushed his mouth again. 'You were making that impossible.'

He didn't deny it, just made any kind of concentration impossible again with his teasing tongue. She sighed, eyes closing, giving in.

But he stopped, smiled once more when she looked at him. 'I have something for you.' He reached a hand under the sofa and pulled out a small rectangular box.

She looked at it and marvelled at how fast her heart could suddenly beat without warning. She knew that brand—the world-famous jewellery store. She told herself to calm down—it wasn't the shape of a ring box—besides, she didn't want any kind of box, she wanted... 'Luca—'

'Open it.'

It took a little more effort than she'd thought it would. When it finally clicked, she stared at the contents. Confusion blinded her. On the backdrop of velvet so navy it was almost black rested the most exquisite bracelet she'd ever seen. It was fine and, oh, how it sparkled, even like that, lying still in the box. Diamond after diamond after diamond, strung together by delicate platinum.

Her heart totally stopped then. What was he doing giving her something like this? She munched the inside of her cheek. What was this for? 'Luca?'

Lying there, looking up into her face, he must have read her unease. 'Don't worry. It wasn't expensive.'

Yeah, right. 'Don't lie to me, Luca.' She shifted the box and met his eyes. 'Not even to be nice.'

He met her gaze square on. 'It wasn't expensive for me. It's just a trinket.'

It wasn't just anything, not to Emily. Questions crowded her head once more. Increasingly nasty questions. Was this part of his usual game plan? Did he buy all his lovers a beautiful piece of jewellery? Was this a little nothing, a bonbon to sweeten the goodbye? Had he bought it himself or got his secretary to race out? Or did he have a stash of them even, in a drawer in his secret bedroom that was as out of bounds as Bluebeard's dungeon? The evil thoughts kept coming, swirling before her and clouding her vision of what was a beautiful bracelet. So classical, elegant and stunning— *nothing* like her.

'Why?' It was the only word she could get out.

He sat up, leaving her lap cold. 'Because I wanted to.'

That simple, huh? *Because he wanted*. That was the way Luca liked to operate—keeping things on a simple plane.

'Why did you want to?' She really, really wanted to understand.

'I just did.' He shrugged. 'You deserve spoiling.'

'What makes you think that?'

'Oh, come on, Emily, it hasn't been easy for you these last few years.'

Her blood chilled. 'Is this about pity, Luca?'

'No. You know it isn't.'

'So what is it, then?'

'I don't know.' He frowned. 'I feel like you've earned it.'

'Earned it *how* exactly?' As his lover? Her blood was ice now and any moment she'd snap.

Silence thickened as she stared at him. He was just as relentless about staring back and his jaw grew ever more square and hard.

Finally he shook his head slowly at her. 'Why do we have to have this in-depth examination of "why"? I just wanted to give you something nice. Get you something nice. I thought it would look pretty. You have the most lovely long arms. Nice wrists.'

Now he was getting frustrated and, despite a film of reservation still keeping her cool, she couldn't stop her small smile. 'Nice wrists?'

'Yes.' His hand encircled one. 'Very fine.'

She looked back at the box to hide her see-sawing emotions. 'Thank you.'

Part of her was thrilled, flattered, flushed…but deeper inside she doubted. Despite its undeniably hefty price tag, it made her feel cheap. Baubles were not what she wanted from Luca. She'd rather have had nothing at all. One moment he was insisting on this being a stringless fling and then he was giving her this? She didn't need mixed messages and he'd just ripped the scab off her vulnerability. Because there was a wound—underneath she'd begun to want more. Words, meaning…and emotion.

Trying to hide that fact, even from herself, she turned into him, breathed in his scent, nuzzled his warm neck, and sought the response that *was* always readily given. The box slipped to the floor as she moved to get closer to him. She silenced herself with the press of her lips to his skin.

Hours later she lay awake but pretended to be asleep. She could feel the restlessness that he was trying to contain. He moved slowly but she felt the bed lift as his weight was removed from it. Felt the brief blast of cooler air as he raised the covers to escape. Now he tucked them back around her. She kept her eyes closed, trying to keep her expression relaxed as if in deep repose, for she knew that the chink in the curtains let in light from the streetlamps and he'd be able to see enough of her features to know.

But she must have done OK because he said nothing, suspected nothing, ran a finger very lightly over her shoulder and then left the room.

The first night he'd said he had to go and do some work. The second night, he'd said he had to check his email. Now he offered no excuse.

At some point *every* night, he left. He didn't want to wake next to her, to start the day with her at his side. It only underlined the level of their relationship—that there wasn't one. And while that was what they'd agreed to, Emily knew it wasn't what she wanted any more.

CHAPTER EIGHT

LUCA appeared only a couple of hours after leaving for work again. Emily was alone at the piano.

'Your friend Pascal phoned.' She stopped playing as soon as she realised he was quietly coming over to her. 'He said he was looking forward to catching up with you tonight at dinner and that he hoped Micaela wasn't on maternity leave yet.'

He halted, halfway across the floor. 'You answered the phone?'

'Yes.' Brows lifted, she matched his hard look.

'Why didn't you let Micaela answer it?'

'Micaela wasn't here,' she replied with care. 'It was just before she arrived.'

'Why did you answer it? Why didn't you just let it ring?'

'Because when phones ring it's normal to answer them. Because it might have been a temp agency. Do I even need a because?' Her hackles snapped up. 'So I answered the phone. I'm so sorry. Was that not on my list of allowable activities?' She shut the lid of the piano. 'Perhaps you'd better write down a list of "dos and don'ts" for me.' She barely paused for breath, realising that her time to renegotiate the rules was right *now*. 'What should I do if someone comes to the door—go hide in the wardrobe?'

He jerked a step away. 'Emily, don't be ridiculous.'

'I'm not. I'm happy to be a holiday fling, but I'm not going to hide away like some sort of secret lover.'

'I don't—'

'If you want a private plaything why not just get an inflatable doll?'

'A doll wouldn't do those sexy sighs the way you do.' He turned his back, about to exit. 'I'll call Pascal and cancel.'

'Why?' Suspicious. There had been such personality in the brief exchange she'd had with the man and she had to admit she was half dying to meet someone Luca dealt with on a personal level rather than an employment one. Until this call she'd been beginning to wonder if there was *anyone* Luca dealt with on a personal level. 'Because I'm here?'

He swung back, looked uncomfortable. 'I have a reputation to maintain.'

What reputation? And how the hell was she going to damage it? 'What's wrong with having a girlfriend?' She saw she'd picked the wrong word in the way he froze. 'A lover,' she immediately rephrased. 'Why do I even have to be defined?' She rapidly changed tack again. 'Aren't I just someone you're helping out for a few days?'

'Because the dinner is business. I keep business and personal separate.'

So he didn't want to introduce her to anyone. 'That's rubbish. That's just a pathetic excuse for not building any

kind of a relationship with your current lover—other than
in bed.' And she didn't believe this dinner was all business—why would Pascal phone so early at Luca's house
if it were? Why would he know about Micaela and her
baby? Wouldn't he just leave a message with Luca's secretary at work? 'Am I really not fit for display? Not good
enough to mix with your friends and associates?'

Only good enough to sleep with? Did he think all he had
to do was toss a few diamonds her way to keep her happy?

'Of course you are.' Luca's face had flushed. 'But I
don't usually have women staying here.'

'Well, I can move out. Shall I go put up at the B & B
down the road? I could earn my crust making beds there.'

'Don't be ridiculous.'

'Well, it's either make theirs, or perform in yours.'

Now he looked really angry. 'You are the one used to
making money on the street.'

She nodded. 'And you're the one treating me like a
whore.'

'I am not and you know it.'

'No, I don't. Have your damn dinner party. I'm quite
happy to go back to the hostel.' She picked up her cardigan,
intending a snappy exit. 'Go screw yourself, Luca.'

He grabbed her arm, ripped the cardy from her fingers
and flung it back across the room. 'No! You don't say
something like that and think you can walk away from it,'
he yelled. 'What the hell do you want from me?'

'I don't know!' she yelled right back. 'But I'll tell you
what I don't want. I don't want your money. I don't want
things from you.'

'Is this about that bracelet? OK, fine. I'll never buy you anything else because it was so damn awful of me. So what's left, Emily?'

'You tell me.'

'I have nothing more to give. You know this. A good time. That's all.'

'A good time is more than just sex. You could give me some respect too. Some *time*.'

'I do have to work, Emily.'

'Twenty hours a day?'

'Usually, yes. But not this week, in case you haven't noticed. I've been home in the middle of the damn day.'

'And for what exactly? A tumble in bed?'

'No-holds-barred sex and nothing else. *Your* idea.'

'The complete holiday package. *Your* idea.'

'What, you're saying the onboard entertainment officer needs to lift his game, that it?'

'Absolutely.' Vexed, wanting to hide the hurt, she rolled her eyes and turned away. 'I shouldn't stay here. I should go.'

There was a long silence.

'Maybe you should,' he said softly. 'But you can't, can you?'

'No,' she admitted. 'Because, fool that I am, I still want you. I find it very difficult to say no to you. You look at me with those eyes, ask me with that voice and while my brain says one thing my mouth says another. Temptation, Luca.' She looked at him. 'You embody it.'

Brooding, almost black eyes dominated his face. 'So do you, Emily.' And then the smallest of smiles pulled his lips.

'I think it's good to take up temptation's offer now and then. The chance doesn't happen all that often.'

Not for her, no, but for him it must all the time. He was exceptionally attractive and there must be a list of women a mile long who'd like to be in her shoes right now. She hated the whole imaginary lot of them.

He sighed. 'I'd forgotten the dinner party. I'll go and tell Micaela now.'

Emily, smarting with insecurity, with the uncomfortable feeling that she'd had to force this little from him, saw a chance to strike back. 'You're going to land a dinner party on her at this late hour?'

He gave her a sideways look. 'Micaela is well used to catering for me. She's completely capable.'

'You're expecting her to serve for you?'

'Of course. That's her job.'

'What about Marco?'

'What about him?' Luca looked mystified.

'Who'll look after him?'

'Ricardo, of course. The child does have a father. Or don't you think fathers are capable of looking after their offspring?'

Not all fathers, no. She winced. His hand lifted, a quick frown tightened his features, but she got in before he could open that can of worms any further.

'I'm sure he's perfectly capable, but I imagine you'll have him off doing some other urgent business,' she blustered.

'Well, I'm not going to get him to drain the pool tonight, Emily,' he said witheringly. 'Look, Micaela and Ricardo have been working for me for years. I pay well above the standard rate and we're all happy. I don't think it's something you need to worry about.'

'Well, have you watched her trying to iron your damn sheets recently?'

'What?' At his stunned look she knew she had him.

'Ironing your sheets. Of all the things—I mean, what sort of la-de-da request is that, oh, lord and master? The woman is swamped in them. What are they—king-size plus?'

'Ironing my sheets?'

Emily nodded curtly as if it were the crime of the century. 'Mountains of the things and she's *so* pregnant.'

'You're right,' he said briskly. 'It's a waste of time, especially while I have you around to rumple them anyway. I'll take them off her list of "dos and don'ts".' Sarcasm all the way.

The victory was bitter and not nearly enough—they weren't his sheets she was rumpling, were they? Not the ones on his bed in his private lair. And his arrogant assumption that she'd still be around to rumple them—even though she would—made her all the more irrationally angry. All the more determined to score a decent point.

'You might own everything in sight, Luca, but that doesn't give you the right to be so arrogant. Is this why you got divorced? Your wife couldn't be bothered putting up with your attitude any more?'

'I'm not divorced.'

'What?'

He'd gone glacial, repeated the words slow and cold. 'I'm not divorced.'

She stared at him. Not divorced? There was a wife somewhere? Harsh, sick anger rose in her chest—acrid, stinging bile burning its way up.

No wonder he didn't want people knowing she was here. No wonder he didn't want her sleeping in his own bed—her scent mixing with that of his absent wife? What, was she on holiday somewhere? Fury clouded her judgment, her logic.

She swore she saw guilt wisp across his face before the heat of anger chased it away. What had happened? Had she left him? He left her? Emily lost it at the thought of his infidelity—her every cell screamed in denial. Even though she knew he must have…he must…

Rage turned everything red. She opened her mouth to hurl the venom at him but he, as visibly irate as she, got in first.

'She *died*.' His lips barely moved as he ground out the answer.

It was a full minute before she moved. Even longer for him—rigid with the effort of containing high-running emotion.

Finally, Emily released a painful breath. Remorse, pity, despair exploded inside. Her eyes, her nose, stung as if she'd sucked in some poisonous gas.

'Luca…' Her voice caught. 'I'm so sorry.' Not just for his loss, but for her thoughts of just a few seconds ago—thoughts that she knew had been written all over her face. 'Why didn't you tell me?'

'Why would I?'

She flinched. That one hurt. Hard and unforgiving and

a bitter reminder of her *nothing* status. Her vision fogged
as she turned away. She heard him swear under his breath.

'Emily—'

'No, you're right,' she gabbled, walking to the door.
'It's none of my business.'

'I'm sorry I snapped.' He grabbed her arm. 'I didn't
mean that.' He held on hard and she had to stop walking.
'It's just that it was a really long time ago and I don't like
to think about it much. Or talk about it. Or anything. Much.'

She blinked. 'I'm sorry too.' She couldn't look at him.
'I shouldn't have been so rude.'

'Stay here. I'll just have a word to Micaela.'

He stood just outside the door and called to Micaela.
They yabbered for a few minutes; Emily understood nothing of what they said. But she understood so much more
of him now: why he held her, and the rest of the world, at
a distance. Not only had he buried his wife. He'd buried
his heart with her.

He reappeared in the doorway. 'Dinner will be at eight.'

'I'm not going to be here, Luca.'

'Yes, you are.' He crossed the room and infiltrated her
space enough to send her pulse crazy. Damn, rational
thought was impossible when all the oxygen seemed to be
sucked away in his presence. 'We're not done yet and you
know it. You just admitted it. Besides—' he inhaled deeply
and seemed to force more lightness in his tone '—you'd be
doing me a favour. In fact I'd really appreciate your company.'

'Why?' What was with this complete, and obviously
concerted, change of heart?

'There are a couple of people coming tonight. Pascal, who you spoke to, I've known for ages. He was my mentor—has a formidable knowledge of the markets and taught me everything. He's also been happily married for the last fifty years. He wants the same for me and has taken it upon himself to find me a replacement wife. He always brings a possible candidate to dinner. This current one is a consultant with the London branch of his company. He's brought her the last couple of times we've met up. Having you there will be a good shield.'

'You want me to—'

'Protect me from the unwanted advances of another woman—yes.' His mouth made the movements of a smile but there was too much of an edge.

'That's ridiculous.' It was ridiculous. As if he'd ever need that. He certainly didn't want a replacement wife. He couldn't have made that clearer to Emily, but that was the point, wasn't it? She was his shield from another woman trying to get close and she was good protection because she already knew her place.

Suddenly she had no desire whatsoever to protect him now. She was hurt and she wanted him to open right up. And while he'd changed his mind about tonight, she didn't have the lack of interest or the dignity to refuse—she wanted to know more before she left. She wanted to know everything. What had happened to his wife? How long was a long time ago? And what was this woman coming tonight like? Why did his old mentor think she'd be a good match for him? Emily's emotions were all at sea and jealousy was the next to fly its flag.

'Have you slept with her?' She made no apology for the rudeness of her question. She just had to know.

'No.' His lips went firm.

'Do you want to?'

'No.'

Uh-huh. Consultants were bound to be beautiful and slim and well maintained as well as brilliant and she refused to believe the woman wouldn't be interested in Luca. There wasn't a woman alive who wouldn't be interested in Luca.

His temper flashed again. 'If I'd wanted to, I would have by now.'

By now she'd thought enough to be able to believe him. He was so determined to compartmentalise his life and he'd be too disciplined to blur the lines. Too hurt by the past?

He bent, glaring right in her eyes, and still felt the need to raise his voice and fire the words in her face. 'This is the thing, Emily—I don't screw around and I don't cheat.' His jaw was tight. 'Eight p.m. Here. Wear something half-decent.'

Emily recoiled at the blunt instruction. It was as if he'd slapped her across the cheek and all her sympathy sank under the force of it. So he did think she'd embarrass him. Did she have no manners? No class? No decent clothes, obviously. And he didn't take her out because she wasn't good enough to be seen with.

For a second he stared at her, a beat of amazement in his eyes, before his frustration blew. A short, sharp, crude oath and he was gone. Three seconds later the house shook as the front door slammed.

CHAPTER NINE

EMILY counted to twenty and then went in search of grissini. She needed something she could snap her teeth on—to crunch away her anger and grind away her guilt, because right now she felt bucket-loads of both.

In the kitchen, Micaela was at the bench, restraint tightening her usually friendly face. As Emily went into the pantry she wondered just how much of that argument she'd heard. Heat scorched her cheeks. So yesterday she and Luca had been at it like rabbits mid-morning, and today they were yelling at each other. It couldn't make for a pleasant working environment. But Micaela was busy making meal preparations and not looking her in the eye.

'Where's Marco?' Another awful thought occurred to her—was the poor kid hiding in his cupboard under the stairs?

'He's at a neighbour's playing today.'

Emily released another difficult breath, glad that he hadn't been around to overhear them fighting. 'I'm sorry if...I...er...'

Micaela put down the knife she was scoring tomatoes

with and turned briskly to face her. 'I want to tell you something. It is personal and I hope you don't mind but I want to tell you.' It was as if she'd been putting the words together in her head for the last five minutes and finally decided to launch forth.

Her grissini suspended mid-air, Emily wondered what the hell it was all about.

'It's difficult for us to get pregnant. We tried and tried for so long. But nothing. Then we found out that we needed help.'

Emily blinked. She didn't know what she'd expected but it wasn't that.

'My family is all in Italy. We didn't have much money and we had no one to turn to.'

Turn to for what? Emily couldn't keep up with the speed of the subject.

Micaela's eyes were dark and shiny and emotion wobbled her voice. 'Luca gave us Marco and he gave us this baby.'

And for one moment, one awful, jealousy-ridden, rottenly hideous moment, Emily thought Micaela meant that Luca had fathered her children.

'He gave us the money.'

Emily put the grissini down and sagged back against the bench. What was it with her and wrong conclusions today?

'For treatment. For doctors.'

Thank heavens Micaela didn't seem to have noticed her almost collapse, too busy getting all the details out.

'We've been going to a private clinic for years. Thousands and thousands of pounds for treatment so we could try and try again—for as long as we wanted to. He said there was no limit. That it was up to us.' She picked up the knife again, head bent as she sliced into the tomato. 'He told us it was part of our health-insurance package as our employer. But it is directly from him.'

She directed a piercing gaze at Emily then, and all her caring and gratitude was evident in the way her eyes were watering and the fierce way she spoke. 'He works too hard. He is too hard on himself. He is a good man. And he deserves…'

'What?' Emily prompted. No wonder they were so loyal to their employer, so happy to drop everything and come running when summoned. No wonder she ironed his damn sheets.

'He deserves to be happy.'

Emily closed her eyes. Yes, he did. But didn't everyone? Didn't she too?

'He should have the kind of happiness he's given Ricardo and me.'

Love. Children. A family.

Now Emily felt worse, because it seemed that Luca had almost had that, only to lose it, and now he didn't want it at all. And she, not realising, had taunted him.

She wished he'd told her before. She'd told him about her parents. But he'd had no intention of ever getting to know Emily well enough to have to bother. Only she'd made him. She rolled the breadstick back and forth on the bench. Thought about what Micaela had told her and why she had told her—because she wanted her to see the best of Luca? 'How long have you worked for him?'

'Almost eight years. He said I should stop when I got pregnant, but I like working. It keeps my mind off worrying.'

Emily understood. Wasn't that what she'd done back home—kept herself busy as a way of burying her fears? And now her lips burned with questions about Luca's past. But she couldn't ask them. It would be prying and Micaela probably wouldn't tell her anything anyway. She'd share her own personal story, but not that of her employer. Her loyalty was too strong and rightly so. Emily didn't want to make her uncomfortable. Besides, she'd rather hear about it from Luca himself.

He was such a challenge to her—and now, with the mention of this woman tonight, she felt a streak of competitiveness too. She'd show him, and all of them, just how damn stylish she could be...

But something 'half decent'? Her pack was filled with lightweight trousers and skirts and old tee shirts. Her wardrobe hadn't been the priority for some time—like, ever. It was Kate who'd had her hair done, who had the fashionable clothes—as the singer centre stage she'd needed to. Emily, the accompanist, had only needed a black top and trousers so she wouldn't stick out.

She looked at Micaela, at the way the Italian was still chic and gorgeous despite having a belly the size of an award-winning watermelon. Emily needed her kind of help. 'Can you recommend a shop that sells nice clothes that aren't too expensive? One that might have something suitable to wear to a dinner party?'

Micaela, her self-possession fully restored, sent her a

broad smile. She didn't just give her the name of the place, she drew her a map.

Luca pushed back from his desk and took a turn around the room. Guilt licked his feet like the burning flames of a small fire that he'd accidentally stumbled on barefoot. Impatiently he moved, trying to stamp out the unpleasant sensation. Adding to that discomfort, irritation whipped at his back. He didn't want to do dinner parties. He didn't want to go out and be social. He just wanted to stay home and be with Emily. The only thing salving the annoyance was the fact that she'd admitted she couldn't leave him yet. Good, because he couldn't let her go.

He wasn't angry because she'd made him think about Nikki, but because she'd so obviously thought the worst of him. But then, why shouldn't she? He'd underlined the temporary, nothing-more-to-it-than-the-physical nature of their affair—of course she probably thought he did it all the time like some cheating stud out for cheap thrills... But her judgment hurt. *What she thought of him mattered*—and that was the real problem.

He paused at the corner of his office where the sheets of glass met, giving a spectacular view over the city. Pascal was the problem too. If it had been anyone else who had called, that argument wouldn't have happened. But for Pascal and Emily to meet? Luca felt so uncomfortable about that.

But he had to host him—Pascal rarely came to London now. Part of him wanted to—but that part was small compared to the part that wanted another night with Emily all to himself. Guilt took another bite. The old man had done so much for him. He owed him. And even though Pascal had insisted that he wanted to see him settled, it wasn't that black and white. He had been there when Nikki died. He was the one person who knew it all. They almost never spoke of it, but that didn't mean it wasn't there.

He walked home—cutting it fine time wise—stopped in the kitchen first off to check if Micaela was holding up OK. He'd had no idea she ironed his sheets—teased her about it and told her to stop. She smiled and waved him away. He breathed deep and savoured the aromas. Of course she'd have it in hand. Emily had that one so far wrong. He paid the couple more than three times the going rate, but only because they were worth it. They were loyal and hard-working and, yes, went the extra mile when he needed them to. Which wasn't anywhere near as often as Emily might think—certainly not since Micaela had got pregnant.

He didn't go in search of Emily, not concerned that she might have moved out after the row that morning. He'd instructed Micaela days ago to let him know if she made any sign of leaving for good. And some more breathing time after this morning wouldn't go astray. He showered and dressed, tucking in his shirt as he walked back down to her room.

He knocked and went straight in. He took one look at her and was glad he'd taken those extra moments to breathe because there was no air getting to his lungs now. They'd shut down. So had everything else in his body, save one organ south of his belt. And then his heart started pounding.

It was just a black dress. Not even that revealing. But those arms and legs were on show, a slight hint of the deep cleavage, and a lot of back. That meant…he fought to focus…

'You're not wearing a bra.'

'Hello to you too.' She turned and gave him a cool look. 'No, I'm not. Is that not decent enough for you?'

When he'd told her to wear something half decent, he hadn't meant dressy. He'd meant something to cover her up. She was all bare arms and legs all the time and he didn't want to be a total picture of distraction when Pascal was here. Like a dog salivating over a particularly juicy piece of meat.

It hadn't come out right, but he'd been too rattled to rephrase. He'd seen the spark in her eye, known he'd scored a hit—not one he'd meant, but at the time he'd felt a gleam of misplaced satisfaction because it had felt as if she was knocking at him left, right and centre. And then he'd just felt wildly angry with her, with himself and with the whole damn uncontrolled mess. But clearly she'd taken it to heart because the woman before him now was the epitome of sultry sophistication.

She turned back to the mirror, lifted her strawberry-blonde hair and twisted it up. He was sorry; he loved the length of it, the depth of colour, wanted to run his fingers into it. Only now, as she secured it with a few clips, her cheekbones were displayed. And the odd strand feathered down, wisping around her ear, her neck, and he wanted to kiss the parts of her they pointed to.

He cleared his throat, looked away. Not tonight—at least, not now. He braced every muscle, determined to calm his raging hormones. He only had to get through a few hours. That was all. He could manage that, couldn't he?

CHAPTER TEN

EMILY concentrated on applying her mascara, trying to apply a brake to the mad acceleration of her heart. Luca crossed the room and picked up the box she'd placed on the table—she hadn't been sure what she'd wanted to do with it.

The diamonds caught the light as he lifted the bracelet out. He walked towards her, holding the chain out straight. 'Wear it for me.'

She met his eyes; the fire burned in them, melting that hard chocolate.

'OK.' It wasn't about the bracelet, it was about him. And she couldn't say no.

He wound it round her wrist and did the clasp. The metal was cold at first but soon warmed against her skin. Glancing back in the mirror, she pushed another pin into her loose topknot and as she did the bracelet slid down her arm a little, catching the light again and sparkling brilliantly. It was beautiful. No other adornment would ever be necessary. It lifted her simple black dress into something stunning and it lifted her status into something nearer his—she couldn't be confused with the waiting staff now. Part of her loved it—how could she not? And yet part of her hated it—and the soulless contract she felt it represented. Was he worried about tonight and how she was going to come across? Was he sprucing her up with an expensive piece of jewellery?

'Am I decent now?' she asked softly.

As she waited she saw his tension increasing, but it wasn't a flush of desire growing; if anything he'd gone paler beneath his brown tan and his body was tense. 'When I asked you to wear—'

'Asked? It was more of an order, Luca.'

'Whatever. I didn't mean dressy. Your arms, your legs poke out from those tee shirts and they tempt me. And now…' His jaw clamped, as if he was holding back more.

'Now what?'

'There's your back. And there's no bra. And you're too beautiful.'

She squared her shoulders. 'Do you want me to change?'

'No.'

She tilted her chin and decided to play with that one advantage she did have.

'Don't look at me like that, Emily.'

'Like what?' OK, so in her mind she was removing his clothes, piece by piece.

'Emily…' He sounded half-strangled.

She ran her hands from his shoulders to his waist. 'You look good too.'

Good enough to eat. She stood on tiptoe so she could press her mouth to his. Only she didn't, instead she took only his lower lip, sucking it into her mouth and then catching it between her teeth to give it a nip, then sucking again. Oh, yes, he was definitely good enough to eat.

He stood frozen, so she did it again, stepping in closer to invade all his space.

His hands smoothed over the curve of her bottom, and as her teeth nipped the second time his fingers curled into her softness and he pulled her right into his hips.

She smiled as she felt his body harden. *This* was the tension she liked to see in him. She held his jaw in her hands, fingers fluttering over the freshly shaved skin, and kissed him some more, teased him some more, tortured him some more. And he, rock-hard, let her. Until he groaned and his hands pushed while his pelvis thrust. One hand went to her dress, lifting the hem.

It was the sound of the door opening downstairs that stopped her. She listened to Micaela greeting the guests, then whispered, 'We can't. They've arrived.'

'We can,' he growled, breathing harsh, grinding his hips against hers. 'They'll wait.'

'You are so arrogant. We *can't* be rude. They're here already.'

'We can. We only need ten, twenty seconds, tops.'

She laughed against his lips. 'Not enough.'

Groaning, he pushed her away. 'Damn it, it'll take me longer to calm down than it would have to follow through on that.'

Giggling, she did a final fuss in the mirror for damage control.

'It's not funny.' He turned his back on her and stalked to the door. She followed him down to the foyer, watching from a distance as he pressed a kiss on the woman's cheek, shook the hand of the older man.

'What's that perfume you're wearing, Luca? So lovely and floral.' She was as stylish as to be expected. Slim, so-phisticated and coyly sharp. 'It really suits you.'

Pascal's sharp eyes flew from Luca's slightly forced smile to Emily's own on-fire face. Emily saw him swap a smile of amusement with the woman and was confused. Surely if Pascal wanted Luca and her to get together he wouldn't be looking so pleasantly surprised about Emily's presence? And as for the unsubtle question mark hanging over her involvement with him…

But Luca was downplaying it. 'Francine, Pascal, meet Emily. She's a friend who's just arrived from New Zealand.'

Unfortunately, the way he was avoiding her eyes pretty much denied the 'friend' status, but Pascal and Francine both smiled and said hello. Emily managed to murmur a similar response.

'How's Madeline?' Luca asked.

'Beautiful as ever,' Pascal replied. 'She sends her love.'

Luca nodded. 'Come through. Micaela has been slaving all afternoon just for you.'

He sent Emily a look then. She refused to bite at it, after all, if she were Micaela, she'd slave too. They went straight to the intimate table in the dining room and caught up on news as their appetiser was served. It seemed Francine was soon heading off to a business school just outside Paris.

'You were at Oxford, weren't you, Luca?' Francine asked.

'For my undergraduate degree, yes, but post-graduate was Harvard.'

Of course. He was elite all over whereas Emily was…

Francine turned to her. 'Where did you study, Emily?'

'I didn't,' she answered, battling the inferior feeling and failing. 'I left school and went straight into work. Retail.'

'Retail?' Francine-the-sophisticated delicately speared a piece of tomato with her fork.

Oh, God, this was a nightmare.

'Yes, you know, a shop assistant. Standing on your feet for hours, dusting, displaying stock, that sort of thing.'

She sensed Luca's posture tighten. What, shouldn't she admit to her working-class history?

'Oh.' Francine brightened. 'I like shopping. What was your speciality? Fashion? Perfume?'

'Sadly no.' Emily smiled sweetly. 'At first it was the hardware department of a bargain outlet store. Cheap power tools, drill bits and gardening implements. Then I moved around departments—footwear, toys, furniture… and I worked in a CD and DVD store at night.'

There, she'd let them know it. She was nothing on their education, their sophistication, their elitism. But she was all about hard work, and prioritising and getting things done. She'd had to. Three loads of washing on before she left the house, making Kate's lunch, leaving something for her father. Racing home to get the washing in off the line in her lunch break and get the next load out there, all the while having dinner slowly cooking in a crockpot. She'd had it all mastered. For years she'd done it all. And now, when she was finally free of it, she felt so empty and so vacant and so out of place.

Pascal was chuckling, but with a kindly twinkle. 'A DVD store? You must know your movies.'

'And music, yes.'

'I love movies.' Francine smiled. 'What's your favourite ever?'

Emily blinked. She hadn't expected them to accept her bald recitation of her utter averageness—or actually be interested.

'If you could have studied, what subject would it have been?' Pascal asked, seeming to understand that it was because she hadn't been able to, not because she had chosen not to.

Emily let a genuine smile out then and decided to sharpen up her act. She'd been verging on rude and that wasn't her. Her defence mechanism was set unnecessarily on high. 'Music and movies, I guess.'

They laughed and fractionally the atmosphere lightened. They discussed the current films on release—half of which Emily had seen on the plane over. She would have relaxed, settled into the swing of it, but for the ominously quiet presence on the other side of her. Each time she glanced in his direction she encountered the frown in his eyes, it made her too adrenalin-charged and aware to truly enjoy the conversation.

She forced attention onto the beautiful Francine—asking her about her upcoming MBA course and then about city life in London. Which shops were the best, which were the tourist spots she shouldn't fail to see...

Francine's coy look resurfaced at that. 'Surely Luca is showing you the best on offer?'

She couldn't have known the significance those words would have. *The best.* Emily turned to look at Luca then, staring him out as he lifted his glass and took more than a decent sip of wine.

'He's trying, I guess,' Emily answered calmly, 'but some things he just doesn't have a clue about.'

His eyes flashed at hers and she felt his knee under the table, pressing hard into hers. A warning if ever there was one.

'Don't worry, Luca.' Pascal laughed. 'You can't be brilliant at everything.'

She could feel his fire crackling. After that she resorted to not looking in his direction at all. She carried the conversation completely with Francine and Pascal while he sat, the almost-silent observer.

Micaela served dessert and Luca insisted she then head home.

'I hope you like it.' Micaela smiled as she said goodbye, but it seemed the smile was directed most pointedly at Emily.

Wondering why, Emily glanced into the bowl. It was the creamy confection that Luca had spooned into her that day in the Giardino.

Emily paused, spoon in hand. Not sure she wanted to taste it again for fear it wouldn't be as sublime as it had been that day. Not wanting to ruin the memory.

'Try it, Emily.' It was the first time he'd addressed her directly all evening and she knew then that he'd ordered it specially.

Just as she lifted the spoon to her lips she felt his hand. Startled, she glanced at him. He held his spoon with his left hand, while it appeared his other rested on his knee beneath the table. But it was on her thigh that his fingers sat. And as she tasted the sweet his fingers slid over the material of her dress, up and down the length of her thigh. She sent him an agonised look but he had his head turned and was talking to Francine.

The pudding was divine—and so was the orgasmic fantasy of sharing it with Luca…on Luca…all over…

She put her spoon down, unable to eat anything more. Barely controlling the urge to part her legs and let his fingers slip all the way up. What was he trying to do to her?

At last the others finished and Emily was glad to be able to scoop up their empty dishes and take them into the kitchen. She insisted the others remain at the table. She needed a breather—not from the guests but from the intensity of Luca, from the pent-up passion she could feel in him and the response he was seeking from her. But as she placed the plates down she heard footsteps behind her in the kitchen and he whispered her name. She turned but he caught her, pulling her backwards into his embrace, lifting her back behind the door. His mouth was hot on the side of her neck—kissing and sucking. His hands were everywhere. She leant back against him, and like kerosene-drenched wood their passion ignited into an inferno.

'Luca?'

He said nothing but kissed her even more fiercely. His hands slid up her bare thighs, lifting under her dress and up to her knickers. But he didn't slide his fingers inside them as she wanted him to. She arched back in invitation. Oh, she wanted everything. Control of the urges suspended between them for hours snapped at the first touch. There was anger and hurt and most of all need.

She forgot everything—where she was, what she was supposed to be doing. All she could think of was Luca and how he felt and how badly she wanted him back deep inside—then it would all be right, right, *right*.

The tips of his fingers stroked over the lace and silk. Close, so close and yet not touching her heat as hard as she needed. His other hand cupped her breast. His thumb worked back and forth over her tight, jutting nipple. And from behind he rubbed against her, pressing his erection against her rounded, hungry flesh.

Sandwiched between his fingers and his aroused pelvis she rocked, seeking satisfaction from both. Wanting the barriers of their clothing gone so she could feel everything fresh and raw.

'Do you want me, Emily?' he muttered, mouth hard against her neck.

'Yes.'

'Shall I bend you over that bench and just—?'

'Oh, yes…' she panted, knees buckling. 'Now. Now!' She was so close she'd climax as soon as he thrust in—she knew it and she wanted it. As hard and fast and as animal as he liked. She couldn't fight her hunger any more, couldn't fight him.

But his hands left her body. He stepped away so fast she staggered—his hands came back again, steadying her.

'Emily,' he panted, more breathless than she'd ever heard him. 'You're right. We can't.'

'What are you doing?'

'Torturing us both.'

'Why?'

He didn't answer directly. She felt his head resting on her shoulder, but he held the rest of him away from her. 'I want you like I have never wanted before.'

There it was again—want. And there was an unmistakable note of agony in there as well. She closed her eyes. He didn't want to want her like this.

'I'd better get back to the others.' He pulled away.

'I need a minute.'

'Of course.' He took another couple of deep breaths and left.

She made it to the bathroom but there was no way she could disguise the colour in her cheeks or the redness of her mouth. It had only been minutes—maybe three? But everything had changed.

CHAPTER ELEVEN

LUCA watched her walk into the lounge. Head high, cheeks flushed. He could almost hear the thunder as the lightning look flashed from her eyes—on fire and unforgiving. It wasn't missed by the others either in a moment of utter silence.

She went to the piano.

'Do you play, Emily?' Francine asked.

'A little.'

'You'll play for us now?'

She nodded. He was relieved because it meant the end of having to hear her conversation for a while and he wouldn't have to meet her eyes again either. That look made him feel worse and he already felt like a jerk. He hadn't meant for it to happen, to get so far out of control. But all through dinner he'd watched her discomfort, listened to her put herself down. He didn't give a damn about whether she'd been to uni or not—nor did the others. Didn't she understand that he knew how hard she'd worked? She'd achieved something far more important than a few choice grades at university—she'd taken on a workload and level of responsibility many people with PhDs wouldn't cope with and she couldn't have done a better job of building her sister's confidence and independence.

But at what cost to herself? Her own life, her own ambition had been put on hold and he wanted to see her take charge of it. Just then he'd wanted to reassure her—let her know how beautiful she was, how bright, how giving—and the simplest way to do that was by showing how much he wanted her. Big mistake—once he'd touched, he'd almost lost complete control.

She played a few chords experimentally. 'I don't have the voice of my sister.'

He tensed, damn her defensive downplaying again.

'And while I love classical, I must be honest and admit I prefer a little blue with my tunes.' Her fingers slid on the keys, adjusting a note here and there and the result became a jazz standard.

Her voice was lower and had a husk to it and he was almost in a puddle. And as she hit her stride there was a raw quality he almost couldn't stand to listen to.

While she didn't have the brilliance of her sister's tone, she had a far greater emotional depth. Luca knew first hand the reservoir of feeling within Emily. It intrigued him, aroused him and scared him.

She kept it short and he was glad because he wasn't sure he could take much more—this looking but not touching was just about killing him. Then Francine asked her to play another. He gritted his teeth.

'Only if you sing this time.' Emily's huskiness was more apparent.

He shifted in his seat, recognising that she was wrung out and frustrated with his inability to do anything about it. Fortunately Francine smiled and sat beside her and did the singing and Luca watched as Emily won her over completely. And then he just watched her. The light played on the diamonds at her wrist just as he'd imagined it would. He would never regret buying her the gift. She did deserve spoiling. It was stunning, elegant and classical—just like her. And also like her, it shone bright with an internal fire. Only now he regretted that he hadn't chosen handcuffs. Then he could chain her to his bed and have her as much as he liked—and keep her from invading other areas of his life. But she was like this force barrelling into him, challenging the things in the world he'd worked hard to establish—like peace, solitude and isolation.

'You find her very beautiful.' Pascal's tone was low and Luca started.

Hell, he'd forgotten the old man was right beside him. He'd forgotten—

'You can't take your eyes off her.'

'I find her frustrating.' As was his attraction to her—uncontrollable, insatiable, undeniable. Even now, right now, he wanted her.

He turned to Pascal, blinked as he looked into those brown eyes that held understanding and just a tinge of sadness—brown eyes that were so familiar and yet for a few moments there had been forgotten. Desolation washed through him. Despair. How could he have forgotten? Guilt seized his heart and he looked quickly away. He'd tried so hard to make eyes just like those happy. And a long time ago, for a few magical moments, he'd succeeded. But then there'd been nothing and there could never be anything again.

'I'm sorry, Pascal.' Sorry for the past, sorry for tonight. Sorry for his failures both then and now. He stood, wanting to end this line of conversation before it even got started. 'Let's go out to the balcony. I'll concentrate better there.'

They could talk work and avoid the personal and Luca could try to go back to denial. But he suspected it was too late. He hadn't been able to control the way she got to him, certainly hadn't been able to hide it. And now he felt his guilt grow. He hadn't wanted to bring pain to anyone.

Pascal and Francine didn't stay late. Pascal explained that he had too much work to do in the morning before flying back to Paris. Emily had sat quietly listening for that last half hour as Luca had taken over the conversational duties and he and the others had talked money and markets and things she had no idea about. She hadn't even been able to look at Luca, had been too wobbly for words.

As Luca was helping Francine with her coat Emily found Pascal standing near her. He spoke softly. 'Don't let him stamp out your fire. It's good for him. You warm him up and he's been cold for too long.' And with that he was gone, following the beautiful Francine down the stairs. Surprised, she stared after him, not really listening as Luca said the final farewells.

The door closed and she blinked. She looked at Luca directly for the first time in hours then and found her fire far from gone. It blazed. He stood, his back to the door. His host facade dropped, leaving him looking big and moody and dangerous.

She shook her head at him, reined in her own frustration as she saw the lines of unhappiness deepening in his features. 'What are you thinking about?'

'The football.' He leaned right back against the door, his edge of sarcasm more bitter than humorous. 'Don't you know there isn't a man alive who doesn't hate that question?'

'Then there isn't a man alive who isn't a coward.' It was her turn to stare him out, waiting for more.

The hint of humour faded totally. 'I don't like feeling out of control and I'm out of control. I was out of control tonight.'

She took a step towards him. 'You once said that things beyond your control scare you. Do I scare you?'

His gaze dropped to her body as she stepped closer still. 'Yes. But I think that, given a little more time, I'll get that under control.'

'Is that what you want?'

'Yes. Just a fling, Emily, one that'll finish soon.'

She stopped walking then. How soon? Because she definitely wasn't done yet.

'Do you want to know what else I'm thinking?' He lifted away from the door.

'I'm not sure.' His honesty wasn't that great so far.

He walked towards her. 'I'm thinking about how much you've achieved, how hard you've worked. And yet you don't recognise it. You sit there and belittle your job and barely mention the reality of your life.'

'I'm not going to trot out the sob story to score sympathy points, Luca. You don't do that either.'

'No, but nor do I put myself down. Be proud of your achievements, Emily. Not many people could have managed all that you have.'

She looked down, watched his broad chest come closer. It was hard to be proud of her achievements when she compared them with those of someone like him or Francine.

He lifted his hand, gently stroked down her arm to clasp her wrist. 'Play the piano for me.'

Music—to soothe the savage breast and the tortured soul? Yes, she would play for him, play for them both.

As he followed her back to the lounge he unzipped her dress. It dropped and she walked right out of it. Embracing the passion still between them, she shimmied out of her knickers as well—naked completely now except for the diamond-encrusted chain that encircled her wrist. If it was going to finish soon, then she was determined to make the most of every moment.

She sat, fingers working over the keys, watching him as he walked round the piano.

'You could have been great.' He unbuttoned his shirt and shrugged it off.

'Maybe.' She knew it was possible. 'But at what price? Years and years of nothing but hard work, giving up so much for such a large battle. Even then the chances of making it are so slim. There were other things I wanted to do with my life.'

'Other things you *had* to do,' he argued. 'You had the option taken from you.'

'Yes,' she acknowledged. 'But what's life for if not to be shared with friends and family?'

'But to give up your own dreams.' He shook his head. 'It's wrong.'

He kicked off his shoes. 'My mother had dreams of performing, but my father decreed that no wife of his would ever work. I think it was the frustration that ate her up from the inside and the bitterness that caused the cancer. You should never give up your dreams, Emily.'

'What dreams?' she confessed. She hadn't had time for dreams, not until now. 'I've never had those sort of ambitions. I'm not after fame and fortune. Kate wants that and good luck to her. But it's not what I want.'

His hands had moved to where his trousers sat loose at his waist, and she smiled as he stripped before her.

'I don't need an audience of thousands to feel appreciated.' She was feeling appreciated well enough now.

'Just the odd four-year-old boy?'

'And the occasional naked man.' One magnificent, harder-than-rock, physically perfect man.

'But you must have some desires, Emily, something you want to do. Everyone does.'

'I guess.' She was still working that one out. Still figuring out what it was that she was happiest doing. Truth be told, aside from the good times with Luca, the happiest she'd been recently was when bashing the keys with Marco.

'You should chase it and grab it. Now you're free to.'

Free? Somehow free felt lonely to her.

He disappeared from view, underneath the piano. Then

she felt his hands at her feet, their slow slide from her ankles to her calves. Her smile returned.

'Play that song again.'

'Which one?' Her mind was slowly blanking everything except the sensations.

'The first one you played after dinner.'

'Why?'

'So I can do now what I wanted to do then.'

She began, and only a couple of chords into it he moved her, sliding her across the piano seat a little so she was clear of the pedals, and then he slid her forward, so she was right on the edge of the seat. She knew what was coming, could feel his mouth moving along the delicate flesh of her inner thighs. Teeth nipping, tongue soothing, lips lush and hungry. His hands pushed on her knees, pulling them wider apart so she was open for him.

Her fingers faltered.

'Keep playing.'

She closed her eyes, unable to deny him or herself. She was used to providing the accompaniment—but not to her own annihilation. For that was what this was. The slow destruction of her mind, her reason, her will. Everything was lost under his onslaught. He was the most sensual creature she'd ever met. And she ached for more of him.

Sweat dampened her skin; her breathing was short and sharp. His hands rose, gently massaging her breasts, thumbs teasing her nipples while his lips kissed and nuzzled. Her hands crashed down on the keys, any keys. Her fingers stretched rigid as the rest of her body went taut, poised on the edge.

The noise was loud and jarring and her cry rose even higher as he burrowed his face between her legs, licking and sucking, and his fingers played her with more skill than hers had ever brought to a piano.

She couldn't bear it any more. 'Luca!'

As she collapsed he lifted her down beside him on the floor, half under the piano. She curled her legs around his waist to maximise the depth. As he slid home she gazed up at him, unable to hide her adoration. 'I'm never going to be able to play the piano again without thinking of you and the most incredible orgasm I've ever had.'

He had ruined her for life.

'It's not over yet. What position do you want?'

'All of them,' she answered, taking everything while she could.

Luca was filled with the scent and sound of her. Her music still rang in his ears. Not the gentle harmony of the piano—he'd waited until that was replaced by the sounds from her mouth as she sighed for him, breathed, pleaded and finally came.

Intoxicating, addictive, and he couldn't get enough. He looked at her. She'd fallen asleep. Reluctantly he left her warm softness. Lifted and carried her to her room. She stirred only slightly. He stood beside the bed with her still in his arms, unable to give her up just yet.

Every night he went back to the private, solitary state of his room. He had to—to keep control of the situation. He had to stay in charge. Had to determine when it would end. Because if he didn't, one day he'd wake up and *she'd* be gone. As Nikki had. He had lost too much too soon. He couldn't go through that again, not ever.

But when he laid her down and covered her beautiful body with the sheet and soft blanket, she opened her eyes. Accusation pointed right at him.

'Why won't you stay with me?'

He straightened, said nothing.

She raised her brows.

'I can't.' But equally he couldn't ignore her demand for answers.

'Do I snore?'

He shook his head.

'Do you snore?'

'Not that I'm aware of.'

'Then what is it you're afraid of? You turn into a were-wolf in the middle of the night? You have bad breath in the morning? Dribble on the pillow?'

His breath of bitter laughter was barely audible. 'You say the most—'

'I say what I think, which is more than can be said for you.'

He sobered instantly and shot the answer out. 'I don't want to hurt you.'

'Who says you will?'

Hadn't he already? He could see it in her eyes, hear the faint plea in her voice despite the defensive bravado. 'I get up really early for my swim. I don't want to wake you.'

Her gaze was relentless as she ignored the fake excuse.

Right, so he had to be honest with her. She deserved

that. 'OK, then. I don't like sleeping the whole night with someone. It's too intimate.'

'Too intimate?' she repeated. 'Too intimate?' Her next repetition was even louder. 'This from the man who likes to…who likes to…' Her blush went from the roots of her hair all the way down.

'Yes,' he agreed. 'I do like to. But that's just sex.'

'Oh, right.' Sarcasm bristling. 'Just sex.'

He turned away so he wouldn't have to look at the confusion in her eyes. 'Don't, Emily. It is all it is.'

But he knew he was the one deluding himself. It was more. They talked, she made him laugh; she made him relax; she made him want—*other* things.

He hadn't been honest at all. It wasn't about her getting hurt. He was the one who didn't want to be hurt. Yet already he was aching.

CHAPTER TWELVE

LUCA woke early in his own room and alone. Only now, for the first time, he felt a finger of regret. Wouldn't it be nice to wake next to Emily's warmth? Then he remembered the madness of those moments in the kitchen where he'd nearly taken her fast and furious while his guests were waiting in the room next door and the finger of regret became a tonne of remorse. Shame filled him. He would never have dreamed of doing such a thing with Nikki. But then he'd never wanted Nikki in this way either—so *desperately*.

He got to work even earlier than usual. But once there just sat at his desk, spinning his chair away from the computer and staring out the window. For years now, he'd pushed the pain out of his head and got on with the job. Determined to prove himself—and hadn't he succeeded at that? He was worth millions…so why did it suddenly feel like nothing?

His thoughts arrowed back to Emily. She was the problem, everything had started to fracture when she'd appeared. This last week had been unnaturally intense—

just the two of them night after night. They were rapidly moving to a level of intimacy that he wasn't comfortable with. Too much, too soon. Wasn't that just the story of his life?

He needed to regain perspective. Maybe they needed to get out more, not be caught so tight in their own little world. If he saw her out and about more, the bubble would be bound to burst. He pulled up his calendar, at the list of events he usually chose to ignore. His ribs squeezed when he saw what was a possibility for tonight. Not ideal. He forced himself to take a controlled breath in and out and decided to do it anyway. It might remind him about what had been real and what was simply a passing fixation.

Decision made, he reached for the phone.

Emily woke to the sound of her mobile, flung somewhere in the room, ringing—over and over. Stumbling over her shoes, the bracelet sliding down her arm, she rummaged and eventually found it. 'Hello?'

'Are you awake?'

'Possibly.' Hell, it was early and she'd been awake half the night thinking about how wrong he was. This wasn't just sex—this was desperation and need. They were fighting for control and battling against surrender—not against each other but against this *thing* sucking them both under.

'Come out with me tonight.' His voice was soft.

'Now I know I'm dreaming.'

'No.' A half-laugh, half-groan. 'Come to a fund-raising ball at the Museum of Natural History.'

A *ball*? 'I can't.'

'Why not?'

'I haven't got anything to wear to a ball, Luca.' She'd barely coped with the dinner party—yes, she'd felt inferior. No way could she manage a ballroom full of those over-achieving, wealthy, beautiful types.

'Wear the dress you wore last night. That'll be fine.'

She hesitated. What was he up to? She knew how badly he wanted to beat out the flame between them. She sensed his struggle. Part of him had wanted to stay with her last night. She'd felt it in the way he'd held her so closely— the tenderness in that long moment before he'd lain her down. But he was determined to deny it whereas she wanted to understand it. And right now she couldn't deny either him or herself. 'OK.'

'I'll pick you up at seven.'

In her heart she knew already. What it was, why it was. She'd been wrong. There was such a thing as love at first sight.

The moment Micaela arrived she told her about the ball.

'What are you wearing?'

Emily shrugged helplessly. 'Just the dress from last night.'

Micaela, ever the efficient, kept loading the dishwasher. 'I have a wrap and an evening bag you can borrow if you like.'

'Really?'

'Leave everything to me.'

In the afternoon she swam, floating in the shallows,

avoiding the deep end of the pool. There was a nervous wobble despite the iron way she was clenching her stomach. She would fight for him. She would do OK.

After a long shower she found Micaela back, ready and waiting with her dress clean and pressed and an array of electrical appliances, make-up and accessories on the table. Micaela did her make-up with a far heavier hand than Emily had ever used. Emily had the suspicion she'd have to use gelignite to get it off but when she looked in the mirror it didn't look overdone at all. Instead Micaela had made her eyes seem an even deeper green, highlighting her pale skin. Then she tied up Emily's hair with the skill of a senior stylist at a first-class salon.

Emily gazed at the older woman. 'Is there nothing you can't do?'

Micaela giggled.

But Emily was deadly serious. 'I can see why he values you.'

'He deserves the best.' Micaela stood back to admire her work. 'He won't be able to take his eyes off you.'

Emily didn't linger near the lounge waiting for him to get home; instead she hid out in her room. There was a soft knock and he opened her door in the same second. Emily chomped hard on the inside of her cheek. His hair was still damp, he was freshly shaven, and the black tuxedo moulded his frame, skimmed over his strength and made him all the more enthralling.

For a moment they just stared at each other. Emotion almost swallowed her.

He lifted his back from the door and walked towards her, purpose evident in his pants. He was halfway there before the instruction from her brain to her body worked and she took a step back.

'No.' She forced her head to shake. 'You're not ruining my lipstick.'

He lurched to a halt. 'What are you trying to do, give me a heart attack?'

Something like that—if she could ever chip her way though the thick ice that his heart was packed in. 'I'm not kissing you before a dinner engagement ever again—remember what happened last night?'

His eyes sparked.

'Behave.' She'd meant it as a sassy joke but it came out too soft, too serious, too real.

'That's the thing, Emily. I don't want to behave when I'm with you.'

Their eyes met and she knew he was recalling as vividly as she how they'd misbehaved last night—how out of control they had spun so quickly. She tried to break the spell. 'Shouldn't we get going?'

'Mmm-hmm.' He didn't move.

She saw that look in his eye grow and, despite her own rush of desire, a vein of disappointment opened up. 'Don't you want to?'

Slowly the expression in his face shut down. 'Of course I do. Let's go.'

Luca listened as Emily chatted with Ricardo in the car. She was babbling. And as they pulled up in front of the magnificently lit building, he saw the nervousness in her face. Then he saw her chin tilt and her shoulders square and they were on their way in.

'Luca, wonderful to see you.'

He said his hellos to the charity chiefs. 'This is Emily, an acquaintance who's just arrived from New Zealand.'

The New Zealand thing did it. Before he knew it she was deep in conversation with one of the driest old guys there about bungee jumping of all things. Grinning, he took a sip of his wine and settled back to watch her win them all over with her smiling eyes and gratifyingly deep concentration as she listened to them warble on. The group of people around them grew as she was introduced to others.

Observing, occasionally adding in a smart comment, he caught the glance passed between a couple of consultants who he knew were complete sharks. For a time there, a few years after Nikki had gone, a few years before now, he'd competed in that after-hours game of drinking and excess and women. Removed his ring and worked hard, played hard. It was an unfulfilling phase that hadn't lasted long and now he concentrated on winning in the business arena alone. But he saw them edge closer, that look in their eyes. Emily was not a toy for them to play with. And at their predatory prowl, his possessiveness was unmasked. He drew her away from the crowd, closer to him.

'What…?' Her words died away as she met his gaze. Who knew what she saw there but colour ran under her skin.

'Dance with me.' He curled his arm around her. As he escorted her to the dance floor he pulled her even closer, took advantage of the slow song to pull her closer still.

Her flush remained, but her brows lifted. 'I thought I was just an acquaintance.'

'It didn't seem polite to add "who I sleep with at every possible opportunity".'

She giggled and they settled into the groove.

'You were nervous about tonight,' he said after a few moments.

'A little.'

'Why?'

She shrugged. 'I'm not very sophisticated or polished. These people all are.'

'You do more than hold your own with them.' Her eyes dropped from his and he gave her a gentle shake. 'You do. You're more genuine, more generous than most of the people in this room. They might have money to give, but you give more of yourself.' He badly wanted her to believe in her own gifts. 'You're a good listener, you're kind, you're funny and you're gorgeous. You had old Thomas all pink and flustered.'

She was all pink now—not from desire but from pleasure. Almost shy, her small smile was sweet. But it was the look in her eyes that really got to him—the green glowing bright and true. 'But most importantly,' he added, needing to lighten up before he said something really stupid, 'you love opera and you love Italian food—thus a truly cultured woman.'

'You're so parochial.' She growled, but she was still smiling.

'Look, you even know long words.'

'And patronising.'

'Don't forget debonair.'

'Arrogant.'

'And a good dancer.'

'Did we mention arrogant already?'

'You love me for it.'

'If I were to love you, it would be in spite of it.'

He chuckled and spun her away from him before pulling her tight again. 'I haven't had this much fun in ages.'

'You mean this much sex.' Her eyes glinted.

'That's true. And, honestly, I've been on the lookout for a secluded corner but there aren't any. Terrible.' He yanked her even closer and brushed his nose against hers. 'But I'm still having fun.'

Her chin tilted. 'So where did you learn to dance?'

'Boarding school. Ms Brady.' He swept her into another turn, then caught her close again, making her thighs sandwich one of his so their hips and torsos were plastered together.

'She might have taught you the waltz but I don't believe she taught you to bump and grind quite like this.' She was breathless now.

'Oh, no. Ms Brady was quite young. It was her first year of teaching...my last year of school...' He waggled his brows.

'Luca!'

He dropped his arm, dipping her head and shoulders backwards down almost to the floor, leant over her and laughed and laughed. Finally forgetting everything except how good he felt when she was close.

Emily came upright, still laughing, and then utterly relaxed into his deliciously tight embrace. She hadn't danced in—

well, ever. She'd always been working, too tired to go clubbing and she'd never been invited to a ball or anything as elite as this. Now she'd discovered how much fun it was, or how much fun it was when she had Luca to lead her—and Luca like this? With his smooth words and even smoother moves that seemed so real and so nice… Oh, she was utterly sunk now.

Several songs later, she slipped away from him. Needing a break from the way he was teasing her—and he was teasing her again. She could see the spark in his eye, he knew exactly what he was doing to her and how hot she was feeling—hot, and so happy.

In the powder room, a woman who Emily knew was one of the bigwigs of the evening came alongside her.

'It's so lovely you could be here,' she said with a bright smile. 'We weren't expecting Luca to come tonight, let alone bring a date.'

Emily simply smiled back, not sure how she should handle this. Luca hadn't exactly introduced her as his date, but then he had just been dirty dancing with her in front of everyone.

'He's a very generous donor,' the woman added.

'Of course.' Emily nodded. He would support cancer research—she could still hear that rough loathing in his voice when he'd told her about his mother dying.

'She was so young.'

Emily nodded again. She must have been as her son was only seven when she died.

'And they'd only just married.' The woman uncapped her lipstick. 'So tragic.'

Emily froze. 'Yes,' she murmured. Just married. The woman wasn't talking about Luca's mother at all. She was talking about his *wife*.

She went back out to the ballroom. He had taken a seat near some other guests but slightly removed—an empty chair between him and the others. That was him, wasn't it? Isolated. He looked up and saw her, a heart-melting smile flashed and he pulled that empty chair a little closer to him. Feeling like a fraud, she sat in it.

'You OK?' he asked quietly in her ear. 'You look a bit pale.'

'Just a bit tired.' She listened to the music and all the while longed to let the pleasure mount as Luca, who had quietly taken possession of her hand, ran his fingers over the links of the bracelet and over her wrist. But she couldn't relax again. She twisted her fingers, to link them through his. He let her, but she knew there was a vast crevasse between them—one she had to try to bridge. 'What was her name?'

He turned a questioning gaze on her.

'Your wife,' she blurted before caution could stop her.

For a moment he looked utterly shocked. Then everything shuttered. And she had to grip his fingers to stop them slipping away from hers.

'What happened to her?' She longed to know. 'What was she like?'

He jerked his hand away then. 'I don't want to talk about it.'

She saw guilt wash over his face just before he clamped down on it and froze over.

* * *

Luca stood, his blood running through him cold enough to make him shiver. 'Do you mind if we go now?'

She said nothing, just rose next to him and pulled the wrap closer about her shoulders. He didn't take her arm, just walked alongside her to the exit. He didn't phone Ricardo, it was faster to get a cab and he needed to move quickly.

He sat on the edge of the seat, staring at the window as they were driven. All he could see was the needle to administer the pain relief, he could smell the antiseptic and he could hear the beep of the machine as every few minutes the medicine was added, drop by drop, trying to keep her comfortable as life ebbed.

But he couldn't see her face. He'd forgotten. *What was she like?* In the second that Emily had asked he couldn't have answered.

'Her name was Nikki.' Reminding himself more than telling her. 'We met at Oxford. Some party or other. She was fluent in French and German. I spoke Italian and Spanish. We joked we'd take over the continent.'

He had loved her, hadn't he? He'd thought he had. Had thought he could feel nothing deeper…but that memory was fading now under the glare of this present madness and he hated that. He felt fickle and disloyal and he wanted to reject the thing that was doing this to him.

'She had brown eyes, dark hair. Tall, slim. French as anything.' He fought to capture her image. 'She was headstrong, a little spoilt. A lot spoilt actually. She could be moody but some of that was…' The memories were all back now. 'She could have gone out with anyone but she went with me.' Vivacious, petulant, young and, all of a sudden, gone.

Afterwards he'd filled his life with work and the drive to succeed—and he had, financially at least. And he'd succeeded in sealing himself away. Not running the risk of loss again, keeping his heart within his control—not wanting or needing anyone else. Because he hadn't had anyone to embrace him, not since he was little—a time he could hardly remember. And when he'd grown up, the one time he'd found someone she'd been taken from him.

'It was so fast. She was always slim but all of a sudden she was skeletal. And before we even knew about it there was nothing they could do to stop it.'

A hand touched his—soft. An even softer voice spoke. 'I'm sorry you lost her, Luca.'

He closed his eyes, clamped down on his jaw. Hating himself all the more because his first thought in response to that statement was just not right. How could he have let a few hot moments wipe all that history out? What kind of man was he?

This lust threatened him, sparked uncontrolled, frankly wrong emotions. He inhaled, fighting the nausea that rose at the mishmash of images in his head. He needed to step back—abstain rather than indulge.

'I'm really tired,' he said lamely as they entered his house. 'I'm just going to go straight to bed.'

'OK.'

He tuned out the soft acquiescence in her voice. He did not want her understanding or interfering or caring. He did not want *anything* from her—especially not her warm and welcoming comfort. He clenched every muscle, walking faster to the private prison that his room had become.

Emily watched him go and felt her heart tearing more with every step. He looked haunted. She shouldn't have asked. Curiosity wasn't good for cats and it wasn't good for her. She ached all over—wishing she could help him, wishing she could help herself. Why was it that she had fallen for someone who couldn't love her the way she needed? Who didn't want her love?

He might think she was good enough to take on a date, good enough to mix with whomever. But none of that mattered now—because how could she even try to compete with his dead wife?

CHAPTER THIRTEEN

THE day was one of the longest Luca had ever endured. His body ached as if he'd been competing in some high-performance multi-sport event. Ha. Some iron man he was. Abstinence was not the answer. He hadn't slept for a second of the previous night. Lying there battling desire and the demons of the past and an anger that he could scarcely control—at the way Emily had invaded every-thing. At the way she'd made him think terrible things. When she had said she was sorry he'd lost Nikki, he'd had his worst moment yet—because right then he hadn't been sorry. He'd just wanted to rewind to those moments on the dance floor with Emily—to go back to forgetting and hav-ing fun.

He felt terrible for that—was all the more determined to find a way to rip her out of his life. But the hunger, the instinct driving him meant he hunted her out the minute he got home, winding his arms around her, hoping she could fill the void that seemed to be gaping wide within him. He looked into her sea-green eyes, saw the new shadows in them, the way her gaze skittered from his.

'I can't seem to stay away from you for long,' he said.

'And that's a bad thing?'

He heard the hurt and felt even more upset. This wasn't her fault. He was trapped—no matter which way he turned he seemed to be doing things wrong.

'I'm sorry.'

'What for?'

For not being what she needed. For not being the man he thought he was. For having the thoughts he did.

He kissed her, the way she ought to be kissed. And in that kiss he felt himself falling, so close to giving in. It seemed as though every time they'd had sex he was stripped of more of his finesse and now he was overcome with the urge to just hold tight and pump—the most basic instinct. Wanting to take her, to fill her, to claim her absolutely. The temptation was so strong—how could it feel so right when in his head he knew it was wrong?

She sat astride him, her skin pale gold, silky soft, and yet he could feel the strength in her thighs as she rode him. Eye sparkling, face flushed, her breasts swaying to the rhythm she was setting. There was no self-consciousness now, just pure pleasure, sensual delight. Only now he didn't think he was going to be able to keep up with her. Only now did he realise this wasn't how he wanted it to be—this wasn't all he wanted it to be. Emotion overwhelmed him.

'I'm going to come.' His voice was hoarse.

'Are you now?' Her eyes flashed. 'I don't think so.'

'I don't think you can stop me,' he gasped. 'I don't think *I* can stop me.'

She knelt up and off him.

Groaning, he shook his head, disbelief flooding him. 'I'm still going to come. Just by *looking* at you.'

He stretched his arms wide, large hands gripping the sheet, trying to stay in control. 'You are magnificent. The most beautiful woman.'

She bent forward, whispered in his ear. 'Don't hold back, Luca. Dive in with me.'

Oh, God, he didn't deserve her, couldn't resist her, gave everything as he gave in. Rolling them both over, he rose high, thrust long and deep and hard and held her tight.

She arched up, her neck bared, her puff of laughter lost in a cry of joyous, erotic freedom. And he was lost—held nothing back, utterly sunk in the blaze of feeling pouring through him.

He'd changed. He was whispering something in his first language. There was almost desperation in his touch. Gone was the languorous lover who skilfully guided them to ecstasy and beyond. Instead his fingers gripped her so hard they pinched and she was sure he wasn't even aware of it as he gathered her even closer and plunged even deeper. His kisses were passionate and landing all over as if he couldn't decide where to go next and was frantically trying to touch her everywhere all at once. And the breathless phrase in Italian was louder now, muttered and repeated and under the onslaught it was easy to remember. After-wards he held her close, raining gentle kisses that soothed her to slumber while over and over he muttered it.

* * *

She woke much earlier than usual. Her legs were weighted down by something hard and heavy—and alive.
Luca.

Shouldn't he have been long gone by now? Warm excitement rushed through her system—but he hadn't gone, he'd wanted to stay. He was tucked up close behind her, his leg and arm thrown over her. Slowly, carefully, she turned. Not wanting to wake him. Not wanting him to leave just yet. She looked at him as he rested, the dark brows relaxed, his mouth full and soft. His broad shoulder a gleaming golden brown, contrasting against the crisp white of the sheets.

His eyes opened and she stilled utterly—her breathing, even her heart, stopped for a beat. Three beats.

The dark chocolate in his eyes was liquid and warm and he regarded her for a long moment in silence. The hard centre was smaller, but it was still there. She watched, anxious that it might grow and that the glow in his face would dim.

But it was his arm that tightened as he pulled her back against him, pushing her down to the mattress again. 'Sleep.'

When next she woke he was kissing her face, gentle kisses on her brow and cheek and jaw, and his hands were stroking down the sides of her torso.

'Morning breath OK?' he teased.

She smiled and inside the flames in her heart roared. She caught his mouth with hers and as the morning sun warmed the bed her confidence surged.

'What does it mean?' she asked.

'What does what mean?'

'*Siete il fuoco della mia anima.*' Nerves suddenly hit as she felt him tense. 'It's what you said to me last night.'

'Oh.' All frozen now. 'It's nothing.' Reluctance written all over him.

She waited.

'It's just a turn of phrase. An expression.' He might still be in her bed but he'd withdrawn so far he might as well be on the moon.

She waited some more but there was nothing else. And her sense of delight burst with a bang. All the good vibes gushed out, leaving her flat and angry.

'Oh, I get it. Nothing special, right?' She sat up, clutching the sheet to her chest. Too hurt to stop herself attacking. 'It's what you say to whoever you're sleeping with. That way it doesn't matter if you forget my name. That sum it up right, Luca?'

'You know there is no one else in my life. You *know*.'

Not right now. Not living.

And what she didn't know was why he was suddenly going cold again when last night had been so incredibly magical.

'Don't complicate this.' He sat up too, pushing the sheet away.

'Don't deny this already is complicated.' This was a mess.

He swung his legs out of the bed. Well, his 'end of conversation' attitude wasn't going to wash with her. And with a reckless courage she didn't know she had, she brought the issue right out into the open.

'Do you feel anything for me, Luca?'

He turned a burning hard gaze on her, clearly angry with the question. 'You know how much I want you.'

Sex. He always brought it back to sex. The lowest common denominator, but surely he recognised how much more there was to bind them? How was it that he could have given so much to her physically—given himself up in her arms—and yet try to remain so withdrawn emotionally? How could he divorce the two so completely? She didn't believe he could and she hated his denial.

She saw his anger rising, but she'd never been angrier herself. He was incredibly strong, incredibly determined. She had one hell of a battle on her hands and she couldn't help the feeling that she'd picked the losing side.

'Get out, Luca, since you so obviously regret being in here.'

He walked. She slumped down in the bed and stared hard and long at the ceiling. Determined not to cry. Determined to get on with her life. Knowing she needed an action plan much sooner than later.

When Luca came up from the most unsatisfying swim of his life he found her on the floor of the lounge surrounded by pamphlets and forms. 'What are you doing?'

'Figuring out my future.'

'Oh.' Every muscle inside got a shot of adrenalin. 'What are you going to do?'

'I'm going to teach music.'

He glanced at the pamphlets. Some were for university courses, some for a college of music—in *Ireland*? Hell, there were some travel ones in there? He grappled with the violent urge to grab them and toss them in the bin and keep her hostage like some fifth-century warlord. The urge itself made him even madder—shouldn't he be feeling relieved? 'Those who can, do. Those who can't, teach.'

'How insulting.' She stood and stomped towards the kitchen. 'Teachers aren't made, they're born.' She whirled back to face him. 'There are a few things I could teach you.'

'OK. That was rude of me.' But the frustration was real. 'Why, when for the first time in your life you're free to do anything you want? Do you want to take a job where it's all about other people?'

'Why do you encourage me to do whatever I want and then knock down the one thing I do want to do? Why can't you understand that I like working with people?'

'But you have so much talent. So much potential—you could do anything.' She could. He wanted to see her seize the opportunity—wanted her to fly.

'I *like* teaching, Luca. I'm sorry if it's not glamorous or good enough for you.'

He drew a breath. Saw he'd really offended her when all he wanted was for her to reach for what she truly wanted. 'Of course it's good enough—'

'I don't need high-powered kudos to prove my worth the way you do.' She was on the attack now.

'What does that mean?'

'Well, come on, Luca,' she sneered. 'How many hours do you have to work? How many quadrillions do you have to make? Who is it you're trying so damn hard to impress, huh?'

'No one,' he choked.

Yeah, right—she didn't even have to say it aloud.

'I work the hours I do because I like the challenge of it. I like to be the best.' Proving a point? Perhaps it had started that way—to be more of a success than his father had been, and utterly without his help or interest. Now it was more of a habit than anything.

'But what about other things, Luca?'

'Like what? I have a great life.'

'You have a half-life. You work so you can escape the things everyone else wants to embrace.'

'Like what?'

'Love.' She threw the word at him.

The silence was sudden and total. He couldn't have moved if he'd tried.

She turned away with a sigh. 'Luca, you've been so generous. I'd been caring for Kate and worrying about finding money for bread for so damn long that I didn't have time to even dream my own dreams. You've given me that time.'

'And teaching really is your dream?'

'Yes. Simple as it may seem to you, it's what I want to do. It's what I'm happy doing.'

Well, OK, then. 'How can I—?'

Her phone buzzed.

'—help.' But she'd answered. Her sister. He could hear her tones even from this distance—asking for a favour. He listened to Emily's replies, her 'yes' and 'sure' and 'no problem, I'll be there' and grew edgy again.

He waited 'til she ended the call. 'Why do you let her take advantage of your generous nature?'

* * *

'She's not…' Emily paused. He didn't get it, did he? She liked to help those she loved—that wasn't being taken advantage of by them, that was doing things because she cared. So she threw sarcasm back at him—proving her own painful point. 'But isn't that what you're doing, Luca? Taking advantage of my generous nature?'

Taking advantage of the fact that she'd fallen for him and could deny him nothing?

Solemn, he met her challenge. 'What if I am? You should cut your losses and run.'

'Maybe I will,' she answered honestly. 'But right now there's this.'

She walked towards him, bolder than ever, kissed him hard. There was no mercy left in the desire that raged between them. But she pushed back before it got too far. 'It's still there. As strong as ever.'

His nod was almost imperceptible but it was enough to give her the shot of courage she needed. She stepped close again, asked very softly, 'Would my loving you be so bad?'

He stood stock-still. Then she saw the flexing muscle in his jaw, the impossible fight to stop colour tainting his cheeks. Then his eyes narrowed and she braced, sensing that he was not going to be nice.

'You're always helping people. *Caring* for people. Where's your selfishness?'

'Everything I do stems from selfishness, Luca. I like to be needed. I have to be needed. If there's no one who wants or needs me, then what do I have?'

'Freedom.'

She shook her head. 'That's not the kind of freedom I

want. I need a community, a family, a place to fit—to be necessary to. Otherwise I'm aimless and lonely. And there's no one for me. I do things for people and hope that one day I'll be given to and cared for too.'

That he would give back to her—just what he could. She'd be happy with that, wouldn't she? But his expression was rock-hard and she tried to hide the fact that he was breaking her heart. She railed against his silence—his denial—wanting to scream with frustration and futility.

'No man is an island, Luca. Not even you.' She began to fail at hiding her frustration. 'You help people too. You try to maintain this distance and you can't.'

His gaze dropped.

'I know what you've done for Micaela and Ricardo. Their family.'

He looked back then, surprised. 'How do you know that?'

'She told me.'

'That's nothing. That's just money.'

'I know about the toy cupboard you keep for Marco. He showed me.'

'Again. Money.'

'Rubbish. That's caring. You *like* these people, Luca. You care about them and you do things for them.'

'It's entirely self-serving. Better to have Marco's little hands occupied with some trains than scribbling on my walls.'

She gave him a yeah-right look. 'Try as you might to deny it, you're involved in these people's lives. Their happiness matters to you. You care about them.' *And you care about me too.*

Their eyes met. She wondered if he'd caught her telepathic add-on.

'You take risks with money. You take huge risks. High risk, high return, right? Ever thought it might be the same with your heart?' She had gone so far, there was no point in holding back. 'And the thing is, Luca, I'm a safe bet.'

'I have to…' He trailed off. 'Go to work. I've really got to go to work.'

For the second time that day she watched him walk away from her. His usually graceful body looked awkward, as if he was having to concentrate hard on every small movement. She wrapped her arms around herself and hugged. Oh, hell, was she deluding herself completely?

OK. So he was still in love with his wife. That didn't mean he couldn't still care about her. This could work. She could settle for that, couldn't she? But suddenly she felt vulnerable and lost. Bitterness surged. Why should she be the one to do the loving all the time? Why couldn't she have someone to love her back completely?

She did, she realised now, want it all. And he wasn't capable of giving it.

He'd got as far as the door when all her selfishness burst out. 'You know I've tried it your way but this whole hedonistic holiday thing just isn't me.' She took a deep breath. 'I need more. I want more. From you.'

He froze, back to her, hand on the door. 'You said you just wanted sex too.'

'I did. I do. But I've changed my mind.' She flung her head up. 'Woman's prerogative.'

His head was bowed. 'Emily, I…'

Hope crashed down as she heard the crack in his voice. 'It's OK. I know already. You don't have to explain.'

He'd buried his heart. He didn't want to try again. His hand tightened on the door. Finally he jerked it open and was gone.

CHAPTER FOURTEEN

LUCA had been trying to catch his breath for hours, his heart thumping one uneven beat ahead of the rest of him. He couldn't sit still, couldn't settle, couldn't concentrate. All he could see was Emily asking him, *Would my loving you be so bad?*

He shut down the computer and flicked off the monitor. There was no point pretending any more. His work day was over before it had even begun.

Siete il fuoco della mia anima—he hadn't realised he'd been saying it aloud. And when she'd said it back to him it had freaked him out—he hadn't wanted to admit it to himself, let alone her. But it was true. *Sua anima…suo cuove.*

The sheer velocity of it stunned him. She was like a meteorite, hurtling into his world, causing chaos and upheaval. The ground was shifting beneath his feet and he was *quaking*. He needed to talk to her, to tell her, to ask her for patience. He knew he'd get it. She was loving and strong but he couldn't quite believe in it yet. He wondered if she was still even there.

He ran. All the way home he ran, not caring about the

strange looks people gave him as he sprinted the mile or so in his three-piece suit.

She was lying on the sofa, reading, looking a little pale and turning even more so as she watched him come near. Did she regret their earlier conversation? He wanted to close his eyes against the depths he saw in hers. The courage.

'Are you OK?' She really did look pale.

She nodded. Emotion rushed through him. Yes, he wanted her to love him. He wanted, he wanted, he wanted—absolutely everything she had to offer he would take. But he didn't think he could do that any more without risk to himself. It meant opening doors he'd tried to seal shut long ago and he didn't know if he had the strength to let her open them.

Who was he kidding? She'd already streaked through them and was firmly lodged in place, wasn't she? Right in his heart. That didn't mean he was happy about it.

'I need some time, Emily.'

'Time for what?'

'To adjust to this. To us.' There had been nothing slow about their affair—and that was as much his fault as hers. He pushed physically, she pushed emotionally. Together that made for one hell of a ride.

And what would she say once she knew it all? If he told her what was really in his heart, would she really still be there for him? He couldn't trust that she would. So it wasn't talking that he'd do yet. He'd love her first, and hold his breath as he told her after.

She winced as she sat up.

'You sure you're OK?' he asked, sitting down beside her.

'Just a tummy ache. I'm fine.'

Anxiety perhaps? He stroked the back of his fingers down the side of her face, wanted to reassure them both with his touch, willing her to understand.

Her expression softened. He couldn't have said a thing then anyway. He opened his arms and she leant into them. He kissed her hair, her cheek, her mouth, pulled her closer.

Another wince.

Concerned, he leaned back to look into her face. 'You're not up to it?'

'No, I want to,' she murmured. 'But…' She was blushing.

He paused. He was so hard, it cost a lot to slow down—she caused irreparable damage to his heart.

'It's just that I'm bleeding a little.'

'Bleeding?'

'Just, you know, a little. It's nothing.'

No, he didn't know. 'But you said you had your period a couple of weeks ago.' Confusion. Fast followed by fear. 'You shouldn't be bleeding now.'

She sat up, wincing again, and then stood, pulling her tee shirt down as she walked away from him. 'I'm a bit out of sorts. I'm fine.'

Out of sorts? Abnormal bleeding was a little more than out of sorts. She wasn't telling him all of it. He could see it in the stiffness of her back. His alarm bells rang louder. What were her other symptoms? How long had she been feeling like this? 'Have you got a headache?'

'If I didn't before I do now.'

He ignored the irony. She was getting more angry, more defensive. So there must be more to it. 'I think you should see a doctor.'

'Luca. I'm fine.'

But anxiety had a hold of him now and thoughts and nightmare visions swirled before him. He went rigid—trying to reject this reality and control the queasiness clogging his ability to process. He stood, headed straight to the phone on the bench. Not again. He was not going through this again.

'You're seeing a doctor. I'll call him right away.' He'd get an immediate appointment. Insist on it. Pay whatever. House call if necessary. He wanted to know what it was and how it could be fixed. *Now*.

Emily stared at the implacable determination driving Luca and exasperation made her raise her voice and overcome her embarrassment. 'Put the phone down, Luca. I'm ovulating, all right?'

That stopped him. 'What?'

'Ovulating. I get a spot of bleeding and tenderness in the tummy. It's called mittelschmerz. It's perfectly normal and lots of women get it.'

'Ovulating?' Clearly dazed, he tried to put the phone back on its base but it missed with a clatter.

'Ovulating.' She nodded.

'Ovulating.' Still confused.

'Happens every month.' She nodded more, exaggerated fashion.

'Ov—'

'Yes, Luca.' Her patience vaporised. '*Ovulating*. You know, where my ovary releases an egg and it goes down the... Do you really need all the details?'

He drew an audible breath and shook his head and she watched as his gaze travelled to her breasts, to her belly. He looked totally blown away. 'Ov… OK… Well… You take a lie-down or something.'

'Right.' She went to her room to escape him as much as anything. She still wanted him, yearned for him. Her body was burning, screaming at her to mate and make love and life with him—literally in heat.

Instead she curled into a ball and wondered how long she was going to have to wait.

She must have fallen asleep because the sun was late-afternoon high in the sky when she came to.

He was standing near the lounge window looking out, but as she walked towards him she could tell that he wasn't seeing any of the spectacular view across the park. His eyes were unfocused, and whatever it was he was seeing, it was causing him pain. His mouth was set, the corners tilting down. Jaw locked. His arms barred across his chest and she could see his hands curled into fists. Fighting.

He turned. His stance didn't relax. If anything he went even more rigid. She forced herself to take another step forward, bracing against the chill sweeping from him to her. His jaw was still locked. She saw the muscle flick as he clenched harder on his teeth.

Her own jaw tensed in response and she had to concentrate hard to be able to move it and use her voice. 'Luca?'

'Emily.' His voice was flat. He seemed to be deciding how to say whatever it was he was going to say. 'I…'

And suddenly, blindingly, she knew. She knew what it

was. And then pride got in there and made her take over. 'You don't want me to stay here any more, do you?'

His eyes met hers. Unwavering. 'No.'

For a second, or maybe longer, she was struck still. Listening, hearing that vehement admission echo louder and louder in her head.

Well, she had asked for it, hadn't she—that he never lie to her? But it was such a shock—that he could go from that adoring lover who'd cradled her to sleep last night to...

That all-preserving pride reared up again. She whirled on the spot.

'You don't have to go right away.'

'No, Luca,' she corrected. 'I do.' As if she were going to hang around for another night after this? What the hell did he expect? Farewell sex?

'Where will you go?'

She paused. Kate didn't need her any more. Luca didn't want her. 'I might try somewhere new.'

She turned her head then, wanting a glimpse of him at this moment—masochist that she was.

His face was pale but set. She knew that determination. He wasn't going to change his mind and she refused to humiliate herself by trying to make him. She'd been trying to do that for too long.

Idly she wondered what her own face was like—because right now, for this second, she felt nothing. Then a touch of irritation flared at the way he was just standing there, staring back at her. If it was over, it was over. He didn't need to watch for the meltdown. She refused to give him the meltdown. God, she'd given him everything else. Dignity was the one thing she had left to hold onto.

'Will you give me a minute? I'd like to get my things together.'

His head jerked. 'I'll go for a walk. Be an hour or so. Then I can drop you wherever you want.'

Stiffly he walked from the room. She stared at the door he'd closed behind him. Seeing through it, at the way he just kept on walking. Just like that.

Had he forgotten he held her heart in his hands? Because he'd just clenched his fists and now her heart was squashed and bleeding and hurting all the more because he'd done it. He'd hurt her and he'd known he would and he hadn't stopped.

Starkly he'd revealed the disparity in their feelings towards each other. Because if he felt for her at all—even as a friend—he wouldn't have done this so cruelly. So coldly ruthless.

She went to the window he'd been frowning out of, looked down to the footpath in front of the building. A second later he appeared. A stupid last curl of hope unfurled. If he looked back up to her...if he looked back up...

But he walked away, no backwards glance, no apparent care in the world.

CHAPTER FIFTEEN

IT WAS warm that late summer evening but Luca felt as if nothing could heat him up—not even the flames of hell. That was where he was now. Locked in a nightmare world of past and present.

His mother had gradually faded away, as if the frustration inside was eating her. The cancer growing and spreading slowly like the poison it was. Nikki's was fast—so fast and there had been nothing they could do to fight it. Memories swirled. He hated them.

To watch someone he loved suffer. To have someone he loved be taken from him wasn't something he could go through again. When she'd winced this afternoon and told him of her tummy ache he'd been consumed by nightmares and demons. Dread fear that she too was going to slip away from him. The fright he'd got was enough to shatter the fragile vision he'd been building—of being with her.

Only then she'd told him. It wasn't a sickness—an unknown cancer killing her. Instead it was her body signalling that it was ready to create life.

A mixture of terror and longing washed through him.

He was never going to marry again, certainly never going to have children. Never going to set himself up for rejection and pain and unstoppable loss. He'd been through enough of that and he'd chosen to live a life that would be satisfied by the challenges of his career. He'd had to pull away from her.

But now, confronted with the prospect of returning to that life, he knew he didn't want to. It was empty, unfulfilling and all the money in the world couldn't buy him what he really wanted. *High risk, high return.* She'd said she was a safe bet...but she wasn't. No one was. There were no answers to the questions that had him trapped.

She couldn't promise not to die, not to leave him.

He walked through the gardens, not seeing the trees or lawn as he grappled with the problem. Desperately searching for the answer he needed because inexorably he was being drawn back to her. He wanted her—he loved her—he had to face it: for as long as she wanted him, he was hers.

And there it was, his answer. If she could promise that she wouldn't leave him for as long as she lived, then he could take it on. Because he would promise the same; he could say nothing truer.

She had been so dignified. So understanding. It hurt him more than if she'd cried. And it angered him too. Why hadn't she fought for him? Why hadn't she yelled at him? He'd wanted her to yell at him, to declare everything again. He'd wanted to hear it from her one more time.

God, he really was selfish.

Why should she? He suddenly saw the unreasonable demands he'd put on her—asking for everything when what had he offered in return? Nothing. Nothing but denial, denial, denial of how much she meant to him. Of what she meant to him.

He couldn't let her go without explaining everything. Whether she would still want to stay after that, he didn't know. Guilt washed through him once more. How he felt just wasn't right. But it was how it was, and he needed to tell her. He could only hope her heart was big enough to still love him once she knew. It was the one thing that brought him a sliver of warmth back.

Emily was just keeping back the tears as she packed. She started by folding her clothing neatly, but a couple of items into it she was frenzied, tossing them into her open bag. She had to get out of there. Hurry before she lost it.

But even as she forced herself to speed up the first tear trickled. Acidic. She was hot all over and her heart was thumping and up in her throat for her to gag on.

'Damn.' She swore, sniffed, stuffed the tee shirt in with the others and wiped her cheek with the back of her hand. Another burning tear streaked down.

Hands gripped her shoulders and pulled her back against a strong, hard body. 'Emily.'

She hardly recognised his voice. But she knew the feel of him. And it was that touch that made her lose it completely.

'No,' she shouted as she turned in his arms. She would not let him try to comfort her. Not now. 'Don't do this to me. Don't DO this!' she screamed at him, pushing him away with every ounce of her strength.

But her strength was nothing on his and his embrace only tightened. 'Stop crying, Emily. Please stop crying.'

'Don't be so cruel, Luca.' She hardly heard the break in his voice through her own sobs of anguish. 'I can't touch you again. I don't want you to touch me again. I can't live through this if you do, Luca. So don't.'

He dropped his arms. His face was white. 'I'm sorry. I—'

'Don't tell me you're sorry!' She smeared tears across her face and sniffed. 'Don't pity me or patronise me!'

'Emily—'

'Just leave me alone!' she yelled at him. 'Why can't you leave me just a shred of dignity? Leave me alone so I can go.' The humiliation was total.

'I don't want you to go.'

She stared at him, almost crumpling under the pain and confusion.

He stared back, stock-still, pale, as low-voiced he repeated it. 'I don't want you to go, Emily.'

Fresh tears filled her eyes and flooded over their rims.

'I know I've hurt you. It was the last thing I wanted to do.'

But she'd always known he would, hadn't she? And so had he. That was why he'd frowned at the beginning. Why he'd tried to impose rules. Why he'd said it so many times—I don't want to hurt you—because he'd known he would. It was why she'd felt that nagging warning. But it was impossible. Feelings, emotions, love seeped between the lines and through the cracks. Mercurial. It couldn't be stopped—well, hers couldn't anyway. He on the other hand? He was the impenetrable fortress. The one who'd locked his heart away for ever and fair enough.

So now she refused to listen. She loved him. He couldn't love her. That was all she needed to know. There was nothing more to it.

'I can't stay here any more, Luca. I can't do this any more.'

The last half hour had been the most hellishly painful of her life and she couldn't cope with it being drawn out another day or two, week or two. It had to be over. Her father had not cared enough to live for her. Kate no longer needed her. And Luca—the man she'd fallen so utterly in love with—didn't want her. And the pain of his rejection was so intense she could hardly breathe, could hardly walk, could hardly bear to stay conscious.

So she fought it, storming past, not wanting him to witness her weakness. Wanting privacy for just a moment of self-indulgence when she could scream and cry before pulling herself back together and getting on with it like the good old trouper she was.

She made straight for the door, heedless of her bare feet. She just had to get out of there *now* because she really was going to howl.

She got as far as the hall when his hand grasped her upper arm and pulled. His other arm came around her waist. By this stage her tears were blinding and she couldn't see where he was half lifting, half dragging her.

A door slammed and his hands left her and she stumbled forward a few more paces.

'Damn it, Luca, what more do you want from me?' She'd offered him everything she had and he'd refused it, yet still he demanded.

She turned to face him. He had his back to the door. Looming big, still pale and more serious than she'd ever seen him.

'Where…?' She trailed off. She knew already.

'My room.' Relentlessly he stared at her. *'Mine.'*

Every cell quivered at the force in his reply. Racked by another sob, she quickly moved, determined to stuff all her emotion back in. Turning her back to him, she blinked and tried to focus on the furnishings, the floor—anything but the misery she'd seen reflected in his eyes. There was no glimmer of hope or happiness there and she didn't want to prolong the agony a minute more than necessary.

There wasn't a thing out of place. The doors to the walk-in wardrobe were open and she could see his suits hanging neatly. There were still no personal touches. No family photos. Only a stack of books and magazines by one side of the bed to indicate some sort of personality inhabited the room. But it wasn't sterile. It was a calm, quiet, restful space. Her shaking inside only increased and she gripped every muscle even harder, trying to piece herself back together and keep it that way. She heard him exhale, a harsh long breath.

'Please let me explain. Please, Emily.'

When had she ever been able to say no to him?

'I need to talk to you about Nikki.'

No. She ached to scream it. Jerked as if to stop herself. Put her hand on her ribcage—trying to protect herself from more pain striking deep. She didn't think she could listen to him and survive.

'Please, Emily. It won't take long.'

He was blocking the door. She had no escape. Head

bowed, fists clenched against her chest, she kept her back to him as she summoned that last grain of courage. She heard every word.

'You know we met at Oxford. She was eighteen, I was almost twenty. I was her first boyfriend and she was the first woman I'd dated for more than a couple of weeks. One day she woke with a bad head. She thought it was monthly. She used to get migraines a bit…' His voice faded. 'I never knew it could be so fast. She had no chance—no time to even *try* to fight it.'

Emily's heart was aching in a different way now. Not just for herself, but for him and for Nikki. She turned and looked at him. He was still focused on her, still relentless, as if he had decided on a path and was determined to take it—no matter what the cost. And there was a cost—she could see it as his eyes grew darker, dominating his whitened face, and she could hear it in his thinning, rasping tone.

'She wanted to get married. It was her wish—one of life's great milestones to achieve before…' He cleared his throat, fought to put strength back into his voice. 'She was going to miss out on everything else. She wanted one moment of happiness. And it was one thing I *could* do for her…' He faded out again. 'She died nine hours later.'

Emily just stared at him. Unable to see anything but the scene he'd painted for her and the unspeakable sadness of that day.

'Don't cry.'

She didn't realise she still was. She wiped away the wet from her cheeks. 'You've never gotten over her.'

'No.' The wince of pain that screwed up his face for a second was as if she'd struck him a mortal blow. 'But not in the way you mean.' His agony seemed to throb in the air. 'It was awful, Emily. And after seeing Mum fade away, and then Nikki be torn down by that hideous disease, I decided no, I'm not going to be in that position again. I put all my energy into my business. I didn't want intimacy. I've never had a relationship since, never spent the whole night with a woman, never had a woman stay in my apartment even. Occasional, casual flings. One-night stands. And then for a long time nothing. Too busy with work.' Flat now, he explained, 'I didn't want a woman—or anyone—to become a necessary part of my life. I didn't want a relationship to form. I didn't want to be hurt when it ended. So I always ended it before it had the chance to begin.'

His hedonistic, no-strings approach hadn't been care-free, it had been underpinned by loss and heartbreak and denial.

'You must have really loved her.'

Her comment seemed to etch greater pain into his face, lines of agony carved deep with a knife and bleeding. 'I used to think I did.' His knuckles were white. 'But do you want to know the awful truth, Emily? Do you want to know what I really feel?'

Silently she waited, because the despair in him was close to the surface now and she wanted to know what it was, why it was.

'*Glad.*' He ground the admission out on a wave of self-disgust. 'Part of me feels glad it happened—that she's gone.' His breathing had gone harsh, his chest jerking. 'Because I. Want. You.'

He looked appalled even as he said it. 'I look back now and wonder if I ever loved her, when how I feel about you is so intense—so all-consuming. So absolutely terrifying. And if I thought losing Nikki was bad, it's nothing on how it would be to lose you.' His voice rose higher and the words came faster. 'It's not that I don't want you. It's that I don't *want* to want you. Not like this. Not when it makes me question everything, not when it makes me feel *relieved* that I'm free to chase you. How awful does that make me? What kind of a man am I?'

He suddenly stopped. Suddenly looked utterly vulnerable, utterly afraid. 'Can you really love a man who thinks like that?'

'Luca, stop.' She took the few paces over to him, grasped his fist in her hands. 'Stop torturing yourself.'

But his heart was rent open and she saw the depth of it—the pain he'd suffered, the loneliness he'd made himself endure and the strength he'd used to seal it all away.

'You did love her. Of course you did. You married her. You gave her what she wanted. You put her first. That is love.' She spoke gently but firmly. 'And you've become the man you are, capable of feeling the depth of feeling that you can, because of her. She taught you love and sacrifice and loss. You did love her.'

'But not like this.' He shook his head.

Emily squeezed her fingers over his. 'It's different. Of course it is. I'm a different person and you're a different person from the one you were back then. It doesn't make the feelings you had for her any less. It's still love. And love isn't measurable, Luca. It isn't comparable. It's just love. And the fear you have of losing me only feels so bad because you've lost before. Not because I'm any more valuable.'

He closed his eyes but she kept talking.

'If she had lived, you would have been happy. We would never have met. We might have passed in the street and you wouldn't have even given me a second glance.'

His smile was faint, as was the slight shake of his head.

Her eyes filled again with the feeling of everything he'd said and hadn't said. 'It's OK to love her, Luca. And it's OK to love me too. It's possible to love more than once, you know.' She took a shaky breath, so badly wanting him to accept her words. 'And you deserve to have been loved by both her *and* me.'

He dropped his face then, hiding the way he was crumbling. And her heart bled for the boy whose mother had gone and whose father had abandoned him and for the youth who had lost his first love so quickly and so cruelly.

She slipped her arms around him and whispered, 'There's a lot to love in you, Luca—there's everything to love.'

His arms snaked around her, pulling her tight as he pressed his face to her neck, and for a long moment he was silent.

'And that's your gift,' he finally mumbled. 'You're so supportive—you have the power to make people feel better.'

'I don't really have a gift, Luca. All I have is love.' And she wanted to give it to him.

His hands tightened. 'That's the greatest gift of all.' He lifted his head and looked at her. 'I don't deserve it for the way I hurt you. But please give it back to me.'

'You already have it. Once it's given, you can't take it back.'

'I know. And now I can't let you go.' He wasn't smiling as he said it. It still troubled him and she knew that if he could, he would let her go. He still felt the fear.

'Do you have a photo of her?' Somehow she had to find peace for them.

He hesitated.

'Show me.'

He stood, and opened the door behind him. She followed him into the next room, eyes widening at the table and bookcases, filing cabinets and high-tech hardware. Some people had a home away from home. It seemed Luca had an office away from the office. He went to the filing cabinet. Opened it and flicked through the obscenely neat files. Her heart splintered more as she saw the way he'd literally tried to put his past in its place and forget about it.

He avoided her eyes as he handed her the picture. It was just a snap. No frame, no album.

Emily looked at the pretty girl, and took in a sharp breath. More tears rolled down her cheeks. She had seen that face before.

'She's Pascal's daughter,' Luca explained, understanding what had made Emily go so still. 'The resemblance is quite something, isn't it?'

Pity swept over Emily. 'Oh, Luca, I'm so sorry.' She felt

terrible. 'And I made you have that dinner with me there. No wonder you were feeling so awkward.'

'And I wanted you to wear something decent—something that would cover you from head to foot and you wore that dress and were so damn irresistible.' He almost smiled. 'Pascal has been unsubtly nagging me to move on for years now. Keeps going on about how wonderful it is to have children.'

'Does he have others?'

'No. It was years of trying before they had her. They would have liked more but it didn't happen for them.'

'Oh, Luca.' Now she saw why Luca had been so determined to help Micaela and Ricardo—wanting them to have it all when his friend had missed out, when he had missed out.

'I guess we're close. We'll always be close.' He looked uncertainly at her, as if asking if that was OK.

'Of course you will.' They had Nikki linking them. Now his parting words to her at the dinner made sense—*he's been cold for too long*. Pascal didn't want that for his son-in-law, he'd been the mentor and guide that Luca had missed out on with his own father and he wanted to see him achieve happiness, not just in his career, but in his personal life too.

'He asked after you last time he emailed.' Luca smiled wryly. 'I think he liked you.'

'I liked him too.' Emily looked at the photo in her hand and then back at Luca. 'Don't confuse the feelings of the past with the feelings of the present. You're a different person now, Luca. She deserves that place in your heart and she would want you to be happy.' She propped the picture up against the lamp on the table. He should have it displayed, just as he should have one of his mum. She'd have a picture of her parents too. She'd see to all that soon. 'She helped make you who you are. And I love the man you are.' She turned to him. 'So strong, Luca.'

'I'm not strong. I've been such a coward and I hurt you. The look on your face...' He paused. 'You deserve better than that. And I'll spend the rest of my life making it up to you.' He glanced over her shoulder to the picture on the desk, seemed to know what Emily was planning, and looked back at her with a new gentleness. 'Thank you for being so generous.'

She shook her head. 'I can afford to be. I have life. I have you.'

His arms swooped around her then and he sighed, pulling her close. 'You gave me such a fright, Emily. I thought you might be sick. I thought I couldn't handle that—but I have no choice.'

And she had one last point to impress on him. 'I've seen what happens when someone gives up, Luca. I've seen someone decide not to bother any more and wither away and die and ignore those who care.' She would be livid if he did that. 'Nikki and your mother would be so angry with you for not living a whole life. Don't use them as your excuse any more. Live now. Live with me. And, heaven forbid, if I do die before you then you just have to pick yourself up and keep on going. Keep on loving.'

But it was her he picked up now, carrying her back through to his bedroom. He laid her down on the bed, looked at her for a long moment before running his hand over her breasts and letting it come to rest low on her belly.

The chocolate in his eyes all sweet fire. 'If we made love now, there's a chance you'd get pregnant?'

'There's every chance, I guess.'

'Is that a risk you're prepared to take with me?'

She'd already gambled her heart on him, so far her reward was priceless and she was starting to hope it was about to multiply many times over. 'High risk, high return, right?'

'*Sì.*' He bent over her, fixing her in place with that burning gaze. 'I've been so wrong. I want to love you. I do love you. So much.'

She melted into the demand of his kiss, softened as he moved his weight onto her. It was a different need he was asking her to fill, no less desperate or passionate, but deeper somehow—total.

'Don't leave me, Emily. Don't ever leave me.' A breathless plea.

She pressed her hand to his heart, feeling the strong beat as she had that first day. 'I'm here, Luca. I'll always be right here.'

There was a brilliance in his face now. '*Siete il fuoco della mia anima*—you are the fire of my soul.' Quietly, deliberately, he translated. '*Mio cuove*—my heart. I mean it. I mean it with all of me—you make me, you are all of me and when I am with you, I know I am alive.'

She cried then, tears of a different kind, tears for herself—of sad relief and sweet disbelief. For the pain and the long years of loneliness and work and heartache— years that she would never regret or resent but was so glad had passed. And he cradled her, comforted her, caressed her. She knew she would never be alone again because her heart was in the care of the strongest, bravest man who was capable of such love. And he showed it to her, kissing away the streams from her eyes, drawing her close, filling her with his strength and holding nothing back. She clung to him, soft and needing every ounce of the sureness of his possession and his passion.

She shuddered in ecstasy as everything he had to offer was given to her, nothing between them now but the powerful surge of love. Every inch of her skin, every muscle, sinew and cell felt it and exulted in it. While she'd had physical completion before, now he gave her emotional fulfilment—telling her with words, eyes and actions how much he loved her. How much he wanted her, needed her and would care for her.

Curled together after, legs and arms and everything between entwined, the warmth having banished the cold and the tears for good, he spoke.

'You haven't said anything about my painting.' He inclined his head and she looked over his shoulder in the direction he'd nodded in.

She hadn't even seen it despite it hanging in perfect position to be viewed from his bed. But now she stared at it. The scene was so familiar. The trees, the topiary… She could almost hear the faint trickle of water from the fountains…could feel the dampness of the air near the grotto…

'I found it in a gallery a few days later and bought it on the spot.'

She studied the richness of it, the graduated greens, the depth and she sank into the memories it invoked: Giardino

Giusti and the most blissful afternoon of her life—surpassed by none until now.

She turned back to his steadfast gaze with a dawning sense of serenity. 'It was the best, wasn't it, Luca?'

'No,' he corrected her with a half-smile, 'it was just the beginning.'

As her inner peace grew she felt his tension rise again. She put a hand to his brow, soothing—everything was right now and he could relax. But his intense look only went more acute, his molten eyes searching right into her, suddenly setting *her* soul alight with wonder.

'Do you think you would marry me there, Emily? In the garden, with a simple ceremony and a picnic under the trees?'

She blinked but she couldn't stop the burning tingle in the backs of her eyes, the unstoppable, infinitesimal nodding of her head and the blossoming of absolute joy in her heart.

'Luca…' the last, the sweetest of her tears spilt, and he had to draw her shaking body even closer to hear her tiny whisper '…I think that *that* would be the best.'

And, one fine day, under a blue sky and green branches, it was.

THE MORETTI HEIR

KATHERINE GARBERA

One

Marco Moretti, by anyone's standards, was a man who had it all. His win today was part of his plan to become the most decorated Moretti driver of all time. His grandfather Lorenzo had won three back-to-back Grand Prix championships—something that Marco had done, as well, but this year he intended to surpass that record.

Both Moretti drivers were tied with three other drivers for the most Grand Prix championship wins, but this year Marco would win a fourth, something he had craved from the time he was a rookie driver.

He had no doubt that he would do it. He'd never failed at anything he put his mind to, and this would be no different. Why, then, did he feel bored and restless?

His teammate, Keke Heckler, was sitting at the banquette next to him, drinking and talking to Elena Hamilton, a *Sports Illustrated* cover model. Keke looked as if he had the world in his hands. All Marco could think was that there should be more to life than racing, winning and partying.

Oh, hell, maybe he was getting sick, coming down with a cold or something.

Or perhaps it was the family curse. Supposedly no Moretti male could succeed in both business and love.

"Marco?" Keke asked in his heavy German accent.

"Yes?"

"Elena asked if Allie was meeting you here later," Keke said.

"No. We're not together anymore."

"Oh, I'm sorry," Elena said.

A few minutes later, Keke and Elena left the table to go dance and Marco sat back against the leather seat and watched the crowd. This party was as much for him as it was for the jet set that followed the Formula One races. He saw other drivers mixed in with the sea of beautiful women, but he made no move to join anyone.

Allie and he had drifted apart during the off-season. It was as if she wanted him only when he was in the spotlight. A part of him craved the quiet life. He couldn't give up the glamour that came with racing, but sometimes when he was alone he wanted someone with whom he could share the quiet times of his life. A companion at the villa in Naples where he retreated to be an average man.

He glanced around the room. None of the gorgeous women stood out—they all were too beautiful for words, but he'd never find a woman here who wanted that type of lifestyle.

What was wrong with him?

He was poised to usher in a new era for Moretti Motors. He and his brothers had grown up in an odd world of wealth and privilege, all the while knowing that they had no riches of their own. Something that he, Dominic and Antonio had changed as soon as they were old enough.

The three of them were now men who commanded respect in the cutthroat business world of automotive design. Under their guidance, Moretti Motors had returned as the leader of the pack for exotic cars. The power of the Moretti engine and the state-of-the-art body design combined to make their cars the fastest in the world, something that Marco was aware of each time he got behind the wheel of his Formula One race car. What more could he want?

His breath caught as he noticed a woman across the room. She was tall—probably almost five-nine, and had hair the color of ebony. Her skin was pale, like moonlight on the Mediterranean. Her eyes... well, it was too far for him to be certain, but they seemed deep and limitless as he gazed at her across the room.

She wore a subtly sexy dress, in the same sky-blue color as his racing uniform. Her hair was caught up and a few curls hung down, framing her face.

Marco slid around the booth to stand up. He was used to letting women come to him, but he needed to meet this woman. Had to find out who she was and claim her as his own.

As he stood up and took two steps toward her, she turned away, disappearing into the crowd. His heart raced as he started after her. But a hand on his arm stopped him.

He turned to see his older brother, Dominic. They were of a height, and both had the same classic Roman features—at least, according to *Capital,* an Italian business magazine. Something that Antonio, their middle brother, liked to tease them about.

"Not now," Marco said, intent on finding the mystery woman.

"Yes, now. It's urgent. Antonio has just arrived and we have to talk." Dominic was very much the leader of their fraternity. Not just because he was the head of the company, but also because he was the engineer of this new wave of prosperity for Moretti Motors.

"Can't it wait? I just won the first race of the season, Dom. I think I'm entitled to one night's celebration."

"You can celebrate later. This won't take long."

Marco glanced back to where the woman had been, but there was no trace of her. She was gone. Maybe he'd imagined her.

"What's up, and where is Antonio?"

"On his way. Let's go to the VIP section to talk. I don't trust this crowd."

Marco wasn't surprised. Dom took no chances when it came to Moretti Motors. He'd been the one to realize that the curse put on their grandfather, Lorenzo, when he was a young man was responsible for their parents losing their wealth. Marco didn't put much stock in curses made by old Italian witches, but his father believed the curse was responsible for their family's change in fortune.

When they were teenagers, he and his brothers had taken a blood oath never to fall in love. They vowed to restore the glory and power of the Moretti name.

Marco and Dom made their way through the crowd to the velvet-rope section of the room. Marco was stopped many times by well-wishers congratulating him on his victory, but he kept looking for that dark-haired woman. He didn't find her. They reached the VIP section and found a quiet area toward the back of the room. It was walled in on three sides and had a curtain for privacy.

Antonio was waiting there for them. "Took you long enough."

"Marco is the champion. Everyone wants a piece of him tonight," Dom said.

"What is the problem?" Marco asked, not interested in having one of their brotherly discussions that led nowhere.

"The problem is the Vallerio family is adamant that we can't use their name on the new production car."

The Vallerio was Moretti Motors' signature car and had been out of production since the sixties. Bringing the model back was Dominic's plan to firmly reestablish their dominance in the market-place.

"How can I help?" Marco asked. "Keke or I can take the stock car to Le Mans and win the Twenty-Four Hours with it."

"Impossible. Their lawyer sent a cease and desist letter to us."

"We need to get to the Vallerio family and con-vince them to let us use the name," Dominic said.

"What do we know about them?" Marco asked, his interest in the dark-haired woman momentarily abated. He knew how important it was that Moretti Motors go ahead with their plans.

"That Pierre Henri Vallerio hated Nonno and is probably jumping for joy in the afterworld at the thought that his descendants have something we need," Antonio said.

"So a family feud…"

"Of a sort. I think they'd say no just to prove they can," Dom said.

"Well, then, I will have to offer them something they can't refuse," Antonio said.

"Like what?" Marco asked. His middle brother was used to winning. Hell, they all were.

"I'll figure it out," Antonio said. "Leave this one to me."

"We can't let this derail us," Dom said.

"We won't," Antonio said.

And Marco knew it wouldn't be a problem for long. The Vallerio's lawyer would be surprised when he had to deal with Antonio.

Virginia Festa had had a moment's panic when Marco left his seat and started walking toward her. She knew enough about him to realize that he liked his women interested, but not obvious. So she turned away hoping…oh, hell, she had turned away due to panic.

Melbourne, Australia, was steamy in March—something that she had anticipated before she'd left her home on Long Island. In fact, she'd planned every detail of this trip with excruciating precision, knowing that timing was everything. But she hadn't anticipated the human element. A mistake she was sure her grandmother had made, as well, when she'd placed the curse on the Moretti men.

She suspected that her grandmother—who had only a rudimentary knowledge of the ancient *strega* witchcraft—hadn't realized that when she'd cursed her lover, Lorenzo Moretti, and his family she was also cursing the Festa women. Virginia had spent a lifetime studying the curse her grandmother had used, trying to unravel the words so she could break it. There was no way to just take the curse back, since her grandmother had been the one who'd spoken the words and she was now deceased.

It totally ticked her off that she had panicked after coming this far. She was putting into action the plan she'd been thinking about since she was sixteen, since the moment she'd discovered the curse her grandmother had placed on the Moretti men and, by accident, the Festa women.

She wiped her damp hands on her classic Chanel gown. She was going to have to try to find Marco again—find him and charm him without giving away her plan. The key was to be vague. She had spent hours studying books on the *strega* spell her grandmother had used to curse the Morettis and looking for a way to break it. She'd determined through her research that to put the plan in action, she had to be anonymous.

She had only her grandmother's memory of the words she'd spoken—words that Cassia had written in her journal and that Virginia had studied. Her grandmother had demanded retribution for her own broken heart, and in doing so, she'd doomed the Festa women to always have broken hearts.

There could be no joining of Festa and Moretti hearts. They had to stay forever apart. But their blood… As she'd studied curses, Virginia found a loophole. Separately, both families were doomed forever. But a child of Festa and Moretti blood could break the curse. A child given to her freely from a Moretti would repay the broken heart her grand-

mother had received from Lorenzo Moretti two generations ago and lift the curse on the Morettis and the
Festas.

Now that the moment was here, she was really
nervous. It was one thing to sit in her condo and
make plans to seduce a man. It was something else
entirely to actually fly around the world and put the
plan into action.

She stepped out of the crowded room and onto the
terrace that overlooked downtown Melbourne. Until
now, the places she'd seen had been only the small
town in Italy where her grandmother had grown up
and her own home on Long Island.

Tonight, standing on this terrace looking out at the
black sky dotted with stars, she felt like she was on
the edge of starting something new. All the *strega*
magic that her mother and grandmother had taught
her had its basis in being outside. She looked up at
the moon shining brightly down on her and took
strength from it.

"It is a beautiful night, is it not?"

The deep, masculine voice sent a tingle down her
spine and she wasn't surprised when she turned
around and saw Marco Moretti standing there.

The panic she'd felt inside the party didn't return.
Instead, as she looked over her shoulder at him, she
felt a sense of power come over her.

"Yes it is," she said.

"May I join you?"

She nodded.

"I'm Marco Moretti."

"I know," she said. "Congratulations on winning today."

"That's what I do, *mi' angela*," he said, grinning at her.

"I'm not your angel," she said, though she loved the sound of him speaking in his native language.

"Tell me your name and I shall call you by it."

"Virginia," she said, very aware that her last name would give her away. So she kept it to herself.

"Virginia…very pretty. What are you doing here in Melbourne?"

"Watching you win," she said.

He laughed out loud, the sound washing over her senses like the warm breeze that stirred around them.

"Will you join me for a drink?"

"Only if we can stay out here," she said. She didn't want to go back into the craziness of the party. Out here, she felt in control and better able to concentrate. Plus, she needed all the *strega* magic she could summon. The night sky filled with stars and the bright moon would help her.

"Certainly," he said. He signaled one of the uniformed waiters and they placed their drink orders.

Once their drinks came, Marco took her elbow and led her farther away from the people lingering on the terrace. The terrace spanned the entire side of the building, and as they walked along, she became very aware of his hand on her arm, of the subtle brush of his fingers over her flesh.

When they reached a quiet area with no one around, he stopped walking and dropped her arm. Leaning back against the railing, he looked at her, his dark brown eyes intense. She wondered what he saw, she hoped she seemed mysterious, sexy, sultry. She was afraid she was going to give up the game she was playing by betraying her nervousness.

"Tell me about yourself, *mi' angela bella*," he said.

She hadn't counted on her senses being engaged by Marco. She'd figured she'd come here, flash some leg and a hint of cleavage, and that he'd be turned on and take her to bed and she'd leave in the morning.

Instead she found that she liked listening to his voice. She loved his accent and the rhythm of his words as he spoke. Liked also the scent of his cologne, and the way that he made her feel like she was the only woman in the world. And of course, that fit what she'd learned about him—that his relationships, while short-lived, were very intense.

"What do you want to know, *mi diavolo bello?*"

He laughed again and she understood why he was considered so charming. Charm imbued every part of him. "So you think I am handsome?"

"I think you're a devil," she said.

"I love the sound of my native tongue on your lips," he said. "Tell me about yourself in Italian."

"I only know a few phrases," she said, "What is it you want to know about me?"

"Everything," he said.

She shook her head. "That would be a very boring tale. Nothing like the famed story of the Marco Moretti."

"I bet that's not true. What do you do?" he asked.

"Right now I'm on sabbatical," she said, which was the truth. She had taken six months off from her teaching job at a small liberal arts college to follow the Formula One racing season and meet Marco.

"Why?"

"I'm going to be thirty next year and I decided it was time to see the world. I've always wanted to travel but never had the time."

"So it's just a happy coincidence that we are both in Melbourne?"

"Yes," she said. A very happy coincidence, put in play by her own actions.

"Melbourne's only the first stop. This is one of my favorite cities."

"What do you like about it?" she asked. She knew little about the man beyond what she'd read on the Internet and in magazines.

"Tonight, I like that you and I are both here."

She shook her head. "That's a corny line."

"It's not a line, but the truth," he said. "Come and dance with me."

She took a sip of her Bellini. She'd caught his attention, diverted the conversation away from herself, and now… "Okay."

"Did you really have to think it over?" he asked, taking her hand in his and drawing her near to him.

"Not really. I just wasn't expecting this."

"Expecting what?"

"To find you so attractive."

He laughed. "Good. I wasn't expecting you, either, Virginia."

"What were you expecting?" she asked.

"Another victory party where everyone pretends that they are happy for me, but no one really cares."

"Is that usually a problem for you?"

"Not really. That's just the way this crowd is. Everyone is here to see and be seen."

His words revealed more than she was sure he intended them to. But before she could ask any more questions, he leaned in, cupped her face and brought his mouth down to hers.

The scent of his Scotch was sweet as he parted her lips with his own. She felt the warmth of his breath and then the gentle brush of his tongue against her mouth.

And in that moment she knew—*strega* magic or not—this was a dangerous mission she'd set for herself. Because not falling for the charming Marco Moretti was going to be harder than she'd ever imagined it would be.

Two

Virginia's plan was working...a little too well. Marco was smooth and charming. She'd expected that. But he was also very funny and a bit self-deprecating.

Everyone wanted a piece of him tonight. A moment to bask in his glory. He had the aura of someone who was going to break that record on wins in the Formula One circuit, and everyone wanted to be close to him.

Since they'd come in from the terrace, she tried to leave a few times, not being comfortable in the spotlight. But he kept her by his side, his fingers linked loosely with hers as they moved through the crowd.

She didn't have to try to be mysterious here. No one knew her, and to be honest, she didn't think anyone wanted to know her tonight. She was simply a pretty woman hanging on Marco's arm.

The feminist in her was a bit outraged to be delegated to nothing more than arm candy.

"I am sorry, *mi' angela,* but winning always means that my time is not my own."

"It's okay," she said. She was learning a lot about Marco from watching him. She wondered if her grandmother had realized what the Formula One lifestyle was like. Was this why Lorenzo Moretti hadn't wanted to settle down with her grandmother? Maybe having experienced the high life, he hadn't been ready to give it up for home and family.

"What are you thinking, *cara mia?*"

"I'm thinking that you can't remember my name so you keep calling me by endearments."

"Virginia, you wound me."

"Doubtful."

He smiled. "I do want to know what you are thinking. You look too serious for a woman at a party."

She didn't know how to respond to that. She wanted—no, *needed*—to be mysterious. She couldn't allow herself to forget for one moment that she wasn't here to fall in love with Marco Moretti. She was here to break a curse.

But when he pulled her into his arms on the dance floor, she forgot about plans and curses. She forgot about everything except the way his arms felt wrapped around her. The way his shoulder was the perfect place to rest her head, which she did for only one second, because the sexy scent of his aftershave was too potent that close.

"I was thinking that at this party, everyone wants something from you."

"Including you?"

Yes, she thought, but didn't say it out loud.

"It's okay, I know you do. Everyone wants something, I want something from you."

"What do you want from me?"

"Another kiss."

Of course he did, and that made her agenda so much easier because she wanted him to want her. But at the same time…

"You're doing it again," he whispered into her ear. "I'm going to think that you aren't happy to be with me."

Shivers ran down the length of her body from her neck to her toes. Her breasts felt heavier all of a sudden, and her nipples perked up, as if they wanted the warmth of his breath against them.

"Of course I'm happy to be with you, Marco. You are the man every woman wants…all you have to do is beckon and any woman here would come to you."

"I don't want any other woman tonight, Virginia, only you."

"Why?" she asked.

"I could say that it is the hint of mystery in those

deep, chocolate-brown eyes of yours. Or the smoothness of your skin against my hand."

"But that's not it?"

"No, *cara mia,* it's not. The reason I want only you is much more base and too demanding to be tamed by words."

"Lust."

"You say it with disdain, but there is a power to lust and to attraction at first sight. From the moment I caught sight of you, I have been unable to think of anyone else."

She smiled up at him and let go of those silly girlish dreams she'd secretly harbored about love. Lust was exactly what she wanted from Marco, and she should be very happy that he felt it.

"It's the same for me."

"Is it?" he asked, drawing his hand down her back. Her skin was exposed by the plunging V at the back of her dress and his fingers felt big and warm against her skin.

He pulled her closer to his body as he spun them around the dance floor. His mouth touched the exposed skin at the nape of her neck. His lips felt warm and moist against her skin as he said something she couldn't understand. All she understood at this moment was that she wanted Marco Moretti.

Her flesh was sensitized to him. She felt alive in this man's arms. Perhaps it was the magic of the night, or maybe it was the peach Bellinis she'd drank going to her head. But deep inside her, where she kept the superstitious part of her soul, she knew it was the curse coming out. She knew this attraction went beyond her and Marco.

It was something cosmic and wonderful, she knew. Especially when he lowered his head to hers. She didn't wait for him to kiss her, but instead rose on her tiptoes and met his mouth with her own.

He brushed his lips over hers before opening them the slightest bit. She felt first the barest rush of his breath over her sensitive lips and then the smooth taste of his tongue.

He kissed her with the kind of passion she'd only read about in books and seen on movie screens. She clung to his shoulders as everything feminine inside of her responded to everything masculine in him.

Kissing Virginia was addictive. Like the rush he got from going over two hundred miles per hour on the track. There was that feeling of being in charge of something he knew he couldn't really control.

Her mouth was sweet and she clung to him like she couldn't get enough of him, either. He maneuvered her off the dance floor, keeping one arm around her waist and tucking her close to his side.

"Where are we going?" she asked. Her voice was breathless and her lips, swollen. There was something almost ethereal about her. He would never have admitted that fact out loud, but having grown up under a very suspicious Italian mother, he believed strongly in things that couldn't be explained.

"To a place where we can be alone. Is that okay

with you?" he asked her. Expectation sizzled in the air between them. He felt almost as if they'd met before. With her, he didn't feel the distance that he felt with most women, as if they had an expectation of something that he couldn't deliver on.

She nodded and smiled. Her mouth was wide and so damned sensuous. He'd never get enough of kissing her. And for tonight, he didn't have to. He ran his hand down the center of her bare back, enjoying the feel of her soft flesh under his fingers.

"I'd like that," she said. There was a hint of shyness in her voice, a timidity at odds with the brazen and mysterious woman he'd known her to be so far.

"Virginia?"

"Yes?"

"Are you sure?"

He saw hesitation in her eyes, but then she nodded her head, curls dancing around her face as she stepped forward. She rose on tiptoes and drew his head toward hers and brushed her lips over his. She kissed him deeply and passionately, arousing him with just that one aggressive move.

"I'm very sure," she said.

"Good," he said, his own voice sounding husky.

He led the way out of the party toward the elevator and almost groaned when he saw Dominic coming. He didn't want to talk to his brother now.

"*Merda,*" he muttered under his breath.

"Excuse me?" Virginia said pulling away from him. "Is everything okay?"

"Pardon me. My brother is heading this way, and with him there is always a discussion about business."

He fought the urge to hit the call button for the elevator again. That would make it look as if he were afraid of Dominic, and that wasn't the case. He just wanted to get Virginia out of the party to be alone with her.

That made him feel a bit odd. He'd never been one of those men who needed to keep a woman all to himself. With Virginia, he realized he wanted just that.

"I didn't realize that a driver would be involved in the running of a company," she said.

"At Moretti Motors we have decided to keep things all in the family. So that means that we all take an active role in running it."

"Doesn't that interfere with your driving?" she asked.

Marco liked being involved in running the company. Dominic, Antonio and he had decided the reason their father had lost his controlling share of the company was that he had not been involved in the day-to-day details. And that was one thing he and his brothers were determined not to let happen.

"Not most of the time…but it can put a crimp in my love life."

She rolled her eyes at that. "Saying things like *that* might be more of a problem for you."

Marco shook his head and gave her a charming smile. The same smile she'd seen when he'd graced the cover of *Sports Illustrated* last year. "Most women don't mind."

"I'm not so sure about that," she said.

"I make up for my…how do you say…ill manners in other ways that women appreciate."

"What ways?"

"I'll show you as soon as we get out of here."

"I'm going to hold you to that," she said. "Should I leave you alone with your brother?"

"No," he said, not wanting her to disappear again. "Dom won't be long."

"Marco, do you have a minute?" Dominic said as he reached them.

Marco tucked Virginia's hand in the crook of his arm, keeping her close to his side.

"Not really. I promised to show Virginia one of my favorite places in Melbourne. I can meet with you tomorrow to discuss the matter," Marco said.

Dominic didn't look pleased, but then his brother rarely did. "That will be fine. But I'm flying back to Italy tomorrow, so my schedule is tight."

"I understand," Marco said. As much as he resented the delay in leaving with Virginia, Moretti Motors was as important to him as it was to Dom.

"Virginia, let me introduce you to my oldest brother, Dominic. Dom, this is Virginia…." He didn't know her last name, he realized. This wouldn't be the first time that he had a one-night stand with a woman whose last name was a mystery to him. So why did it bother him?

"Affascinato," Dominic said.

"The pleasure is mine," she said.

"Did you enjoy the race today?" he asked.

"I missed it," she said, blushing.

Marco found that odd. Most of the women who followed the circuit never missed a race. He looked down at her. "You did?"

"My flight was late. I was upset, but I had this party to look forward to."

"Where are you from?" Dominic asked.

"The United States," she said.

"Most Americans prefer NASCAR racing. Do you follow that sport, as well?" Marco asked, realizing that with his brother here he was learning more about her than he had all evening, talking to her.

"No. I've always been in love with the glamour of Formula One."

He raised one eyebrow at her. "What do you think is glamorous about it?"

"This party, for one," she said. "Oh, look, the elevator is here."

The doors opened and Marco wondered at her vague answers. Was she hiding something? She wrapped an arm around his waist and squeezed him closer to her. "You did promise to show me your favorite sight in Melbourne."

"Indeed I did. *Ciao,* Dom."

"*Arrivederci,* Marco."

Virginia didn't say much as they got in Marco's sports coupe convertible. She recognized it as a Moretti model. The car was pure luxury on the inside and all speed under the hood. She'd never feel confident enough to drive a car like this, but Marco handled it like the professional driver he was.

As they left the hotel behind he glanced over at her. "So you're from the States?"

She'd known he was going to ask questions. She'd done a good job of keeping her past vague and the spotlight on him, but the conversation with Dominic had probably made him realize how little he knew about her.

"Yes. Long Island. Where did you grow up? I know Moretti Motors is based in Milan, but do you live there?"

"I have a villa in Milan, and my family has an estate outside of the city."

"Do you like living in Milan? I've never visited there," she said. She was very aware of the Moretti family estate in San Giuliano Milanese. Her grandmother had gone there to curse Lorenzo, and there was a faded picture of the Moretti estate hanging on

her wall back home. Her grandmother had be-
queathed it to her along with her journal.

"It's a fashionable city and there is always something to do there." He shrugged as he glanced over
at her. "It's home."

She envied him the feeling of belonging in Milan.
It was there in his voice and his words. Unlike she,
who'd never fit in anywhere, he had a place that he
called home. And that was a big part of why she was
determined to break the curse her grandmother had
placed on them by accident. She wanted—no,
craved a home and a family. She was tired of always
being alone. Her mother and grandmother were both
deceased, and no matter how hard she tried, the
bonds of family seemed to always be just out of her
reach.

Having his child would give her a chance at happiness. A chance at that elusive dream she'd longed
for. Once she broke the curse, she would marry and
give her child a father and siblings.

"We're here." Marco's words startled her from
her thought.

She glanced out the window as a uniformed valet
came to open her door. The high-rise building was
a monument to modern architecture, its lines distinc-
tive and clean.

"Good evening, Mr. Moretti."

"Good evening, Mitchell."

Marco led the way into the foyer and to a bank
of elevators.

"I thought you were taking me to see your favorite
spot in Melbourne."

"I am. My penthouse has a spectacular view of the city. It's amazing," he said, glancing down at his titanium watch. "In about two hours, the sun will come up and you will be amazed at how beautiful the sunrise is here."

"Will I?"

"Yes, I think you will," he said. "Unless you'd rather I take you back to your hotel."

She shook her head.

The elevator arrived and they entered. They were alone in the marble-floored car, and as soon as the door closed Marco entered a code on the keypad and the elevator started to move. He drew her into his arms and lowered his head, kissing her.

She felt the return of the passion he'd evoked in her on the dance floor. Her body longed for his. She'd missed his touch during the twenty-minute drive, and she wondered how much of this feeling was due to the magic spell she'd cast earlier to help her break the curse. She wasn't a practicing witch, but she figured she'd better enlist as much help as she could before she came to Melbourne. How much of it was due to the fact that she needed him to be obsessed with her?

And how much, if any of it, was real?

When the doors opened, he broke the kiss and ran his hand down her bare arm, linking their fingers together. She squeezed her hand against his and followed him eagerly into the foyer of his home.

"I have this entire floor. Would you like a drink?"

"That would be nice," she said.

He led the way into the living room. There were floor-to-ceiling windows that lined the wall and a sliding door that opened onto a huge balcony. Marco kept one hand on the small of her back as they walked across the room.

She felt a slight bit of panic as she realized this was it. She was going to sleep with this man, whom she'd known for less than five hours, and then she was going to walk away. It was what she'd planned for more months than she could count, but now that the moment was here…

She stopped in the middle of his living room as a surreal feeling swamped her. She was aroused, every inch of her skin sensitized from his kisses and touch. As she glanced at the Monet painting hanging on one wall and felt the thick Arabian carpet under her feet, she knew she was really here, that this wasn't something she was imagining. Yet, at the same time…

"Would you like to step outside? We can sit in the hot tub and have that drink."

She glanced at Marco, with his strong Roman features, and saw in him the glimpse of her future. She wasn't going to let panic or doubt swamp her, and give up everything she'd ever wanted.

She needed Marco Moretti, and it seemed that he wanted her tonight. And that was all she needed. She repeated that in her head as she stepped out onto the balcony and let the warm air wrap around her.

Three

Marco poured a glass of champagne for each of them. He wasn't inept when it came to taking care of the women in his life, despite the fact that Allie had often complained he paid no attention to her. The fact was, he was careful to pay only a certain amount of attention.

He was careful not to let his emotions get involved, always leery of falling for a woman and thereby ruining his life.

His mobile rang and he cursed out loud as he saw from the caller ID that it was Dominic.

"What do you need now?" he asked in Italian.

"Just wanted to remind you to be careful with

Virginia. We can't risk anyone falling in love, especially now."

"Mordalo," he said to his brother.

"I'm not jerking your chain, Marco. You know that falling for a girl isn't something we can do."

He glanced across his penthouse apartment to the balcony where he could see Virginia leaning against the railing. She didn't *look* dangerous. He saw nothing in the woman to indicate she could bring about the downfall of Moretti Motors.

"She's just a woman, Dom," he said, even as, deep inside, a part of him protested. But the truth was, his priorities were simple—racing and winning. Moretti Motors and then enjoying life. And Virginia was a woman who would make his life very enjoyable tonight.

"Make sure you remember that."

"I always do. I think you're afraid that Antonio and I are too much like you."

There was silence from his usually loquacious brother. Dom had fallen in love in college, and that one, brief lapse in his vigilance served as a constant reminder to Dom that all women had the potential to tempt any of the Moretti men.

"I don't know what I fear. Just be careful, Marco. This is the year that everything will change. We have worked hard to get to this point. We are launching the revamped Vallerio model. You will surpass the Gran Prix record for most wins…."

"I am aware of that. *Buona notte,* Dom."

"*Buona notte,* Marco."

He hung up the phone, thinking of his oldest brother. Antonio often complained that Dominic needed to get laid so that the old boy would relax. But Marco suspected that Dominic's heart was the most vulnerable of all of the Moretti men.

"Marco?"

"Coming, *mi' angela.*"

A warm, gentle breeze stirred the air around the balcony as he approached Virginia. Her hair lifted in the wind and for a minute it seemed as if she were part of the night. As if this was the only place she could exist. Almost as if she were a fantasy. But she was a flesh-and-blood woman, as he'd ascertained by kissing her and holding her in his arms.

"I thought you'd changed your mind," she said.

"Not at all. I just wanted to make sure I had everything perfect," he said, handing her the glass of chilled champagne.

"Is this part of the charm you promised to show me earlier?"

"Do you think it is?"

She laughed, and the sound was like music on the wind. He closed his eyes and let the worries that his brother always reminded him of disappear. For tonight he was nothing more than a winning driver with a beautiful woman.

"I'm not so sure."

He arched one eyebrow at her. "What will it take to convince you?"

"I'm reserving judgment until morning."

He handed her the champagne flute, which she took.

"To your victory on the track today," she said.

He tapped the lip of his glass against hers. *"Grazie."*

He kept eye contact with her as he took a sip of the sparkling wine.

"To mysteriously beautiful women," he said, lifting his glass toward her.

"Grazie," she said with a shy smile. "But I'm not beautiful."

"Let me look again," he said.

She stood still, a hesitant, almost fragile smile on her face as he stared at her features. Her wide brown eyes seemed luminous and filled with secrets. The thick eyelashes that surrounded them and the light dash of makeup on her lids made them look exotic.

Her high cheekbones and creamy skin were next. He lifted his free hand and traced the line of her brow and then down the side of her face. Her nose was thin and long, marking the elegance of her face, but it was her mouth that entranced him.

Her upper lip was a bit fuller than the bottom one, and both were rosy red and so soft to his touch. He ran his thumb over her mouth, tracing the bow at the top and then stroking her bottom lip.

"I see nothing to change my opinion," he said.

"Maybe in your eyes I'm beautiful, but I promise you other men don't see me that way," she said.

"The eyes of other men don't matter, *mio dolce.*"

"No, they don't…I just…I've never done this before," she said suddenly, her words coming out in a rush.

"Come back to a man's apartment?" he asked, unable to help feeling a bit honored and possessive of the fact that he was the first man she'd felt this strongly attracted to.

And he couldn't deny the attraction between them. He hoped she'd never know how much he wanted her and how much power that gave her over him. He needed her in ways he was only beginning to realize.

"Yes…I'm a bit nervous."

"It's not too late to leave. We can finish our drinks and I can take you back to your hotel."

Virginia realized that Marco was making very sure she couldn't say he coerced her into anything. Or perhaps he was just being a gentleman. What did it say about her that her first thought was that he was protecting himself?

But there was little he could do to protect himself against her. She wanted nothing more than this night in his arms—and his sperm.

She felt cold and calculating, thinking the words. She knew that every night millions of people had one-night stands and it meant nothing.

But she didn't. She had been pretty sheltered all of her life. After being told early on that love and romance were not in the cards for her, she'd become determined to find a way to make her romantic dreams come true.

She knew that her motivation for being here was breaking the Moretti curse. But when he'd described her just a moment ago, talked about a beauty she just couldn't see when she looked in a mirror, she felt as if this encounter meant more than she knew.

She felt as if Marco wasn't just the means to an end. That he wasn't just another victim of a long ago, bitter love feud between their families…felt as if he could be the man who would make her fall in love with him.

And love for Festa women wasn't a good thing.

"Virginia?"

She shook her head to clear it. Glanced up at the moon and gathered the strength she needed to forget about consequences and right and wrong. For this one night, she wanted to just enjoy the moment with this man.

"I'm not leaving," she said.

He smiled at her, and she realized just what true male beauty was. It was his smile when he looked at her.

"Are we going to just stand here and wait for sunrise?" she asked.

"Not at all. I thought we could sit in the hot tub and relax. Enjoy the champagne and the rest of the evening."

The warmth of his hand on the center of her back

and the low thrum of the hot tub located on the end of the balcony settled her nerves. She let go of all the planning and concentrated on the fact that she was here with a charming and sexy man.

"I'd like that," she said.

"There's a changing room over there stocked with robes," Marco said, his voice deep and dark in the moonlit night. He gestured to the small building next to the tub.

Having spent most of her adult life waiting for this exact moment, she knew it was time for her to act. But action was the one thing that had always scared her. Her grandmother had loved Lorenzo Moretti and that single act had completely ruined Cassia's life.

Perhaps sensing her unease, Marco said, "Do you know about the stars?"

"What?"

"The stories of the different stars and why the constellations fill the sky," he said. Wrapping his arm around her waist, he led her to a double lounge chair and gestured for her to sit down.

She did, and Marco sat down next to her. He put his arm around her shoulder and shifted until she was lying next to him with her head on his shoulder.

She looked at him and knew without a doubt that he had sensed her keyed-up nerves. And she wondered if this was a sign from the universe that she should give up on her plan. Was there a side effect she'd missed when she'd determined the way to break the curse on their families was by getting pregnant with Marco's child?

"The sky is different here," Marco said. "In the Northern Hemisphere, where we both live, you can never see the Southern Cross."

She stopped worrying about seduction and re-laxed against him. "I had heard that. Where is the Southern Cross?"

He pointed at the sky. "Right there…do you see it?"

Her gaze followed the line of his arm, and she saw four stars in a diamond shape in the sky. The Southern Cross. "Does it have a legend with it, like Orion or Sirius?"

"Not really. Because it is visible only from the Southern Hemisphere, we have no Greek or Roman legends associated with it."

"What is that constellation?" she asked pointing to another one.

"That is Leo. Egyptian priests used to be able to predict when the Nile would flood based on its position in the sky."

He talked about other constellations and she began to see beyond the international celebrity race car driver to the man beneath. He was used to moving in a world of privilege and wealth, yet tonight he was just a man.

"How did you become interested in stars?"

"My father. He isn't into racing or cars…not the way a Moretti should be." He turned on the lounge chair so that he was leaning over her. "But he loves legends and the past…he has spent a lot of his life reading about stories of old."

"Where are your parents now?"

"In San Giuliano Milanese. It's where our family home is."

"Are you close to your parents?" she asked.

"In some ways. I've always shared a love of the night sky with my father. When I was younger, most of my time alone with him was spent outside at night, looking through the lens of his telescope."

Being an only child, she'd had too much time alone with her mother, who had been very sad most of the time.

"Why didn't your father like cars?" she asked. She knew that Giovanni Moretti was rumored to have been too easygoing to run the big automotive company. That he wasn't interested in business… only in making love to his wife.

"He liked them, he just loved my mother more. So business didn't hold his interest."

"Yet, it does hold yours," she said.

"Tonight I can see why my father was distracted," Marco said.

She thought she saw surprise in his eyes as he revealed that, but he recovered quickly, leaning in close to kiss her. His kiss was soft and slow, one of seduction rather than full-out passion.

He swept his hand down the side of her body, unerringly finding the zipper in the side of her dress.

Instead of unfastening it, he simply traced his finger over the seam.

His mouth moved along her jawline with small, nibbling kisses, then dipped lower to caress the length of her neck. She shifted in his arms, trying to bring her body into full contact with his as he continued to tease her.

Her breasts felt sensitive and the skin of her arm beaded with goose bumps as he continued to move his hand over her body. She wanted more.

Marco had always had an innate gift for seducing women. Dom had suggested it was because he was Italian and wooing women had been bred into him, but Marco thought it was more than that. He'd never been callous in his seductions and he'd walked away from women who he knew would regret having made love to him when they woke in the morning.

But he couldn't walk away from Virginia. He surprised himself with the depth of the need he had for her. Still, if he made this about the physical, then his emotions would recede and she would be nothing more than a passionate memory for him to look back on, years from now.

The rich darkness of her hair contrasted with the creamy whiteness of her skin. He drew down the zipper at the side of her body and watched as the sky-blue material gaped open. He slipped his hand under the fabric and touched her skin.

Her breath caught and she shifted in his arms, turning on her side so they were now facing each other. He reached between them and drew her hands up to the first button on his shirt.

Staring into her wide, chocolate-colored eyes, he saw the shyness that was so much a part of her melt away as her fingers brushed against his chest.

Blood rushed through his veins, pooling in his groin and hardening him as she started unbuttoning his shirt. Her fingers were cool against his skin as she worked her way down his body. When she finished unbuttoning the shirt she pushed it open and he shrugged out of it.

He growled when she leaned forward to brush kisses against his chest. Her lips were soft and not shy as she explored his torso, and he felt the edge of her teeth graze his pecs.

He watched her, his eyes narrowing and his pants feeling damned uncomfortable. Her tongue darted out and brushed his nipple. He canted his hips forward and put his hand on the back of her head, urging her to stay where she was.

"Where did you get this?" she asked, one finger tracing over the scar under his left nipple.

"Tony pushed me out of the fig tree in the back-yard when I was eight and I landed on a hoe that the gardener had left lying on the ground."

"Did it hurt?" she asked. She braced one hand on his chest as she leaned over him.

He shifted under her and lifted her in his arms so

that she straddled him. He leaned up and kissed her lips. "At the time it hurt very much."

"I'm sorry," she said, leaning down to lave the spot with her tongue. "I have a scar, too."

"Where?" he asked.

She blushed and then shrugged her shoulders, pulling her right arm out of the dress. The bodice loosened and the other sleeve slid down her left arm until the dress pooled at her waist. She wore those strapless bra cups that were clear in color. He could see all of her breasts and yet as he reached up to touch them, he felt only fabric and not the sweetness of her flesh.

"The scar isn't on my boobs," she said, with a little laugh.

"No?"

"No," she said. "It's here."

She pointed to her right side an inch below her breasts. It was long, almost two inches, and had faded with time.

"How did you get this?" he asked, stroking a finger down the length of it. She shivered in his arms and rocked against him. His erection twitched against her core.

"Trying to climb into the window of our house. My mom locked the keys inside."

"I'm sorry," he said. He lifted his hips to tip her body toward him. He found the scar with his lips and rubbed his hands over her naked back, enjoying the feel of this warm woman in his arms.

She put her hands on his shoulders and eased her way down his chest. She traced the muscles of his abdomen and then slowly made her way lower. He could feel his heartbeat in his erection and he knew he was going to lose control if he didn't slow things down.

But another part of him wanted to just sit back and let her have her way with him. When she reached the edge of his pants, she stopped and glanced up his body to his face.

Her hand brushed over his straining length. He removed the bra she still wore and then lifted her up so that her nipples brushed his chest.

"Hmm…that feels so good," she said.

"Does it?"

"Yes."

Blood roared in his ears. He was so hard, so full right now that he needed to be inside of her body. But he had to take care of details first.

"*Cara mia,* I hate to ask this, but are you on the pill?"

She pulled back for a second. "I'm…yes."

"You are taking the pill?" he asked.

She nodded. "And I don't have anything else you need to worry about. What about you?"

"I'm clean."

"Good," she said.

He pulled her closer and kissed her until she relaxed. Then, impatient with the fabric of her dress, he shoved it up to her waist. He caressed her creamy thighs. God, she was soft. She moaned as he neared

her center and then sighed when he brushed his fingertips across the crotch of her panties.

The lace was warm and wet. He slipped one
finger under the material and hesitated for a second,
looking up into her eyes.

They were heavy-lidded. She bit down on her
lower lip and he felt the minute movements of her
hips as she tried to move his touch where she needed
it.

He pushed the fabric of her panties aside and
lightly traced the opening of her body. She was so
ready for him. It was only the fact that he wanted
to bring her to climax at least once before he
entered her body that enabled him to keep his own
needs in check.

She shifted against him and he entered her body
with just the tip of one finger. He teased them both
with a few short thrusts.

"Marco…" she said, her voice breathless and airy.

"Yes, *mi' angela?*"

"I need more."

"Is this better?" he asked, pushing his finger deep
inside of her.

"Yes," she said. Her hips rocked against his finger
for a few strokes before she once again needed more.

"Marco, please."

He pulled his finger from her body and traced it
around her pulsing center of her need. Her eyes
widened and she moved frantically against him. She
leaned forward, her breasts brushing against his

cheek as she braced her hands on the back of the lounge chair.

He turned his head and drew one beaded nipple into his mouth, suckling her deeply as he plunged two fingers into her body. He kept his thumb on her center and worked his fingers until she threw her head back and called his name.

He felt her tighten around his fingers. She kept rocking against him for a few more seconds and then collapsed.

He tipped her head toward his so he could taste her mouth. He told himself to take it slowly, that Virginia wasn't used to him. But one taste of her lips and he was out of control.

He kissed her and held her at his mercy, caressing her back and spine, scraping his nails down the line of her back down the indentation above her buttocks.

She closed her eyes and held her breath as he returned his fingers to one nipple. It was velvety compared to the satin smoothness of her breast. He brushed his finger back and forth until she bit her lower lip and shifted on his lap.

She moaned, a sweet sound that nearly did him in. He reached between them and unzipped his pants, freeing his erection. She cried out softly as he brushed the tip against her humid center.

She reached between them and touched him, her small hand engulfing the length as she shifted to put the tip inside her body.

He held her still with a hand on the small of her

back. He had a lap full of woman, and he wanted
Virginia more than he'd wanted any woman in a
long time. Maintaining control was harder than it
had ever been. Dangerous. He knew better than to
let this mean anything more than a passionate encounter.

This was about the physical. One night together.

She rocked her hips, trying to take him deeper,
and he knew the time for teasing was at an end.

"Marco?"

"Hmm?"

"Are you going to take me?" she asked.

"Do you want more?" he asked.

She leaned down and sucked his lower lip into her
mouth, biting gently. "You know I do."

"Beg me to take you, *mi' angela bella.*"

"Take me, Marco. Make me yours."

He did want to make her his, in this moment with
the night sky around them, the Southern Cross shining in the sky, he was away from Italy and the curse
that had dogged the Moretti men for too long.

He was going to claim Virginia as his…even if
only for this one night.

He gave her another inch, thrusting his hips up
into her sweet, tight body. Her eyes were closed, her
hips moving subtly against him, and when he blew
on her nipples he saw gooseflesh spread down her
body.

He loved the way she reacted to his mouth on her.
He sucked on the skin at the base of her neck as he

thrust all the way home, sheathing his entire length in her body. He knew he was leaving a mark with his mouth and that pleased him. He wanted her to remember this moment and what they had done when she was alone later.

He kept kissing and rubbing, pinching her nipples until her hands clenched in his hair and she rocked her hips harder against him. He lifted his hips, thrusting up against her.

"Come with me," he whispered to her in Italian.

She nodded and he realized she understood his native tongue. Her eyes widened with each inch he gave her. She clutched at his hips, holding him to her, eyes half-closed and her head tipped back.

He caught one of her nipples in his teeth, scraping very gently. She started to tighten around him. Her hips moving faster, demanding more, but he kept the pace slow, steady, building the pleasure between them.

He varied his thrusts, finding a rhythm that would draw out the tension at the base of his spine. Something that would make his time in her body, wrapped in her silky limbs, seem to last forever.

"Hold on to me tightly."

She did as he asked and he rolled them over so that she was beneath him. He pushed her legs up against her body so that he could thrust deeper, so that she was open and vulnerable to him.

"Now, Virginia," he said.

She nodded and he felt her body tighten. Then she

scraped her nails down his back, clutching his buttocks and drawing him in. Blood roared in his ears as he felt everything in his world center on this one woman.

He called her name as he came. He saw her eyes widen and felt the minute contractions of her body around his as she was consumed by her orgasm.

He rotated his hips against her until she stopped rocking against him. She wrapped her arms around his shoulders and kissed the underside of his chin.

"Oh, Marco," she said. "Thank you for making love to me."

"You're very welcome, Virginia."

She wrapped her arms around him and held him close. "I never thought it would be like this."

"Like what?"

"So incredible. Being with you is just…well, I had no idea it would be so raw and intense."

He laughed. "That's because you hadn't made love with me before."

She tipped her head back and in her eyes he saw a vulnerability that he didn't understand.

"I think you are right."

Marco stretched and rolled over as the morning sunlight spread across the floor of his bedroom. The pillow next to his was rumpled and the sheets still smelled faintly of sex and Virginia's perfume.

"Cara mia?"

There was no answer as he stood up and stretched.

There was a glass of juice on his nightstand. He smiled as he reached for it. Maybe Virginia was making breakfast for them.

He walked slowly through his penthouse. All of Melbourne was spread out before him, and he thought for a moment about his life and the fact that he seemed to have it all. He wondered about the curse of Nonno's that had doomed their family. He'd never put too much stock in it, preferring to believe that he had control over his own destiny, but Dom had loved and lost badly, so perhaps there *was* something to the Moretti curse.

He scrubbed a hand over his face. Why was he thinking about that damned curse this morning?

He didn't want to admit it was because he liked Virginia. He was tempted to postpone his travel plans today. Stay in Melbourne with her as long as he could before commitments would demand he leave.

And that was the true measure of why she really did need to leave. He'd find her, eat whatever it was she'd fixed for him and then send her on her way.

"Virginia?"

Still no answer. The kitchen was empty. Maybe she was on the balcony. He remembered that last night she'd really enjoyed being outside. He stopped in his office, noticing that the papers on his desk were askew, as if someone had riffled through them. Knowing how important it was to keep the Moretti Motors secrets, Marco started to grow concerned.

Had Virginia been in his penthouse just to find out what Moretti Motors was doing?

Hell, now he was getting paranoid like Dom. She hadn't asked a single question about the company and hadn't really seemed interested in it.

He finally got to the balcony and it was empty, as well. He realized she was gone. He knew it wasn't hard to leave. The keypad at the elevator only prevented people from entering.

Marco clenched his fists, angry that Virginia had left before he'd had a chance to...hell, he wasn't ready for her to leave yet. He'd thought about changing his entire day for her, and she was gone.

Four

The race in Barcelona, Spain, wasn't any different from the two previous races for Marco. He did press conferences, attended Moretti Motors functions and as far as his brothers and his teammate Keke were concerned, he was the same ambitious winning driver he'd always been.

But inside Marco seethed. At first, when he'd discovered he was alone in Melbourne, he'd been concerned about Virginia, worried that their night of passion had overwhelmed her. But as time had gone on he'd realized that she'd been after just that one night with him.

He also realized that she didn't want to be found. And that shouldn't have been a big deal. He was aware that if she'd stayed, he would have hustled her out of the penthouse and then gone on with his life. He wasn't looking to settle down. He had made a promise to his brothers that he wouldn't break, and he had no time in his life for romantic complications.

So why, then, was he still so angry when he thought about the way she'd left him?

"Marco?"

"*Sì?*"

"We have to meet with the officials in a few minutes…are you okay?" Keke asked.

"Fine. Just going through the race in my head."

"Are you free for dinner tonight? Elena's family is in town and we're going out with them."

Keke and Elena were getting more serious with each month that passed, and he appreciated his friend always including him, but Marco was starting to feel like a third wheel with them.

"My parents are coming to the race, so I'm going to spend the evening with them."

"You can invite them, as well."

"What's up? Don't you want to be alone with Elena's parents?"

Keke flushed. "It's not that. I'm going to ask her to marry me and I would like to have you there. I don't have any real family, you know?"

Marco understood. "I'd be honored to join you. In fact, Dom has reserved a restaurant for our evening so that we would have privacy…would you like to use that location?"

"I made reservations at Stella Luna," Keke said.

"Then we will join you there. What time?"

"Nine."

Marco looked at the German, wondering what this would mean for their friendship. He knew no matter how much a man wanted his relationships to remain intact, once a man got married, his life changed. "Congratulations, *amico mio*."

"Thanks. I…if she says yes, will you be my best man?"

"She will say yes, and I will be your best man."

Keke left a few minutes later and Marco called his parents and brothers to invite them to join Keke's dinner celebration.

Marco had a moment's pause, as he always did when he thought of marriage. The plan that he and Dom and Tony had concocted when they were young boys meant that they'd probably never marry for love. And he envied his friend that relationship.

He left the garage and found a group of fans waiting for autographs. He stopped, smiled for photos and signed hats and shirts, all the while scanning the crowd for Virginia's face. He was a sap and an idiot to keep looking for her. She was gone. And he needed to move past that one night in Melbourne.

But he couldn't. She was the one who left. A part of him acknowledged that it was wounded pride that made him want to see her again. Another part, the baser part, wanted to see her again for purely sexual reasons. He wanted to take her and enslave her with the passion that ran between them. Bind her to him and then when she was well and truly his…leave her so that she could experience what he'd been going through.

He was lucky his racing hadn't suffered, but at this point in his career he knew how to shut out everything except the race when he got behind the wheel.

"Marco, wait up," Dom called as he walked across the field toward him.

"What is it?"

"I got your message about tonight and I'll try to be there. But I may not be available."

"Is something going on?"

"I think we have a spy in our company. I might have to return to Milan to take care of the matter."

Marco's eyes narrowed. *The ruffled papers on my desk…*. "Why do you think that?"

"I ran into Dirk Buchard today in the owner's lounge, and he mentioned rumors of a new car design from ESP," Dom said.

ESP Motors had been formed by Nonno's archrival on the Grand Prix track. Moretti Motors had outshone ESP at the time. One thing that had been in Lorenzo's favor was the fact that he had the Midas touch when it came to business. "What about the design?"

"I might be paranoid—"

Marco snorted. His brother wrote the book on paranoid when it came to guarding business secrets. "*Might* be?"

"Whatever. But he mentioned something that is on the new Vallerio model. And no one outside of you, me, Antonio and our R & D team has seen that."

"You don't have to stay for the race if you want to go back to Milan and do some more research," Marco said.

"I want to. I think you race better when Tony and I are here."

"I agree. I like to remind you both that I'm faster than either of you can ever hope to be."

Dom punched him in the arm. "Speed isn't the only thing that matters."

"In our world it is."

"True enough. Speaking of speed, did you get the e-mail I sent about the new marketing campaign?"

"Yes. I like it. I think it'll be just what we need to launch the new Vallerio."

"I agree."

Marco thought for a moment. "Is it possible that someone could have figured out what we were doing by studying the cars? I'm using similar technology in my race car this season."

"I'll know more after I go back to the Milan office."

Marco looked at his brother and thought of how hard they'd all worked to distance themselves from the fiasco that had been Moretti Motors under his father's management. At times like this, Marco felt like no matter what they did, they were always going to be struggling.

The only times he didn't feel that way were when he was on the track…and when he'd slept with Virginia. That night, he'd realized he could find peace in a woman's arms.

Virginia landed in Barcelona on Saturday morning. Last week, when her period had started, she'd had a genuine excuse to return to Marco. Clearly their one night of passion hadn't born fruit. She had been happy, because she'd missed Marco. And she knew that was a problem. What if her actions just perpetuated the curse on both families?

The truth was, she didn't care. Every night she'd been away from Marco, she'd dreamed of him, rich and vivid images of the two of them together.

And not just making love.

She'd had strong visions of her and Marco with children dancing around them.

She collected her luggage and found the car she'd hired to take her to the hotel. She wished her grandmother was still alive so she could ask her about the curse she'd put on Lorenzo.

But she had no one. There had been a bit of sadness laced in the knowledge that she wasn't pregnant. For the first time, she understood why her mother had been so happy to have her. A child meant the end to the loneliness that seemed to haunt each generation of Festa women.

She meant to end that loneliness.

"Welcome to Barcelona," the liveried doorman at the Duquesa de Cardona Hotel said.

She'd chosen a luxury boutique hotel in the heart of Barcelona's Gothic district. She smiled at the doorman as she exited the cab and walked into the hotel. It was odd to be traveling so much, yet at the same time, she felt like she was finally alive.

All those solitary years of staying at home on Long Island, going to school as a child and young woman and then teaching—it had been a life of nothing but routines; and now she had a mission. Something to fill her days. She felt alive for the very first time.

She had no idea how to contact Marco and knew she'd have to spend the day by herself until the race tomorrow. She wasn't even sure if she'd be able to get close enough to see him and had no idea what she'd say to him when she did get there.

She checked into her room and changed her clothes. She thought about hanging out in her room, but she didn't like the thought of waiting around for Sunday.

She knew that changing her life this year was about more than breaking the curse. She needed to find a way to be the woman she'd always dreamed of being. If she was going to be a mother, she didn't want to be like her own mother had been, that solitary figure who rarely smiled and never left their small house. She needed to get out and experience life.

She went to the F1 track and watched the practice

session, making sure to stay out of Marco's sight, but getting as close as she could to him.

He looked thinner than he had been in Melbourne, but he smiled for his fans and signed autographs. She started to approach, but there was no way to get through the throng of people. And then Marco waved to the crowd and turned away.

She watched him until he disappeared into the garage area, and then she left the track. In her year of figuring out how to get close to Marco, she'd gone online to the F1 message boards and made friends with a lot of people. Using those contacts, she'd been able to get into the exclusive parties after the racing events. Even the VIP areas.

She took a cab to the Picasso Museum, because the thought of going back to her hotel room was unbearable. She strolled through the museum and lingered in front of a Picasso painting titled *The Embrace,* which the artist had completed in 1900. It struck Virginia how little couples had changed over time. Nothing was more soothing than standing together wrapped in each other's arms.

"It's beautiful, isn't it?"

She glanced at the woman who'd spoken. She was tall and slender and very beautiful.

"Very."

"I love Picasso's work, before he started doing the abstract stuff."

"Me, too. He reminds me a little of Pissaro in some of his early work."

"I'm not that familiar with Pissaro. Just Picasso. Are you in town for the race?"

"Yes. How did you know?"

"I saw you at the party in Melbourne. My boy-friend is Keke Heckler."

"He's on the same team as Marco Moretti." Virginia didn't know if Marco had mentioned her after their night together. She realized that she hoped he hadn't. She didn't really want anyone to know about what had happened between them, especially since she had no idea how he'd felt the next morning.

She'd left while he was sleeping, afraid that if she stayed there in his arms, she'd forget her plans and resolve and just stay with Marco until he tired of her. Leaving like that was something that she suspected her own mother had done with Virginia's father.

"Yes, he is. We didn't meet at the party, but I saw you dancing with Marco. I'm Elena Hamilton."

"I'm Virginia," she said.

"I have a confession," Elena said. "I followed you here because I was curious about you."

Virginia tensed. "Why?"

"Because Marco has been asking about you. Questioning everyone, to see if they know your last name or where you went. Keke said he's never seen Marco so angry when he thinks no one is looking."

"I don't know what to say."

"Marco's like a brother to Keke. And I've come to know Marco, as well. He means a lot to me, and I don't want to see him being used."

Virginia was glad to hear that. Glad that Marco had good friends who looked out for him. "I'm not using him."

Elena glared at her. "I don't believe you. Just know that I'm watching you."

Virginia nodded as the other woman walked away. It might be harder than she'd thought to have a second night with Marco.

Marco finished the Catalonia Grand Prix in second place, but he didn't mind not winning this week. Keke had been unstoppable on the track. His friend and teammate had a string of good luck going that stemmed in part from his recent engagement to Elena.

Marco smiled along with everyone else. Dominic was happy, because a win for the Moretti team kept them ahead of Ferrari and Audi, which was really all Dom cared about.

Marco rubbed the back of his neck, realizing he wasn't as joy-filled as he should be. He needed to get away from Keke and the rest of the crowd.

He started to leave when he saw the familiar brown hair that he'd been searching for at each race since Melbourne. *Virginia.*

She was here. And he was going to get some damned answers about where she'd been and who she really was.

Fans swarmed around him as he made his way over to her. He didn't have time for smiles or photos, but he made himself take the time. His popularity was one of the things that was important to the success of Moretti Motors. He signaled Carlos, his security guard.

"Keep that woman here," he said, pointing to Virginia.

"Yes, sir," Carlos said, and went to Virginia's side. She arched one eyebrow at him and he guessed that she didn't like that he was keeping her from leaving. Too bad.

He took his time flirting with the women fans who were always waiting for him. They liked to pose with him and have their pictures taken. Today while Virginia was waiting, he said no to no one.

Why was she back? he wondered as the last of the fans moved away. He signaled to Carlos to bring Virginia to him. She didn't look pleased, but he didn't care. He wasn't going to give her any further ground. He was in charge, and it was about time she figured that out.

She slowly walked toward him, hips swaying with each step, drawing his eyes to her body. He was intimately familiar with her curves and longed to touch her again. When she was within arm's reach, he took her wrist in his hand and pulled her to him.

She gasped as her body came into contact with his. He was hot and sweaty from the race and he was pumped with adrenaline and something else. Something he didn't want to define.

"Hello, Marco."

"*Bongiorno,* Virginia."

"You raced well today," she said.

She was nervous. And that pleased him. She *should* be leery of him. He'd never hurt her physically, but he was angry with her and he wanted her to know it.

He cupped her jaw gently and tilted her head back. "I want answers."

"I'll give them to you," she said. Her eyes were wet as he lowered his head, taking her mouth with his.

This was no gentle seduction. He meant to be masterful, to remind her that he wasn't a man to be toyed with. That his passion—and hers—belonged to him.

He forced her lips wide and thrust his tongue deep into her mouth. She clung to his shoulders, her fingers gripping him tightly.

He heard a small sigh escape her and he softened his embrace—wrapped one arm around her and hugged her to him. God, he wouldn't have thought it possible, but he'd missed her.

"Come with me," he said. The track wasn't the place for this kind of reunion. She nodded, speechless, and he led her to the motor home he used as a dressing room and place to relax at the races.

He had a million questions to ask, but touching and caressing her made him want to take her. He needed to establish his dominance over her. She'd left him, and while it was true that one-night stands weren't out of the ordinary for him, he'd always been the one to leave.

"Why did you leave the way you did?"

She folded her arms. Her short, emerald-green designer dress brought out the creaminess of her skin. He tried not to notice.

"I...I didn't want to wait around for you to tell me to leave."

"Why do you believe I would have done that?"

"Marco, I know the type of man you are."

"What kind of man am I?" he asked, curious to know what she thought she knew about him.

"You have a reputation of living fast and large on the track and off. And I knew, just as I know now, that a simple girl from Long Island has little chance of slowing you down for long."

There was a certain amount of truth to that. But he suspected that wasn't the only reason she'd left. In fact, the more he thought about it, the more convinced he became that there was more to Virginia than met the eye.

"I have never hurried a woman out of my bed."

"It wasn't you."

She lowered her gaze to the side and walked around the living-room area of the luxury motor home. She paused to look at the picture of his family on the wall. From over her shoulder, he saw his family all posed in front of the main Moretti Motors plant in Milan.

"Then what made you leave?"

"It was me," she said, turning to face him. "I wasn't sure I'd be able to leave gracefully if you were awake and I had to walk away from you. So I skulked out while you were sleeping."

"Why are you back?"

She took a deep breath and walked over to him. She brushed her fingers over her bottom lip, which was swollen from his earlier kiss.

"I'm back because I missed you, Marco. And I couldn't stop thinking about you."

He didn't admit that he'd missed her, as well. "Good."

"Good?"

"Yes. I have to shower and change, then we will go for an early dinner."

He walked away from her before she could answer. She was here, and he was suddenly determined that she would never leave him again.

Five

Marco's attitude made it difficult for Virginia to do anything but follow him. He'd showered and changed in the motor home and then come out smelling wonderfully masculine, and she felt very much like a school girl enamored with a boy. Though there was nothing boyish about Marco. He was all man.

A man who was determined to set the rules of their…"relationship" didn't seem the right word to describe what was between them. But he was definitely letting her know that he was in charge.

Whereas in Melbourne he'd wooed her, this time he simply took charge. And as they drove through Barcelona, she admitted to herself that she secretly liked the forcefulness of Marco.

To lessen some of his impact on her, she gazed out the window. Barcelona was a beautiful city. Very Mediterranean in feel. Whenever she traveled outside of the United States…as if she was a world traveler, she thought. But both times, she had left her home country, she noticed how different the world was. She loved the architecture of the old buildings. She loved the streets lined with people walking from place to place. And she loved the way that Marco fit into this world. This was his place, and she felt very much the intruder tonight.

But then she'd always felt like an intruder, and being in beautiful Barcelona wasn't helping.

"What are you thinking?" he asked.

She didn't want to tell him what she was really thinking. She cast around her mind for something to say and remembered that Picasso painting in the museum where Elena had cornered her.

"About a painting I saw earlier at the Picasso museum."

"Which one?"

"*The Embrace*. Are you familiar with it?"

"I am. My mother is an art history teacher."

"Really? Did you grow up surrounded by art?"

He shrugged. "Not really. She tried to expose us, but we were more interested in cars and engines."

"All of your brothers?"

"Yes. And my father."

"How did your parents meet?" she asked. She'd heard via the grapevine that Giovanni and Philomena had a love match. That their love had meant the destruction of Moretti Motors.

"My mom was hired to buy art for the lobby of our building. My father took one look at her and forgot all about cars and racing."

"Was he a driver like you?"

"No. He did one twenty-four-hour race with his cousins when he was in his twenties, but didn't care for it."

"What's a twenty-four-hour race?"

"An endurance race that involves a team of at least three drivers."

"And you drive for twenty-four hours?"

"In shifts…usually each guy drives for three hours."

She couldn't imagine what would make someone want to do that. But then again, she was a little unsure of why Marco raced. Wanting to go fast, she understood. She even got that he wanted to beat other people on the track—but racing as a calling she didn't really get.

"Is it fun?"

He laughed a little. "No. It's more. It's exhilarating and a bit of a headache. There's nothing else like it."

"Do you drive through towns or around tracks?"

"Tracks, usually," he said. He drove through the streets of Barcelona with skill and competency, which really didn't surprise her.

"Have you done one?"

"Every year my brothers and I participate in at least one."

This was his world, she realized. She wondered if the child they had would be like Marco. Would he have the need for speed? And what would being raised so far away from the racing world do to the child?

For the first time, she realized that, while her plan was to fix this generation, she had no way of knowing what the fallout of her solution was going to be.

"I like the track at Le Mans. We've done charity events, too, where we compete against other car companies."

"How is that different from what you do each week? Is it friendlier?"

"Not really. But we do raise money for charity. One charity rule requires you to have a woman driver for one leg."

"Who do you guys use?"

"No one. We haven't participated in that one…my family is cursed."

"Cursed?" She wondered how much he'd tell her about the curse and whether she should pretend that she didn't know what he was talking about.

"It's an Italian thing," he said. "Our curse involves women."

"Being around women?" she asked, wondering how much he knew of the actual curse.

"No. But being involved with a woman. Okay,

here's the truth, Dom has always been afraid that either Tony or I will weaken and fall in love with a woman, and then our family curse will kick in. So that's why we've never participated in that particular race. I think he fears that if I met a woman who loved racing as much as I do, I'd fall for her."

Virginia didn't like the sound of that. That Marco wasn't going to fall in love. But that shouldn't matter to her, she wasn't after his heart, only his child. "You seem very successful, to be cursed."

He turned into a parking lot and pulled into a space, but made no move to turn off the car or get out. "It's not a curse like that."

"What kind is it?"

"As I said, it's one that involves women."

"From where I'm sitting, you seem to do okay with women."

"I do. But I never *fall* for a woman."

"So, do you want to fall in love?" she asked. She wondered if he was lonely like she was at times. It didn't matter how full his life was. Because of her grandmother, he could only be lucky in business or in love. Never both. And since he'd chosen business, that meant a lonely life.

"No," he said with a smile. "I'm still young and have my life ahead of me."

"Indeed. What about racing? Are you going to retire?"

"Not for another few years," he said, turning off the ignition and looking at her.

The smell of his aftershave and the leather of the seats overwhelmed her, and she was very aware of the fact that she'd made small talk to cover her nervousness about being alone with Marco again.

This was something she hadn't planned for. Being with Marco again wasn't going to be easy, because each time she was with him she didn't want to leave. But more than that, she realized that he wanted answers from her, and she was going to have to keep on her toes to stay one step ahead of him.

Marco led the way upstairs to his apartment. He hated staying in hotels, and since Moretti Motors always had a driver in F1, over the years the company had bought residences in all of the major cities where the races were held.

He was trying to be genial and laid-back, though he really wanted answers. But after that one passionate outburst he'd had back at the track, he knew he needed to rein himself in.

He didn't want Virginia to realize how much she'd gotten to him. And she had. Until he'd seen her again, he hadn't realized that he'd been searching for her in every crowd—that he'd been waiting for her at each race. And that each win and each loss was marked by the fact that she wasn't there.

He'd never let anyone have that kind of power over him. He didn't think he'd "let" Virginia. For some reason, she was the one woman who could make him react this way. Only finding out every detail of who she was would give him the peace he needed.

Dinner had yielded few answers. She was very clever at keeping the conversation off herself and on him. But he was determined to learn more about Virginia, and he wanted to do it without asking her flat out for the answers. She'd set the rules of their game by disappearing and by the very mystery of who she was.

"You're staring at me," she said.

"You're a beautiful woman. Surely I'm not the first man to stare at you."

She shook her head. "I'm not really beautiful."

"Beauty is in the eye of the beholder, and I find you captivating."

"Marco."

"Yes?"

"Please don't say things like that."

"Why not?"

"Because I'll be tempted to believe you, and you just said that you weren't interested in any woman for the long term."

"I did say that, didn't I?"

"Yes."

"But you're not really interested in the long term, either, are you, Virginia?"

"I don't know," she said.

He had no idea what she meant by that comment. Maybe she was just as confused about what was happening between them as he was. But she'd left after one night. Most women didn't do that.

He wasn't being a chauvinist or anything like that. His experience had shown him that women stuck around for a while. That only when they were convinced a man wasn't going to be the right one for them to spend their lives with did they move on.

"A woman who leaves while a man is sleeping surely isn't looking for 'happily ever after'…though I thought most American women were."

"Why would you ever think such a thing? American women are independent."

"My mother watches *Desperate Housewives*." To be honest, he wasn't too sure about that show as a standard for American women. But Elena was American, and she wanted to be married.

"That's a TV show."

"Television shows are made popular by the way they exaggerate real life."

"Marco, that makes no sense."

"You are simply saying that because you don't agree with my theory."

"Okay, if you're right about TV echoing life, how do you feel about movies?"

"I think that, to a certain extent they reflect the view of what they are representing. You know, I'm not saying that movies and television programs are real life, simply that they mirror an attitude of the culture that produced them."

She was so bubbly with her passion for discussing this. He liked it because he could tell that she wasn't planning what she would say to him. She wasn't keeping this conversation all about him, the way she had during dinner. This was something real. An indication of the woman who was Virginia.

He still didn't know her last name, but he would before morning. He hoped to spend this night uncovering *all* of her secrets.

He would know everything about her body, of course—he was already intimately acquainted with the sounds she made when her body was suffused with pleasure. Now he wanted to know what made her mad. What made Virginia cry? What made her laugh and smile? He needed that knowledge and he would be ruthless about getting it.

"Did you see the movie *Talladega Nights?*" she asked him.

"Yes. It was quite funny, with that Will Ferrell."

"Um…by rights I should assume you are like the French driver in the movie."

It took him a moment to figure out that she was trying to say he might be gay. He saw the sparkle in her eyes. She was teasing him. He knew he shouldn't feel good about that fact, but he did.

He closed the distance between them, tired of not holding her in his arms. The last month had been too long. He'd focused on racing and on the promo events that went with the Formula One season, but every night he'd had passion-filled dreams of Virginia and he wanted to make them a reality.

"I think I've proven that I'm more interested in women than men," he said, drawing her into his arms. "But perhaps you need another demonstration?"

She put her hands on his face and rose up to kiss him with the gentle passion he associated only with Virgina.

"I have no doubts that you are interested in women. I was trying to make a point," she said.

"Instead, you proved that Americans think Frenchmen are gay. It matters not to me. I'm Italian, and interested in only one woman tonight."

"Me?"

"You," he said, sweeping her up in his arms and carrying her down the hallway and into the bedroom.

He put her on her feet next to the bed. As he stroked one finger down the side of her neck and traced the soft fabric neckline of her dress, shivers spread down her body. His fingers were warm against her skin and she wasn't really listening to what he was saying.

She simply watched his lips to see if he was going to kiss her. That was what she really wanted and needed. She had missed him. And though she'd had other relationships before Marco that one night in his arms had far exceeded what she'd expected. He'd marked her indelibly and she'd been unable to forget his touch.

"I'm almost afraid to believe that you are really here."

"I am here," she said. Truly, she was afraid to believe that he'd taken her back into his arms so easily.

He leaned down, his lips brushing over hers. They were so soft, yet so commanding. And as he sucked her lower lip into his mouth and laved it with his tongue, she stopped thinking and just gave herself over to the feelings that were swamping her.

When she was standing naked in front of him, he traced the scar under her breast. "Do you realize that this is one of the only things I know about your past?"

She felt a frisson of fear at his words. He could never know about her past. His family and hers were enemies. Real life Capulet and Montague stuff.

"My past isn't important, Marco. Only what we have when we are together. Make love to me."

"Why?"

She felt more vulnerable now than she had just a second before. "I want to know that I'm really here in your arms."

He bent down to trace the scar with his tongue. His hands cupping the weight of both her breasts, one long forefinger stroking up and over her nipples. She shivered in his embrace, needing more of him. He made her react so quickly…he was like a flame she couldn't stay away from.

She tunneled her fingers through his thick black hair and held his head to her body. He murmured something in Italian against her skin. Then she felt his lips against her breast. His mouth moved over the skin, tongue licking and teeth lightly scraping until she was desperate for more of him. She needed more than just his mouth lightly touching her.

His hand on her other breast just kept stroking lightly, until she couldn't stand it a second longer. She pulled his head up to hers and kissed him deeply, sucking his lower lip into her mouth and biting him. She shifted in his arms until her breasts were pressed to his chest.

The cool fabric of his shirt shocked her naked skin. She hadn't realized he was still fully dressed and she was wearing nothing but her silky thong. The thought of being naked in his arms was very arousing.

He stood back up and lifted her onto the bed. Pulling his mouth from hers, he bent down to capture the tip of her breast. His hand still played at her other breast, arousing her, making her arch against him in need.

She reached between them and stroked his erection through the fabric of his pants, spreading her legs wider so that she was totally open to him. "I need you now."

He lifted his head. The tips of her breasts were damp from his mouth and very tight. He pressed his chest against them.

She reached up to unbutton his shirt. "Leave it. I need to be inside you now."

She nodded, and instead fumbled with his belt, finally getting it unfastened. Then she couldn't get the button at his waistband open. "Damn it."

He laughed softly and brushed her hands aside so that he could unfasten his own pants. She heard the swish of fabric and then felt the warmth of his erection against the center of her body. He rocked his hips against hers, rubbing the length of his arousal against her feminine core.

She needed him inside her. She reached between them and took him in her hand, positioning him for easy entry. But she could get no more than the tip inside her body.

He held his hips still, and no matter how she squirmed or moved, he wouldn't budge. Finally she looked up at him. "What are you waiting for?"

"I'm waiting for you to really want me."

"I do. I want you inside of me right now. I feel like it's been a lifetime since we were together, and I've missed you so much." The words wouldn't stop coming, and she knew she'd revealed too much, but she couldn't help herself. "Please, Marco," she said again. She ran her hands down his back, cupping his buttocks and trying to draw him closer to her.

He gave her barely an inch. "That's all you get."

His words were breathed right into her ear and almost made her climax. She shifted in his embrace, trying to take him deeper.

"Marco, please, I need more."

"No. You were a bad girl."

"When I left?"

"Yes," he said, pulling his hips back and thrusting into her again, still just an inch.

She wanted him madly. She needed to feel him deeper inside of her body instead of just at the threshold.

"Marco."

"Yes, Virginia?"

"I'm sorry I left."

"That's good, *cara mia,*" he said, giving her another inch.

She shivered around him and felt the first fingers of an orgasm dancing up her spine. She clutched at his buttocks and tried to draw him deeper.

"Marco…"

"I want your promise that you won't leave me again."

"I promise."

"You said that too quickly, Virginia. Do you mean it?"

"Yes, I mean it."

"If I give you all of me, then I'm going to expect you to stay in my bed until I ask you to leave."

She looked up into those obsidian eyes of his and knew he was serious. This was more to him than just a teasing game that lovers play. And she couldn't help but want to give him that promise. It might be hard to keep, but she'd try. "I will stay until you ask me to leave."

He stared into her eyes for a long moment before he thrust all the way into her body. She felt marked by his possession, that he'd changed her and she'd never be the same again.

She slid her hands down his back as he thrust deeper into her. Their eyes met. Staring deep into his eyes made her feel like their souls were meeting. She felt her body start to tighten around him, catching her by surprise. She climaxed before him. He gripped her hips, holding her down and thrusting before he came with a cry of her name.

She slid her hands up his back and kissed him deeply. "You are so much better than I dreamed you were."

His deep laughter washed over her and she felt like she'd found her place here. And that was very dangerous thinking, because if she belonged with Marco, then what was she going to do when she had to leave him again?

Six

Marco woke in the middle of the night and sat bolt upright in his bed. The voice of his grandfather echoed in his mind, saying something about being too late.

Marco scrubbed a hand over his face and reached for the light on the nightstand, flicking it on before he remembered he wasn't alone. *Virginia.*

She was really here. After they'd made love she'd fallen asleep in his arms. And he hadn't minded. Because the last thing he'd wanted to do was question her when he felt so vulnerable. Damned if this woman didn't make him feel…weak.

Well, out of control. Like he had the very first time he'd gotten behind the wheel of a Moretti F1 racing machine. Virginia lay curled on her side facing him, one of her hands reaching toward him, the other curled under her chin.

Asleep, he could study her without having to admit to anyone that he was obsessed with her. He knew that Dominic had been particularly glad when they'd met that morning in Melbourne and Virginia hadn't been with him.

Had his brother seen something in Virginia that had made him wary of the attraction she had for Marco? Or was it simply Dom's normal fear that a woman would distract him from the quest to take Moretti Motors to the top?

It wasn't like Marco was ever really alone. There were always beautiful women who were more than willing to hang on his arm and go back to his place for a night. What had been different with Virginia? Or had it been *his* reaction that had made Dom more watchful?

Marco didn't know if he and his brothers had made a wise decision when they'd vowed to avoid women who could make them feel. Marco couldn't speak for his brothers, but he was tired of the emotional wasteland that was his past relationships.

He let no one close to him. And at the end of the day, he was alone. Of course he had his brothers, and together the Morettis were strong—but there were times when he longed for the happiness his father had found with his mother.

The kind of happiness that stemmed from love.

He shook his head to clear it. He wasn't the kind of man who needed love. He needed a powerful engine under his control. He needed the thrill of pitting himself against the other top race car drivers in the world. But *love?* He didn't need that.

He pushed himself out of the bed and flicked off the light so he wouldn't disturb Virginia.

Why did she make him feel? He was thirty-six years old and he had a good life. Why was he suddenly asking questions and looking harder at the choices and decisions he'd made?

He walked to the wet bar and poured himself a Di Saronno. He tossed the drink back and walked around the darkened living room. The lights of Barcelona competed with the stars in the sky. He'd like to blame his restlessness on Virginia and the questions he still hadn't asked her, but he knew it was more than that.

He leaned against the French doors, staring out at the night sky over Barcelona. It was quiet now, and he had the feeling that he was alone in the world. His thoughts swirled and he realized that winning the Grand Prix World Championship this year wasn't going to be enough for him. Because once he had another championship under his belt, there would be nothing left for him in the world of Formula One racing.

He felt sometimes as if he didn't know who he was if he wasn't behind the wheel of a race car. Being the face of Moretti Motors was fine, but that wasn't much of a career. And to be honest with himself, he'd known he'd always been a little bit embarrassed by the way women flocked to him and photographers sought him out.

He walked back to the bar and refilled his glass again.

"Marco?"

He turned to see Virginia standing in the shadows of the hallway.

"*Si?*"

"What are you doing?"

"I could not sleep. Did I disturb you?"

She walked toward him and he saw that she wore his shirt. He liked the way she looked in his clothes. When she was close enough, he reached out and pulled her closer, tucking her head under his chin and simply holding her.

"What are you thinking about? The race earlier?"

He was tempted to say yes. It would be easy to say that he was rerunning the race and trying to figure out when he'd lost, but his mind wasn't on Formula One or even Moretti Motors. It was on this woman.

"No. I'm not dwelling on the race."

"What then?" she asked, pulling back to look up at him.

"I was thinking that I don't know your last name or what you do for a living. Yet, you know what my mother's career is and a million other details of my life."

She flushed. "Is that important to you?"

"Yes," he said. "It is."

She hesitated. Then, "I'm Virginia Festa. I was born in Italy, but moved to America when I was a year old. My mother, Carmen Festa, was a school-teacher."

"What about your father?"

"I never knew him. He died before I was born."

The name Festa sounded familiar to him. "Where in Italy were you born?"

"In Chivasso."

He stiffened. That was where Cassia had been from. The woman who'd cursed his grandfather and by default all of the Moretti men. He had no idea what the old witch's surname was, because his grandfather always just referred to her as that witch. But there was something about hearing the tale of Virginia's life that put him in mind of his own family's curse. He hadn't believed in the curse until Dom's doomed love affair. That had been the incident that had made both him and Antonio consider what their *nonno* had believed.

Lorenzeo had told the tale of a girl from his village whom he'd promised to love, a girl whose heart he'd broken. In return, that girl had cursed him.

"So it was just you and your mother?"

"No. My grandmother lived with us, as well."

"Just three women?"

"Yes. My grandmother had done something rash when she was a young girl, and I think her actions doomed us all."

Virginia didn't know if it was because they were standing in the dark or because of the comfort she drew from standing in Marco's arms, but she suddenly wanted to talk about her past. Talk about the path that had led her to his bed so that maybe, at some point in time, he'd understand what she'd done.

"What does this have to do with the secrecy you've kept?" he asked. He drew her over to the leather couch and sat down. She sat next to him, drawing strength from him.

Virginia realized that she was saying too much. That she should just retreat back to the bedroom or use sex to distract him and then disappear again in the morning.

Except the last month had given her too much time to think, and retreating to her lonely life wasn't what she wanted. She liked Marco. That was something she'd forgotten to factor into her calculations— the human emotions part of the curse-breaking. She'd always understood that her grandmother had been truly heartbroken when Lorenzo had refused to return to their village and marry her. But she hadn't realized that emotions might be the one key component to spell-casting that she hadn't accounted for. To be fair, she wasn't a witch and didn't regularly practice magic. Her entire training—if you could call it that—had simply been to study the practices to find a way to break the curse.

It was a basic thing, using emotions, and something she shouldn't have forgotten. But this spell, the only spell she'd ever tried…

"Virginia?"

"Hmm?"

"I asked you a question."

She smiled up at him. In the dark, his obsidian eyes were fathomless and she realized that she was falling in love with him. Was it only because she'd selected him to father her child?

"That's right, you did," she said.

"Are you okay?" he asked, the Italian accent making his words seem more carefully spoken.

"Yes, I am… Actually, no, I'm not. I guess because it's the middle of the night, I thought that telling you about the past would somehow make everything okay, but now I'm not sure."

"I'm not following," Marco said.

"You asked me whether the mysterious way I've acted about my life has anything to do with everything between us….well, it has nothing, and everything. I'm not sure how to say this," she said, losing her nerve. The middle of the night was a stupid time to make decisions. She knew that, but here she was anyway, about to tell Marco…

"*Mi'angela,* don't do anything you don't want to. I simply asked because…hell, I asked because I want answers. I'm tired of searching for your face at races and realizing that you aren't there—and that I don't know enough about you to find you."

"I guess that my second thoughts aren't fair to you."

"Second thoughts about what?"

"Telling you the truth."

"Have you been lying to me?"

"Not really lying, just omitting stuff. Actually, I wish you'd just figure it out so I wouldn't have to tell you."

"Figure *what* out?"

She took a deep breath as Marco shifted on the couch and moved away from her. She was on her own any way she sliced it, and she had to remember that only a child would change either of their lives.

"I'm the granddaughter of the woman who cursed your grandfather. Cassia Festa, my grandmother, was heartbroken when your grandfather, Lorenzo, refused to marry her."

He stood up, cursing as he paced away from her before returning to stand in front of her, hands on his hips.

"I know this story. So, out of spite she put a curse on my family—on the men—so that no Moretti man could have both happiness and fortune."

Virginia nodded. It was hard to explain Cassia's actions to someone who'd never known her. "She wasn't a happy woman."

"Yeah, like the Morettis have been happy…we lost our home, Virginia."

"I'm sorry. It wasn't like she prospered after doing such a thing to your family."

"Why are you here?" Marco demanded. "Did the women of your family think of another curse to heap on us? I have to warn you, Virginia, it's too late. My brothers and I have made up our minds that love isn't something we aspire to."

She shook her head. He was angry, and she acknowledged that he had a right to be. But that didn't mean she liked the way he was yelling at her. She took a few steps away from him then stopped. She knew Marco wasn't going to reach out and hurt her, and she had lied to him.

"I am not here to place another curse on you. The women of my family…well, there's just me. Cassia died a lonely, bitter woman, and my mother lost the only man she loved. And I…"

"What?"

"I have spent the last two years of my life studying the curse and trying to figure out why my grandmother never married and had only one child, a daughter—my mother. And why my mother's life followed the same pattern. And I realized something as I looked at my family and the curse my *nonna* put on you. She cursed you with an ancient spell. One that has a backlash to keep the balance."

"I'd like to say I care, but right now I'm too pissed off."

"I don't blame you. But you are hardly a man who hasn't had affairs before."

"True enough. But I've *never* left woman in the middle of the night."

"I'm sorry, but if you will just hear me out. There is a silver lining to this."

He shrugged again. "What did you mean by balance?"

"The balance of justice. The balance of everything in nature. The curse gave my grandmother what she desired, but it also required that she give up something to get her wish. And she craved Lorenzo's unhappiness. She needed him to feel the same heartbreak that she had felt...."

Marco went to the wet bar and poured himself two fingers of Scotch. "Cassia sought revenge because she was jilted. And she got it. My *nonno* was unhappy in love all the days of his life. His marriages failed, though he did get sons whom he worshipped. My own father couldn't make the business successful, but he had the love of my mother to make up for it."

"I had heard that about your family. I'm glad that you and your brothers grew up in a house filled with love."

"Are you?" he asked caustically.

"Yes. My own home was filled with bitterness. With that expectation that life wasn't anything but a series of disappointments."

"Indeed, it can be. Why don't you tell me why you are really here? Is it for money?"

"No, Marco, I don't want your money. I want your progeny."

Marco wasn't sure he could handle any more surprise announcements from Virginia.

"My prog— You want to bear my child?"

"Yes," she said.

Marco poured another glass of Scotch and tossed it back. His emotions were in turmoil. This night was turning into an all-out high-speed ride. It was something he'd only ever experienced with Virginia. With her, he never knew what to expect and couldn't plan beyond the road he could see in front of him.

Then he realized what she'd said. She wanted his baby, so did that mean...

"Did you lie to me when I asked if you were on the pill?"

She flushed and turned away.

That was all the answer he needed. "God, is there one thing you've said to me that is the truth?"

"It's not like that. I mean—well, it is like that, but I've been lying to make things right. Doesn't intention count for anything?"

"No. Hell, I don't know. Why me?"

"Um...well, it doesn't necessarily need to be you. Just a Moretti man."

"So, again I ask, why me?" he asked, becoming even more incensed. He was half-tempted to call his lawyers and find some reason to drag her into court.

"You were the easiest Moretti brother to get close to. And when I looked at you and your brothers, I just felt drawn to you."

He'd felt a spurt of jealousy when she'd said it didn't have to be him. That jealousy was assuaged a bit when she said she was drawn to him, but he didn't like the fact that to Virginia he was just a means to an end.

"Why do you want my baby, Virginia?" he asked, still trying to get his head around the fact that she'd lied about birth control. He came from a loving family. He was always very careful to make sure he didn't have any consequences from his affairs.

She twisted a long strand of her hair around a finger and walked a bit closer to him. She wore only his shirt and he realized how small and vulnerable she looked. With only the faint lights from the bedroom and balcony illuminating the room, she seemed ethereal.

But he didn't want to trust the vulnerability he saw in her. She'd lied to him.

"It's all tied to the curse."

"Tell me more about this."

"Well, I think that when my *nonna* cursed your *nonno* Lorenzo, she cursed herself. It was as if by denying Lorenzo true happiness, she eliminated it from her own life and from that of successive generations."

"Your mother wasn't happy?"

"She fell in love with my father and they were happy for about three months before he was drafted and sent to war. I was born, and three days later she received word that he had been killed. She was brokenhearted for the rest of her life."

"But you were born in Italy?"

"Yes. Just after my father left, Nonna's mother

fell ill and she and my mom went back to Nonna's village to help. When Mom discovered she was pregnant, they decided to stay for a while. After word came of my father's death, I think Nonna hoped some nice Italian man would fall for Mom and marry her, but nothing worked out. We moved back to the States when I was one."

"And your *nonna?*"

"She'd had an affair with someone in her village. I don't know who, but the scandal of her pregnancy caused her to leave the village and move to the United States, where my mother was born."

Marco was getting a pretty grim picture of Virginia's family life and he could see why she'd want to find a way to lift the curse. But that didn't explain why she wanted his child. And he was just realizing that every time he'd made love to her, he hadn't used a condom.

"How did you connect the tragic past of the women in your family with me?"

"It is the only thing that makes sense. I finally pieced it together when my mother died and left me my grandmother's journal. I learned a lot about the *strega* way and the curse my grandmother had put on your family. Until then, I had no idea she'd done that. I just figured we were unlucky in love."

"You, too?"

She looked up at him, and he realized he was getting closer to the truth. This was a very personal mission for Virginia. He rubbed the back of his neck.

He was mad at her for tricking him and lying to him, but he wanted to get past this.

"Yes, me, too. I didn't want to spend my entire life alone and unhappy the way my mother and my *nonna* did. So I started researching the *strega* way and curses. I knew the curse my *nonna* had used, because Mom had given me Nonna's journal.

"When I started reading the history of love curses, I realized that they had repercussions on the lives of whomever was placing the curse."

"How do you hope to break the curse?"

"By having your child. The merging of Moretti and Festa blood in a new generation will bring together what was torn apart and reverse the curse. But I don't think we can fall in love."

"I'm not going to fall in love with you," Marco said, not liking the way she assumed he'd fall for her. She'd done nothing but use him for sex and lie to him. The irony of her actions wasn't lost on him. He was well aware that for his entire adult life he'd treated women as his playthings. "And I'm not sure about you having my child."

She flinched and wrapped her arms around her waist. "I'm not asking you to fall in love with me."

"So you are really here to help me out?" he asked.

She bit her lower lip. "Well, you and your brothers and your children."

"What will happen to this baby you want to have?" he asked. He'd been the victim of a fraudulent paternity suit when he was twenty-one and had vowed to never allow himself to be used like that again.

"I will raise it. You wouldn't be responsible for the baby at all."

He rubbed the back of his neck. He didn't think he could turn his back on his own child. Family was the cornerstone of everything he did—even racing. "I'd want my child to know me."

"Then of course we can work something out," she said. "I wouldn't keep your child from you."

Marco put his empty glass on the counter of the bar and walked back to Virginia. He stopped when barely a foot separated them.

"Tell me the wording of the curse."

"I can let you read Nonna's journal if you like, but I don't think I should say the words aloud. They are very powerful."

"Fine. Get the journal for me, please."

Marco watched her leave. She came back a few minutes later with a worn, leather-bound book. She untied the ribbon around the middle and opened it. He saw his grandfather's name on the first page. In Italian, there was the undying love of a young woman. Cassia wrote about her hopes and dreams. He put his hand over Virginia's to keep her from turning the page.

Marco knew he had to get over his anger if he was going to figure out how to move forward from this.

"Do you want to see the curse?" Virginia asked.

"Yes." He lifted his hand.

She flipped the pages to about three-quarters of the way through the journal. There was the same handwriting, only it seemed angrier. The curling script of earlier had become shorter and more compact, the lines of ink slashing across the page.

My love for you was all-encompassing and never-ending, and with its death I call upon the universe to bring about the death of your heart and the hearts of succeeding generations.

As long as a Moretti roams this earth, he shall have happiness in either business or love but never both.

Do not disdain the powers of a small body. Moretti, you may be strong, but that will no longer help you. I am strong in my will and I demand retribution for the pain you have caused me.

"What makes you think having a child will break this curse?" he asked.

"The part that speaks of retribution. My grandmother wanted to create a family with your grandfather, and since he denied her that and placed racing above her, she wanted to deny him love forevermore."

Marco looked at the words again. He noticed a different handwriting in the column. These words were in English and not in Italian. "Is this your handwriting?"

"Yes. I have spent a lot of time researching the words Nonna used, so I could figure out how to break the spell."

"Can't you just reverse it?"

"No. I can't. Nonna could have, but she's dead."

"Okay, let me make sure I have this right. You are here to get pregnant so you can break the Moretti curse?"

She nibbled on her lower lip and then nodded.

"What's in it for you?"

"It will keep me from ending up bitter and alone like my mother and grandmother did. And it will give me the chance at a future with a husband and more children."

He looked at Virginia, pictured her growing big and round with his child, and felt a primal rush. He wanted to plant his seed in this woman. Not just because it might break the curse on all the Moretti clan, but because on some primitive level he believed that Virginia was his.

He made a gut decision. "Okay. In the morning I will have a contract drawn up that details this arrangement. You will travel with me for this racing season until you are pregnant. Then you will live in a house I pay for until the child is born. I think I should like for you to continue to live there with the child and raise the child close by me. I will have free visitation of the child."

She put her hands on her hips. "You will not be making all the rules of this arrangement, Marco. I'm not going to just do what you tell me to."

He reached out and grabbed her wrists, drawing her into his arms. "I think you will, Virginia. Because without my 'rules' you will have nothing."

Seven

Marco knew this meeting wouldn't be easy. Dom had always had a thing about their family curse, and bringing it up wasn't going to go over well. But since he'd called everyone last night and asked them to meet this morning at his parents' townhouse in Milan, he had no choice but to follow through.

"Bon giorno," Marco said as he entered the sun-room.

His mother rose and gave him a kiss on the cheek and his father hugged him close. As much as Marco was an adult, he still liked the feeling of coming home.

"What was so urgent we had to meet so early in the morning?" Tony asked, sipping his morning espresso.

Marco took a seat across from his mom and next to Tony. He served himself some food, even though he didn't feel like eating.

"It involves the family curse," Marco started.

The silence was electric. Then Dom spoke. "What about it? You know this is a crucial year for us. Does this have anything to do with that woman you were with in Melbourne…Virginia something?"

"Yes, it does."

"I knew it." Dom said. "I had a bad feeling about her."

"Maybe you were picking up on the fact that she's Cassia Festa's granddaughter."

Dom's face reddened. "Don't mention that name in our house," he said.

"What does she want with you, *mi figlio?*" asked his father.

"She says she's figured out a way to break the curse that Cassia put on Nonno and the family."

His mother leaned across the table. "How? Lorenzo asked every witch he knew, and all of them said that without the exact wording, it was impossible."

Marco stood up. "Virginia claims that the way to break the curse is for her to have my child."

"What?" Dominic yelled, his voice booming across the room.

"Marco, that sounds crazy," his father said.

"I thought so, too, but…just listen to this. When Cassia put the curse on Lorenzo, she was angry at the death of her dream—husband, family and future. So she wanted to punish him in the same way. Make it so he could never have it all. But when she cursed him, she also cursed the Festa women. None have found happiness in love. Virginia has studied the wording of the curse and believes that if she bears a Moretti heir, the curse will be broken because Lorenzo's legacy will fall to a Festa."

"Who would raise your child?" his mother asked.

"I am having our attorney work on the details. I want to share the responsibility." He paused, considering whether or not to share the rest. "Virginia thinks one key to breaking the curse is that she and I can't fall in love."

"Is that a possibility?" Tony asked.

"No," Marco said, quickly denying the charge. He wasn't going to entertain the thought of Virginia meaning more to him than an affair.

Dom nodded. "So, what do you need from us?"

"I'd like the both of you to come to the offices with me this morning to talk to our attorney. I told Virginia we had to have a contract if this was going to work."

"I agree," Dom said. "We'll be there."

"What about your mother and I?" his father asked.

"I think you two should wait to meet her for now."

His mother nodded. "I agree. But we do want to meet this girl soon. After all, she'll be the mother of our first grandchild."

* * *

The thing about the Moretti family, Virginia realized the next morning as she sat in a corporate boardroom at a prestigious law firm, was that they were a *family*. That Marco and his brothers all stuck together as a group was abundantly clear to her, and as she sat at the far end of the table by herself, she felt very small and alone—and very wistful.

She never had the kind of bond that Marco had with his brothers, and she wanted that. Not only for herself, but for any child she might have.

"Virginia, do you agree to the terms?" Marco asked.

She hadn't been paying attention and knew better than to just say yes. "May I have a few minutes to review everything?"

"Certainly," Marco said.

Dominic Moretti was an intimidating man, and he looked like he wasn't pleased to give her a few more minutes. In fact, his face had gotten tighter as she'd explained what she wanted and Marco's attorney had taken notes, then relayed the terms of the contract Marco was proposing back to her. Antonio, Marco's middle brother, said very little at first, but surprisingly, he'd been the one to add a few stipulations in her favor.

Virginia didn't have the money to hire a good attorney, and she certainly had no friends here in Europe who could recommend a solicitor. But that was neither here nor there. She knew what she

wanted, and this was nothing more than a formaliza-
tion of everything she and Marco had talked about
the night before. But hearing it in this sterile setting
made her feel kind of cheap and unsure of herself.

Dominic, Antonio and their lawyer left the room,
but Marco remained.

"Do you understand everything as it's laid out?"

"I think so. I just don't want to throw away all my
rights without thinking this through."

"I'm not going to agree to anything less than
what's been laid out."

"I know," she said. Part of what drew her to Marco
as a man—aside from his being a Moretti—was the
forceful and determined way he lived his life. He
was a winner on and off the track, and she doubted
that he'd settle for less than he wanted.

"So what's the hold up?" he asked.

"Nothing. If you must know, I wasn't focused
enough to comprehend everything when the lawyer
was talking, so I just want a chance to read over the
contract."

Marco came close to her side of the table and
leaned against it. He was dressed in a fine Italian suit
and he looked so good that it was all she could do
to pretend she wasn't entranced by him. She hoped
she was successful and he didn't notice the way she
stared at him as if she were fascinated by him.

"Go on then," he said. "Read over it."

But she couldn't. The scent of his cologne teased
her with every breath she took, and she was hyper-

aware that he was standing close to her. All she wanted to do was move beyond the lawyers and the contract, to the next step—living with him until she was pregnant.

That wasn't something she'd ever dreamed she'd have, and she wanted to begin this phase of her life. Even though they'd have this contract between them, for the first time in her life she was going to have someone to share her days with.

Her mother had never really been a participant in Virginia's life. From the earliest memory, she'd known that her mother was simply existing until Virginia was old enough to survive on her own.

She pulled the papers closer to her and skimmed over them. They had been prepared in Italian, but there was a translation into English. It didn't matter to her what the papers outlined. She knew that if she didn't break the curse she was going to spend the rest of her life alone, and probably sad and bitter.

She took a deep breath and signed the papers. And then pushed them to the center of the table. She stood up. "Okay, that's done. Let's get out of here."

"Not so fast. You didn't even read the contract."

"I skimmed it, and as you said, it's not as if I have much choice. You have something I want. Something I'm willing to do anything to get. So in a way, I've already signed a contract. I want your child, Marco."

"Why is having my child so important to you?" he asked. "It sounds like it goes beyond breaking the curse."

"You won't understand," she said. A man who knew what a real family was, a man who had the support of his parents, brothers and friends, would never be able to comprehend what kind of lonely and isolated life she'd had. There was nothing she wouldn't trade to have someone special in her life. She wasn't willing to be the sad by-product of a long-ago curse, the way her mother had been.

"Try explaining it to me. I'm a very smart man."

She smiled up at him. "I know you are. It's one of the things that attracted me to you."

"Dominic and Antonio are smart, as well. So why *my* baby?"

"I don't care about your brothers. From the first moment I realized the way to break the curse, I knew that you were the one I wanted."

"So not just any Moretti would do?" he asked, stroking his finger down the side of her face.

She caught his hand and kissed his fingers. "Exactly. It was you or no one."

It was only at this moment that she realized the truth of her words and how important he was to her. And she made a promise to herself. She wasn't going to let herself fall for him, because Festa women and Moretti men weren't meant to be in love.

Lorenzo and Cassia had proven how disastrous that could be.

Marco was used to traveling and doing promotional events. He gave interviews to both broadcast and print media and was entirely at home in front of the public. He had always craved the spotlight and freely admitted that he liked the attention.

It wasn't that he was an egomaniac, it was simply that he liked all the fuss. And now, in Monte Carlo, it was even better, because when he left this press event he'd be going back to his villa where Virginia was waiting for him. It was as if he'd finally found what he'd been looking for, a surcease from the manic lifestyle he'd been living to try to prove to himself that he had a life.

"What's your hurry?" Keke asked as Marco tried to sneak out the back door of a party sponsored by Moretti Motors.

"I'm not in a hurry," Marco said.

"Yes, you are. It has been this way since you hooked up with Virginia in Spain. I'm engaged to Elena, and I'm not as desperate to get back to my woman as you are."

"I'm not desperate, Keke."

"I didn't mean that in a bad way. I think it's good that you have something other than Moretti Motors to fill your life."

"I've always had more than the company. I'm known the world over for my party lifestyle."

"I am, too—that's why I know how empty it is. There's a difference between filling time and actually having someone to spend it with. Someone who means something."

"Keke, when did you get to be a philosopher?"

"I know that I'm not a smart man, but having Elena in my life made me realize what I'd been missing."

"What does that have to do with me?" Marco asked.

"Seeing you with your Virginia reminds me of me and Elena." Keke shrugged. "I'm starting to think there's more to life than racing...like maybe it's time for me to retire and settle down."

Marco looked at his old friend. He and Keke had been teammates for the last five years. Keke was older than Marco, and maybe it was those four years age difference that had Keke talking like he was, but there was a sincerity in Keke's voice that made Marco hesitate.

"I'm not retiring, and Virginia is just a girl."

Keke raised both eyebrows at him. "Whatever you say, man."

Elena interrupted them before Marco could comment, and then he watched as his friends walked away from him. Was he desperate for Virginia's company? Was that why he hadn't sent her away immediately, as soon as she'd started going on about breaking the curse?

A part of him knew it was because he'd never fully believed in the curse. What he did believe was simpler. He wanted Virginia, and the contract gave him a safe reason to be with her. He didn't have to worry about marriage or expectations of love from Virginia. But her having his child was huge. Having a legal agreement seemed to make things simpler—unless he was just fooling himself.

He made his way to the waiting Moretti Motors convertible that he'd left in the drivers' parking lot. He liked the city of Monaco. He'd grown up coming here every year to watch the races with his grandfather. The Grand Prix de Monaco was one of the most famous.

Even the car he was driving had been his grandfather's. He'd always felt a special connection to Nonno Lorenzo, one that his brothers hadn't shared. Nonno had said it was because they both had a passion for speed. And Marco had to agree. But now, staring down at his grandfather's car, he wondered if there was more to him than racing. Was there more to the man he'd become than what he was—the face of Moretti Motors?

Did he really need there to be?

He ran his hand over the hood of the car, feeling the power and the miles that the car had traversed. There was a bond between man and car. It was something that he'd never really talked about, but this old car of Nonno's had always been like an extension of himself.

"Ciao, fratello," Dominic said as he came up behind him.

"Ciao, Dom. What's up?"

"Antonio and I need to see you tonight. We strongly suspect that we have a corporate spy."

Since Dom had been worried about a leak when

they'd spoken in Melbourne, Marco wasn't surprised by this news. "I'm seldom at the office, Dom. I doubt that I know the spy."

Dominic pushed his sunglasses up to the top of his head. "The leak could be anyone. And I want both you and Tony to go over the information that has been leaked to see if either of you have insight into how it is getting out. You know our F1 program better than anyone. And I hesitate to mention this, but...we hardly know Virginia, and she's been living with you."

Marco narrowed his eyes and thought about the freedom he'd given Virginia at all of his homes. Right now she was alone at their family villa on the outskirts of Monte Carlo. And while Marco himself didn't go to the corporate offices, Dominic's office faxed him a daily report to keep him apprised of the progress on the new Vallerio production car.

"Do you believe that Virginia is responsible for this? The first leak happened before we even met."

"We need to rule out the possibility of her involvement. Someone may have used her as pawn. What do you think?"

Marco had no real evidence, but his gut said that Virginia wasn't interested in anything other than his sperm. She'd been up front and honest about everything since the night she came clean. "I will ask her."

"Do you think that's best?"

"Yes. She will not lie to me."

"Be careful, Marco, I don't want to see you hurt."

"By a woman?"

"Her grandmother is the one who cursed our family," Dominic said.

Dominic had a point, but then his oldest brother often did. "*Arrivederci,* Dominic."

"We will have dinner tonight at nine at the villa. Will we see both you and Virginia?"

"Yes. And by then I'll know if she's the spy."

Marco got into the Moretti sports car that had been his grandfather's. He really hated to think how similar he and Lorenzo were in many things. He was determined that they wouldn't both let the distraction of a Festa woman ruin their lives.

Virginia sat down on a stone bench and breathed deeply. She loved the gardens at the Moretti family villa in Monte Carlo. It had been only two weeks since everything had come out—since she'd told Marco what she wanted from him. She spent a lot of time in the huge, fragrant garden courtyard in the center of the villa. Every room in the villa opened into the courtyard. The second-floor rooms had balconies, too, and she had enjoyed sitting on theirs in the quiet by herself while Marco went to the track to do his qualifying.

Since she wasn't a race fan, she didn't mind not being at the track, but she was starting to desperately need to be in Marco's company, and that wasn't good. She had to remember that this relationship was temporary, and that once she was pregnant it was going to be "*ciao,* baby."

"I thought I'd find you here," Marco said. He wrapped his arms around her from behind and pulled her close. He nuzzled his head next to hers and dropped a kiss on her neck. "What are you doing out here all alone?"

"Enjoying the garden. It's so pretty and peaceful."

"And that's what you need? Is my lifestyle too intense for you?" he asked.

She started to say no, she didn't mind it at all. But since there was no future between them and she needed to keep her emotional distance from Marco, she held her tongue. This wasn't really a relationship, no matter how much it might feel like one when his arms were wrapped around her.

"Yes, it is. I don't really like all the attention you get. It's tiring to have to keep smiling all the time."

Marco tipped her head back and kissed her. The beginning twinges of desire raced through her body. She turned in his arms and lifted hers around his shoulders.

His tongue thrust past the barrier of her teeth and tasted her deeply, and she realized that this was what she'd been waiting for.

How could she miss one man as much as she missed him when he was gone?

When he lifted his head a few minutes later, Marco said, "The attention will wan once the season is over."

At first she had no idea what he was talking about. She wanted to take his hand and lead him to the quiet corner of the garden where there was a marble bench and enough privacy to allow them to make love.

"What?"

He smiled down at her. "What are you thinking about?"

"Making love to you."

"Truly?"

"Yes," she said. All she'd thought about while he was gone, was that the physical was all she really had of Marco and all she could ever really claim of him. And with that thought had come the creeping idea that maybe, if she played her cards right, the desire between them could spark into something else. Something lasting. And then she wouldn't be alone anymore.

She ran her hands down the front of his chest, lightly scraping her fingers over the fine, Italian Merino summer wool sweater he wore. He caught her hand and drew it lower until it was over his zipper. She cupped his lengthening erection in her hand and rose, going on tiptoe to kiss first his jaw and then his earlobe.

"We have a dinner date," Marco said.

"With whom?"

"My brothers," he said, drawing her hand away from his body. "We need to talk, Virginia."

"Now?" she asked, not ready for a serious conversation.

"Unfortunately, yes, we need to talk now. Then we can get back to you seducing me."

She flushed and smiled at him. "What do we need to talk about?"

He led her into the formal living room. "Can I get you a drink?"

She raised both eyebrows at him. "Am I going to need one?"

He shrugged in that European way of his. She was coming to know that Marco gave away very little of himself. And that made her feel always at a disadvantage. "I'll just have Pellegrino with a twist of lime."

"Have a seat, I'll get our drinks."

She sat down and then realized that she was being a little too biddable. But she really had no choice. She hadn't had a choice for most of her life, and all of sudden that seemed to boil up inside of her. How long was she going to let the actions of others dictate her life?

She stood up, ready to take action. "What is this about, Marco?"

He turned with both of their drinks in his hands. "Sit down and we'll talk."

"I feel like you're calling me on the carpet," she said. He reached her side and handed her the sparkling water.

She took a sip and tried to marshal her thoughts. But Marco was close to her, and the only thing she wanted was to have peace between them. For the attraction between them to continue to grow....

Oh, no! she thought. She *was* falling in love with

Marco Moretti. And to him she was nothing more than a summer mistress. A woman who'd signed a contract to have sex with him until she was pregnant.

"Virginia—stop it."

"Stop what?"

"Whatever it is you're thinking."

"I just want to know what is going on. Why do you need to talk to me?"

"There has been a leak at Moretti Motors. Proprietary information has shown up in our competitor's offices, and we need to find out how."

She was surprised by the topic. His company had nothing to do with her. "What does this have to do with me?"

"The information started showing up approximately three weeks ago," Marco said, tipping back his Scotch and draining it in one long gulp.

"Again I say, what does this have—" She put her drinking glass on the table as she connected the dots. "You think *I'm* the spy?"

"Are you?"

Eight

Marco watched Virginia for some kind of reaction. At first she seemed to cave in on herself, and then he saw anger. But anger didn't necessarily mean innocence. Yet in this case, he had the feeling that Virginia *was* innocent.

For one thing, she'd shown very little interest in Moretti Motors, although that could have been her plan.

"Are you going to answer me?" he asked, walking to the wet bar to pour himself another two fingers of Scotch.

"Do I really have to? I mean, are you serious that you think I'm giving information to another company?"

"I am serious," he said, turning back to face her. He'd never really trusted any woman. Maybe that was why his relationships were all short-term. He'd always put it down to the time he spent on the track.

"I don't know anything about your business, and I don't really care about it. This obsession you Moretti men have with Moretti Motors is detrimental to your lives. I think that Nonna had a point when she cursed your *nonno*."

Marco had no idea where she was going with that line of thinking, though to be honest he wondered if there wasn't a hollowness in being so obsessed with the company. His parents had never cared that Moretti Motors wasn't the leader in automotive design under his father's tenure, and they were insanely happy together.

"So my family deserves to be cursed."

"That's not what I meant," she said.

"What did you mean?"

"Just that Moretti men seem to think the world revolves around their car company."

"Don't paint my brothers with the same brush as you paint me. You don't even know them."

"From things you've said, it's pretty clear that the company is all you guys think of. There is more to life than being the best automotive company in Italy."

"We are the best in the world."

She raised her hands and turned away from him. He thought about pushing this argument until she got fed up and walked away entirely. He didn't need the distraction that she presented. He didn't need this vulnerability he'd discovered in caring for her.

Damn. When had that happened? He hadn't meant for Virginia to mean any more to him than any woman in his entire adult life had meant. But somehow, she did.

That was why her answer to his question was so important to him. He wanted to be able to trust her.

"Just answer the question, Virginia. Did you pass anyone information on our new Vallerio production car?"

"What is that?"

"A new luxury production car that is the fastest in the world and also one of the most expensive. We are launching the car later this year…but you already know that, don't you?"

She crossed over to him and stopped less than a foot away, putting her hands on her hips. "No, I don't. I don't even know who your competitors are."

"Has anyone approached you and asked about the Vallerio car?"

"No. How would I pass information, anyway?"

"You'd take it from my home computer or from the faxes that I get from the head office and then copy it and take it to your contact."

"You've obviously given this a lot of thought. Why would I do this?" she asked.

"The information is worth a lot of money," Marco said. He wanted to make very sure that Virginia understood where he was coming from.

"I don't need money, Marco."

She was really ticked off and he didn't blame her. "I didn't miss it. But Americans are obsessed with money."

"The same way that Morettis are obsessed with Moretti Motors. That's a path to emptiness, Marco, and I for one am not interested in an empty life. Have you learned nothing about me in the weeks we've been living together?"

He reached out and snagged her wrist, drawing her into his arms. She squirmed, trying to push away. "I'm still mad at you."

"I know," he said. But seeing the passion and anger in her had turned him on. And now that he knew she wasn't a corporate spy, he wanted her again.

"I think you owe me an apology," she said.

He leaned down and pressed his lips to hers, seducing her with his mouth. He didn't let go of her, but he felt her soften against him.

"You hurt my feelings," she whispered when he lifted his head.

"I did?"

"Yes. I don't like that. I don't want you to have the power to hurt me, but you already do."

He held her closer. He'd never thought of Virginia as fragile. The way she'd come to him and strategized to have his child spoke of strength, and he didn't like the thought that he might be a vulnerability for her.

"I'm sorry," he said at last. "We've known each other only a short time, but I know you wouldn't lie to me about your involvement."

He kissed her again, trying to say with actions the things he had no words for. He couldn't—*wouldn't*—tell her that she had made him vulnerable. Vulnerable men made mistakes, because they had something to lose.

Marco was just realizing that he did have more to lose than just money for Moretti Motors, and he didn't like that. He had to figure out a way to insulate himself from the feelings Virginia evoked in him.

Virginia didn't want to stop being angry at Marco, but she did. Life was too short, and her time with Marco was limited, so she let her anger go. She knew that he'd asked because he didn't know her—four weeks was hardly enough time to build complete trust—but she'd hoped that they were working toward that. Regardless of what happened between them as a couple, she knew that once they had a child, they'd have to depend on and trust each other.

She twined her arms around his neck and held him close, resting her head against his shoulder. She wanted to pretend that falling for Marco wasn't going to adversely affect her, but it already had. She was changing in an attempt to please him, and letting go of her anger was just a little thing—one of the many that didn't really matter to her as much as time in his arms did.

"Mi scusi, il Signore Moretti," Vincent said from the doorway.

Virginia liked Marco's butler. The man traveled with Marco and made sure that Marco had everything he needed.

"Sì, Vincente?"

"Your parents are waiting for you in the study."

"Tell them we will be right there."

"Sì, signore."

Vincent left and Virginia felt a sense of reluctance to meet Marco's parents. They had to know that her grandmother was the reason for their family curse.

"I think I'll go freshen up first," Virginia said.

"You look fine. There's no need to do anything."

"Yes, there is."

He arched one eyebrow at her. "What reason?"

"I don't want to meet your parents unless I look my best."

He leaned over to kiss her and she let the caring that she felt for him surround her. She felt safe with Marco, which was silly, considering he had the power to ruin her life.

"You look wonderful. They aren't shallow people."

She suspected that. Marco couldn't be the man he was without having been raised by two extraordinary people.

"I just…"

"What?"

"Do they know that I'm Cassia's granddaughter?"

"Yes, they do. Why does that matter?"

Virginia pulled away from him. There was no way for him to really understand the bitterness her *nonna* had felt toward the Moretti family. It was impossible to think that the Morettis wouldn't feel the same way toward her. That they wouldn't resent the fact that her *nonna* had ruined any chance at complete happiness for them.

"What are you thinking?"

"Why?"

"Your eyes are suddenly very sad," Marco said, carefully running his finger over her eyebrows.

"I'm thinking that if my grandmother hadn't cursed Lorenzo, your family would be a lot happier and so would mine. I don't want to see your parents knowing that."

"My parents are the happiest couple I've ever met. They don't feel the burden of the curse."

"Are you sure?"

"I promise you. I think because my father followed his heart, he has no conflict. Not the way Nonno Lorenzo did."

That made an odd sort of sense to her, and she had a moment of clarity about the curse. *What if it isn't really a curse against happiness, but a curse that dealt with not really knowing what you wanted?* Cassia and Lorenzo had each wanted something different.

Cassia wanted Lorenzo and needed him to be happy with her love and living in their small village. Lorenzo needed Cassia to understand his love of cars and speed and his need to make a fortune before he could settle down with her.

With a bit of twenty-twenty hindsight, she realized that Lorenzo had loved cars and racing more than he ever could have loved Cassia.

She pulled away from Marco. Was she simply stepping into her grandmother's shoes? Letting herself fall in love with a man who would never fall in love with her?

"Come and meet them. I think you will see that they aren't at all unhappy with the way things have worked out."

"I wonder why not?" she asked. Her grandmother had been utterly miserable every day of her life. She'd kept a picture of Lorenzo in the kitchen and every morning Cassia would look at him and curse him. *Every day.*

Her earliest memories were of a certain disdain… okay, to be honest, it was a hatred of the Morettis. Only as she got older and could ask questions did she realize that hatred wasn't helping the Festa women.

"Because my father finds absolute joy in my mother. He likes cars, but as he said to me when I was eight, there is nothing in this world that can compete with my mother's smile."

"He really said that?"

"Yes, he did. Then he kissed her when she came

out to bring us some lemonade. To an eight-year-old boy, it was a bit on the gross side."

"What was gross about it?"

"Kissing," he said with a big grin. Then pulled her close and kissed her.

He whispered something in Italian that she couldn't translate, and although she didn't want to look at it too closely, it felt to her that Marco was starting to care for her, too. She knew that she could never be more than second in his life, behind his love of racing and speed, but at that moment she wondered if that hadn't been Cassia's mistake with Lorenzo—not realizing that she could still love him even if he loved something else more than her.

"Ciao, Mamma e Papa," Marco said as he entered the den. Virginia was still a bit reluctant to meet his parents, but she stood by his side.

His father was seated at the desk in front of the iMac computer and his mother was perched on the desk next to it. They were both staring at the screen.

"Ciao, figlio," his mother said. "Your papa is trying to show me the Moretti Motors Web site…have you seen it?"

"Not yet. What is the problem, Papa?" Marco asked as he walked into the room. *"Mamma e Papa,* this is Virginia Festa. Virginia, my parents—Gio and Phila."

"It's a pleasure to meet you both," Virginia said.

"We're pleased to meet you, too, Virginia," his mother replied. Phila gave Marco a hug and a kiss and ran her hand over his hair the way she always did. He hugged his mother close for a minute and then leaned over his father's shoulder to see what the problem was. To say that Gio Moretti wasn't too tech-savvy was a major understatement.

"*Ciao,* Virginia," Gio said. "This is on the company intranet, and I think I entered the proper password...."

"Let me see what you typed in," Marco said, working over his father's shoulder. His mother drew Virginia aside and they began to talk quietly.

He'd always been aware that his parents were special. They had that something that just always made him happy to be with them.

That didn't mean he hadn't gotten into his fair share of trouble as a teen, but he'd always been aware that his parents had a bedrock of love for him and his brothers.

Virginia's cell phone rang and she excused herself to answer it. Even though she was on sabbatical from her work as a college professor of anthropology, she had students sometimes call to ask for her expert opinion. He was impressed by her knowledge and the rapport she had with her colleagues and students.

"She's a nice girl, Marco. I didn't expect that."

"What did you expect, Mamma?"

"I don't know. I just wanted to make sure you were okay and that this girl wasn't taking advantage of you," Phila said.

Gio got up from the computer and wrapped an arm around Phila's shoulder. "Antonio told us about the spy and Dom's suspicions, so we thought it was time to meet this girl."

"So you came to Monte Carlo?"

"Well, that, and I promised your mother a week at sea on our yacht."

"Marco, we are concerned about you and your brothers." Phila said.

"Don't be. We are big boys."

"I know that. How is the curse-breaking going?"

"Mamma, are you asking about my love life?"

She blushed and smacked his arm. "No, I'm not. I really don't want to see you bring a child into this world without loving the mother."

He watched his father hug his mother. "Tell us more about Virginia. Why does she want to end the curse? Cassia certainly never wanted to."

"How do you know that?"

"Nonno went to her when he was in his fifties and tried to rebuild the trust that had been broken. But she refused."

Marco didn't know that Lorenzo had done that. "I don't know about Cassia, but Virginia said that the women in her family have been doomed to live solitary lives devoid of love. She thinks if she has my child, the Morettis and the Festas will be free."

His mother walked over to him. "Do you like her?"

"Mamma, of course I do. She's very smart and sexy."

"Good. Will you two stay together after the baby?"

"I don't think so, Mamma. Remember, she believes that we can't fall in love, or the curse won't be lifted."

"I don't like that," Gio said. "We want a chance to know this grandchild of ours."

"I will have joint custody of the child, so you two will be able to see the baby."

"How will that work? It's silly to have a child, knowing that you aren't going to stay with the mother," Phila said. "Have you thought this through, Marco?"

"*Sì*, Mamma. I have thought about it a lot. Having a child is the thing that will break the curse."

"Are you sure that Virginia isn't interested in the Moretti fortune?"

"No, Mrs. Moretti, I'm not interested in Marco's money," Virginia said as she came back into the room.

His parents turned to face her. "This just doesn't make a lot of sense to me," Phila said.

"Mrs. Moretti, if there were another way to break the curse, I'd do it. But this is the only thing there is."

Phila put her hands on her hips as she looked at Virginia. "How did you figure this out? When Marco told us about this plan, I thought it was crazy."

"Well…my grandmother and mother both lost their men before they could marry. Both of them were pregnant at the time their lovers died, and both of them never loved again."

"I'm sorry to hear of such heartbreakingly lonely lives," Gio said. "But how did you reach the conclusion that having Marco's baby will fix this?"

"I studied the Strega lore that Cassia used to curse Lorenzo. There is more to love curses than just making it so the lover of the one spurned doesn't fall in love again. It has a backlash on the lover placing the curse."

Virginia explained her reasoning to his parents. Her body seemed to vibrate with passion as she stated her belief.

"Until the curse in broken, Festa descendants will have no happiness in love. And I'm tired of being alone. The only way to fix this is for me to have a Moretti baby."

Nine

After Monte Carlo and spending time with all of Marco's family, Virginia felt like nothing could ever be that intense. Dinner with his brothers had been nice, and she saw how close the three of them were. It was obvious to her that Dom wanted to make sure she wasn't the corporate spy, but by the end of the evening she felt confident he knew that the only thing she was interested in was Marco and breaking the curse on their families.

Still, the Morettis didn't really seem to like her. They weren't rude or mean to her, it was just that… she guessed it was that they didn't trust her not to hurt Marco.

Which she thought was silly. Marco wasn't the

kind of man who'd let any woman hurt him. He was careful to make sure that she was only allowed to participate in his life in two areas—in bed, where he made love to her, and in public, in front of the camera, where he made it seem as if she were his newest plaything—which she guessed she was.

The trip to Canada had been pleasant. She'd enjoyed being in Montreal, and Marco had taken two days out of his schedule to visit her home on Long Island. They'd made love in her bed in the small bedroom of the house she'd grown up in, before heading back to France, where they were now. It was the end of June and they were in Magny-Cours for the Grand Prix de France.

They were south of Paris and she liked the area. The race fans were sophisticated and some of them were cordial to her. Others thought she was distracting Marco and made no bones about wanting her to leave him to racing.

They were staying in a chateau owned by a friend of Marco, Tristan Sabina. The chateau was like something out of a fairy tale and the Loire Valley was charming.

Yet Virginia couldn't relax. She'd been feeling a bit nauseous for the last few days, and this morning had thrown up after Marco left for the track to take his practice runs.

She suspected she might be pregnant. She'd asked Vincent to get a pregnancy test for her. She was both hopeful and frightened to learn the result.

She was falling more in love with Marco each day. It was the little things he did, things that she knew probably meant nothing to him. Little things such as finding a book of poems by Robert Frost, who she loved. Or sitting on the balcony late at night and talking about the constellations and the legends that surrounded them.

She'd ordered a book of Russian legends off the Internet for him, and it was supposed to be delivered today. She knew he'd enjoy it, and that gave her pleasure.

A part of her knew that what they had wasn't real. But this quiet time together was nice.

There was a knock on the door of the suite. She walked across the marble floor, loving the life she was living. She had to stop for a minute and remind herself that she wasn't dreaming. That she was really here in France.

She opened the door to find Vincent standing there. "*Ciao,* Vincent."

"*Ciao,* Miss Virginia. You have a guest waiting downstairs."

"Who is it?"

"Miss Elena."

Keke's fiancée. They hadn't spoken since Spain, when Elena had warned her to watch herself around Marco.

"I'll be right down to see her. Where is she?"

"I asked her to wait in the courtyard. I know you like to be outside."

"*Grazie,* Vincent."

Vincent left and Virginia took a quick minute to fix her hair and make sure she looked presentable. It was hard to feel confident in her looks when she was in the same room as the former *Sports Illustrated* model. But Virginia decided she wasn't going to let Elena's looks intimidate her.

She went downstairs and stepped out into the courtyard. It was a huge landscaped area complete with a hedge maze. She saw Elena sitting on a bench a few feet away. The other woman turned and smiled at her as she approached.

"Thank you for seeing me."

"You're welcome. Why are you here?"

"Two reasons."

Virginia was a little leery of hearing them. "And they are?"

"Well, first I want to apologize. I was worried about Marco and I shouldn't have followed you like I did when we were in Catalunya."

"That was okay. I think it's great that you care so deeply for Marco."

Elena smiled at her. "I don't have a lot of friends, because I'm a bit...well, Keke says I have a forceful personality, but others have called me a bitch, and I'm sure I came off that way to you."

She smiled at the other woman, thinking that Elena was actually a very nice woman who cared deeply for the people she called friends.

"You didn't. Please don't worry anymore about what was said in Spain."

"Good. The other reason I'm here is to see if you want to sit with me at the race this weekend."

"Um...I'm not sure I'll be attending."

"I think it bothers Marco that you aren't there. When Keke and I talked about it, I realized that you might not feel comfortable with the other wives and girlfriends because you don't know anyone...so I wanted to invite you to sit with me."

"I'd like that, but to be honest I can't stand it when Marco is racing. I keep worrying that he's going to lose control of the car and crash."

"I worry about the same thing with Keke, but these men of ours, they know what they are doing. They've both been driving fast all their lives. I have a feeling the only place they feel alive is behind the wheel."

Virginia kept up the small talk with Elena, but a part of her mind was on the fact that Elena had named her real fear. That Marco would never be able to love anything other than the speed he found on the race-track.

Since he'd started living with Virginia, Marco had started a new ritual the night before race day. It involved dinner alone with her under the stars while they talked about whatever innocuous topic either of them came up with. Both of them avoided mention of their families and their pasts.

Tonight, when he came out to the courtyard where he was meeting Virginia, he saw that the table was set for four and not two. There was a wrapped package with his name on it and a note in Virginia's handwriting that told him she was waiting for him inside the maze.

This villa had been his grandparents'. And though he barely remembered his Nonna Moretti, he had happy memories of the time that he'd spent here as a boy. His brothers and he would spend endless hours at the Grand Prix track, and his parents—who never seemed interested in racing—would actually attend the races here, even though Nonno had long since stopped racing.

"Virginia, *mi' angela,* where are you?" he asked. The maze in this garden was familiar to him, and he knew there were many hidden benches and places to get lost. As a child, when his brothers were ganging up on him, he'd come out here and hide. He'd had his last conversation with his grandfather in this garden, on a bench in the center, near the fountain that was topped with a statue of Nonno Lorenzo's prized Moretti Vallerio open-wheel race car.

"Come and find me." Virginia's voice came from farther up the path. It was soft, and he heard a hint of laughter in the tone.

"Aren't we a little old for hide-and-seek?" he asked, but continued down the path toward the center of the maze.

"Are we?" she asked. Again her voice came from

farther up the trail, but this time it sounded as if it came from the left.

Usually, he didn't like to play games. His life wasn't the kind where he often had time for these kinds of amusements, but with Virginia he was finding he was a different man.

No longer the driven Formula One driver who was focused on speed and winning.

"I had hoped to make love to my woman, but if you prefer playing childish games…"

She giggled. And he smiled. From what he'd come to know of Virginia, she'd had too little happiness in her life. And as silly as he thought this game was, he didn't mind doing this for her.

Plus, he was intrigued. She'd gotten him a gift and he wanted to find her and learn what it was. He'd never received a gift from a lover when it wasn't a holiday or his birthday.

What had she gotten him? And why?

"Marco…" she called softly, and he realized she'd stopped moving.

"Yes?"

"You're supposed to say 'Polo.'"

"Why?"

"It's a hiding game that kids play in the pool."

He was certain he had narrowed down her location. But wasn't ready to end the game yet. "But it is also my name."

"I know. I was wondering if you'd played that game as a child," she said.

He smiled to himself, realizing that she'd forgotten the rules of her own game. Perhaps she'd even forgotten that she was hiding from him.

He stepped around a bougainvillea bush and onto the cobblestone path that led to a small alcove near the back of the walled garden and maze.

"No, I spent most of my time watching *Speed Racer* and building race cars in the garage with my brothers."

"Cars? Why am I not surprised?" she asked, but her voice had moved again.

"Were you distracting me, *mi' angela?*"

"*Sì!*"

There was a kind of joy in her voice that he hadn't experienced in his own life in so long. He realized suddenly that winning another Grand Prix championship wasn't going to bring him that joy. This was what was missing from his life. He wasn't lonely. How could he be with a family the size of his? But he had forgotten how much *fun* driving used to be. Back when winning a race meant something more than another notch on his place in history. And maybe winning the record-breaking championship would restore his joy for driving, but…what if it didn't?

For so long, he'd had all of his hopes on the fact that racing would always be in his blood, but he was finding that maybe that wasn't so.

He didn't say anything else—and pushed those

thoughts from his mind. They wouldn't serve him well tonight, or at tomorrow's race.

He stood quietly and listened, slowly sorting out the sounds of the fountains in the garden and the sounds of his own breath.

He heard the small scrapping of shoes against cobblestone and realized that Virginia was moving again.

He pivoted in the direction in which he thought he'd heard her, but the path was empty.

He started in that direction, when he felt the air change behind him and her arms come around him, her hands covering his eyes. He felt the brush of her breasts against his back as she rose onto her tiptoes and whispered in his ear. "Guess who?"

He reached up and caught her hands in his, drew them down to his mouth where he kissed them as he turned to face her. Staring down at her, he realized that the joy he'd been searching for was right here. A feeling he'd previously experienced only when pulling gs as he went through the turns on the racetrack swamped him, and he realized that he had fallen for this woman.

Virginia was in a good mood, having decided to just enjoy the time she had with Marco. But although he kissed her with all the passion he usually showed, there was something dark and brooding about him as she looked up into his eyes.

She realized then that life seldom went as planned. She *knew* that, she thought with disgust. *Hadn't she learned anything during her childhood?*

"Why are you hiding in the garden?"

"I wanted a chance to be alone with you before Keke and Elena arrived for dinner."

"You invited my friends for dinner?"

"Yes. Is that okay?"

"Sure, I'm just surprised. You haven't seemed too interested in any part of my racing life."

"I didn't want you to think I was just after you for the attention that follows you around," she said. "I saw a special on television once, about some women who hired photographers to follow them out when they went clubbing so that they'd look famous."

Marco rolled his eyes. "Was this in Europe?"

"No, the U.S. But still, people do like the attention."

"But you don't."

"No," she said, taking his hand and leading him around the corner in the path to where she'd set up an ice bucket with a bottle of champagne.

"What's this?"

"I really wanted this night to be memorable for both of us because, well…" How was she going to say that she was pregnant and there was no longer a need for them to stay together? She'd never had a problem finding the right words. Never had any problem saying what was on her mind, and she'd never cared what the consequences were, but tonight…she didn't want her time with Marco to end.

And she had set this up—as *what?* She started to feel very vulnerable and a bit stupid. He was going to see through the night she'd planned and realize that she wanted to stay with him.

What was wrong with her? Where was the clear-headed reasoning she'd always had when it came to anything in her love life?

"What are you trying to say?"

She shrugged and realized she didn't want to say anything about the baby just yet.

"Let's have something to drink." She knew that drinking alcohol wasn't recommended for pregnant women, so she planned to have just a sip of the champagne.

"Are we celebrating something?" he asked.

She wondered if he already suspected that she was pregnant. She'd been nauseous for the last ten days or so.

"I want to toast the qualifying time you posted today. I think you made a new track record."

"Yes, I did. But that is what they pay me for."

She arched one eyebrow at him. "Really."

"Well, that is what Antonio always says. That I'm paid to be the best so that the world will speak the name of Moretti the way they talk about Lambor-ghini or Andretti."

"I think your brother is making light of your ac-complishments. They should be praising you for doing your job so well. And we will definitely toast your new record."

Marco drew her over to the champagne stand. He poured the drink into the glasses by the bucket for both of them and offered one to her. "To fulfilling our duty."

"Yes." She tapped her glass to his and took a small sip, letting the sparkling wine sit on her tongue until the bubbles dissolved. In this part of the world, the champagne was good. Even labels she hadn't heard of before were exquisite.

"I noticed a package with my name on it...."

She smiled at him. "I got you a little something. It's kind of a thank-you for the gift of these days we've spent together."

"I have enjoyed our time together, too. In fact," he said, drawing her over to the marble bench, "sit down, Virginia."

She loved the way he said her name, the emphasis he put on the different syllables and the way that his accent made her name sound exotic. It made her feel like she was something more than just plain old Virginia Festa.

She sat down and Marco settled onto the bench next to her. She set her champagne flute on the bench and turned to face him.

He took her hands in his, and she wondered if this was going to be it. The point where he acknowledged that they really had no reason left for staying together.

A knot formed in the pit of her stomach and she almost jumped up and walked away. No matter what he said to her, there was no happy way for the relationship to end for her. Breaking the curse had seemed simple and straightforward when she'd plotted it out. But the reality of Marco had changed everything. He had ripped away her safety net and left her vulnerable. Because as she looked up into his deep, chocolate eyes, she knew that she never wanted to leave him. She never wanted to be anywhere other than by his side.

In childhood, she'd believed that once the curse was lifted from her she'd find a good man, fall in love and live happily ever after. She knew now that wasn't the case. She was never going to meet another man like Marco. And she'd already given him her heart....

Why didn't falling in love make this right? She had truly believed that love made the impossible possible.

"Why do you look at me like that?"

"Like what?"

"Like I'm about to do something hurtful to you. I don't like it when you are sad, Virginia."

"I'm not sad," she said. And she wasn't. She was bittersweet, she thought. "What were you going to say?"

He rubbed the back of his neck. "Stay with me until the end of the race season. I know we said you would stay until there was a child, but regardless of any pregnancy I would like for you to continue traveling and living with me until October."

"I'd like that." She took a deep breath. "Um...I took a pregnancy test today, Marco."

He stilled. "Why didn't you tell me this right away?"

"I couldn't find the words," she said. "I am pregnant."

He smiled at her. "Excellent. Then that means we are on our way to breaking the curse."

"It also means we don't have a reason to stay together," she said.

"I want you to stay with me. We're friends now, aren't we?"

"Yes," she said. "Does this mean we won't be lovers still?"

He shook his head. "I don't want the life we've had to change. We can live together until the child is born, and then we will begin our agreed custody."

Virginia felt like she'd gotten a reprieve and that there was now a bit of hope for the future—for a real future with her and Marco and the tiny spark of life within her womb.

Ten

Marco won in France, came second in the British Grand Prix and then won again in Germany. They'd passed the halfway point in the racing season, and it was sweltering this first week in August. Now they were in Budapest, a city he'd always loved.

Virginia had confirmed that she was indeed expecting his child. He'd hired a physician to travel with them and monitor her, after they'd had a scare with spotting and feared she might lose the baby in Germany.

Now he was at the track garage, avoiding Keke and his brothers. It was odd. They all wanted to talk to him about the same thing—Virginia. But where

Keke thought that having a woman in his life and finding a connection with Virginia was the best thing that could happen to Marco, Dom and Antonio both thought he was putting their future in danger.

His brothers had cornered him last night and told him he was putting Moretti Motors in jeopardy by staying with Virginia and taking the risk of falling for her.

He was somewhere in between his brothers and his friend. He didn't like the new vulnerability he felt, now that Virginia was in his life. Asking her to stay with him for the rest of the season was an easy decision. He'd had mistresses before. But he'd expected his feelings for her to wan the way they had with other women.

Instead, his feelings were growing deeper. He missed her when she wasn't around. She rarely came to the track with him, and a part of him wondered why she wouldn't watch him race.

He acknowledged that he'd never really driven for anyone other than himself. Even though Antonio and Dominic told him repeatedly that it was his duty to drive and win, Marco did it for himself. He needed to be out on the track, beating everyone else and getting the adulation and the praise that came from winning.

He looked around the garage, realizing that this was one place in the world where no one expected anything of him. Winning was expected when he was on the track, but here in the garage, with his car nearby and the smell of tires and oil filling the air, he was just another driver.

"Marco Moretti?" a man called from the opening that led to pit row. The man was of average height, with thinning hair that he had unfortunately combed over his pate. He wore wrinkled khaki pants and a long-sleeved black T-shirt.

"*Sì?*" he asked.

"I'm Vincenzo Peregrina, with *Le Monde,* out of Paris. I'd like to talk to you for a few minutes."

Marco glanced around, looking for his crew chief, but everyone had left for the afternoon. If he hadn't been lingering in the hopes of avoiding his brothers, he wouldn't be cornered.

"I don't have the time right now, but you can contact Moretti Motors and make arrangements through my office," Marco said. He reached into his pocket and handed the other man his card.

"This isn't about Moretti Motors."

"Then what is it you wish to speak to me about?" he asked the other man. He didn't mind doing interviews and found the media to be very helpful most of the time. But this man wasn't part of the entourage that he usually dealt with.

"The young woman who is traveling with you."

"You're not with *Le Monde.*"

Vincenzo shrugged. "Would you have talked to me if I'd said I was with *Hello!* magazine?"

"Doubtful. As I'm not going to speak to you about this subject," Marco said. He saw Pedro, one of the security team who worked in the garage area, and signaled to him.

"Good day, Mr. Peregina."

Pedro reached for Vincenzo's arm, but the other man put his hands up. "I'm going. But you should know that just because you ignore my questions doesn't mean I'm not going to find out who she is."

"Your questions are of no concern to me," Marco said. He left the garage and went to the drivers' lot where his convertible waited. He climbed into the car and sat there for a few minutes. Maybe it was time to stop avoiding his brothers.

He didn't want the media to swarm around Virginia. He wanted to keep her private.

He dialed Dom's mobile. It was time to bring the full force of Moretti Motors into his personal life.

"This is Dominic."

"Dom, cio e Marco. I need to talk to you."

"I've got ten minutes before I have to go to a press conference about the new Vallerio."

"Did you find the leak?"

"No. But Antonio is putting together two sets of information, and we think we've narrowed the suspects down. We will see what information our enemy has, and then we should know who is our spy. Is that what you were calling for?"

"No, Dom. I just had a tabloid reporter ask me about Virginia, and I'd like to make sure that no one comes close to her. I do not think she is accustomed to talking to the paparazzi."

"That usually doesn't bother you."

"What do you mean?"

"Your women…you usually leave them to deal with the press on their own."

"Virginia is different."

Dom sighed. "That is what I was afraid of. We need to meet in person."

"Why?"

"Because you are forgetting about your blood vow to Antonio and me."

"What are you talking about?"

"You are allowing yourself to fall for her."

He uttered a curse under his breath, and his brother said nothing. Marco wasn't about to admit to Dom that it was too late, he'd already fallen for Virginia.

Virginia enjoyed dinner out with Marco. They went to an exclusive restaurant, and on the drive back he put down the top of his car. The Budapest skyline conjured up fairy-tale settings. The castle in the background and the warm evening air made her relax, and she forgot all the worries she'd been carrying around with her.

Marco had been treating her like she was fragile, and a part of her thought that he also saw her and the baby in her womb as something precious to him. Something that he wanted to protect and keep safe.

She turned her head against the leather seat and looked at his profile as he drove. He reached over and took one of her hands, brushing his lips against her palm before he placed her hand on his thigh.

He drove with the superb skill that she expected of him. And his concentration when he was on the road was intense. She was coming to realize that it was the same intensity he brought to everything he touched.

"What are you thinking about?" he asked.

"That you are a very protective man," she said.

He didn't respond, just glanced over at her.

"It makes me feel special to be with you like this."

He lifted her hand again, kissing her knuckles this time. "You are special to me."

"You are to me, as well, Marco. I never expected my quest to free my family from the curse to turn out this way."

He steered them through the streets back to their hotel. "What did you expect?"

"To be honest, I don't know. I haven't really dated all that much, so I don't have a lot of men to compare you to."

"And how do I fare compared to these few other men?" he asked.

She took a deep breath and the magic that was this night in Budapest filled her. "There is no comparison. You are so much more than I ever expected to find in any man."

"You make me sound—"

"Like what?" she asked, wondering if she'd revealed too much. But she had the feeling that he must have already guessed the depth of her love for him. She tried to keep her feelings to herself, but she was struggling with that.

"Like someone who's better than I really am. Please don't see me for anything more than what I am."

"What are you?"

"A Moretti. My loyalty is always going to be to my blood. My family comes first, and then racing."

"And I'm a distant third?" she asked.

She'd already known he didn't care about her in the same way she did for him. It had been obvious from the beginning that there was much more to Marco's love life than there had ever been to hers.

He was a worldly man, and that had never really bothered her until this moment.

"Not a distant third," he said. "I'm actually not sure where you fit. As the mother of my child, I think that makes you family."

She knew that Marco wasn't one of those men who felt comfortable discussing his feelings. He often told her how he felt about her body in very explicit terms when they made love. But he never spoke of his emotions.

He pulled the car to a stop in front of their hotel and she climbed out when the valet opened her door. Marco was already coming around the car, tossing his keys to the attendant.

"Excuse me, ma'am. May I have a word with you?"

Virginia glanced over at the man in wrinkled

khaki pants who was standing off to the side of the valet stand.

"No, you may not," Marco said. Wrapping an arm around her shoulders, he led her into the hotel and straight to the concierge desk.

"There is a reporter outside who is bothering us. He does not have permission to speak to us and I don't want anyone on your staff giving him information about where we are staying."

"Yes, sir, Mr. Moretti. I will take of the problem immediately. Perhaps you'd like to move to one of our other properties in Budapest."

"No, I would not. I have to race in the morning and I trust that your security staff will ensure my privacy."

"Of course we will."

Marco led them from the desk to the elevator. Once the car doors closed behind them, Virginia turned to him.

"What was that about?"

"That man is a reporter for a gossip magazine. He is digging around, trying to find out who you are."

"Thank you for making sure that I didn't talk to him. But I really don't have anything to hide. I mean, I don't mind answering a few questions, if that means he'll go away and leave you be."

Marco drew her closer to him. "*I* mind. I don't want him writing about you. I don't want the world to know the details of my personal life."

"If I didn't already love you, Marco, I would now," she said, and then realized what she'd done.

She put her hand over her mouth. "I mean…"

He pulled her into his arms and kissed her deeply, his mouth moving over hers with skill and passion. Bringing her body to life. Making her crave so much more than his mouth on hers.

"I'm very happy to hear that you love me."

Marco lifted his head when the doors opened on their floor. He kept one arm around Virginia as he led the way down the hallway to their room. Her confession made him feel ten feet tall. Somewhere deep inside he was relieved that she cared as deeply for him. But mostly, he just felt a primitive need to reaffirm the bonds between them. To ensure that she knew she was his and that no other man would ever have a place in her life like he did.

He wasn't sure if that meant he loved her or not, and he didn't care. Right now he needed to make love to her. To cement in both of their minds how deeply she was his.

He unlocked the door and led her through the suite to the balcony. He wanted to make love to her with the night around them and the beautiful city of Budapest spread out in front of them.

"Why are we out here?" she asked, her voice soft.

"I thought it only fitting that we celebrate out here under the night sky. Since the moon and the stars are what brought you to me."

"Did they?"

"Well, it may have been a *strega* curse, but the

strega get their strength from the moon and the night sky—"

"So they do."

She was so beautiful in the moonlight. It wasn't that she was classically beautiful, but there was something about Virginia that always drew his eyes to her. She imbued a certain sexiness that never failed to make him hard. Tonight, standing in the minimal light, with her hair hanging around her shoulders, she was breathtaking.

He ran his finger down the side of her face, caressing her cheekbones and her long neck. He reached the pulse at the base and felt it pounding heavily beneath his finger. "Are you excited?"

"Yes."

"Good," he said. He continued caressing her skin, tracing the seam where her flesh disappeared under the gauzy fabric of her dress.

She shivered with awareness and her nipples tightened against the bodice of her dress. He lowered the straps on her sundress so that the bodice hung loosely over her breasts.

"Take your top down for me," he said.

"Out here?"

"Sì," he said. He stepped back and watched her. He wanted her to want this moment as much as he did. And he liked pushing her past her own sexual barriers. Slowly, she lifted one arm and then the other. She kept her breasts covered, one hand holding the fabric against her chest.

"Are you sure you want me to take this off?" she asked.

He nodded. "Do it now, *mi' angela.*"

Shaking her head and letting her hair fall around her shoulders, she let the bodice fall slowly away from her skin. Her breasts were full, her nipples tight, begging for his attention. She looked so sexy at that moment that he was almost overwhelmed, but he attributed it to the fact that he hadn't made love to her today.

He stepped to her and leaned down to lick each nipple until it tightened. Then he blew gently on the tips. She shivered, her hands coming up to frame his head. She arched her back and thrust her breast against his lips. He sucked her deep into his mouth and felt as though he could find that one thing he'd always been thirsting for in her body.

He wrapped his arms around her waist and drew her to his body. He attended her other nipple, and then tried to push her dress down her body, but it was too tight at the waist.

He found the zipper and lowered it. Her dress fell to her feet and he stepped back to look at her. She wore only a mint-green-colored thong and a pair of sexy heels. Her hair was tousled around her shoulders, her nipples red and beaded from his attention and her lips were swollen, begging for more of his kisses.

He caressed her body, sweeping his hands down her sides until he reached the satin fabric of her panties. He grasped either side and pushed them down her legs. Now she was completely naked.

"Now you are as nature intended for you to be," he said.

"Am I?" she asked.

"*Sì*. You are exquisite. And I cannot wait to thrust myself deep into your body and feel your silky limbs wrapped around me."

"You are a tad bit overdressed."

"Then undress me," he said.

She pushed his jacket off his arms, but instead of letting it fall on the floor, she took it to one of the patio chairs and draped it over the back. He enjoyed watching her naked body as she moved around the patio.

She unbuttoned his shirt next, taking her time to caress each bit of skin that she revealed. She lowered her head and dropped nibbling kisses on his chest. She pushed the shirt off and carried it over to the chair where she'd placed his jacket.

He realized that the minx was teasing him, and he was enjoying the hell out of it—and her. But he needed her. He wanted—no needed—to be buried inside her now. He was hard and he knew he would probably climax as soon as he thrust inside of her. But he wanted to make sure she came at least once before he did.

He lifted her up once she was back within arm's grasp and carried her back inside their suite. He set her on the couch in the living room.

"I need you. Now."

She nodded. "I need you, too, Marco. So much."

"Show me how much," he said.

She parted her legs and he saw the glistening of her body's moisture.

"Open yourself for me," he said.

Her thighs twitched and she drew her own hands down her body. But she hesitated at the top of her thighs. "I'm not sure I can...."

He took her hands in his and brought them to her mound. "I want to taste you, Virginia. Don't you want to feel my mouth on you?"

He kissed her lips again. Thrust his tongue deep inside her mouth and sucked on her lower lip before leaning back to see her reaction.

She nodded and he felt her hands move between them.

The pink of her flesh looked so delicate and soft with the red rose petals around it.

"Hold still," he said.

He leaned down, blowing lightly on her before tonguing that soft flesh. She lifted her hips toward his mouth.

He drew her flesh into his mouth, sucking carefully on her. He held on to her thighs, holding her in place as he carefully tasted her essence. He wanted to strip away all of her barriers, so that she'd never forget this night and the confession she'd made in the car.

He felt the frantic movements of her hips against

his mouth and then her fingernails dug into his shoulders. He lifted his head to look up at her.

Her eyes were closed, her head tipped back, her shoulders arched, throwing her breasts forward with their berry-hard tips, begging for more attention. Her entire body was a creamy delight.

He lowered his head again, hungry for more of her, feasting on her body the way a starving man would. He used his teeth, tongue and fingers to bring her to the brink of climax, but held her there, wanting to draw out the moment of completion until she was begging him for it.

Her hands grasped his head as she thrust her hips up toward him. But he pulled back so that she didn't get the contact she craved.

"Marco, *please.*"

He scraped his teeth over her clitoris and she screamed as her orgasm rocked through her body. He kept his mouth on her until her body stopped shuddering, and then slid up her.

"Your turn," she said, drawing him up next to her on the couch. She reached for his belt and he lowered his zipper while she unfastened it. He lowered his pants and boxers in one quick move. She took his erection in her hand and followed with her tongue, teasing him with quick licks and light touches.

He arched on the couch, thrusting up into her before he realized what he was doing. He pulled her from his body, wanting to be inside her when he came.

He pulled her up his body until she straddled him. Then, using his grip on her hips, he pulled her down while he slid into her.

He pulled her legs forward forcing them farther apart until she settled even closer to him. He slid deeper still into her. She arched her back, reaching up to entwine her arms around his shoulders. He thrust harder and felt every nerve in his body tensing. Reaching between their bodies, he touched her between her legs until he felt her body start to tighten around him.

He climaxed in a rush, continuing to thrust until his body was drained. He then collapsed against her.

"You are mine now, Virginia Festa."

"And you are mine, Marco Moretti."

"For now," he said.

Eleven

Virginia was happy to be back in Valencia for the Grand Prix of Europe. It felt like her life with Marco had started in Spain. She and Elena were in the pit area, hanging out together. The last three weeks since Budapest had been the best of her life.

She and Marco had turned a corner in their relationship, and contrary to ruining things, her confession had drawn them closer. Marco blew her a kiss from behind the wheel of his race car as he went out for a practice run on the track.

Elena slipped her arm through Virginia's. "I'm so happy for you and for Marco. He's needed a good woman in his life for a long time."

"Has he?" she asked. Though she knew it was silly, she was jealous of the women in Marco's past.

"Yes, he has. He and his brothers made that silly vow, and I thought that Marco would never date a woman like you."

"What vow?" she asked. She knew that no one, save for the Moretti brothers, knew about her contract with Marco.

"The one they took never to fall in love."

Virginia swallowed hard. She told herself that the vow Marco had made long ago had nothing to do with her. She was here to break the curse anyway, even if he had made a deal with his brothers.

There was a loud screeching sound of wheels on asphalt, and then a boom that shook the ground around them. Since her back was to the track, Virginia had no idea who had crashed. Elena's face went deathly pale as she stood next to Virginia. She gripped the other woman's hand as she turned toward the track.

Flames and smoke engulfed the car and she couldn't make out anything other than the sight of fire trucks rushing to the scene. Everyone went still. The only sounds were those coming from the emergency vehicles. No one spoke in the pit area until, finally, a man that Virginia didn't recognize came over to them.

"Keke isn't responding on the radio. They are cutting him out of the car now."

Elena started sobbing and Virginia saw her own

fears realized in Elena's eyes. "Is he alive?" Elena cried.

"Yes. I will take you to the hospital where he will be airlifted."

"Yes. That will be fine. But I can't leave here until Keke does."

"Do you want me to come with you?" Virginia asked. She wrapped her arm around the other woman. She had no idea what to say, how to offer comfort. Part of her was still afraid that Marco wasn't all right, though he hadn't been near Keke.

Her heart was racing. The acrid smell of smoke filled the air and the JumboTron screen rebroadcast the crash in slow motion. Virginia knew that if it were Marco's crash, she wouldn't be able to watch it, so she drew Elena away from the pit area and to Keke's trailer.

"How are you feeling?"

Elena said nothing, but silent tears ran down her face. Virginia hugged the other woman close. This was horrible. They knew nothing, and Virginia realized that the officials mustn't have heard anything yet. Elena needed someone to tell her something.

She saw a race official and waved him over. She used her rudimentary knowledge of French to try to communicate with him. "Have you had any word on Keke's status? His fiancée is beside herself."

"Nothing yet. Ms. Hamilton is welcome to go to the official trailer and wait there for word."

The official moved on.

"Do you want to do that?" she asked Elena.

"Yes. I think that would be good. Oh, God, Virginia, I'm so scared."

"Don't worry. Everything will be okay," Virginia said, then realized that she had no idea if everything was going to be okay. But she refused to think negatively. She offered a quick prayer that Keke would survive his crash.

"Let's go," she said to Elena.

When they got to the trailer, the officials were immediately very helpful in getting Elena a comfortable seat and a drink, but they had no information. After ten minutes, Elena turned to her.

"I can't take this. I just need to know that he's alive."

"Okay. I will go find out what I can. You wait here, so the officials can find you."

"Thanks."

Virginia raced back to the viewing area. She saw Dominic Moretti walking through the pit and ran over to him. If there was any man who could get answers for her, it was a Moretti.

"Dominic, do you know what's happening?"

"I'm not sure. How's Elena?"

"Beside herself. We can't get any information from anyone. I'm not even sure who to ask. But she needs something—to know Keke's status."

"I will see what I can find out."

"Grazie," she said, but didn't let go of his arm.

"Was there something else?"

"Um…have you heard from Marco?"

Dom grasped her shoulder in a very reassuring way. "He's fine. Still out on the track. They won't let him close to Keke's car, either. I'll tell him that Elena is anxious to hear from her man, in case he gets to talk to Keke."

"That would be great. Would you tell Marco… just that I'm glad he's okay."

"I will relay your message to him. Keep close to Elena. Here is my mobile number so we can keep in touch."

She programmed Dom's cell number into her phone so that she'd have it.

Keke was pulled from the wreckage of his car and airlifted to the local hospital. Marco had to finish his lap and still hadn't qualified. But knowing his best friend was in the hospital tinged everything.

Almost forty minutes after the crash, they were all back in the garage. Still wearing his jumpsuit and sitting on a chair drinking a bottle of water, Marco waited for the officials to reopen the track. Virginia had phoned to say that she was going to accompany Elena to the hospital. There had been fear and worry in her voice, and he hadn't had the words to soothe those fears.

He had no idea what was going to happen with Keke. He'd lost only one other friend to racing, but they all knew that it was a risk, driving at superfast speeds in cars designed more for speed than safety.

"Do you have a minute for us?" Dom asked as he and Antonio came into the garage area. His brothers looked tired and worried.

"Yes. What's up?"

"Are you okay?"

"Sure. Crashes happen. Remember the twenty-four hours at Le Mans, when we were kids? Everyone thought Nonno wouldn't walk away from that… but he did."

Dom and Antonio both looked at him and Marco knew they were two of the few people in the world he couldn't fool with his glib tongue.

"It really does not matter how many crashes we've seen. Keke is your best friend."

"I know, Dom. I keep seeing it replaying in my head. Keke—is better than he drove today."

Dom pulled a chair up next to him and sat down. "What do you mean? You think he deliberately crashed?"

"No. Not at all. He is too professional to do something like that. I think that he has something to lose now, and that made him second-guess his instincts."

Marco didn't say it out loud, but he was thinking that he had something to lose now, too. The new life that he was starting to carve with Virginia. He hadn't said anything to her, but he'd been thinking that once the racing season ended he'd go back to the States with her for a few weeks. Maybe convince her to move to Europe permanently.

"How do you know this? Did Keke say something

that made you think that Elena was a liability?" Antonio asked, as he leaned his hip against one of the big toolboxes in the area.

Marco shook his head. "Nothing like that, Dom. It's just that you get to know a man after spending so much time together."

"The same way that brothers know each other," Antonio said. "We look at the world the same way because we have a shared past and dreams of a successful future."

"Exactly," Marco said. He knew his brother was trying to allude to the fact that Marco had let Virginia grow too close.

"Let's discuss something else. Elena went to the hospital and will let us know once Keke is out of surgery."

"That is good. I'll head over there when you go out to take your qualifying laps," Dom said. "We need someone from Moretti there."

"Yes, we do. Is there any chance that the wreck could have been caused by sabotage?" Antonio asked.

Marco hadn't even thought of that. Had he used his perception of how Keke felt about Elena to color his version of what had happened on the track? "Why do you ask?"

"Because someone is out to ruin us. The corporate spying is one thing, but now that we are on to them, maybe they've changed tactics," Antonio said.

"It could be, but security here is very tight. Pedro would be the one to ask, but I have to warn you, he'll be offended that you are asking. He prides himself on being the best in the business."

"If he's the best then he won't mind a few questions," Dom said. "I'll talk to him."

"We need to be very careful for the rest of the season," Antonio said. "Marco, have you noticed anyone around here who shouldn't be?"

"Just a reporter who was sniffing around for information on Virginia."

"Are you sure he was a reporter?" Dom asked.

Marco rolled his eyes at his brother. "I'm not an idiot. Of course I'm sure he was a reporter."

"It never hurts to double-check. Speaking of which, we want to ask you something that is probably not any of our business."

Antonio, who always looked vaguely bored by the goings-on at the track, suddenly seemed very serious. They leaned forward in his chair.

"What is it?" he asked, alarmed by the way his brothers were acting.

"Do you remember the vow we took as boys?" Dom said.

"Yes, I do," Marco said. He thought of little else lately, with Virginia coming to mean more to him. He wondered if he was fooling himself when he thought that he could easily control his emotions toward her.

"Well, we are concerned," Antonio said. "I know that Virginia believes having your child will break the Moretti curse, but we're not so sure. And you are getting very serious about her."

"Since when does my love life concern either of you?"

"Since you are looking at her the way that Papa looks at Mamma. You know what that means as well as we do."

"She means nothing to me."

"Yeah, right. You are living with her beyond the original terms of the contract. You are warning paparazzi away from her and making sure that she's cosseted everywhere you travel."

"She's my mistress, Antonio. I think it's okay to treat her well."

Antonio and Dom both stood up. "Make sure that's all she is. We have all worked too hard to rebuild Moretti Motors to see it all fall apart because you fell for some skirt."

"I'm very aware of what Virginia means to me, and I'm not about to let either of you down," Marco said. He stood up and turned to go to his car, and saw Virginia standing in the shadows.

Virginia wasn't feeling her best after leaving the hospital and her wild taxi ride back to the track. She'd been out of sorts and not feeling too good already, and now her stomach was doing flips, because of worry, she suspected.

Seeing Marco had made her feel better, until she'd realized that he and his brothers were discussing her. And that he had just said she meant nothing to him. She was no different from the other women he'd been with in the past, according to what he'd just told his brothers.

She wanted to get angry, but she couldn't. She was still too happy to see him alive.

"I am sorry you had to walk in on this conversation," Dominic said. "How is Keke?"

"He's stable. Elena will be able to see him when he comes out of surgery. She's still at the hospital."

"*Grazie,* Virginia," Antonio said. "You are a good friend to Elena."

"I know it wasn't in the normal mistress arrangement for me to be nice to the fiancée of the second Moretti driver, but I figured I'd make the effort."

Antonio gave her a strained smile and said goodbye to his brothers before leaving. Dominic said nothing, and Marco had a tight, angry look on his face.

"Do you have a minute to talk?" she asked Marco.

"A few moments. Dom, will you leave us?"

"*Ciao,*" Dominic said as he left.

Marco turned and walked to his private trailer. A couple of his crew members were inside, but they left as soon as Marco entered with Virginia in tow.

He stopped in the middle of the trailer and turned to face her once they were alone. "I am sorry you had to hear that."

"I'm not. It's better for me to hear the truth. I had been fooling myself that even though you couldn't say the words, you still loved me."

"*Dio mio,* Virginia—"

"I know. You never said anything that would lead me to believe you cared for me. It was my own delusion. I think, once I realized the man you are…well, the man I thought you were…" She couldn't go on. She was going to start crying and that was the absolute last thing she wanted to do right now. "It doesn't matter," she said at last.

"Virginia, *mi' angela,* please don't let my words wound you. I meant nothing by them."

He came to her and tried to draw her into his arms, and she was tempted to go because he'd hurt her deeply and she wanted to be soothed by him. But at the same time she heard his voice in her mind. Heard him say that she was nothing more than a mistress, and she knew that if she had any chance of coming out of this relationship with her pride intact she needed to stand on her own.

She stepped back from him and he dropped his arms. "I do not know what to say," he told her.

"You didn't have that problem earlier when you were with your brothers," she said.

"That wasn't a conversation you were meant to hear," he said.

"I know. Believe me, you've done a great job of acting like you really care about me…but I guess that's what you usually do with your mistresses.

"I have no idea why this behavior surprises me. I knew that you were like this when I picked you as the Moretti brother I would seduce."

Marco put his hands on his hips. She saw the lines of stress on his face and also the flash of anger. "I'm not some kind of cad when it comes to women, Virginia. The women I am involved with—you included—have always come to me wanting something in exchange."

"How nice of you to point that out," she said sarcastically. She knew she should leave before she said something stupid, but she was too angry and too hurt to just walk away. She wanted Marco to feel the same pain she felt. That emotional pain that she honestly didn't know if she'd ever recover from.

"I'm not the one who slept with you and walked away," he said.

"No, you're not," she said quietly. "You also aren't the one who fell in love. Maybe this is the way it's supposed to be," she said. "I mean, I'll have a child and you'll have your life, which will continue on as usual. The curse probably demands that I shouldn't fall in love with you."

Marco remained quiet, and she knew she had to leave before she broke down and started crying. She had no idea that silence could hurt her this deeply.

"I guess I'll be on the next plane back to the States," she said.

"Virginia…I never meant for you to get hurt. I only wanted to keep you safe and happy."

"Well, you did a good job of that."

"Did I?"

"Yes."

"Then what has changed? Why are you leaving me?"

Virginia looked at him. He was a smart man, and she knew he had enjoyed the fact that she did love him. But there was no way she could continue to live with him when their versions of reality were so markedly different.

"I guess, now that I know how you see me...I can't keep telling myself that someday you're going to realize that the only way to truly break this curse is to fall in love and live your life in a fully realized manner."

Marco reached for her, and she felt his hand on her face. She knew this was the last time he'd touch her, and she leaned into that touch for a minute. "I'm sorry for making this goodbye so messy. And for not staying until the end of the season."

She kissed him on the lips and walked away while she still had the strength to do it.

Twelve

Marco didn't want to admit it to himself, but he thought he'd made a mistake when he let Virginia walk out on him. He'd won the Grand Prix championship, and in a few short months, Moretti Motors would release their new Vallerio model, if Tony had his way and successfully acquired the use of the name. His brother was already in negotiations to get that deal moving forward.

So Marco had no reason to feel like something was missing in his life—except that his arms felt so damned empty every night. He needed her back. Sometimes he thought he caught a wiff of her perfume in a room and would walk in expecting to see her, only to find that it was empty.

Empty.

God, how had he not realized that he was letting himself become the same man Nonno had been? He was letting racing and his public take precedence over his life.

He needed to do something, find a way to get Virginia back. But how?

He got his mobile out and called Keke.

"I need a favor," he said before Keke could ask why he was calling.

"What?"

"I'm going to get Virginia back and…"

"Are you coming to me for woman advice?" Keke asked, laughing.

"No, I'm coming to you because I need someone to help me coordinate things in the U.S."

"How can I help?" Keke asked.

Marco outlined his plan to his friend and a few hours later was on a commercial flight to the United States. Never before had he been so nervous. Not even when he got behind the wheel of his first F1 driving machine. And now he knew why. Racing was what he did, but Virginia was his life and his love, and he didn't know if he could survive without her. If this was how Cassia had felt for Lorenzo, Marco understood why she'd cursed him when he'd chosen racing over her.

He also thought maybe it was time for a Festa and a Moretti to fall in love and right the wrongs of the past.

* * *

Virginia spent the rest of the summer and the beginning of the fall in her quiet home on Long Island. She grew each day with her pregnancy, and the baby—a boy—was doing very well. She was still on sabbatical and enjoyed the quiet days at home.

She avoided newspapers and television and anything that might show her a glimpse of Marco. She'd learned the hard way that seeing him even on a magazine stand was enough to trigger a deep sadness inside her. A part of her wanted to say to hell with pride and return to him.

She really missed him.

But she also had to live with herself, and somehow she knew that loving a man who thought of her as nothing but a mistress wasn't a good thing.

It was a rainy Saturday in early November, and she was painting the nursery for the baby. She dreaded the thought of the upcoming holiday season—of spending another one all alone. But she rubbed her small pregnancy bump and realized that in a year's time she wouldn't be alone anymore.

She'd have her baby, and together the two of them would celebrate all the holidays. She was toying with naming the baby Lorenzo to appease the curse that Cassia had set. Maybe if she named her child for the man who'd originally been cursed, Fate would be happy with her and leave her be.

Her doorbell rang and she looked at her watch. That should be Elena. Her family lived in the Lake

George area of New York and she and Keke had spent the last few months there.

Keke had recovered nicely from all his injuries and had decided to retire from racing. He'd taken up a new gig, as a male model and commentator for a European sports channel.

Today they had both promised to come and help her with her room renovation. She had been grateful for their friendship. She'd never realized how alone she was in the same small town she'd grown up in. But she was grateful that Elena and she had become fast friends in the months they'd spent together on the Formula One racing circuit.

The doorbell rang again, and she realized she was dawdling. She didn't know if it was the pregnancy or what, but her mind tended to wander lately. Usually it wandered to Marco.

She opened the door. "Come on in."

"*Grazie,* Virginia."

It was Marco. Marco was standing on her front porch, wearing a pair of wool trousers and a black turtleneck, as well as a long trench coat. The rain had wet his jet-black hair.

"What are you doing here?"

"I hope you don't mind, but since you wouldn't return any of my calls, I persuaded Elena and Keke to let me come and help you today."

"That's…why?"

"Because we need to talk. May I come in?"

She stepped back and let him enter her house. As

he took off his coat and hung it on the coat rack she had by the front door, she realized how much she had missed him. He smelled just as good as she remembered and her arms were literally tingling with the need to wrap around him.

"You are staring at me," he said.

"I'm sorry. Why are you here?"

"Because I realized that I can't live without you. I don't care if my brothers believe that love is the one thing that will doom Moretti Motors. I need you in my life."

She wasn't sure she'd heard him correctly. "I don't—"

"Don't overthink this. I lied to you that day in Valencia, when I let you believe you were nothing more than a mistress to me. My life has been hollow and empty without you."

She couldn't say anything, but when he drew her into his arms she went to him, wrapped her arms around his lean waist and held on. "Marco, is this for real?"

"Sì, mi' angela, ti amo."

She tipped her head up to look at him, to see if the love he'd just spoken of was reflected in his eyes. And it was. She saw the sincerity there.

"I know I have no right to hope that you still feel the same way about me."

"I do still love you. It's been agony living without you," she said. "But I figured that was the only way to appease the Fates."

Marco shook his head. "The only way to appease the Fates is for us to be together. To raise our son and give him brothers and sisters."

"Are you sure?"

"Yes," he said. "Will you marry me, Virginia?"

"Yes!" She threw her arms around him and kissed him with all the passion and love she'd been storing up since they'd parted in August.

"What about your brothers?"

"I told them that we were all wealthy and that we would continue to focus on making our new production car very successful, and that was all we needed to do to break the curse."

"And they were okay with that?" she asked, not wanting his brothers to dislike her.

"Not really. But I told them that, regardless of whether you are with me or not, you own my heart and soul."

* * * * *

ALESSANDRO AND THE CHEERY NANNY

AMY ANDREWS

This book is dedicated to all
good fathers and their sons.
Little boys need their daddies too.

Amy Andrews has always loved writing and still can't quite believe that she gets to do it for a living. Creating wonderful heroines and gorgeous heroes and telling their stories is an amazing way to pass the day. Sometimes they don't always act as she'd like them to—but then neither do her kids, so she's kind of used to it. Amy lives in the very beautiful Samford Valley, with her husband and aforementioned children, along with six brown chooks and two black dogs. She loves to hear from her readers. Drop her a line at www.amyandrews.com.au.

CHAPTER ONE

NAT DAVIES was instantly attracted to the downcast head and the dark curly hair. There was something about the slump to the little boy's shoulders and the less than enthusiastic way he was colouring in. He seemed separate from the other children laughing and playing around him, and it roused the mother lion in her.

He was the only stationary object in a room full of movement. And he seemed so…forlorn.

'Who's that?' she asked, bumping Trudy's hip with hers to get her boss's attention.

Trudy stopped chopping fruit and followed Nat's gaze. 'Julian. It's his second day. Four years old. Father is ooh-la-la handsome. Italian. Perfect English. Just moved from London. Widower. Recent, I think. Doesn't smile much.'

Nat nodded, well used to Trudy's staccato style of speech. 'Poor darling.' No wonder he looked so bereft. 'How awful to lose your mother at such a young age.' Not that it mattered at any age really. She'd been eight when her father had left and it still hurt.

Trudy nodded. 'He's very quiet. Very withdrawn.'

Nat's heart strings gave another tug. She'd always had

a soft spot for loners. She knew how it felt to have your perfect world turned upside down while life continued around you. How alienating it could be. How it separated you from the bustle of life.

'Well, let's see if I can fix that,' she murmured.

Nat made a beeline for the lonely little boy, stopping only to grab a copy of *Possum Magic* off the bookshelf. In her experience she found there was very little a book couldn't fix, if only for a short while.

'Juliano.' Nat called his name softly as she approached, smiling gently.

The little boy looked up from his lacklustre attempt at colouring in a giant frog. His mouth dropped open and he stared at Nat with eyes that grew visibly rounder. She suppressed the frown that was itching to crease her forehead at the unexpected response. Surely he was used to hearing his name spoken in Italian?

He was looking at her with a mix of confusion and wonder, like he was trying to figure out if he should run into her arms or burst into tears.

She kept her smile in place. '*Ciao*, Juliano. *Come sta?*'

Nat had learnt Italian at school and spent a year in Milan on a student exchange after completing grade twelve. Given that she was now thirty-three, it had been a while since she'd spoken it but she had been reasonably fluent at one stage.

Julian's grave little face eked out a tentative smile and Nat relaxed. '*Posso sedermi?*' she asked. Julian nodded and moved over so Nat could share the bench seat with him.

'Hi, Juliano. My name's Nat,' she said.

The boy's smile slipped a little. 'Papa likes me to be called Julian,' he said quietly.

The formality in his voice was heart-breaking and Nat wanted to reach out and give him a fierce hug. Four-year-olds shouldn't be so buttoned up. If this hadn't been St Auburn's Hospital crèche for the children of hospital staff, she might have wondered if Julian's father had a military background.

Maybe Captain Von Trapp. Before Maria had come on the scene.

'Julian it is,' she said, and held out her hand for a shake. He shook it like a good little soldier and the urge to tickle him until his giggles filled the room ate at her.

She battled very uncharitable thoughts towards the boy's father. Could he not see his son was miserable and so tightly wound he'd probably be the first four-year-old in history to develop an ulcer?

She reminded herself that the man had not long lost his wife and was no doubt grieving heavily. But his son had also lost his mother. Just because he was only four, it didn't mean that Julian wasn't capable of profound grief also.

'Would you like me to read you a story?' Nat pointed to the book. 'It's about a possum and has lots of wonderful Australian animals in it.'

Julian nodded. 'I like animals.'

'Have you got a pet?'

He shook his head forlornly. 'I had a cat. Pinocchio. But we had to leave him behind. Papa promised me another one but…he's been too busy…'

Nat ground her teeth. 'I have a cat. Her name's Flo. After Florence Nightingale. She loves fish and makes a noise like this.'

Nat mimicked the low rumbling of her five-year-old tortoiseshell, embellishing slightly. Julian giggled and it was such a beautiful sound she did it again. 'She's a purring machine.' Nat laughed and repeated the noise, delighted to once again hear Julian's giggle.

As children careened around them, immersed in their own worlds, she opened the book and began to read aloud, her heart warmed by Julian's instant immersion into its world. Page after page of exquisite illustrations of Australian bush animals swept them both away and by the end of the tale Julian was begging her to read it again, his little hand tucked into hers.

'I see you've made a friend there,' Trudy said a few minutes later, plonking a tray of cut-up fruit on the table in front of them and calling for the children to go and wash up for afternoon tea.

Julian followed the rest of the kids into the bathroom, looking behind him frequently to check Nat was still there. 'I hope so, Trude,' Nat replied.

If anyone needed a friend, it was Julian.

An hour later the chatter and chaos that was usually the kindy room was filled only with the beautiful sounds of silence as the busy bunch of three- to five-year-olds slumbered through the afternoon rest period. Nat wandered down the lines of little canvas beds, checking on her charges, pulling up kicked-off sheets and picking up the odd teddy bear that had been displaced.

She stopped at Julian's bed and looked down at his dear little face. His soft curls framed his cheeks and forehead. His olive complexion was flawless in the way of children the world over. His mouth had an enticing bow shape and his lips were fat little cherubic pillows.

Unlike every other child in the room, he slept alone, no

cuddle toy clutched to his side. With the serious lines of his face smoothed in slumber he looked like any other carefree four-year-old. Except he wasn't. He was a motherless little boy who seemed to carry the weight of the world on his shoulders.

More like forty than four.

He whimpered slightly and his brow puckered. Her heart twisted and she reached out to smooth it but he turned on his side and as she watched, his thumb found its way into his mouth. He sucked subconsciously and her heart ached for him. He seemed so alone, even in sleep. It was wrong that a boy who had just lost his mother should have nothing other than a thumb to comfort him.

She made a mental note to talk to his father at pick-up. Ask him if Julian would like to bring along a toy, something familiar from home. Maybe she could even broach the subject of counselling for Julian. Something had to be done for the sad little darling. Someone had to try.

It may as well be her.

It was early evening when Nat found herself curled up in a bean bag with Julian in Book Corner, reading *Possum Magic* for the third time. The room was once again quiet, most of the children having gone home, their parents' shifts long since finished. The few remaining kids had eaten their night-time meals and were occupied in quiet play.

Despite her best efforts to engage him with other children, Julian had steadfastly refused to join in, shadowing her instead. Nat knew she should be firmer but in a short space of time she'd developed a real soft spot for Julian.

His despondent little face clawed at her insides and she didn't have the heart to turn him away. He looked like he was crying out to be loved and Nat knew how that felt. How could she deny a grieving child some affection?

She didn't notice as she turned the pages that Julian's thumb had found its way into his mouth or that one little hand had worked its way into her hair, rhythmically stroking the blonde strands.

All she was really aware of was Julian's warm body pressed into her side and his belly laugh as she mimicked Grandma Poss and Hush on their quest to find the magic food. As ways to end the day went, it wasn't too bad at all.

Dr Alessandro Lombardi strode into the crèche. He was tired. Dog tired. Emotional upheaval, months of no sleep, moving to the other side of the planet and starting a new job had really taken their toll. He wanted to go home, get into bed and sleep for a year.

If only.

He pulled up short in the doorway as his son's laughter drifted towards him. It had been months since he'd heard the sound and he'd almost forgotten what it sounded like. And after an arduous day it was a surprising pick-me-up.

His midnight-dark gaze followed the sound, his eyes widening to take in the picture before him. His son cuddled up next to a woman with blonde hair and blue eyes exactly like Camilla's. His fingers absently stroked her hair while he sucked his thumb, just as he used to do with Camilla.

His welcoming smile froze before it had even made a dent into the uncompromising planes of his face. He crossed the room in three strides. 'Julian!'

Nat felt the word crack like a whip across the room and

looked up startled as Julian's thumb fell from his mouth and he dropped his hand from her hair as if it had suddenly caught fire.

She didn't need Trudy to tell her Julian's father had arrived. They were carbon copies of each other. Same frowns, same serious gazes and brooding intensity, same cherubic mouths.

But where Julian's appeal was all round-eyed child-hood innocence, his father's appeal was much more adult. There was nothing childish about his effect on her pulse. He looked like some tragic prince from a Shakespearean plot to whom the slings and arrows had not been kind.

Put quite simply, at one glance Julian's father was most categorically heart-throb material. A tumble of dark hair, with occasional streaks of silver, brushed his forehead and collar, a dark shadow drew the eye to his magnificent jaw line and that mouth…

She knew without a doubt she was going to dream about that mouth.

She suddenly felt warm all over despite the chill that blanketed her as cold dark eyes, like black ice, raked over her. Nat was used to men staring. She was blonde and, as had been pointed out to her on numerous occasions, had a decent rack. She was no supermodel but she knew she'd been blessed with clear skin, healthy hair and a perfect size twelve figure.

Until today she'd thought living in Italy had immunised her against being openly ogled. As an eighteen-year-old blonde with pale skin in a country where dark hair and olive complexions were the norm, she'd certainly attracted a lot of interest from Italian boys.

But there was nothing sexual about this Italian's

interest. Rather he was looking at her like she was the wicked witch of the west.

And he was definitely no boy.

'Julian,' he said quietly, not taking his eyes off the strange woman who was eerily familiar. From the way she folded her long pale legs under her to the blonde ponytail that brushed her shoulders and the fringe that flicked back from her face, she was just like Camilla.

His gaze strayed to the way the top two buttons of her V-necked T-shirt gaped slightly across her ample chest. They lingered there for a moment, unconsciously appreciating the ripe swell of female flesh. It had been a long time since he'd appreciated a woman's cleavage and he quickly glanced away.

His gaze moved upwards instead, finding the similarities to Camilla slapped him in the face again. Same wide-set eyes, same high cheekbones, same full mouth and pointed chin complete with sexy little cleft that no doubt dimpled when she smiled.

Hell, he must be tired, he was hallucinating.

He held his hand out to his son. 'Come here.'

Julian obeyed his father immediately and Nat felt the beads of the bean bag beneath her shift and realign, deflating her position somewhat. She looked up, way up, at a distinct disadvantage in her semi-reclined state on the floor.

From this angle Julian's father looked even more intimidating. More male. His legs looked longer. His chest broader. He loomed above her and she was torn between professionalism and just lolling her head back and looking her fill.

She couldn't remember ever having such an immediate response to a man.

His pinstriped trousers fell softly against his legs, hinting at the powerful contours of his quadriceps. The thick fabric of his business shirt did the same, outlining broad shoulders and a lean torso tapering to even leaner hips.

Unfortunately he was still staring down at her like she was one of those insects who ate their young and reluctantly professionalism won out. She floundered in the bean bag for a few seconds, totally annihilating any chance of presenting herself as a highly skilled child care worker before struggling to her feet.

Snatching a moment to collect herself, she smiled encouragingly at Julian. She noticed immediately how, even standing next to his father, Julian still looked alone. They didn't touch. There had been no great-to-see-you hug, he didn't take his father's hand, neither did his father reach for him. There was no affectionate shoulder squeeze or special father-son eye contact.

It was obvious Julian wasn't frightened of him but also obvious the poor child didn't expect much.

Nat returned her gaze upwards. Good Lord—the man was tall. And seriously sexy. She smiled, mainly for Julian's benefit. 'Hi. I'm Nat Davies.' She extended her hand.

Alessandro blinked. He'd braced himself when she'd opened her mouth to speak, half expecting a cut-glass English accent. But when the words came out in that slow, laid-back Australian way, still unfamiliar to his ear, he relaxed slightly.

The similarities between this woman and his dead wife were startling on the surface. Same height, same build, same eye colour, same blonde hair worn in exactly the same style, same facial structure and generous mouth. Same cute chin dimple.

No wonder Julian had taken a shine to her.

But looking at the fresh-faced woman before him, he knew that's where the similarities ended. This woman exuded openness, friendliness, an innocence, almost, that his wife had never had.

Her hair had been dragged back into its band, rather hurriedly by the look of it, with strands wisping out everywhere. It hadn't been neatly coiffed and primped until every hair was in place.

And Camilla wouldn't have dared leave the house without make-up. This woman…Nat…was more the girl-next-door version of Camilla. Not the posh English version he'd married.

Even her perfume was different. Camilla had always favoured heavy, spicy perfumes that lingered long after she'd left the room. Nat Davies smelled like a flower garden. And…Plasticine. It was an intriguing mix.

Most importantly, her gaze was free of artifice, free of agenda, and he felt instantly more relaxed around her then he ever had with Camilla.

Alessandro took the proffered hand and gave it a brief shake before extracting his own. 'Alessandro Lombardi.'

Nat blinked as the fleeting contact did funny things to her pulse. His voice was deep and rich like red wine and dark chocolate, his faint accent adding a glamorous edge to his exotic-sounding name. But the bronzed skin that stretched over the hard planes and angles of his face remained taut and Nat had the impression he wasn't given to great shows of emotion.

No wonder Julian rarely smiled if he lived with Mr

Impassive. Nat looked down at Julian, who was inspecting the floor. 'Julian, matey, would you like to take *Possum Magic* home? It's part of our library. Maybe your papa could read it to you before bed tonight.'

Nat watched as Julian glanced hesitantly at his father, his solemn features heartbreakingly unhopeful.

Alessandro nodded. '*Si.*'

Nat passed the book to Julian, who still looked grave despite his father's approval. Did he think perhaps his father wouldn't read him the book? She had to admit that Alessandro Lombardi didn't look like the cuddle-up-in-bed-with-his-son type. 'Go and find Trudy, matey. She'll show you how to fill out the library card.'

They watched Julian walk towards Trudy as if he was walking to his doom, clutching the book like it was his last meal.

Nat's gaze flicked back to Julian's father to find him already regarding her, his scrutiny as intense as before. 'Senor Lombardi, I was—'

'Mr, please,' he interrupted. Alessandro was surprised to hear the Italian address. Surprised too at the accuracy of her Italian accent. 'Or Doctor. Julian knows little Italian. His mother…' Alessandro paused, surprised how much even mentioning Camilla still packed a kick to his chest. 'His mother was English. It was her wish that it be his primary language.'

It was Nat's turn to be surprised. On a couple of counts. Firstly, Julian knew a lot more Italian than his father gave him credit for if today was anything to go by. And, secondly, what kind of mother would deny their child an opportunity to learn a second language—especially their father's native tongue?

But there was something about the way he'd faltered when he'd talked about his wife, the hesitation, the emptiness that prodded at her soft spot. He was obviously still grieving deeply. And maybe in his grief he was just trying to do the right thing by his dead wife? Trying to keep things going exactly as they had been for Julian's sake. Or desperately trying to hang onto a way of life that had been totally shattered.

On closer inspection she could see the dark smudges and fine lines around his eyes. He looked tired. Like he hadn't slept properly in a very long time.

Who was she to pass judgment?

'Dr Lombardi, I was wondering if Julian had a special toy or a teddy bear? Something familiar from home to help him feel a little less alone in this new environment?'

Alessandro stiffened. A toy. Of course, Camilla would have known that. There was that mangy-looking rabbit that he used to drag around with him everywhere. Somewhere…

'I've been very busy. Our things only arrived a few days ago and there's been no chance to unpack. We're still living out of boxes.'

Nat blinked. Too busy to surround your child with things that were familiar to him when so much in his world had been turned upside down?

'This is none of my business, of course, but I understand you were recently widowed.'

Alessandro saw the softness in her eyes and wanted to yell at her to stop. He didn't deserve her pity. Instead, he gave a brief, controlled nod. *'Si.'*

If anything, he looked even bleaker than when he'd first entered but despite his grim face and keep-out vibes Nat was overwhelmed by the urge to pull them both close and hug them. Father and son. They'd been through so much and were both so obviously still hurting. She couldn't bear to see such sadness.

'I was wondering if Julian had had any kind of counselling.' *Or if the good doctor had, for that matter.* 'He seems quite...withdrawn. I can highly recommend the counselling service they run here through St Auburn's. The child psychologist is excellent. We could make an appointment—'

'You're right,' Alessandro interrupted for the second time, a nerve jumping at the angle of his jaw. 'This is none of your business.' He turned to locate his son. 'Come, Julian.'

Nat felt as if he had physically slapped her and she recoiled slightly. Alessandro Lombardi had a way with his voice that could freeze a volcano. He was obviously unused to having his authority questioned.

She'd bet her last cent he was a surgeon.

She watched Dr Lombardi usher his son towards the door. Julian partially lifted his hand, reaching for his father's, then obviously thought better of it, dropping it by his side. He turned and gave her a small wave and a sad smile as he walked out the door, and Nat felt a lump swell in her throat.

They left side by side but emotionally separate. There was no picking his son up and carrying him out, not even a guiding hand on the back. Something, anything that said, even on a subliminal level, I love you, I'm here for you.

Nat hoped for Julian's sake that it was grief causing this strange disconnectedness between father and son and not something deeper. There was something unbearably sad about a four-year-old with no emotional expectations.

Having grown up with an emotionally distant father Nat knew too well how soul destroying it could be. How often had she'd yearned for his touch, his smile, his praise after he'd left? And how often had he let her down, too busy with his new family, with his boys? Even at thirty-three she was still looking for his love. She couldn't bear to see it happening to a child in her care.

But something inside her recognised that Alessandro Lombardi was hurting too. Knew that it was harsh to judge him. As a nurse she knew how grief affected people. How it could shut you down, cut you off at the knees. He had obviously loved his wife very deeply and was probably doing the best he could just to function every day.

To put one foot in front of the other.

Maybe he was just emotionally frozen. Not capable of any feelings at the moment. Maybe grief had just sucked them all away.

She sighed. It looked like she'd also developed a soft spot for the father also. Yep, it was official—she was a total sucker for a sob story.

The next day Nat had finished her stint in Outpatients and was heading back to the accident and emergency department for her very late lunch. She'd been sent there to cover for sick leave and was utterly exhausted.

She didn't mind being sent out of her usual work area and had covered Outpatients on quite a few occasions since starting at St Auburn's six months ago but it was a full-on morning which always ran over the scheduled one p.m. finish time. There hadn't been time for morning tea either so her stomach was protesting loudly. She could almost taste the hot meat pie she'd been daydreaming about for the last hour and a half.

Add to that being awake half the night thinking about

Julian's situation, and she was totally wrecked. *And then there'd been the other half of the night.* Filled with images—very inappropriate images—of Julian's father and his rather enticing mouth.

She'd known she was going to dream about that mouth.

'Oh, good, you're back. I need another experienced hand,' Imogen Reddy, the nurse in charge, said as Nat wandered back. 'It's Looney Tunes here. Code one just arrived in Resus. Seventy-two-year old-male, suspected MI. Can you get in and give the new doc a hand? Delia's there but she was due off half an hour ago and hasn't even had time for a break. Can you take over and send her home?'

Nat looked at the bedlam all around her. *Just another crazy day at St Auburn's Accident and Emergency.* And they wondered why she kept knocking back a full-time position. Nat's stomach growled a warning at her but she knew there was no way she could let a seven-months-pregnant colleague do overtime on an empty stomach.

She smiled at her boss. 'Resus. Sure thing.'

Nat stopped just outside the resus cubicle and pulled a pair of medium gloves out of a dispenser attached to the wall. She snapped them on, took a deep breath, flicked back the curtain and entered the fray.

'Okay, Delia. You're off,' she said, smiling at her colleague who happened to be the first person she saw amidst the chaos. 'Go home, put your feet up and feed the foetus.'

Delia shoulders sagged and she gave Nat a grateful smile. 'Are you sure?' She turned and addressed the doctor. 'Are you okay if I go, Alessandro? You're getting a much better deal. Nat here is Super-Nurse.'

Alessandro? Nat swung around to find Alessandro Lombardi, all big and brooding, behind her. The bustle, the sounds of the oxygen and the monitors around her faded out as she stared into those coalpit-black eyes.

They were alert, radiating intelligence, but if anything he looked more tired than he had yesterday. He stared back and Nat felt as if she was naked in front of him.

She dropped her gaze as some of the images from last night's dream revisited. *Bloody hell. He* was the new doctor? Working part-time generally kept Nat out of the loop with medical staff rotations and she'd just assumed Imogen had meant a new registrar. Surely Julian's father was a little too old to be a registrar?

So much for her surgeon theory.

Alessandro took in the woman who had been the cause of another sleepless night. A new cause, granted, but still a complication he didn't need. She was different today, out of her shorts and T-shirt. Very professional looking in the modest white uniform with the zip up the front. Her hair was a little neater in her ponytail and in this environment he felt on a more even keel around her.

Still, his gaze dropped to the zip briefly and before he could stop it, an image of him yanking the slider down flitted across his mind's eye.

He looked at Delia briefly. 'Yes. We've met.'

Then he turned back to the patient and Nat felt thoroughly dismissed. If only he knew what he'd done to her in her dreams last night...

Had she had time she might have been miffed but her patient caught her attention. 'Super-Nurse, hey?' he croaked behind his oxygen mask.

Nat dragged her gaze away from the back of Alessandro's head to look at the patient. He was sweaty and grey with massive ST changes on his monitor.

Multiple ectopic beats were worrying and as she watched, a short run of ventricular tachycardia interrupted his rhythm.

His heart muscle was dying.

He was also in pain despite the morphine that she noted had already been administered, but there was still a twinkle visible in his bright eyes. He was obviously one of those stoic old men who didn't believe in complaining too much.

'Yes, sir.' She reached for his hand and gave it a squeeze. 'That's me. To the rescue.'

The patient gave a weak chuckle. 'Ernie,' he puffed out. 'Looks like I'm in safe hands, then.'

Nat glanced at Alessandro. She hoped so. She hoped he was better at doctoring than he was at communicating. At fathering. 'The very best.'

'What's the ETA on the CCU docs?' Alessandro asked no one in particular.

Seeing Nat Davies from the crèche was a bit of a surprise but he didn't have time to ponder that, or her damn zip, now. He had to focus on his patient, who needed that consult and admission to the coronary care unit pronto.

Ernie's ECG was showing a massive inferior myocardial infarction. They were administering the right drugs to halt the progress of the heart attack but these patients were notoriously unstable and with age against him, Alessandro worried that Ernie would arrest before the drugs could work. Or that his heart was already too damaged.

'Couple of minutes,' someone behind him said.

As it turned out, Ernie didn't have a couple of minutes and Alessandro's worst fears were realised when the monitor alarmed and Ernie lost consciousness.

'VF,' Nat announced as the green line on the screen developed into a series of frenetic squiggles. Her own heart rate spiked as a charge of adrenaline shot through her system like vodka on an empty stomach.

Alessandro pointed at Nat. 'Commence CPR. I'll intubate. Adrenaline,' he ordered. 'Charge the defib.'

Nat hiked the skirt of her uniform up her thighs a little as she climbed up onto the narrow gurney. She planted her knees wide and balanced on the edge of the mattress, a feat she'd performed a little too often, as she started compressions.

Any ill will she may have been harbouring towards Dr Lombardi fizzled in an instant at the totally professional way he ran the code. It was textbook. But that wasn't doing him justice. It was more than textbook. He didn't see a seventy-two-year-old man and give up after a few minutes. He gave Ernie every chance. It wasn't until the down time reached thirty minutes that he finally called it.

He placed his hands on Nat's, stilling their downward trajectory. 'Thank you,' he said. Then he looked at the clock. 'Time of death fifteen twenty-two hours.'

Nat looked down at his hands. She could just see her own through the gloved fingers of his. She noticed for the first time his sleeves were rolled back to reveal the dark hair of his bronzed forearms and she absently thought how strong they looked. How manly.

She glanced at him and their eyes locked, a strange solidarity uniting them. She could see the impact of this loss in his bleak stare. As she watched, his gaze drifted briefly south, lapping her cleavage, and she felt her nipples bead as if he'd actually caressed them. When he looked back at her, all she could see was heat.

Two beats passed and then as quickly as the heat had come it disappeared and he was removing his hands, extending one to help her off the gurney. Dragging her gaze from him, she accepted, easing back to the floor.

Her knees nearly buckled and Nat snatched her hand away, grabbing for the edge of the trolley to steady herself.

'Are you okay?' he asked as he watched her wobble slightly.

Nat rubbed her at her knees. 'Fine'

Except, staring down at Ernie, she knew it wasn't. Ernie was dead. And whatever was going on between her and Alessandro didn't matter next to that. Neither did it matter that she'd only known Ernie for only a handful of minutes—he was still dead. Gone. The twinkle in his eyes extinguished for ever. In fact, it made it worse that she didn't know him. It was wrong that a person should die surrounded by strangers.

She felt as she always did, overwhelmingly sad.

Alessandro nodded. 'We need to talk to his family.'

His cold onyx gaze bored into hers with an air of expectation, no trace of the heat from a moment ago.

Looked like she was going with him.

Confronted with the businesslike professional, she wondered if she'd imagined the fleeting glimpse of sorrow and passion she'd seen. Her tummy growled again and she bargained with it for another half an hour.

Alessandro strode briskly ahead and Nat worried as she followed him. Sure, the view was good. His trousers hugged the tight contours of his butt and each stride emphasised not only the power of his legs but pulled at his shirt, emphasising the broadness of his back.

But none of that meant this man was remotely equipped

to talk to grieving relatives. He was still grieving himself. Had Ernie's death resonated with him? Had this death reminded him of his dead wife, of his own grief?

He was obviously a consultant, she didn't think for a moment this was his first time. But if he was as emotionally disconnected with this family as he was with his son, it could be disastrous for them. As a nurse she was used to being involved in these conversations but did he only want her there to fill in the emotional gaps for him? Was she going to be left to pick up the pieces like she'd done too many times before in her career because too often doctors were ill equipped for this sort of situation?

She contemplated saying something. But despite the brief flare of desire that had licked her with heat, his terse *This is none of your business* from yesterday still rang in her ears and she didn't want to annoy him before this heart-wrenching job. But he seemed as tense as yesterday, as distant, and not even the growling of her stomach could override the foreboding that shadowed her as she tried to keep up with his impossibly long stride.

Telling someone their husband/child/mother/significant other had died was always dreadful. As a health-care worker, Nat would rather clean bedpans all shift than witness the devastating effects of those awful few words. But she knew Ernie's wife and kids deserved the truth and she knew they'd have questions that only someone who had been there could answer.

And that was her.

She couldn't back away from that. No matter how much she wanted to.

Much to her surprise, Alessandro again totally confounded her. He spoke softly, his accent more apparent as he gently outlined what had happened and how they'd tried but in the end there had been nothing they could do to bring Ernie back. The family cried and got angry and asked questions and Alessandro was calm and gentle and patient.

He was compassion personified.

And at the end when Ernie's wife tentatively put out her hand to bridge the short distance between Alessandro and herself and then thought better of it and withdrew it, it was he who reached out and took her hand.

It should have melted her marshmallow heart in an instant. But it didn't.

It reminded her of yesterday and Julian reaching for his father's hand and it had the opposite effect. She was furious. It felt like a red-hot poker had been shoved through her heart. She wasn't sure if it was the lack of food or the lack of sleep but she felt irrationally angry.

Was this man schizophrenic? Was he some sort of Jekyll and Hyde? How could he offer Ernie's wife, a relative stranger, the comfort he denied his own child?

He'd shown this family, this previously unknown collection of people, more sensitivity, more emotion, than he'd displayed for his four-year-old son. Yesterday she'd thought he was emotionally crippled. Grieving for his wife. Today, as they'd walked to do this, she'd worried about it again. Worried about his ability to empathise when he was buried under the weight of his own grief.

But it wasn't the case. He was obviously a brilliant emergency physician with a fabulous bedside manner. He just didn't take it home with him. To the most important person in the world. To his own child. To his son.

* * *

They left Ernie's family after about twenty minutes and Nat had never been more pleased to be shed of a person in her life. She steamed ahead, knowing if she didn't get away from him she would say something she would regret.

Alessandro frowned as Nat forged ahead. She seemed upset and as much as he didn't want anything to do with the woman who could almost have been Camilla's twin, they worked together and he knew that sudden death, such as they'd both just been part of, took its toll.

He caught her up. 'Are you okay?'

'Fine.' She repeated her response from earlier.

Except she wasn't. It didn't take a genius to figure out that something was bothering her. He grabbed her arm to prevent her walking away any further. 'I don't think you are.'

Nat looked at his bronzed hand on her pale arm. She looked at him. *Oh, Senor, you really don't want to mess with me now.* She pulled her arm away but he tightened his grip.

Heat radiated from his hand and spread up her arm to her breasts and belly. Damn it, she did not want to feel like this. Not now. She was mad. *Furious.* She sucked in a breath, ragged from her brisk walk and the rage bubbling beneath the surface.

They were standing in the corridor facing each other and it was as if time stood still around them and they were the only two people on the planet. Nat couldn't believe how it was possible to want to shake someone and totally pash their lips off at the same time.

'I'm fine.' The denial was low and guttural.

Alessandro could see the agitated rise and fall of her

chest, see the colour in her cheeks. His gaze drifted to her mouth, her parted lips enticing.

He dragged his gaze away. 'I don't believe you. I know these cases can be difficult—'

Nat's snort ripped through his words and gave her mouth something else to do other than beg for his kiss. 'You think this is about Ernie?' She stared into his handsome face, at his peppered jaw line. How could she want someone who was so bloody obtuse?

'It's not?'

Nat snorted again and she knew she couldn't hold it back any longer. 'Tell me, how is it that you can reach out and hold a stranger's hand and yet you can't offer your own son the same comfort?'

Alessandro froze at the accusation in her words. He dropped his hand from her arm as if he'd suddenly discovered she was suffering from the ebola virus. Nat watched his black ice eyes chill over as he paled beneath his magnificent bronze complexion. But she was on a roll now and she'd come this far.

'Nothing to say?' she taunted.

'Oh, I think you've said enough for both of us. Don't you?'

And before she knew it he'd turned on his heel, his rapidly departing figure storming along the corridor ahead.

She sucked in a breath, her body quivering from anger and something else even more primitive. She guessed she should feel chastised but she couldn't. If he could show this level of compassion at work, even if it was just an act, he sure as hell could show it at home.

If she could save Julian from the emotional wasteland

she'd trodden, trying to please her father throughout her childhood, then she would. Attraction or no attraction.

So, no. She hadn't said enough. Not nearly enough. Not by a long shot.

CHAPTER TWO

Two weeks later Brisbane was in the throes of an unremitting heatwave. The power grid couldn't keep up with consumer demand for ceiling fans and 24-hour-a-day air-conditioning. Tempers were short. Road rage, heat stroke and dehydration were rampant.

Even in a city that regularly sweltered each summer, the temperatures were extreme. But this was spring and totally ironic when the other side of the world battled the looming pandemic of a horrible new strain of influenza and unseasonal snow was causing general havoc.

Nat actually looked forward to stepping through the doors of St Auburn's and being enveloped in a cool blast of air. Anywhere was better than her hot little box the real estate agent euphemistically called a townhouse in a breezeless suburb blistering beneath the sun's relentless rays.

Not that it would matter soon, seeing that it looked like she was going to be evicted by the end of the month.

Nat stepped into the crowded lift on the eighth floor, pondering this conundrum yet again. She'd just transferred another heat-stroke victim to the medical ward and was returning to the department. She squeezed in and, noting the ground-floor button had already been pushed, let her mind wander to the phone call she was expecting from the realtor any time now. She would find out today whether she could get an extension on her lease.

It wasn't until the lift emptied out over the next few floors and she had some more room to move that she was even aware of her fellow travellers. Two more people got out at the fourth floor and she was suddenly aware of there being only one other person left. Big and looming behind her. A strange sixth sense, or possibly foreboding, settled around her and she glanced quickly over her shoulder.

Alessandro Lombardi stared back at her, one dark eyebrow quirked sardonically. *Hell.* She had only seen him very briefly and at a distance in the last couple of weeks since she'd basically accused him of being a terrible father. He was wearing a pale lemon shirt and a classy orange tie. A stethoscope was slung casually around his neck.

In short he was looking damn fine and her hormones roared to life.

She turned back to the panel, pressing 'G' several times as the door slowly shut, her heart beating double time.

A fleeting smile touched Alessandro's mouth as he stared at her back, her blonde ponytail brushing her collar. It was the first time he'd been close to her since her outburst a little while ago. But he'd certainly heard her name frequently enough. Julian had spoken of little else. He'd heard it so often he'd started to dream about her.

He moved to stand beside her. 'Good afternoon, Nat.'

Nat took a steadying breath. 'Dr Lombardi,' she said, refusing to turn and face him. She jabbed at the 'G' several more times—why was this lift so damn slow?

'Be careful. You'll break it.'

She could detect a faint trace of amusement in his voice but today with the heat and the eviction hanging over her head she really wasn't in the mood. She hit it one more time for good measure.

Which was when the lift came to a grinding halt, causing her to stumble against him. She heard him mutter '*Porca vacca*' as he was jostled towards her and she supposed, absently, a profanity was better than an *I told you so*.

His hand cupped her elbow and the lights flickered out. It was a few seconds before either of them moved or spoke. Alessandro recovered first.

'Are you okay?'

His big hand was warm on her arm and for a second she even leaned into him, her pulse skipping madly in her chest as her body tried to figure out what was the bigger problem. Being stuck in a lift. Or being stuck in a lift with Alessandro Lombardi.

'You know,' she said, moving her elbow out of his grasp, 'when they teach you a foreign language it's always the swear words you learn first?'

Alessandro chuckled. 'Guilty.'

His low laughter sounded strange coming from a man who had thus far looked incapable of anything remotely joyous. But it enveloped her in the darkness and made her feel curiously safe.

The lights flickered on, or at least one of them did, and Alessandro braced himself for the lift to power up and lurch to a start. When nothing happened he looked down at Nat, who was looking expectantly at the ceiling. He hadn't realised they were standing so close.

Her flower-garden scent wafted towards him and when her gaze shifted from surveying the ceiling to meet his, the urge to move closer, to stroke his finger down her cheek, was a potent force.

He took a step back. His attraction to this woman was a complication he didn't need. 'I'll ring and see what's happened.'

Nat nodded absently, also backing up, pleased to feel the solidness of the wall behind her. For a moment there, maybe it had been the half-light, his eyes had darkened even further and she could have sworn he was going to touch her. *In a good way.*

She felt as if there wasn't enough air suddenly and took some calming breaths. She wasn't the hysterical type and now was not the time to become one.

Nat listened absently as Alessandro had a conversation with someone on the other end of the lift's emergency phone. It was brief and from the tone it didn't sound like they were getting out any time soon.

He hung up the phone and turned to her. 'There's a problem with the city grid. Something to do with the heat wave. The emergency power has kicked in but two lifts have failed to start. They're working on it.'

Nat licked her lips, the thought of spending time with him in a confined space rather unsettling. Did he also feel the buzz between them or was it all one sided? 'Did they have any idea how long it might take?'

'No.'

'*Porca vacca,*' she muttered, figuring Alessandro's instinctive expletive was as good as any. In either language.

Alessandro suppressed another chuckle. He could see her gaze darting around the lift and he wondered if she was trying to calculate carbon-dioxide build-up or was looking for an escape hatch. 'You're not claustrophobic, I hope?'

Nat shook her head. 'No. I'm afraid you'll be disappointed if you're waiting for me to turn into a hysterical female.'

Was he disappointed? Certainly Camilla would have thrown her first tantrum by now, demanding to speak to someone in authority. He much preferred Nat's calm resignation. 'Good.'

Nat glanced at him briefly and quickly looked away. He loomed in the dim light and with each passing second he seemed to take up more room. 'Well, no point in standing. Might as well get comfortable for the long haul.'

She sat then, cross-legged on the floor, her back pressed to the wall. She looked up at him looking down at her and was reminded of their first meeting when she'd had the bean-bag disadvantage. He was looking at her with that now familiar coolness in his eyes.

'Sit down, for God's sake,' she grouched.

Alessandro frowned. Nat Davies was one bossy little package. He slid down the wall, planting his feet evenly in front of him, his knees bent. 'Are you always this disagreeable?'

Nat, who was excruciatingly aware of his encroaching masculinity, shot him a startled look. She opened her mouth to protest. No, she wasn't. Despite her father's desertion and the recent ending of a long-term messy relationship that would have caused the most congenial woman to become a bitter hag, she was essentially a very agreeable person.

Perennially happy. Everyone said so. She almost told him so too. But then a quick review of the twice she'd spoken to him had her conceding that his comment was probably fair.

She raised her gaze from the very fascinating way his

trousers pulled across his thigh muscles. 'I owe you an apology. For the other day. After Ernie. I was out of line. It was none of my business.'

Alessandro was surprised by her admission. It was refreshing to be with a woman who could apologise. 'You did overstep the line a little.'

Nat wanted to protest again, justify her reaction as being in Julian's interests, but he was right. 'I get too involved. I always have. The matron where I trained said I was a hopeless case.'

Alessandro smiled grudgingly. He removed his stethoscope and loosened his tie. It was already starting to get stuffy without the benefit of the air-conditioning. 'There are worse human flaws.'

He knew that only too well.

Nat stared at how even a small lift to his beautiful mouth transformed his face. Combined with the now skew tie and the undone top button, revealing a tantalising glimpse of very male neck, he really was a sight to behold. She smiled back. 'She didn't think so.'

Alessandro straightened a leg, stretching it out in front of him. He shrugged, looking directly at her. 'We'd just lost the battle to save a man's life. Death affects everyone in different ways.'

The teasing light she'd glimpsed briefly snuffed out and he seemed bleak and serious again. An older version of Julian. She hesitated briefly before voicing the question that entered her head. But they had to talk about something. And maybe he was looking for an opening? 'How long ago did your wife die?'

Alex felt the automatic tensing of the muscles in his neck. A fragment of a memory slipped out unbidden from the steel trap in his brain. Opening his door on the other side of the world to two grim-looking policemen. He drew his leg up again.

Nat watched him withdraw, startled by a twist of empathy deep inside.

Oh, no. No. No. No.

Alessandro Lombardi was a big boy. He didn't need her empathy. It was bad enough that she was sexually attracted to him. He didn't need her to comfort him and fix things too. His wife was dead—she couldn't fix that. Only time could fix that.

'I'm sorry. There I go again. None of my business.'

No. It wasn't. But he was damned if he wasn't opening his mouth to tell her anyway. 'Nine months.'

Nat was surprised. Both that he had responded and by the nine months. She'd known it was recent but it was still confronting. No wonder they were both so raw. 'I'm so very sorry,' she murmured.

Alessandro watched as her gaze filled with pity, the blue of her irises turning soft and glassy in the gentle light. He couldn't bear to see it. A sudden black fury streaked through him fast and hot like a lightning bolt from the deep well of self-hatred that bubbled never far from the surface. He didn't deserve her pity. He wasn't worthy of it. All he deserved was her contempt.

This was why he'd left England. To get far away from other people's pity. Their well-meaning words and greeting-card platitudes. Knowing that he had driven her to her death, that he alone was responsible…the hypocrisy had eaten him up inside.

Looking into Julian's face every day was more than he could stand. It was much easier not to.

He dropped his gaze. It took all of his willpower to drag himself back from the storm of broiling emotions squeezing his gut. 'Nat,' he said to the floor, before raising his face to meet hers, 'is that short for something?'

There had been a moment, before he'd looked down, when she'd glimpsed a heart-breaking well of despair. But it was shuttered now, safely masked behind a gaze that could have been hewn from arctic tundra.

He was obviously still deeply in love with his wife. It was also obvious he wasn't going to talk about it with her.

'Natalie,' she said, taking the not-so-subtle hint. 'I was supposed to be a boy.'

'Ah.'

'Nathaniel. Nat for short.'

She told the story she knew off by heart, careful not to betray how inadequate it made her feel. How she'd never felt like she quite measured up because her father had wanted a boy. 'My parents had kind of got used to thinking of me as Nat so they decided on Natalie.'

'Nathalie.' Alessandro rolled the Italian version round his tongue. 'It's pretty. Much prettier than Nat.'

It certainly was when he said it. His accent made a *th* pronunciation shading it with an exotic sound plain old Nat never had. Coming from his lips it sounded all grown up. No girl-next-door connotation. No one-size-fits-all, unisex, if-only-you'd-been-a-boy name.

In one breath he'd feminised it.

And right then, sitting on the floor in the gloom of a broken-down lift, she could see how women fell in love at first sight. Not that she was quite that stupid. Not any more. After Rob she knew better than to get involved with a man who was in love with another woman. Even a dead one.

But raw heat coated her insides and she squirmed against the floor to quell the sticky tentacles of desire.

'I prefer Nat,' she dismissed lightly, brushing at imaginary fluff on her skirt.

Alessandro dropped his eyes, watching the nervous gesture. It was preferable to the vulnerability he'd seen in her unmasked gaze.

'Ah, yes, Nat. Nat, Nat, Nat. I hear that name so often at home these days I'm beginning to think you must have magical powers. I think you could give Harry Potter a run for his money.'

Nat, pleased to be off more personal subjects, laughed out loud. Right. If she had magical powers she sure as hell would have used them shamelessly to her advantage long before now. Made her father love her more. Made Rob love her more. Made them stay.

'Julian talks about me?'

Despite not wanting to, Alessandro noticed the way her uniform pulled across her chest. The way the slide nestled in her cleavage. It had been such a long time since he'd noticed anything much about a woman at all but it was becoming a habit with this bossy, talkative Australian nurse.

He sent her a tight smile. 'Nonstop.'

Nat grinned. 'Sorry.' But she really wasn't. It made her happy to think she was making a difference to the serious little boy who came to the crèche. She knew she looked out for him on her days there and her heart melted faster than an ice-cube in this damn heat wave, when his sad little face lit up like a New Year's Eve firework display the moment he spotted her.

Alessandro shrugged. 'I'm pleased he...has someone.' Even if hearing her name incessantly meant she was never far from his thoughts. Even if that transferred into the rare moments of sleep he managed to snatch during nights that seemed to last an eternity. Those few precious hours were suddenly full of her. Bizarre erotic snapshots the likes of which he hadn't experienced since puberty.

Just another reason to despise himself a little bit more. Camilla hadn't even been dead a year and he was fantasising about some…look-alike-but-not Australian bossyboots, like a horny teenager.

'He's a great kid, Alessandro.'

Her voice had softened and he could tell she held genuine affection for Julian. He wished his own relationship with his son was as uncomplicated. When he looked at Julian he saw Camilla and his guilt ratcheted up another notch. 'I know.'

And he did know. But he didn't know how to reach a child who was a stranger to him. He didn't know how to look at his son, love his son and pretend that he wasn't the reason Julian's world had been torn apart.

Perhaps if they'd been closer…

They looked at each other for a long moment, the air thick between them with things neither of them were game enough to say aloud. A phone ringing broke the compelling eye contact and it took a few seconds for Nat to realise it wasn't the lift emergency phone but her mobile.

She pulled it out of her pocket. 'Huh, look at that,' she mused. 'Good reception. Go figure.' She looked at the number on the screen and gave an inward groan. Great timing.

It was difficult for Alessandro not to eavesdrop. It was impossible to even pretend he wasn't. There was him and her in a tiny metal box, not much light and nothing else to do. He did try to feign disinterest, pulling his pager out and deleting the build-up of stored messages, but it was obvious she was having problems with her lease.

When Nat pushed the 'end' button on her phone with a grimace he said, *'Problemo?'*

Nat sighed and stuffed the phone back in her pocket. 'You could say that.'

'Sounds like you're having trouble with your landlord.'

Nat gave a derisive snort. 'That's an understatement. I've been given two weeks to move out.'

Alessandro dropped both of his legs, stretching them out in front as he crossed his arms across his chest. 'Let me guess. You have lots of loud parties and are behind on your rent?'

Nat, aware that his legs were a good deal closer now, flicked him a *funny ha-ha* look. The fact that he was even attempting humour wasn't enough to lift her out of the doldrums.

Where the hell was she going to go? 'The owners want to move back in.'

'Can they do that?'

Nat shrugged. 'The lease is up.'

'Ah.'

She sighed. 'Yes. Ah.'

'Have you thought of buying? It's a buyers' market at the moment with the world economic situation and interest rates being at an all-time low. I bought my place in Paddington for a very good price.'

'I have bought a place. A unit not far from St Auburn's. I bought it off the plan. It was supposed to be finished two months ago but with all that winter rain we had it's behind schedule.'

'Ah.'

Nat's legs were starting to cramp in her cross-legged position so she also stretched her legs out, her modest uniform riding up a little and revealing two very well-defined kneecaps and a hint of thigh. 'I only took a six-month lease because the project manager assured me the project would be on time. Damn man is as slippery as an oily snake.'

Alessandro's gaze dropped to the narrow strip of thigh visible between her knees and hemline before he realised what he was doing. He dragged his attention back to her frowning face. 'Do you not have a man, a husband or boyfriend, who can deal with these things for you?'

If she hadn't already been annoyed at the world—heat wave, broken lift, difficult landlord—Nat might have laughed at his typical Italian male assumptions. But unfortunately for Alessandro, she was.

'I don't need a *man* to deal with stuff for me,' she said sharply.

Frankly she was sick of men. It was because of a bloody man she was in this pickle to start with. Eternal spinsterhood was looking like a damn fine alternative these days. Although the presence of a six-foot-nine Neanderthal next time she visited her half-complete unit did hold some appeal.

Alessandro held up his hands in surrender, not wanting to get into a debate about gender roles with her already looking like she was spoiling for a fight. Things were different these days, which was a good thing. And this wasn't Italy. Besides, they might well need to preserve oxygen.

'Have you not got family here you can stay with?'

She shook her head. 'All my family live in Perth. In Western Australia. I've only been in Brisbane for six months.'

'You are a long way from home, Nathalie.'

His voice was low and it slithered across the floor of the lift like a serpent, inching up her leg, under her skirt, gliding across her belly and undulating up her spine, stroking every hot spot in between. She was one giant goose-bump in three seconds flat.

The ease with which he accomplished it was shocking but she was damned if she was going to let her body do the talking. She raised an eyebrow, going for sardonic. '*I'm* a long way from home?'

He chuckled. *Well deflected. 'Touché.'* There were a few moments of silence as they both contemplated the floor. Alessandro had the feeling there was more to the Nat Davies story. He checked his watch. Ten minutes. How much longer?

It seemed stupid to sit in silence.

'So why did you leave Perth? Was there a reason or did you have a crashing desire to see Queensland?'

Nat gave a nonchalant shrug. 'I had a fancy to see the sun rise over the ocean.'

Alessandro smiled at her flippant reply. He was pretty sure it ran deeper than that. It took one damaged soul to recognise another. 'I get the feeling there may have been a man involved?'

Nat contemplated another snappy quip but she'd never been able to pull flippant off for very long. 'There was.'

'What happened?'

Nat repeated her earlier eyebrow rise. 'I think this is where I tell you it's none of your business, isn't it?'

Alessandro nodded his head, a small smile playing on his lips. 'I do believe so, yes.' He shrugged. 'Just trying to pass the time.'

Nat regarded him for a few moments. Why did she feel so compelled to talk to him? One look at him and she lost her mind. She didn't bother to point out they could pass it just as easily by talking about his stuff because frankly she was tired of listening to men talk about women who used to share their lives.

'It became…untenable.' She waited for the barb in her chest to twist again, like it always did when she thought about Rob and their crazy crowded relationship. Her, him and his ex-wife.

Curiously it didn't.

Alessandro nodded. So they were both running away…

'So I left. I didn't plan to leave Perth but then I hadn't planned on it being so hard to still move in the same circles.'

She glanced at him, wondering what he was thinking, wondering if he empathised. Was that why he'd moved to the other side of the world? To escape the memories that were there, waiting around every corner? 'When the property settlement came through I just…left. Took my half and relocated.'

Alessandro nodded. 'That took courage.' He knew how hard it was to up sticks.

'Yeah, well, it doesn't seem so brave now, does it?'

Alessandro crossed one outstretched leg over the other at the ankles. 'Do you have a plan B?'

'The rental market in Brisbane is tight. I only need a couple of months but no one's going to be keen to rent to me for such a short time.'

Alessandro nodded. He'd tried to get a short-term lease so he didn't have to rush into buying but there'd been nothing available and he'd taken the plunge and bought instead.

'I don't really know anyone well enough to crash with them for long periods of time, apart from Paige who I went to school with in Perth. She works in Audiology and part time in the operating theatres at St Auburn's. I stayed with her for a couple of weeks when I first arrived but her husband walked out two years ago and she has a three-year-old with high needs. I can't impose on them again.' She shrugged. 'The short answer is, I don't know. But something will show up. It'll work out, it always does.'

As soon as the words were out the lights flickered on in the lift and the air-conditioning whirred to life. Nat laughed. 'See?'

Alessandro smiled, picking up his pager and stethoscope off the floor as the lift shuddered and began its descent. He vaulted to his feet and held out a hand to her. She hesitated for a fraction and then took it. He pulled her up, the lift settling on the ground floor as she rose to her feet, causing her to stumble a little.

Nat put her hand against his chest to steady herself, aware that his other arm had come around to help. She copped a lungful of something spicy and for a brief dizzying second she considered pushing her nose into the patch of neck his skew tie had revealed to see if she could discern the exact origin. His lips were close and his gaze seemed to be suddenly fixed on her mouth and all she could think about was kissing him.

His heart thudded directly below her palm and the vibrations travelled down her arm, rippling through every nerve ending in her body, energising every cell.

The lift dinged and saved her from totally losing her mind. 'Oops, sorry,' she said, pushing away from him, uncharacteristic colour creeping into her cheeks.

The doors opened and a small crowd of maintenance people as well as department staff were there to greet them, clapping and cheering.

Nat risked a quick glance at him, dismayed at the heat she saw in his eyes again. Her blush intensified. She high-tailed it out of the lift without a backward glance.

Alessandro had not long been home with Julian early that evening when the doorbell rang. He opened it to a middle-aged woman and ushered her in. Debbie Woodruff was the tenth applicant for live-in nanny he'd interviewed.

He had no intention of the crèche being a long-term solution for Julian. Yes, it was open 24 hours a day and Julian seemed to like it there, at least when Nat was on anyway, but he'd already been dragged halfway round the world. His son deserved stability. And that was one thing he could give him.

Debbie seemed very nice and was plainly well qualified. Julian was polite, as always, saying please and thank you as Camilla had taught him, eating carefully, playing quietly. But he wasn't enthused. And Alessandro had to admit he wasn't either.

He wasn't sure what he wanted. Someone to love Julian, he guessed. Not for it just to be another job. A pay cheque. What his son needed was a mother.

His mother.

Guilt seized him as he saw Debbie out. The one thing Julian needed the most, and he couldn't give it to him. It was his job. He was the father. He was supposed to provide for his son.

Alessandro entered the lounge room. Julian looked at him but didn't smile or acknowledge him. He sat next to his son and wished he knew how to bridge the gap. Wished his father had been around to be a role model for him, instead of the distant provider. Wished he hadn't let Camilla distance him from his own son.

He looked down at Julian, who was watching television. 'Did you like her?' he asked.

Julian turned and looked at his father. 'She was okay.'

Hardly a glowing endorsement. 'Have you liked any of them?'

Julian shrugged, looking at him with big, solemn eyes.

'Who do you like?' he asked in frustration.

'Nat,' Julian said, and turned back to the TV.

Of course.

Great. Nat, who couldn't mind her own business. Nat, who spoke her mind. Nat of the lift. Nat of the zipper. Nat, who he'd dreamt about every night since they'd met.

Anyone but her.

Alessandro looked down at his son and sighed. Julian wanted Nat. And that was all that mattered.

Nat it was. That he could do.

CHAPTER THREE

ALESSANDRO spotted Nat at the dining room checkout the next day and hurried towards her. He was just in time to hear the waitress say, 'Eight dollars and twenty cents, please.'

He fished out his wallet and handed over a twenty before Nat had even zipped open her purse. 'Take it out of this,' he said.

Nat felt every nerve ending leap at his unexpected appearance. She glanced back at him, her heart doing a funny shimmy in her chest at his sheer masculinity. She frowned, both at her unwanted response and his motivation to pay for her lunch. 'Thanks. I pay my own way,' she said, presenting her own twenty.

The waitress looked from her to Alessandro and Nat couldn't help but notice that when he wanted to, Alessandro Lombardi could indeed pull a hundred-watt smile. His face went from darkly handsome, deeply tortured widower to blatantly sexy, Roman sex god. His curved lips utterly desirable.

After another stifling night with only a fan that seemed to do nothing other than push the hot air around and little sleep, it was especially irksome.

He pushed his money closer. 'Keep the change,' he murmured.

Nat rolled her eyes as the waitress practically swooned as she reached for his crisp orange note. She stuffed hers back into her purse, picked up her tray in disgust and left him to it. Within seconds she could sense him shadowing her.

'Italian women may think it's charming to be taken care of but I don't,' she said, steaming ahead to a table that overlooked the rose gardens St Auburn's was famous for. 'So don't pull your macho rubbish with me.'

Last time she'd let a man pay for her, she'd been sucked in to wasting five years of her life on him.

Alessandro pulled out her chair for her as she angled herself into it and ignored her glare. 'I wanted to talk to you about Julian. I thought the least I could do was buy you lunch while you listened.'

Nat eyed him across the table. She folded her arms. She was damned if the man didn't already know her Achilles heel. She'd spent the morning with Julian and he hadn't seemed any worse than normal. Not that that was much re-assurance. 'Is he okay?'

Alessandro's gaze was drawn to the way her crossed arms emphasised the shape of her breasts. She was in crèche clothes today—shorts and T-shirt—and he noticed how her shirt displayed their full, round shape to perfection. He wondered for the hundredth time how they'd feel in his hands. In his mouth.

Damn it!

That wasn't why he was here. He was here for Julian. Not for himself. But it was fair warning that gave him pause. Nat would be very distracting should she be crazy enough to agree to his plan.

'Of course,' he dismissed, annoyed at himself. Seeing her confusion, he hastily added, 'I just wanted to ask you something.'

Nat opened up her packaged egg and lettuce sandwiches and took a bite, intrigued despite herself. 'Ask away.'

If anything, he looked more tired than she'd ever seen him. His hair look more tousled, like he'd been continually running his hands through it, and the furrows in his forehead were more prominent.

'How come you work at both the crèche and the hospital?'

She quirked an eyebrow. Not quite what she'd been expecting. 'You have to ask me that after Ernie?'

He regarded her for a moment. 'So it's a self-preservation strategy?'

'I prefer to call it a happy medium. Too many hospital shifts and I get burnt out. But I miss it if I'm away too long.'

'The best of both worlds?'

She shrugged. 'I like to temper the Ernie days with the Julian days. Both workplaces let me have permanent shifts. No weekends, no night duty. Two days at St Auburn's gives me my hospital hit, keeps my hand in, let's me know I'm alive. Three days at the crèche restores my sanity. It keeps me Zen.'

Alessandro considered her statement. How many years had it been since he'd felt Zen? Definitely not for the last five years at least. Definitely not with her keeping him constantly off balance. 'Do you have child-care qualifications too?'

She narrowed her eyes. Why did this suddenly feel like a job interview? 'I've done my certificate and have a child health qualification.' She cracked open the lid on her can of soft drink and eyed him over the top as she brought it to her mouth and took a swallow. 'Why?'

Alessandro noticed the sheen to her lips and the way her tongue slid between them, lapping at the lingering moisture. He wondered what guava-and-mango-flavoured Nat tasted like.

Inferno! Concentrate, damn it!

He cleared his throat. 'I think I have a solution to your eviction situation.'

Nat felt his gaze on her mouth as if he had actually pressed his lips to hers. Her eyes dropped of their own volition to inspect his. They were generous, soft. Lips made for kissing, made for whispering.

'Oh, yes?' she said cautiously, dragging her attention back to his eyes. Eyes that told her he knew exactly where hers had been.

'You can stay with me.' He watched her pupils dilate and her glance encompass his mouth once again. 'And Julian.'

The canteen noises around them faded as his suggestion stunned her. Live under his roof? A man who, fully clothed, grim faced and utterly inaccessible, made her heart flutter like an epileptic butterfly? What the hell could he do to her in his own place, where the pretence of professionalism didn't exist? Where he'd be all relaxed and homey and…wearing less. What did he wear to bed? She had the feeling he'd be a nothing kind of guy.

'Just until you're unit is built, of course.'

Nat blinked as her mind shied away from images of Alessandro in bed. Naked. 'But…why? I barely know you.'

Alessandro shrugged. 'I have the room, you need a place. And you'd be doing me a favour, helping with Julian. I haven't been able to find a suitable live-in nanny and Julian adores you.'

She frowned. 'You want me to be a…nanny? I already have a job. Two, actually. Which, by the way, I love.'

Alessandro shook his head. 'No. I don't expect you to give up your jobs. Julian can still go to the crèche but he could go and come home with you, which means he wouldn't have such long days there. And he wouldn't have to go on weekends and when I'm called in at night.'

Nat listened to his plan, which sounded very reasonable. So why did it seem so…illicit?

'I'd pay you, of course. And it would be rent free.'

Of course. Nat reeled, her brain scrambling to take in his offer. She looked at him all big and dark and handsome and completely macho Italian with the added grimness that made him heart-breakingly attractive. She didn't know much right at this second but she did know saying yes to Alessandro Lombardi was a very stupid idea.

'No.'

Alessandro's brows drew together. 'You've had another offer?'

Nat contemplated lying. But it really wasn't her way. Already her cheeks were growing warm just formulating a falsehood. 'No.'

He shrugged. 'Then it's settled.'

Nat looked at the haughty set to his jaw and bristled at his arrogant assumptions. 'No.'

'I don't understand. What's the problem?'

The problem was that Alessandro Lombardi was a very attractive man. The mere thought of sharing a living space with him was breathtakingly intimate and already her pulse raced at the thought. She knew enough about herself to know she had a soft heart. And he was still in love with his dead wife. And she wasn't stupid enough to get herself embroiled in that kind of scenario again.

'Ah,' he said as she averted her eyes from him. 'You worry about what people will think? You have my word I have no ulterior motive. I have no…' He searched for the right word, looking her up and down with as much dispassion as he could muster. 'Agenda. Your virtue is safe with me.'

Because it was. His attraction was just physical, a combination of libido and abstinence. Easily tamed.

Nat felt his gaze rake her from head to toe and obviously found her wanting. She felt about as attractive as a bug. One of the really ugly ones. It wasn't something she was used to. 'Gossip does not bother me.'

'Then what?'

She stared at him exasperated. The man was obviously not used to hearing no. 'I don't have to account to you, Alessandro,' she said testily, placing her packaging back on her tray and rising. She wished she had any other reason for turning him down other than his irresistible sex appeal.

But she had nothing. 'I'm sure you're quite unused to hearing the word no. I'm sure you just snap your fingers and women fall all over themselves to do your bidding. But I'm not one of them. The answer is no. Just plain no. No equivocations, no justifications. Just no. Get used to it.'

Alessandro couldn't believe what he was hearing. She was right, once upon a time he had been a finger snapper but that had all ended with Camilla. She turned to leave and he reached across, grabbing her arm. 'Wait. I'm sorry, Nathalie, I didn't mean to be so…'

Nat shivered. She didn't know if it was from his touch or the way her name sighed from his lips like a caress. She turned back. He seemed so perplexed and she felt her anger dissipate as quickly as it had risen. 'Italian?'

Alessandro smiled and dropped his hand. 'You have knowledge of Italian men.'

'I lived in Milano for a year. A long time ago now.'

Ah, that explained her grasp of his language. 'There was a man there?'

Nat gave a wistful smile. She'd lost her virginity in Italy. She'd been eighteen and hopelessly enamoured. 'A boy. It didn't last long. I was a little too…independent for him.'

He nodded. 'So you know we're not very good at asking for things.'

A shard of a memory made her smile broader. 'I don't know. I seemed to remember he was very good at asking for some things.' It had been a heady few months.

Alessandro gave her a grim smile, inordinately jealous at the tilt of her lips and the far-away look in her eyes. 'I meant help. Italian men like to be…men. Yes?'

Nat returned to the present. Yes. She did know that.

'I need help with Julian. We are not…close. Since his mother died…it's been difficult. He doesn't let me in… he's very unhappy.'

Nat swallowed at the raw ache in his voice. It clawed at her soft spot. 'His mother just died, Alessandro. He's grieving, just like you. He's allowed to be unhappy. There would be something wrong if he wasn't. He needs time.'

Alessandro shut his eyes briefly against the pity he saw in her gaze, her words stabbing into his soul. If only she knew. 'I can't bear to see him like this. He likes you,

Nat. He smiles, laughs when he's around you. I miss hearing him laugh.'

Nat felt helpless, trapped by eyes that were deep black wells of despair. She'd seen him with his son, maybe had judged him harshly. Too harshly. At least he seemed willing to try. At least he wanted to reach out to Julian.

'Please, Nathalie. If you don't feel you can for you, please do it for Julian.'

His plea was so heartfelt it oozed past every defence she had. She stood staring hopelessly at him, like a rabbit caught in headlights. Knowing she should run like the wind but powerless to do so.

Alessandro saw the compassion in her eyes and knew he'd touched her, could see that he'd struck a chord. 'He needs a woman's touch, Nat. A mother.'

His words stuck in her tightened throat, dragging her out of the compassionate quicksand she'd been sucked into. A mother? She shook her head. He was wrong. Didn't he know that children needed their fathers too? That without their father's love they grew up only half the person they could be? Always wondering. Always yearning.

Damn it—she'd known them for a fortnight. She didn't owe this man anything. Or his little boy. They weren't her responsibility. He wanted to take the easy way out? Use her so he could remain emotionally distant? So he didn't have to try? A substitute mother? He wanted her to be his enabler? She wouldn't. Julian needed his father, just as she had needed hers, and she would not let Alessandro shirk his duties as her father had shirked his.

He had to find a way through this himself. A way to connect with his son. One day he would thank her for it.

She took a deep breath, gathering her courage, breaking away from the spell he'd woven with his beautiful accent and his tragic gaze. 'Children need their fathers too.'

And she turned and walked away, not looking back. She had to protect herself. Alessandro and Julian were a delightful package, right up her bleeding-heart alley. Too easy to fall for.

She'd barely recovered from her last relationship. A man who had claimed to love her yet all the while had still been entangled with his ex-wife. She knew how vulnerable her heart was and she'd be stupid to repeat that mistake again.

So she didn't turn back, even though she could feel his gaze boring a hole between her shoulder blades. Even though her marshmallow centre blazed hot and gooey, berating her for her callousness, urging her to turn around.

It was time to protect herself for a change. Long past time.

Alessandro was more aware of her than he'd ever been when he picked Julian up from the crèche at five that afternoon. It was one of the first days he'd managed to get away on time and Nat was still there. In fact, Julian and Nat were sitting at a table doing a jigsaw puzzle.

It was hard to look at her and know that he had laid himself bare to her, taken a leap of faith, and been rejected. He supposed he was as proud as the next man, maybe prouder. He certainly didn't make a habit of asking anyone for help. He certainly wouldn't again.

He strode towards them, stopping a few feet away. 'Come, Julian, it's time to go.'

Nat's gaze travelled all the way up to the forbidding planes of Alessandro's regal face, etched with lines of tiredness, his beautiful mouth a bleak line. He barely acknowledged her, barely acknowledged his son. He obviously hadn't taken her rejection well.

But she had no intention of letting him take his disappointment out on her or his son. She climbed out of the low kiddy chair and stood. 'Julian, matey, why don't you go and get the picture you drew for your papa today?'

He nodded a silent assent and she watched his unhurried pace as he made his way, slump-shouldered, to his open wooden locker. No welcoming embrace for his father, no jubilant tearing around at the thought of going home. She glanced at Alessandro and caught him also tracking his son's movements.

'He drew a picture especially for you,' she murmured.

Julian hadn't seemed overly excited when she'd suggested that he draw a picture of Papa at work but, then, excited just wasn't a state he ever seemed to inhabit. But he'd attacked the picture with vigour and had spent a long time getting it right, choosing the colours carefully, brightening up the background. And when he'd showed it to her she could see pride and accomplishment in his dark little eyes, so like the ones in front of her.

Alessandro pulled his gaze back to her. 'That's nice.'

Nat cringed at the politeness of his tone but refused to be swayed. She was offering him a chance to bridge the gap with his son. 'You want to know how to connect, Alessandro?' She kept her voice low. 'It's not that hard. Smile at him, touch him, praise him. Show some affection.'

Alessandro felt each suggestion slice into him. If only it was that simple. Camilla was dead because of him. Could any amount of affection make up for that? How could Julian ever forgive him? He clenched his jaw, refusing to comment. Nat could not possibly understand what they'd been through.

He was conscious of her beside him—silent, judge-mental—as Julian made his way back to them. He stopped in front of them and held out the picture. Alessandro took it. He didn't want to, he wanted to throw it aside and sweep the boy into his arms, but the memory of Julian's stiff little stance from months ago still clawed at his gut. He couldn't bear two rejections in one day.

Alessandro's gaze went instead to the picture. It was done in crayon. The background was red and purple and quite cheery. The sun shone in one corner and there were trees with possums. The detail was remarkable.

He was in the foreground, nothing more than a stick figure with a stethoscope around his neck, his mouth a grim slash in his otherwise nondescript face. An adult, maybe Nathalie, had written across the bottom in neat teacher handwriting—'*My papa is a doctor. He works very hard.*'

Alessandro gripped the page hard. *That was it?*

Nat was too busy watching Julian to notice the play of emotions across Alessandro's face or the way the paper tore slightly beneath the vice-like grip of his fingers. The little boy's expression was heart-breaking. He was looking up at his father with such hope, his face full of anticipation.

'That's wonderful, Julian,' Alessandro forced out through the chokehold around his throat.

As Nat watched, Alessandro patted his son on the head and Julian's face broke into a broad grin, happy for even that tiny crumb of affection. Not that Alessandro noticed, his gaze still firmly fixed to the picture.

She couldn't believe what she was seeing. She suddenly wished she'd let Julian do rock art so she could beat Alessandro around the head with it. What the hell was the matter with him? Couldn't he see his kid was crying out for love, dying to be swept up and showered in his father's adoration?

It was like her childhood all over again. Once her father had moved on to his new family it hadn't seemed to matter what she'd done, he'd never seemed to notice. And it had hurt—man, had it hurt.

Alessandro dragged his attention away from the picture, his heart heavy. 'Come on, Julian. Get your stuff, it's time to go.'

Nat shook her head. That was it. She couldn't stand watching this…farce of a relationship any longer. Alessandro was obviously clueless. Someone had to teach him how to be a father. And regardless of every flashing light blaring at her, regardless of the attraction that simmered between them, she knew she had to be the one.

She just couldn't witness Julian's emotional isolation one second longer. She couldn't bear him to go through what she'd been through. It was like an arrow through her heart.

'Can I move my stuff in on the weekend?' she asked as Julian's lacklustre pace obeyed his father's instructions. 'There isn't much. Most of its in storage.'

Alessandro was wound so tight it took a couple of seconds for her question to penetrate the barbed wire he leashed his thoughts with. His head snapped around. Had he really just heard what he thought he'd heard? Her gaze was open, steady. It took him all of about two seconds to realise she was deadly serious.

Suddenly the tension that had been holding every muscle taut since she'd rejected him earlier, since Camilla had died, since before then even, since their hasty nuptials, relaxed. It was as if she'd taken bulk cutters and hacked through barbed-wire in one fell swoop.

Everything was going to be all right.

Alessandro nodded. 'That would be most suitable.' He delved into his pocket and handed her a card. 'My number.'

Nat took it hesitantly. For someone who had just got precisely what he'd wanted, she couldn't tell the damn difference. His gaze was carefully masked but she saw the flare in his pupils at the same time she felt a corresponding thrum in her blood as their fingers brushed.

The intensity frightened the hell out of her. 'This is purely business,' she said, lowering her voice. 'Nothing but convenience.'

Alessandro didn't have to ask her to explain. He got the subtext loud and clear. Her husky voice, the slight tremble in her finger tips, the brief widening of her eyes. He knew she was as tuned into their vibe as he was. He bowed slightly. 'Of course.'

He opened his mouth to elaborate further, to assure her, as he had that morning, that her virtue was safe, but Julian joined them and Alessandro nodded at her briefly, said, 'Until tomorrow,' and bade her goodbye.

Nat looked at the card, the pads of her fingers still burning, and wondered what the hell she's got herself into.

Nat pushed the doorbell to the enormous house on a Saturday morning that was already proving to be another scorcher. Her hair fluttered as a warm breeze whipped through the shady portico. She felt jittery but forced herself to concentrate on the wind's caress.

The door flung open and Julian stood there, his curls

bouncing slightly as his body trembled with what she could only describe as excitement. Or the nearest thing she'd ever seen in this little boy.

'Nat!' he exclaimed. His dark eyes, so like his father's, literally sparkled as he shifted from foot to foot. 'Papa told me this morning you're coming to live here.'

Nat couldn't help be infected by his barely suppressed enthusiasm. 'Just until my house is finished, matey.'

He grabbed her hand and dragged her inside. 'I hope it never finishes,' he declared.

'Gee, thanks.' Nat laughed as a cloud of cool air enveloped her, instantly dispelling the heat and stroking her exposed arms and legs with icy fingers. She looked up and saw the recessed vent in the ceiling. Ducted air-conditioning. She closed her eyes against the pleasure.

Bliss—instant bliss.

Her eyes fluttered open as Julian again tugged at her hand and she looked around at the large entrance area dominated by white walls, white tiles, white carpet and a large white staircase. She could see boxes left and right in her peripheral vision.

'Come on. I'll show you my room. You're right next door.'

'Julian.'

Julian dropped her hand as Nat glanced up to find Alessandro lounging in a doorway directly to her left, a mug in hand. He was wearing a snug white T-shirt that emphasised the rich golden colour of his skin and every muscle in his chest. His trendy khaki cargo-style shorts rode low on his hips. His feet were bare.

The man had a rumpled look about him, his hair tousled, his jaw unshaven. He looked like he hadn't slept very much and that she could relate to. She'd been awake half the night regretting her decision.

He held her gaze through thick dark lashes and she felt a rush of warmth to places that not even the air-conditioning could cool down.

'Don't crowd Nathalie.'

She opened her mouth to tell him not to call her that. She couldn't live under his roof if he was going to caress her name with his lips like that every time he addressed her. But she saw Julian's excitement ebb and decided to drop it. For now.

'I would love to see your room. Then I have a surprise for you.'

Julian smiled at her and grabbed her hand again, pulling her towards the ugly monolith that passed as a staircase. She could feel Alessandro's eyes on her as they ascended and forced herself to walk, not run.

Alessandro tracked her path up. She was wearing her standard attire of shorts and T-shirt. Neither were particularly risqué. The mocha shorts came to mid-thigh, the T-shirt was neither low cut or excessively clingy. But there was something about the sway of her hips and the bob of her ponytail that tightened his groin.

Hell. He pushed off the wall and headed straight for the coffee pot.

Nat couldn't believe the clinical wasteland Julian and Alessandro lived in. It was all white—everywhere she looked—and littered with unpacked boxes. Most of the five upstairs bedrooms, two lounge areas and what she presumed was a study were practically bare—except for a few essential pieces of furniture and, of course, the ever-present boxes.

Julian's room wasn't much better, with a bed, a bedside table with a lamp and a couple of books spread on the floor.

There was no colour, no bright quilt or curtains. In fact, there hadn't even been any curtains hung at all. Which made the white of the room even starker as the bright sunlight pushed through the glass.

Maybe Alessandro's wife had been one of those minimalist freaks?

She must have betrayed her feelings because Julian said, 'We haven't got round to unpacking yet. Papa's been very busy.'

Nat's heart nearly broke at the defensive tone and his worried frown. She gave him a bright smile. 'That's okay. I'm here now. I can help with that stuff.'

Julian brightened. 'Your room is next door.'

They went in and she plastered a huge smile on her face as Julian looked at her for any signs of dislike. The room, like Julian's, had a bed and a bedside table. No curtains. But it did have a vent in the middle of the ceiling and it was blissfully cool. 'It's perfect,' she said.

They were walking out when Julian stopped in the hallway and turned to face the end. 'That's Papa's room.'

He pointed to the closed door like it was a forbidden kingdom. Nat bit back her disapproval. Man, Alessandro was clueless. A far-away room dominated by a closed door? What the hell did he think his son, his four-year-old son, would read into that?

She really did have her work cut out for her.

Nat gave his shoulder a squeeze. 'Want that surprise now?'

Julian looked up at her and nodded enthusiastically, a wide grin firmly in place. She smiled back at him and they made their way downstairs.

'Wait here, it's in the car.' Nat injected a conspiratorial note into her voice.

She was back at the door in a minute—thankfully. The heat seemed even worse after the cool ecstasy of Alessandro's house. She stuck her head round. Julian was waiting there, anticipation lighting his dark features.

'Shut your eyes,' she requested. 'Hold out your hands.' Julian obeyed instantly. 'No peeking,' Nat warned as she adjusted the package in her arms and passed it gently into Julian's waiting arms.

Julian eyes flew open. 'A cat.'

He looked at Nat with utter wonder and squeezed the animal close, rubbing his face into her soft fur. Flo purred appreciatively. In his excitement he even forgot about the weird stiltedness between him and his father and called out to him.

'Papa, Papa, look, a cat. Nat has brought her cat.'

Alessandro appeared in the same doorway as before. Great. A cat. He regarded it warily. Pinocchio had been Camilla's cat and had positively hated him.

'You didn't say anything about a cat,' he murmured, keeping it low for his son's benefit. Not that it mattered. Julian was totally preoccupied by the ball of fur purring like an engine in his arms.

Nat raised an eyebrow at his disapproving frown. 'You're allergic?'

'No.'

Ah. 'If the cat goes, I go.'

Alessandro sighed. He believed her. And how could he deny his son the obvious pleasure? 'The cat's fine. Just keep it out of my room.'

Nat didn't think that would be much of a problem. Flo wasn't one for wasting her time on people who didn't care for her. Especially not when there was a little boy who was obviously going to dote on her.

They watched him for a few moments. 'I trust your room is to your liking?' Alessandro enquired.

To her liking? That was a bit optimistic. 'It's fine. Thank you.'

Alessandro had heard the word *fine* enough in his marriage to know that coming from a woman's lips it didn't always mean fine. *'Problemo?'*

Nat hesitated. But, hell—she had to live here. 'Is there a reason for all the white?'

Alessandro frowned. He looked around. He supposed it was a bit stark. 'No. There's plenty of colourful things— paintings, rugs and so on in the boxes. I just haven't had a chance to unpack yet. This is the first weekend I've had at home since I started at St Auburn's.'

'So you won't object to me adding a bit of…colour, then? I can unpack the boxes if you like.'

'I don't expect you to do that,' he dismissed.

She shrugged. 'It's the least I can do for free rent.' And it wasn't good for Julian to live in such a cold space, devoid of warmth.

He looked at his son, still talking to the cat like a new best friend. 'You're here for Julian, not to be a housekeeper.'

She shot him a pained expression. 'Alessandro, if I have to live in this white palace for even a day, I'm going to go snow blind. Please let me do this.'

Alessandro gave her a grudging smile. Funny how he hadn't really noticed it until she'd pointed it out. 'As you wish.'

Frankly, if she could make Julian this happy in just a few minutes she could paint rainbows all over the house and sprinkle it with glitter.

CHAPTER FOUR

ALESSANDRO and Julian helped her carry her meagre belongings up from the car. Alessandro withdrew the minute the job was done and she had to admit to being relieved. His presence in her room was too…dominant and she found herself questioning her sanity—yet again.

Julian hovered while she unpacked, leaping at the chance to help her distribute her bits and pieces around the room. Then Flo entered the room and he sat on the floor with the cat nestled in his lap, happy to just observe as he petted the purring animal.

A lava lamp brightened things up considerably in the stark room, as did the orange and russet bedding. Her Turkish rug covered most of the hideous white carpet and Impressionists prints along with her much-loved Venetian masks added colour to the walls. Finally she looped some rich purple gauzy fabric she'd bought in China along the curtain rod, letting it drape haphazardly over the bare window.

She stood back and admired her work. Not bad for an hour's work. At least the room no longer looked like the inside of an igloo.

'What do you reckon?' she asked Julian.

Julian beamed at her, raising Flo to his face and stroking his chin along the top of her soft head. 'It's… beautiful,' he sighed.

Nat laughed. The awe in his voice was priceless. 'Do you think you could do this to my room? Make it like my old one? Before Mummy died?'

Nat felt her heart lurch in her chest at his matter-of-fact words. She scanned his face for signs of distress or grief but found none. Instead, he was looking at her as if she were Mary Poppins and had done it all with a snap of her fingers.

'Sure,' she replied. 'We'll go through the boxes tomorrow and see if we can find all your stuff.'

Nat heard Flo's half-hearted protesting miaow as Julian bounced on his haunches and squeezed her a little too tight. His eyes sparkled and he looked like a normal excited four-year-old.

And she knew in an instant that coming to live under Alessandro's roof had been the right thing.

'Right. Well. I'm starving.' She looked at the slim rose-gold watch that adorned her wrist. Midday. She saw Julian yawn in her peripheral vision and his eyes drift shut briefly as he continued to rub his chin against Flo's head. They'd been having such fun she'd forgotten he was only four and still needed his afternoon sleep.

She realised he would need lunch before going down for his nap. 'Boy, look at the time! Let's get something to eat.'

Julian followed her down the stairs, Flo bundled up in his arms, purring loudly as she wallowed in cat heaven. He led her to the kitchen and Nat braced herself to face Alessandro again. He was working on a laptop at the dining table, which was through an archway to the right off the massive gourmet kitchen gleaming in all its stainless-steel and white-tiled glory.

Alessandro looked up from the recent on-line health alerts from the Australian government concerning the spread of the deadly swamp flu which, due to international travel, could easily be on Australia's shores before they knew it. If he was going to be treating cases of it in his emergency department, he wanted to be forearmed.

Julian was smiling and chatting away and Nat's cheeks were all pink as she conversed with Julian. 'I trust you've settled in?'

Nat nodded, her gaze settling on his broad shoulders. 'Yes, thank you. Julian and I are going to attack his room tomorrow.'

Alessandro nodded. 'As you wish. I'll locate his boxes and take them up there in the morning.'

'Thank you.'

His gaze held hers, boring into her, like he already knew her, and she suddenly felt out of breath. A lock of hair fell across his forehead and her fingers tingled with the desire to push it back. She could actually see herself doing it in some weird slow-motion flash. Except he didn't have a shirt on. And neither did she.

Nat dragged her gaze away and nervously looked around for something to do. Anything. The stainless-steel fridge was right there and she reached for the door with relish. 'I was just going to make some lunch for Julian and I before he goes down for his nap.'

She stared in the fridge unseeingly for a moment while her pulse settled and her knickers unknotted. 'Shall I make you something as well?' she twittered.

'There's not a whole lot there, I'm afraid. I really need to do a proper shop.'

Nat blinked as the contents, or lack of them, slowly came in to focus. She blinked again. *Now, that was the understatement of the year.* She turned to him. 'What have you guys been living on?'

Alessandro shrugged. He hated shopping. Camilla had always taken care of that. Nothing had been right since she'd gone. 'I usually just pick up a few bits and pieces after work every second day or so.'

Nat pursed her lips. 'Hmmm.' She shut the fridge and glanced briefly at Alessandro. She located the pantry and found it similarly devoid of food. It was obvious they'd just been living from day to day. Was the man totally clueless? Didn't Alessandro know that kids needed a sense of permanency, long-term planning to feel secure? Especially ones whose whole lives had just fallen apart?

'Looks like we go shopping after your nap.'

Julian beamed. 'Can I ride in the trolley? Mummy used to let me ride in the trolley.'

She glanced at Alessandro and saw him visibly pale, his face possibly the grimmest she'd seen yet. She supposed he only used a basket to shop for his bits and pieces and that would seem rather boring to a four-year-old.

Her heart ached anew for both of them. Julian was too young to understand the things that his father was struggling with. 'Yes, you can ride in the trolley. Maybe Papa would like to come with us?'

Nat watched as both father and son tensed. Julian turned hopeful eyes on hers before he looked away, rubbing his chin along Flo's head, and she had to stop herself from going to him and pulling him close.

Alessandro watched in despair as his son fell silent and his little shoulders stiffened. He'd hoped if he didn't push, if he gave his son room and space, that Julian would turn to him eventually but hearing the word *Mummy* fall from his lips had been like a knife plunging deep into his gut and twisting mercilessly. Maybe his son would never let him closer? Maybe Julian also blamed him for Camilla's death?

'I have these journals to catch up on,' Alessandro said, turning back to his lap-top.

Nat stared at two downcast heads. So alike but so disconnected from each other. For a second she felt helpless, but not for long. These two needed intervention and it seemed the universe had decreed she was the one to do it. And she wanted Julian to be close to his father. She wanted to give the little boy the gift of the father-child relationship. She didn't want Julian growing up feeling somehow not whole, as she had. She would never wish those feelings of isolation on anyone, never mind a small child.

But it was plain neither of them were going to make it easy. *She sure had her work cut out for her.*

Alessandro followed the sound of chatter and his nose into the kitchen around five o'clock. The smell of garlic and basil, the aromas of his childhood, and Julian's laughter drew him and he was powerless to resist.

Nat and Julian were cooking. Julian was sitting on the bench next to the cook top, a large metal spoon in hand, stirring something in a saucepan as he fired a hundred questions at Nat. He could see the backs of her long legs, the outline of one very cute derrière and the swish of her ponytail as she chopped and talked and dipped her finger into the saucepan, savouring the taste.

'More salt, Julian.'

Alessandro watched as Julian picked up the salt grinder and handled it as well as a four-year-old could be expected to. He was concentrating hard, his little pink tongue caught between his teeth. It was awkward and he dropped it. Nat was quick, though, and saved it from landing in the pot.

'That's fabulous, Juliano.'

It was on the tip of his tongue to reprimand her for using the Italian form of his name. Despite Camilla insisting it appear on his birth certificate, she actually hated it and had insisted their son be called the anglicised version. But right now he couldn't deny how good it was to hear his son's name being pronounced in the way of his ancestors.

And Julian was smiling at her, swinging his legs as they dangled over the edge of the counter. He was enjoying himself and Alessandro didn't have the heart to spoil that.

'Something smells good.'

Nat faltered as he announced his unexpected presence. She felt every molecule in her body stand to attention. Her nipples jutted against the lacy fabric of her bra, as hard as bullets. Julian's chatter ceased instantly and she noticed his legs stopped swinging in her peripheral vision.

Alessandro noticed it too but steadfastly ignored it as he pushed into the kitchen. 'What are you cooking, Julian?' he asked.

Julian shrugged. 'Spaghetti. The proper stuff. From Milano.'

Alessandro's heart nearly stopped at the perfect way Julian pronounced Milan. He'd always hoped any child of his would be bilingual but Camilla had been adamant.

'Ah.' Alessandro kept his tone light. 'The proper stuff tastes best.'

Camilla hadn't been much of a cook. She'd normally bought pre-prepared food from exclusive delicatessens or supermarkets. Julian had certainly been the best-fed toddler in London, with gourmet treasures bestowed on him every day. When they'd entertained it had always been catered.

But not only had Nat filled his fridge and his pantry and their lives in just half a day but she'd also filled his kitchen with incredible aromas. His stomach growled and he absently realised he was hungry. He couldn't remember the last time he'd eaten for any other reason than as fuel to keep his body going.

When he'd given her his card to go shopping that afternoon he'd imagined she'd buy enough food to get them through the week, but she'd gone way beyond that. He'd helped them unpack and had been amazed at the items she'd considered necessities.

She'd apologised profusely for the amount she'd spent. He had shrugged it away—money wasn't any impediment for him. Besides, when you'd lost all that he'd lost, it truly meant nothing.

Nat felt rather than saw Alessandro lounge a hip against the bench not far from her. She could also sense that the lovely homey atmosphere from a minute ago had vanished. Julian was tense and she couldn't bear to see a four-year-old so…stiff.

Flo chose that moment to rub against her legs and miaow loudly. *Bless her!* 'Julian, sweetie, would you like to feed Flo?'

Julian brightened. 'Could I?'

'Of course. You know where her bowl is in the laundry and you know where the little sachets of food we bought for her today are. Maybe your papa could help you open one and he could show you how to feed her?'

Nat glanced at Alessandro, praying he'd take the bait. The long journey back to each other had to start with one step.

Alessandro considered her for a moment. Tendrils of hair had escaped her ponytail and framed her face in almost angelic frothery. 'Good idea,' he said, holding her gaze for a moment longer before skirting her and approaching his son. He grabbed an unprotesting Julian under the arms and swung him down to the floor.

'Where's this food, then, Julian?'

Nat kept stirring, not daring to turn around or interfere in any way. Their conversation was hardly natural—in fact, it was so stilted she wanted to cry—but they had to start somewhere. She was relieved though when Julian called Flo and they both left the kitchen. Her shoulders were aching and she slumped a little as the tension left the room and headed to the laundry.

Five minutes later, though, he was back. He didn't have to say a word, she could just feel the hairs of her nape standing to attention. She turned and saw him watching her from the doorway, all dark and brooding, his shadowed gaze heavy against her chest. 'That was quick,' she murmured, turning back to the spaghetti.

'He seemed much more interested in the cat.'

She stirred the sauce. 'That will fade. Give him time.'

Alessandro approached. This was a great angle but he preferred her front. Her open gaze, her perfect mouth. He turned as he reached the bench so his backside leant against it, facing in the opposite direction from her. 'It smells great.'

'Thank you. I figured I couldn't go too far wrong in this house with some pasta and sauce.'

Alessandro allowed a ghost of a smile settle on his lips. He turned so his hip nudged the bench and he was on his side, facing her. 'May I?'

Nat nodded. She stepped back a pace as Alessandro quickly dipped his finger in the sauce. She watched fascinated as it disappeared past his lips, his mouth slowly revealing a totally clean finger.

Damn. It was good. Almost as good as her dilated pupils as her eyes had followed his actions. 'Hmm,' he murmured, licking his lips to savour the residue as he held her gaze. 'You've done this before.'

Nat took a second to pull her body back into line but her voice was still annoyingly husky. 'My host mother in Milano taught me her secret family recipe for Napolitano sauce.'

Ah. Definitely the aromas of his childhood. 'You don't have to cook, you know. Or clean. Or unpack boxes.'

Pleased to be back on firmer ground, she nodded. 'I know. But I enjoy it. It's not much fun cooking for one. I usually don't bother, I'm afraid.'

In truth she missed cooking. And all the other homey things about being a couple. She'd loved cooking for Rob, they'd loved cooking together. It felt good to be doing it again. Even if it this wasn't any kind of cosy, lovey-dovey relationship.

His gaze on hers was intense and rather unnerving in his grim-faced way. She broke their connection, looking down into the saucepan and giving it another stir. 'I still think it's missing something,' she muttered as she tried to collect herself, blunt herself to his wounded charm.

She dipped the spoon in, blew on it out of habit and

brought it to her lips, sipping the rich sauce and not tasting it at all. His eyes were still on her and he was making her nervous. Her hand trembled and the spoon tilted, spilling some of the lukewarm sauce down her chest. It landed on the soft swell of cleavage just visible above the v of her neckline.

Her eyes flew to his, startled by the occurrence. His gaze had already sought it out, tracking the slow trek of the sauce as it unhurriedly made its way south. He licked his lips, involuntarily, she thought as his heated look enveloped her in a raging stupor.

All she could do was watch as he openly stared. Her nipples were the only things moving, scrunching as his hot gaze lapped fire at her skin.

Alessandro could no more have ignored the dictates of his body than flown to the moon. He wanted to taste it, taste her, so badly he couldn't think of anything else. 'I'm good with ingredients. Let me try.'

His voice was like sludge oozing over her and she didn't stop him, just shut her eyes as his head lowered and his mouth closed over the swell of her breast as his tongue lapped at the sauce.

Someone groaned. Was it her? Or him? Looking down at his dark head, she had an insane urge to bury her fingers in his hair, hold him there. Arch her back. Beg for more.

Alessandro felt a strange spiralling out of control as Nat's ripe flesh almost flowered beneath his tongue as he ran lazy strokes over the tempting swell. She tasted sweet and spicy and very addictive. Elicit. Heady.

'Nat, is it okay if Flo goes outside?'

Alessandro lifted his head as if he'd been zapped with a cattle prod, moving away a few paces as Julian's voice called to them from the other room. What the hell was wrong with him? He had his head in the cleavage of someone he barely knew when his wife hadn't even been dead a year.

Julian's mother.

'Sure it is,' Nat called. She'd spun back to face the cook top, desperately trying to ignore how her skin still flamed where Alessandro's mouth had been.

Julian entered the kitchen, oblivious to the ragged-breath adults, Flo in his arms. 'She ate up all her fish and milk but I think she wants to play.'

Nat turned to face him, plastering a smile over the confusion storming her body. 'Of course she does. Flo loves the great outdoors.'

Alessandro gripped the bench at her blatantly husky tone. 'Not too long, Julian,' he said tersely, distracted by his stupidity. 'Dinner isn't far away.'

Nat saw the confusion in Julian's eyes at his father's harsh tone and watched as he bit into his bottom lip. 'It's okay,' she said gently. 'I'll call you when it's ready.'

Julian nodded, looking deflated, and slumped off. She turned to Alessandro to chide him for his reaction. Yes, she understood where it had come from, but Julian was only four. Except he was gone. Nothing but air where he'd been. She looked to the right in time to see the broadness of his shoulders as he strode out the archway and out of reach.

Nat stayed in the lounge room till late, watching television that night, too keyed up to sleep. Julian had long since gone to bed and Alessandro, who, apart from a brief appearance to help them search for another knife, fork and plate in the mountain of boxes and eat his dinner, had taken his laptop into his equally barren study and not come out.

A light movie was on and Nat had a headache from forcing herself to concentrate on it and not on what had happened in the kitchen earlier. But force herself she did. What had occurred could never occur again. There was no point building castles in the air with a man who was obviously still so messed up over his dead wife that he hadn't even been able to look at her.

No matter how much he stirred her pulse and her senses and every feminine instinct she had. It was time to rely on other instincts—survival instincts.

The movie ended and she reluctantly made her way to bed. Alessandro's door was open at the end of the corridor, she noticed, but doggedly diverted her attention from it. She checked on Juliano, half expecting to find Flo still curled up with him, but the warm spot where the cat had obviously recently been lying was vacant. She pulled up his covers and turned out his lamp.

She wondered into her bedroom, expecting to see Flo stretched out on her bed. But, no, the cat wasn't anywhere in the bedroom. She knew she wasn't downstairs because she'd just come from there.

'Flo?' she whispered into the darkened hallway, sticking her head out of her open doorway. A distant miaow turned her head in the wrong direction and Nat stared down at the partially open end door. She knew without a doubt that Flo was in Alessandro's bedroom.

Keep the cat away from me. That's what he'd said. *Oh, hell!* She'd done enough damage for one day—she needed to get Flo out.

She tiptoed down the hallway. The thick carpet muffled

her footsteps perfectly, she just hoped it also stifled the hammering of her heart. She was sure Alessandro was still in his study, so it was just a matter of sneaking in, grabbing Flo then getting the hell out.

As she drew level with the doorway she whispered, 'Flo,' again. The damn cat miaowed contently and Nat thought seriously bad thoughts about her pet for a moment or two. She gingerly poked her head over the threshold. A low lamp threw a small glow around the room but otherwise the room was empty. Flo sat in the middle of Alessandro's bed, cleaning herself on his espresso-coloured bedding.

'Flo,' she whispered, half scandalised, half scared out of her wits. She did not want to be there but she knew Flo well enough to know that she wasn't going to voluntarily leave—not until after she'd groomed herself anyway.

'Flo,' she whispered again, more loudly, moving closer, trembling too much to notice the minimalist quality of the rest of the house carried through to his bedroom, which had equally sparse furnishings. 'Come here—now! Alessandro will not be amused.'

Flo stopped her fur licking momentarily and regarded Nat with half-closed eyes before stretching her leg in the air and cleaning it with long firm kitty strokes from her little pink tongue.

Nat almost screamed in frustration, knowing she was going to have to climb onto Alessandro's enormous bed and retrieve the recalcitrant cat.

She was two paces away from the bed when a door behind and to the left of the bed suddenly opened and a semi-naked Alessandro appeared before her. His hair was wet and the only thing stopping him from being totally naked was one white towel riding low on his lean hips.

She didn't mean to ogle but she also couldn't look away. The soft lamp bathed his body in a beautiful bronze glow and, backlit by the en suite light, his face looked more dark, more dangerous than ever.

Her mouth dried in an instant. 'Oh…er, sorry. I didn't know you were…Flo came in.' She pointed to the guilty party like a lawyer holding up exhibit A in a courtroom. The guilty party purred loudly into the tense silence. 'I was just trying to…retrieve her.'

Alessandro hadn't had a woman in his bedroom in a long while. And especially one he'd not long licked Napolitano sauce off. She was wearing the same clothes and the memory came back to punch him in the gut. The taste of her skin, the whimper that had gurgled from her throat, her uneven breath.

He stuck his hands on his hips to quell the surge of lust and the urge to do something more…productive with them. Whether she knew it or not, and he suspected she didn't, her gaze on him was frank and he could feel himself reacting under the towel.

They really needed to clear the air—before he totally embarrassed himself. 'I apologise for this afternoon.'

Nat shook her head, trying desperately hard not to think about that afternoon while he'd stood before her in just a towel. Avoidance was looking good right now.

'I gave you assurances that your virtue would be safe.'

'Don't worry about it,' she dismissed, her voice practically a squeak.

Alessandro shook his head. 'No. I mustn't…I can't… get involved. My wife…I think it best if we just forget it. It…won't happen again.'

He raked his hand through his wet hair, hating how disjointed he sounded. Hating how the possibilities between them could never be explored. She was nodding at him vigorously and he was pleased she understood.

'You have my word, Nathalie.'

And that's where it all fell part for her. He couldn't call her Nathalie and not expect her to melt into a puddle. Not the way he said it—like a sigh, like a whisper from the devil.

A startling urge to cross to him and whip his towel away was so strong she could actually see it in her mind's eye. Thankfully Flo chose that moment to miaow loudly and spring up from her reclining position, rubbing herself against her owner.

Thank god for kids and animals—where would they have been today without either of them? *Naked on the kitchen floor. Going at it on his bed.*

She blinked.

'Of course. It was just…' She stroked Flo's fur as she cast around for something to say, some syndrome or insanity plea to blame it on. But with him nearly naked before her, her brain wasn't functioning that well.

'Impulsive.' She picked Flo up and squeezed her tight. 'You're right, it won't happen again.' She backed out slowly. 'Sorry,' she said again. 'About the…' She gestured to his nakedness but couldn't bring herself to say the words. 'Anyway…'

And with that rather inarticulate ending, she turned on her heel and fled the room.

CHAPTER FIVE

THE next morning Alessandro and Julian were up when Nat wandered downstairs. She'd heard the muted noise of the television a little while ago but had lain in bed, wide awake, putting off the inevitable. She'd felt hot and restless all night, despite the air-conditioning, images of Alessandro's perfect flat abdomen and the hot lick of his tongue taunting her through elusive layers of sleep.

The very last thing she wanted to do was face him again. But after a while she knew being a coward wasn't the answer either and she hauled herself out of bed, and showered and dressed to face the day.

Alessandro looked up from his bowl of cereal when she entered the kitchen. He was shirtless and his hair was rumpled. He looked tired, his eyes bleary, like he'd slept even less than she had. And yet still he looked better than any man had a right to.

She really, really needed to talk to him about wearing a shirt.

She gave him a bright smile and kept her eyes firmly trained on his chin. 'Where's Julian?'

Alessandro, who'd stopped chewing in mid-mouthful,

swallowed. Nat looked fresh and earthy, her hair loose around her shoulders, her cheeks pink. She was wearing a sundress that sat wide on her shoulders with thin straps that tied in bows and a scooped neckline that drew the eye.

He dropped his gaze back to his bowl. 'Watching television.'

Annoyed at his shirtless state, she advanced into the kitchen and headed for the coffee pot. 'Why aren't you in there with him?'

'I asked him if he wanted me to watch with him and he said no.'

Nat shook her head. 'Don't ask next time.' *Hell, it wasn't rocket science.*

Alessandro frowned at her grouchy reply. 'I'm trying not to push him too hard.'

She opened her mouth to tell him that it was okay to push a little in some situations but Julian bustled into the room and she tore her gaze from Alessandro's.

'Nat! Oh, Nat! You're here. You're really still here!'

Julian launched himself at her, throwing his arms around her legs and squashing his cheek against her thigh. She laughed as she hugged his little body to her legs. 'Of course, silly. I can't leave until my house is built!'

She grinned and ruffled his hair, glancing at Alessandro. He was watching them, his face grave and brooding. Her smile slowly disappeared. Was it hard for him to watch Julian being affectionate with another woman? Someone other than his mother? Did it emphasise his loss even more? Did it twist the knife just a little bit deeper?

She peeled Julian off her. 'I'm making toast—do you want some?'

Julian clapped his hands. 'I love toast!'

Nat busied herself with Julian, chatting away as they shoved slice after slice of bread into the toaster. When they were done she carried it over to the central station where Alessandro was apparently reading a journal. She helped Julian climb onto the stool opposite his father and then plonked the loaded plate in the middle. She topped up their coffees and sat down next to Julian.

'Toast,' she said, not quite looking at Alessandro. 'Eat up. We made enough to feed an army.'

Julian giggled and she grinned down at him but all the while she was hyper-aware of Alessandro and she almost sagged against the counter when his long bronzed fingers reached for a slice. She'd felt his gaze, heavy and intense, on her the entire time they'd been at the toaster and it had been unnerving.

Nat wished she knew what he was thinking behind the brooding mask. Was he remembering what had happened in this kitchen only yesterday or her unscheduled visit to his room last night?

If only she knew.

For his part, Alessandro had been trying *not* to think about what would happen if he pulled one of those little bows sitting snugly atop her shoulders. How easy would it be? Just reach out and tug. Would her whole dress just slide off?

Sitting opposite him, the bows in his direct line of vision taunted him even further. He wasn't following the conversation and was surprised to find he'd somehow managed to pick up a piece of toast and eat it. He tuned back into the chatter when he became aware that both Julian and Nat were looking at him expectantly.

Well, Nat was anyway. Julian was looking wary and the

sparkle in his eyes was gone. 'I'm sorry,' he apologised looking from one to the other. 'I wasn't listening.'

Nat gave him a reproving look. 'I was just assuring Julian you were going to help us with the boxes today. Get his room decked out.'

Alessandro looked at Julian. His son didn't seem too enthused by the idea. He was sitting painfully straight in his chair, like a little soldier. 'Ah…well.' He glanced at Nat whose brow had furrowed and then back at his son who seemed to be holding his breath. 'I do have some work to catch up on.'

Nat glanced down at Julian whose bottom lip wobbled and then sharply at Alessandro who was staring down at his journal. She glared at his head but it remained stubbornly downcast. 'Julian, why don't you see if Flo wants a piece of toast?' She scooped up the last cold piece. 'Take it out to the laundry and break it into small pieces.'

Julian squirmed down off the chair enthusiastically and skipped out of the kitchen. Alessandro watched him go.

Nat took a deep breath and gently put down her coffee mug. 'What the hell is wrong with you?' she demanded. 'I just offered you the perfect opportunity to spend time with your son.'

Alessandro gave her a hard look, his eyes chilly. 'He doesn't want me to help. I'm not going to force myself on him.'

Nat got off her stool and stormed over to the coffee pot, pouring herself another. She turned to face him, leaning against the bench, pleased to be far away from his naked chest.

'Sometimes you have to push, Alessandro. He's four. Sometimes children need to be led. You two have to meet in the middle, start doing things together, and this is a perfect place to begin.'

'And what if it has the opposite effect? What if he can't handle what's inside, what if it brings up stuff he was just getting over?'

His eyes were dark and troubled. His frustration and resistance filled the space between them and Nat suddenly understood that this might not be about Julian at all. 'Ah. I understand what this is really about.'

Alessandro snorted. *He was pleased somebody did.* Nothing had made sense for quite a while now. 'Oh, yes?'

'I know that what's in those boxes may be hard to deal with for you. They're your memories. Of your wife and the life you had with her, the one you left behind. But they're his memories too, Alessandro. He's on the other side of the world, far away from everything that's ever been familiar to him. Even his relationship with you is different now. He needs his things around him. And not just in his bedroom but all around him. And he needs to feel like this is home. Not some temporary, half-lived-in dwelling.'

She drew breath for a moment then plunged on again. 'You wanted me to help. You wanted him happy and laughing again. Well, it starts here, Alessandro. And you need to be part of it. You might be surprised what he can handle.'

Alessandro blinked. Maybe she was right. Maybe this was more about him? Maybe the boxes were a bridge too far for him at the moment and he'd been resisting them because of the emotions they were bound to stir? The guilt had been too much to bear as it was.

But if it helped reach Julian…

He stood. 'Okay, sure. That makes sense.'

Nat, who'd open her mouth to strengthen her argument, firmly closed it. He picked up his mug and moved towards her, heading for the sink, his abdominal muscles shifting enticingly with each footfall. She told herself not to look but it was compelling scenery. She gripped the mug hard in case she reached out and touched.

He paused at the sink and drained the contents of his mug. Nat's gaze followed his movements, admiring the glide of his bronzed skin over toned muscle. He placed his mug inside the bowl and it wasn't until he was facing her that she realised he was saying something.

Nat dragged her gaze from the strip of hair that arrowed down from his belly button. 'Huh?'

Alessandro felt desire slam into him right where her eyes had been, as if she'd lapped at his belly button with her tongue. She was looking at him, her eyes slightly glazed, and for a moment they just stared at each other. Her bows taunted him and he curled his fingers into his palms.

'I said when do you want to start?'

Nat's brain grappled with the simple sentence, her annoyance growing. Oh, for crying out aloud, it was just a chest! No reason to lose her mind. Every man had one. Rob had had one. Except, of course, she'd never felt this inexplicable primal swell of lust at the mere sight of Rob. Not even in the beginning.

'Soon. A few minutes.' She pushed away from the bench, the need to get the hell away from him becoming imperative. 'And for God's sake,' she snapped, annoyed at him. And herself. 'Put a shirt on.'

Alessandro stared after her as she stormed out, pleased she and her damn bows were out of sight. Even if his erection wasn't.

* * *

Fifteen minutes later they were all sitting on their haunches in Julian's stark room with one of the two boxes marked *Child* in front of them. Alessandro took a deep breath before taking a Stanley knife to the packing tape.

Nat could see he was nervous. Hell, so was she. After all, Alessandro could be right—what if this whole thing backfired and Julian couldn't handle the memories? What if it upset him too much? If he became inconsolable? But she knew, deep down, that whatever the emotional fallout, father and son needed this.

His biceps drew her gaze, bunching and moving beneath his sleeves as he opened the flaps. She shut her eyes against the temptation—obviously a shirt made little difference to her wandering gaze.

Alessandro opened the box and there, on top, sat Julian's old rabbit.

'George!' Julian snatched up the rather forlorn-looking creature that had obviously seen better days and gave it an enthusiastic hug. 'I missed you, George!'

Watching the reunion, Alessandro felt utterly dreadful. Julian could have had George weeks ago. He hadn't even been aware that the toy had been packed. Or even noticed that Julian had been without him until Nat had prompted him that day at the crèche.

What kind of a father did that make him?

He glanced at Nat and she smiled at him and nodded. 'What else have we got in here?' she prompted.

Julian clung to his rabbit and peered into the box expectantly. They pulled out clothes and toys and books and colourful wall hangings and an exquisite mobile of stars and moons. They were made of brightly coloured glass that formed a whirlpool of colour when the pieces twirled.

'This is beautiful,' Nat gasped as Alessandro lifted it from the box. She could tell it was hand-made, the crafts-manship patently obvious.

'Nonna gave it to me.'

Alessandro looked at his son as Julian reached out and pushed one of the stars with a finger. He smiled. 'That's right.'

His mother had brought it in Murano when she'd been visiting relatives in Venice. He remembered how Julian would lie on his back for ages as a baby in his cot and watch the constellations swing above him in a kaleidoscope of colour.

Julian looked at his father and clutched George tighter. 'Can you hang it above my bed like in London?'

Alessandro expelled a breath he hadn't even realised he'd been holding. It was probably the first time Julian had directly addressed him for anything remotely personal. He nodded. 'Of course.'

They spent a couple of hours putting things to rights in Julian's room, hanging and placing, father and son inter-acting properly for the first time. And when they'd finished, the room was hardly recognisable. It actually looked like a child lived in it instead of a robot.

There was one thing left in the box and Nat reached for it. It was a box of fish food. She held it up and raised her eyebrows at Alessandro. Julian looked at it and held out his hand for it.

He turned to his father. 'It's Gilbert and Sullivan's food.'

Alessandro looked at the tin. He had bought the fish for Julian's third birthday. Julian had thought he was

Superman. Camilla, however, had not been impressed. She certainly hadn't mourned their passing.

'You had fish?' she addressed Julian.

Julian nodded. 'Daddy bought them for my birthday. But they got sick and died.'

'Ah.' Poor kid. His mother had died, his fish had died and he'd had to leave his cat behind. She waited for tears or withdrawal but he seemed quite matter-of-fact. She glanced at Alessandro. He seemed more affected, the ghost of a smile she'd glimpsed a moment ago gone.

Alessandro's heart thudded in his chest as he contemplated taking the next step forward. 'I can buy you some more,' he offered tentatively.

Julian's face lit up. 'Really?'

'Really.'

Nat felt a lump lodge in her throat at the fragile connection that was being built in just two hours between father and son. Sure, there was a long way to go but it was a start. Alessandro glanced at her and smiled. Actually smiled.

And despite her resolve to keep some distance from him, she grinned back like an idiot.

A couple of days later Nat was working triage when her friend Paige walked through the doors, cradling her listless-looking three-year-old daughter McKenzie. The child looked pale, her limbs mottled.

Paige had been through the wringer in the last few years. McKenzie, a twin, had been born at twenty-seven weeks. She and her twin sister, Daisy, had been very frail and while McKenzie had defied the odds, Daisy had died after a four-month, uphill battle.

It had been a devastating time, compounded by her husband leaving shortly after and McKenzie's chronic health issues. Paige looked tired and pinched around the mouth, her brow furrowed. A far cry from the vibrant woman she'd known back in Perth.

Nat didn't know how she kept going. Not only did she care for her high-needs daughter but she also had to work part time as Arnie, her ratfink ex, refused to pay for anything more than he absolutely had to.

'Paige, what's wrong?' she asked.

'It's McKenzie. I think she's got another chest infection.'

Nat heard the tremor in her friend's voice and ushered her into the privacy of the small triage room. Paige looked as if she was at breaking point and Nat knew her friend, who was running on pride alone, would hate to break down in front of an emergency room full of strangers.

Paige sat in a chair, hugging McKenzie close. She turned beseeching eyes on Nat. 'She's due to have her operation next week, Nat.' She rocked slightly, choking on a sob. 'It took me eighteen months to get her off oxygen and two years to get her to ten kilos and we've had to postpone it three times. Not again, please not again.'

Nat gave Paige's shoulder a squeeze. 'Hey, one step at a time, okay? Let's get her seen to first, huh? I'll just take her temp.'

Paige looked at Nat as she placed the digital thermometer under an unprotesting McKenzie's arm. She gave her friend a watery smile. 'Sorry. Of course. It's just I don't know if I can take much more of this. Thank God for Mum and Dad or I would have gone mad years ago.'

Nat laughed. Paige's parents had been a terrific support after Arnie had abandoned their daughter. 'You're doing fine, Paige. Just fine.'

The thermometer beeped, confirming an alarmingly high temp. 'When did you last give her something for her fever?' Nat asked gently.

'Just before I got in the car,' Paige said.

Nat placed a stethoscope in her ears and listened to McKenzie's chest. It sounded like a symphony orchestra conducted by a tone-deaf conductor inside her chest— wheezing, squeaking and crackling away. She slipped a saturation probe onto McKenzie's toe and the number only read 90 per cent. Paige looked at Nat and worried her bottom lip with her teeth.

'Come on. Come through and I'll get Alessandro to look at her.'

Paige stood. 'I hear he's excellent.'

Nat nodded, avoiding her friend's gaze. 'The very best.'

Nat set Paige up in a cubicle and placed a set of nasal prongs on McKenzie's face. The child, well used to the plastic in her nose and too sick to care, didn't protest. Nat used a low-flow meter to set the oxygen at a trickle. She smiled at Paige, her heart going out to her utterly exhausted friend. 'I'll be right back.'

Nat found Alessandro in the cubicle they used for eye patients. It was set up with a special microscope for high-powered viewing of the eye. She'd triaged Bill Groper fifteen minutes ago after a workplace accident had seen boiling fat splashed into his eye.

Alessandro was leaning forward in his chair, his feet flat on the floor, his legs wide apart to accommodate the low table the microscope rested on. He was staring into the eye-pieces, examining his patient's eyes. Bill sat opposite, his chin on the plate, looking in from the other side.

She noticed immediately how the position emphasised

the broad expanse of Alessandro's back and how it tapered down to narrow hips. One strong leg, bent at the knee, was positioned slightly out to the side and the dark fabric of his trousers pulled across his thigh, outlining the slab of muscle she knew, from living in close proximity, defined his upper leg.

She waited for him to finish, knowing that Paige needed time to pull herself together and McKenzie's condition would benefit from the supplemental oxygen.

'You certainly did a good job of it, Bill,' Alessandro murmured. 'Bull's-eye on your cornea.' He pulled away from the eyepieces. He noticed a figure in his peripheral vision and felt his abdominals contract. He didn't have to turn his head to know it was Nat. His body seemed to have a sixth sense when she was around.

'Never do anything by halves, Doc.'

Nat felt a similar awareness and sensed rather than saw his momentary eyelid flicker, which told her he knew she was there. It was probably imperceptible to most, but after a few days of cohabitation and an almost electric awareness of him, she was coming to know all his cues—both obvious and subtle.

Alessandro continued with his patient. 'It's not too bad, though, only superficial by the look of it. Some antibiotic eyedrops should work like a charm.'

Nat lounged against the doorframe and waited. She was used to him ignoring her now anyway. It was a policy they'd both adopted. And as far as it went, it wasn't such a bad idea. There was an attraction there. He knew it. She knew it. It hummed between them like a palpable force, like powerful magnets irresistibly drawn to each other.

But acknowledging it out loud was just plain dumb when neither of them was going to do anything about it. So they were polite. They addressed each other when required and worked together with utter professionalism. In short they carried on as if nothing had ever happened.

Like he'd never licked Napolitano sauce off her chest.

Alessandro stood and Nat spoke. 'Excuse me, Dr Lombardi. I have a patient you need to see.'

Alessandro looked at her fully then and gave her a brief nod before turning back to his patient. He held out his hand and shook Bill's. 'I'll send someone in with some drops for you.'

Nat stepped back from the doorway as Alessandro headed towards her. She could see tension in his shoulders as the looseness with which he'd shaken Bill's hand disappeared and his face drew back into grim lines.

'Three-year-old ex-twenty-seven-weeker. Twin one. Twin two died at four months of age.'

She fell into step beside him, ignoring the lurch of her cells, and launched into the standard summary she'd give any doctor she was handing over to. Here at St Auburn's she was a nursing professional and she would be professional if it killed her. Even if she did want to find the nearest vacant room and tear all his clothes off.

'Chronic neonatal lung disease, oxygen dependent for first two years of life, recurrent chest infections, failure to thrive. I think she's brewing another infection. Febrile. Sats ninety on room air. Bilateral chest crackles. Listless. Cool peripherally and mottled.'

Alessandro nodded as they walked. 'What was her birth weight?'

Nat struggled to keep up with Alessandro's stride,

which seemed to lengthen with each footfall. 'Twelve hundred grams.'

'How many days ventilated.'

'Twenty.' The answers to his spitfire questions were well known to her but his emotionless firing of them was irritating.

'Which cube?'

'Eleven,' she said as they drew level with the central nurses' station.

Alessandro nodded. He could smell that flower-garden scent he was becoming so familiar with and, as usual, he had the craziest urge to bury his face in her neck. It didn't seem to matter how fast he walked, he couldn't outrun it. 'Chart?'

She handed the thick file to him but kept hold of it. Alessandro frowned at her. *'Problemo?'*

'Paige is that friend of mine I told you about in the lift that day. She lost a baby, her husband walked out and she's dealing with McKenzie's fragile health. McKenzie's implant operation has been postponed three times in the last year and she's supposed to go in next week for it and that probably won't happen now so Paige is…a little emotional at the moment. Just…I don't know…' She looked at his grim face. 'Smile or something.'

He clenched his jaw and, ignoring her jibe, cut straight to the chase. 'Implant?'

'Sorry,' Nat dismissed, letting go of the chart as she realised she'd left out a vital part of patient history. 'Cochlear implant. McKenzie's profoundly deaf.'

Alessandro looked down at the bulging chart and then back at her. 'Are you coming?'

He didn't wait for an answer and Nat followed him in.

The harsh screech of the curtain as he snapped it back didn't bode well and she castigated herself for irritating him just prior to seeing Paige.

Alessandro's gaze encompassed the mother and listless diminutive little girl, hearing aids firmly in place. He gave Paige a gentle smile. She looked utterly exhausted. She looked like he'd felt for the last year and he felt an instant surge of empathy. 'Hello, I'm Alessandro,' he said, and signed it too.

Nat's eyes bugged, as did Paige's. 'Oh. You sign?' she exclaimed.

Alessandro gave a self-deprecating shrug. He had learned the English sign language when he'd moved to London which he believed was similar to what they used here. 'In a fashion.' He smiled. 'I have an aunt in Italy, who's profoundly deaf. I spent a lot of time there as a kid. She was like a second mother to me. My cousin Val, her son, is a renowned cochlear implant surgeon in London.'

He signed as he spoke without giving it conscious thought. Not that McKenzie cared or could probably even understand his mixture of sign language but it was second nature to him when he was in the company of a deaf person.

Nat shook her head, marvelling at the change in Alessandro when he was with a patient. He was great with McKenzie, getting her X-rayed, admitting her for intravenous antibiotics when the films revealed bilateral consolidation and quickly and efficiently placing a drip.

He was especially good with Paige, chatting about sign-language differences and asking her about the scheduled operation. He was like a different man.

Involved. Animated. Connected.

Now, if he could just be more like that at home she could walk out of their lives in a couple of months knowing it had all been worth it.

Even if it meant having to go to bed every night with a fire in her belly and a buzz in her blood that wouldn't quit.

CHAPTER SIX

ON FRIDAY Nat was sitting on the quiet mat at crèche with Julian and another boy, Henry. She was trying to encourage a friendship between them. Henry was a nice kid who had been trying to engage Julian for a little while now with not much success.

It wasn't that Julian didn't like Henry—she could tell he did. But he still shied away from other kids, preferring to keep to himself or follow her around. Julian was more than happy to play and talk with Henry as long as she was there as well.

Henry had brought in some photos of his family holiday to New Zealand and they were going through them. There was a beautiful shot of Henry and his mother. He was sitting in her lap, facing the camera. She had her arms crossed across his front, pulling his back in tight to her chest. They were looking at each other, she looking down, Henry looking up and laughing. A massive mountain gave the background some perspective.

Julian took the photo reverently, being careful to only touch the corner as he'd been taught. 'Is that your mummy?'

Julian didn't take his eyes off the photo and the look

on his face was heart-breaking. It suddenly struck Nat that there were no photos of Julian's mother anywhere. She'd been so distracted by the starkness of the never-ending white, so snow blind, she hadn't even thought about that.

Goodness, her mother had practically set up a shrine to her father after he'd gone. Despite the fact that he'd deserted them. But she'd been determined to maintain contact, to keep his memory fresh for Nat's sake.

Pity her father hadn't tried as hard.

But there wasn't even a framed picture for Julian to put on his beside table. No family portraits hung on the wall. Come to think of it, not even Alessandro had pictures of the wife he so obviously mourned. Not in his office or his bedroom. It was almost as if she never existed at all.

Was it too painful for him to even look at her? Was his grief still that profound?

And why did the thought depress her so much?

She made up her mind to ask Alessandro about it tonight after Julian went to bed. It seemed to have become her role to ask the hard questions. To be the bad guy. It certainly hadn't taken her long to realise that as much as Alessandro wanted to reach his son he was still floundering and relied heavily on her to facilitate it. They both did. She was like the buffer between them, the referee, and her ruling was final.

Alessandro seemed more than happy for her to take up where his wife had left off. Be some kind of substitute mother to Julian. And she knew that was about his grief more than shirking his duties, that he'd been knocked sideways and was groping in the dark. But she wasn't living with them so Alessandro could hide from his son, to maintain his emotional distance.

She was there until her unit was built and in the meantime she was in Julian's corner. He was a four-year-old child and, God knew, he needed someone in his corner.

Surely there were pictures somewhere? Even one? Alessandro might find it too painful to contemplate but watching Julian now it was obvious he yearned for that connection. If he was to ever recover from his tragic loss, he needed to be able to openly grieve and he needed his mother's life, her existence, to be acknowledged.

'And next Grandma Poss and Hush went to—'

'Hobart!'

Alessandro chuckled. 'For?' he prompted as he turned the page.

'Lamingtons!'

Julian just couldn't seem to get enough of this damn book—it was their second time through tonight. He seemed to forget everything as the story unfolded. About Camilla. And being dragged halfway across the world. And the stiltedness of their relationship.

At the moment Alessandro was propped against the head of his son's bed, his legs stretched out in front, his son cuddled into his side, Julian's curls tickling his chin.

Nat had been right. This was a special time of the day.

But as happy as he was, it was moments like this that the vile sting of regret was at its most potent. He'd been so busy in London, so involved with his career, with making consultant, that he'd let Camilla drive a wedge between him and Julian.

His guilt at entering into the marriage for all the wrong reasons had convinced him his strained relationship with Julian had been his due. Some kind of cosmic payback.

But, then, he'd never imagined his son would be mother-less and he would have the sole care of his child.

A virtual stranger…

'Nat bought me a lamington yesterday.'

Alessandro absently rubbed his chin against Julian's soft curls, savouring the texture and this time together. Soon the book would end and Julian would become awkward with him again. Three nights ago Nat had insisted that bedtime was a special time and bedtime stories were a father's role and firmly shoved the book at his chest.

Julian had pouted and begged her to do it but she had just smiled at both of them, kissed Julian goodnight and left them to it. And now here they were, both enjoying the night-time ritual.

Enjoying going to another world far away from their own and all its baggage.

'Did she, now?' he said good-humouredly. 'Did it make you invisible?'

Juliano giggled. 'No. But it tasted dee-licious.'

Alessandro smiled to himself as an image of delicious Nat with Napolitano sauce oozing a tempting streak down the swell of her breast rose in his mind. Not what his son had meant but he couldn't think of a better description.

Had a woman ever tasted so sweet?

Not that it mattered. It wouldn't matter if she tasted like fairy floss, cinnamon doughnuts and dark chocolate gelato all rolled in one. He was paying penance and Nat, who'd no doubt been sent by the devil to tempt him, was definitely off limits.

Nat could hear a low murmuring of voices as she collected her pyjamas from beneath her pillow. A high-pitched giggle carried easily, followed by a deeper, richer baritone that seemed to slither into her room on serpent's wings.

She smiled at the baby steps of progress. Demanding that Alessandro be proactive was doing the trick. She tiptoed down the short distance of hallway between her room and Julian's, unable to resist taking a peek. The sight that greeted her was heart-warming. Father and son stretched out on the bed in the way of father and sons the world over.

Alessandro was still in his work clothes. But he'd taken his tie off and loosened the top two buttons of his duck-egg-blue shirt. His feet were still encased in his socks. He looked relaxed for a change. Younger, even. Devoted, certainly.

Also hot, sexy and virile. What was it about seeing a big man with a small child that was irresistibly attractive?

Julian's little body was curled up, knees to chest, snuggled into Alessandro's side. His small hand rested on his father's shirt, making it seem positively diminutive against the sheer size of Alessandro's chest. He was looking at his father as he read the story like he could leap tall buildings in a single bound.

No one watching this scene would guess at the strange relationship that had existed between the two of them. The stilted politeness, their mechanical interactions, the distance. Right now it was as it should be and her foolish soft heart practically over flowed with joy.

She tiptoed away, a small smile curving her soft mouth, knowing that things were looking up and she was part of it.

An hour later, Nat, her heart thudding in her chest, knocked on Alessandro's office door. It wasn't shut, just pulled to, but, still, it was a barrier she didn't feel comfortable breeching without an invitation. He shut himself away every night after Julian went to bed. The relaxed man who lay with his son disappearing the second he walked out of Julian's room.

His message couldn't have been clearer—back off. Keep out. He'd said they should pretend it had never happened and he was hell bent on leading by example.

She heard his soft '*Entrato*' and hesitated briefly, girding her loins for the forthcoming battle. One thing she'd learned very quickly had been that Alessandro was an intensely private man. She didn't think he'd take too kindly to her entering these particular waters. He didn't talk about his wife, he hadn't even let her name slip. Nat had no way of knowing how he'd react to the photo issue.

But she'd made a commitment to herself that she would raise this with him, for Julian's sake, and she wasn't going to back down. She took a breath and pushed open the door.

He was sitting in his black-leather, Italian-designed swivel chair. His computer was on. Open textbooks cluttered the surface of the desk and the floor around his feet. Piles of medical journals, some open, littered the area as well in some kind of order…she guessed.

The rest of his office was still stark. The walls were bare and the whiteness was harsh in contrast to the cluttered desk area. She made a note to attack those boxes this weekend. Surely Alessandro wanted familiar things around him too? Maybe he'd appreciate a photo of his wife for his desk?

He'd changed out of his work clothes into his pyjamas. Boxer shorts, the soft clingy kind often seen on models, not the loose, silky ones. They came to mid-thigh and revealed more than they covered. As did a snug-fitting white T-shirt. He'd avoided being 'undressed' around her, for which she was most grateful.

The occasional glimpses she'd caught of him *sans* shirt had been hard enough.

His hair was damp as if he'd not long been out of the shower. A soft lamp spread a glow around the office and settled against the angles of his face, emphasising the richness of his bronze complexion and shadowing his mouth. He looked dark and dangerous and breathtakingly good-looking.

Her very first thought was to turn around and run.

Alessandro raised an eyebrow. 'You wanted something?'

Nat swallowed. His voice was a low purr, like Flo's— on steroids. *God help her, she did.* She wanted him like she'd never wanted a man before. Not even Rob. She shut her eyes against the image of her and him going for it in his big old chair that flashed briefly through her mind.

No! They couldn't do this.

When she opened them again his dark gaze netted her in its web. It was if he knew exactly what she'd been thinking.

Alessandro flattened his bare feet in the carpet so he wouldn't leave the chair and cover the short distance between the two of them and snatch her into his arms. Nat's gaze had licked all over him and become all heat and steam and he suddenly felt like he was sitting in a sauna or a hot spring. He kept his gaze trained on hers despite the compelling tug to let it wander down over her cleavage and further to her long bare legs and feet he could see in his peripheral vision.

Inferno! This was crazy. 'Nat?'

His voice was steely now, pulling Nat back from temptation. 'I wanted to talk to you about…' she swallowed '…something.'

Alessandro's gaze took in her mouth as she talked and

her nervous throat bob. The strange urge to stroke a finger down the ridge of her windpipe, place kisses along it, came upon him and he curled his hand around the arm of the chair, anchoring himself. 'Okay. So talk.'

Nat nodded, still uncertain how to go about asking the question. 'I was wondering if…' He was staring at her mouth and she couldn't process anything. She took a second. Probably best to just say it. 'You had any photos of your wife?'

Alessandro's gaze flicked back to her eyes in an instant. He felt the tension that was never far way come back into the muscles of his neck. 'What for?'

Nat heard the note of foreboding, the no-trespassing in-flection in his wary voice. And the urge to flee became an imperative. Her heart beat loud enough that she felt sure that Alessandro must be able to hear it. 'I thought it would be nice for Julian to have a picture of her on his bedside table. Maybe one of them together?'

Alessandro stiffened, an immediate denial rushing to his lips. They'd made real progress this week. He couldn't bear to see Julian return to the practically mute little boy he'd been in those few days and weeks after Camilla's death.

His son was moving on, he didn't want to take him back. 'I think that would make him unbearably sad again.'

Nat steeled herself to be the bad guy again. 'His mother's dead, Alessandro. He's allowed to be sad.'

Alessandro shook his head. She didn't know how hard it had been. 'It's too awful to watch.'

Nat nearly gave up then and there. The anguish in Alessandro's voice cut her to the quick. But she knew enough child psychology, as should he, to know he wasn't doing his son any favours. 'You can't protect him from that. It's healthy to be sad, to cry, to grieve. You can't fast-forward this bit by pretending she didn't exist.'

Alessandro's head snapped up. 'I'm not doing that,' he denied, ice lacing his voice and turning his obsidian eyes flinty.

Alessandro's fervent denial flared out at her like a striking snake. 'There's not a single photo of her anywhere, Alessandro,' she persisted, keeping her voice even and gentle. 'You loved her. She was the mother of your child. I know it's hard for you to have reminders of her around —'

Alessandro's snort interrupted her. 'You have no idea.'

Nat frowned, surprised at the derision in his voice but ploughed on anyway, not sure she'd ever be brave enough to say it again. 'He's four, Alessandro. You know I'm right. Put aside the father, the husband, for a moment and think like a doctor. Like the good doctor you are. You know I'm right. You know this is good grief resolution strategy.'

Alessandro cursed her for being right. 'And what if I can't look at her?' he demanded.

How long had it been since he'd looked at Camilla's face? Conjured her up? He'd been trying so hard to banish the years of baggage he'd steadfastly refused to imagine her at all.

Of course, he didn't have to look too far for a reminder. But funnily enough, the physical similarities between Nat and Camilla didn't strike him any more—hadn't since that first meeting. They were two different women in so many ways. Too different to be mistaken as the same one.

Nat swallowed. She felt his pain all the way down to her toes and felt dreadful, pushing. 'I'm not asking you to commission a six-foot mural on one of these god-awful walls. Just a photo for Julian's bedside table. So he knows she existed and she loved him and she's looking over him.'

Alessandro wished it was that easy. Could he look at that photo every time he entered his son's room? Could he look at it and not feel the knife twisting a little deeper?

He looked at Nat's earnest face and sighed. Hadn't she been right about everything else? Hadn't she helped him reach out to his son already? Of course he could do it, if it helped his son mourn.

'There are framed photos,' he sighed. 'A few. In one of the boxes.'

It had been his intention to get around to putting them out. In their house in London, photos of her, of them, as a family had been everywhere. They'd been so hard to look at afterwards. The hypocrisy had been torture. And frankly he'd been enjoying the emotional freedom.

Nat felt her heart sink at both the defeat in his voice and the thought of having to search through the remaining mound of boxes. Whoever the packing company had been, they'd done a lousy job. Most of them were marked miscellaneous so the photos could be anywhere.

But it was a start, a concession. And there was no rush now that Alessandro had consented—they'd find them some time in the next few weekends and with Alessandro on the same page it would be a good avenue to open discussion. And in the meantime they could sound Julian out about the idea.

She noticed how tired he looked and suppressed her natural soppy-female instinct to go to him. She wanted to put her arms around him, hug him, give him a place to rest his head. But she knew it would be a mistake. The urge to comfort might be her motivator but she doubted it would stay that pure for long.

'Thank you. This is the right thing to do, Alessandro.'

Alessandro heard the note of genuine belief in her voice. She stood in his doorway, oozing certainty and confidence. God, he felt so out of his depth sometimes. And yet here she was in her T-shirt and shorts, all perfect and Zen and centred, telling him it was going to be all right.

He wished she'd come nearer. He wanted to put his arms around her, bury his face against her belly. Absorb some of that Zen she had going on. Maybe feel her hand sifting through his hair. 'I hope so,' he murmured.

Nat was almost paralysed by the longing she saw in Alessandro's gaze. Was it desire to connect with his son or just plain old desire?

Desire with a capital D?

His eyes roamed over her and her skin felt like it was on fire. The room had become a furnace, heat roaring between them. She opened her mouth to say something but, as if he knew he'd already given away too much, he swivelled the chair back around to face his desktop monitor.

She stood in the doorway for a few moments, staring at the back of his chair, trying to catch her breath. This was a good thing. Something happening between them would be dumb—way dumber than Rob. He was doing them a favour.

And one day, she had no doubt, she'd truly appreciate his resolve. But right now a long lonely night stretched endlessly ahead.

Nat woke in the wee small hours to Flo miaowing and nudging her. Rain drummed on the colour bond roof. She wasn't surprised. The day had been humid and a storm had been brewing as she'd climbed into bed. She stroked Flo,

lying there for a second just enjoying the noise and luxuriating in being dry and snuggled beneath the covers. But
Flo persisted with her nudging and Nat reluctantly got up.

'All right, bossy-boots. I know you like to frolic in the
rain, you crazy cat.' She picked up a purring Flo. 'Come on.'

Familiar now with the layout of the house, Nat made her
way downstairs in the dark and opened the laundry door for
Flo to go out. She watched the cat bound into the rain and
grinned. Silly animal—giving up a dry warm bed snuggled
into a doting little boy to chase a few raindrops around.

Nat shut the door, knowing Flo would be happy out
there for hours. She stopped and grabbed a drink of water
in the kitchen and headed back to the stairs. A chink of
light from beneath the office door caught her gaze. Good
grief! Alessandro was still up?

She knocked lightly on the door and waited for his gruff
'*Entrato*' but nothing. She pushed it open slowly, expecting him to swivel around with an annoyed look on his
face. Instead, he was bent forward in his chair, head on
desk, amidst the clutter of textbooks, his eyes closed.

'Alessandro?' she whispered, approaching carefully.
He didn't stir and she stood for a moment just looking
down at him. His black hair fell across his forehead, dis-
armingly innocent, just like Julian's did when he slept.

But the dark growth shadowing his jaw and his softly
parted lips were one hundred per cent adult.

It was a shame to wake him—he always looked so tired.
In fact, even asleep he looked utterly exhausted. But he'd have
a hell of a sore neck in the morning if he stayed like this.

'Alessandro,' she called again as she gave his shoulder
a gentle shake.

Alessandro startled, sucking in a breath and sitting bolt

upright as he dragged his body out of the sticky depths of slumber. His hand automatically went to the twinge in his neck as his brain scrambled to get up to speed.

Nat standing in his office. Nat standing really close in his office. Nat wearing some clingy T-shirt dress thingy with no bra standing close in his office.

'I'm sorry,' he murmured, struggling with the urge to drop his gaze to the bounce of her unfettered breasts in his peripheral vision. 'I must have fallen asleep.' He used both hands to rub his neck for fear of where they'd go if they weren't occupied.

He had a red mark on his cheek where it had been stuck to a textbook and Nat had a crazy urge to stroke it. 'What are you doing up so late?' she whispered. She wasn't sure why she was whispering. It just seemed appropriate in the dead of night.

Alessandro shrugged. 'I've been working on St Auburn's readiness for pandemic status should the dreaded swamp flu reach our shores.'

'It's two-thirty in the morning,' she chided. 'The swamp flu can wait. Go to bed. Get some sleep.'

Alessandro let his hands drop. If only if was that easy. 'I can't sleep,' he murmured. 'I never sleep.'

Nat felt his weariness, his anguish, right down to her toes. He looked totally wretched and her instincts cried out to comfort him. 'Oh, Alessandro,' she whispered.

She didn't give a second thought to moving closer, sliding one hand behind his neck and one into his hair, cradling his head, pulling it against her belly. 'I'm so sorry.'

Alessandro's arms automatically encircled her waist, drawing her closer. He shut his eyes as he leaned into her, his face pressed into her nightshirt. She smelled like soap and rain and flowers. And he wanted her. 'I'm tired. I'm so tired.'

'Shh.' She cradled his head and rocked slightly. 'I know. I know.' Because she did know. She knew what it was like to grieve the end of a relationship. To lose someone close.

He pressed a kiss to her belly and looked up at her. She was so beautiful. Her eyes were shimmering pools of empathy, her skin was glowing and her mouth was beckoning. He wanted to crawl into a nice, big warm bed with her and stay there for ever. 'Nathalie.'

Nat shook her head. She knew that look in his eyes. Knew for damn sure it was reflected in hers. 'Don't call me that.' Her voice shook. She hated how husky it sounded.

He rubbed his chin against her stomach. 'Why? It suits you.'

Her abdominal muscles rippled beneath his stubble as if he had licked them and deeper down other muscles stirred deliciously at the way he'd sighed her name. Her hand drifted down from his hair to his face. She rubbed gently at the red mark on his cheek with the back of her hand. 'Because I like it too much.'

They stared at each other for the longest time. They didn't move. All that could be heard in the small office was the rain on the roof and the staccato rhythm of their breathing. It was Alessandro who made the first move, applying pressure through his arms, bringing her down onto his lap, their heads close. Their lips closer.

Nat didn't protest, mesmerised by his eyes, by the desire that gleamed there. That they could be cold like black ice one moment and warm like sable the next. She wasn't supposed to be here, doing this, but she also knew she was utterly powerless to resist. She could almost feel his mouth on hers, taste it, and she wanted it so badly anticipation hummed through her system.

Alessandro's hand crept up, brushed against her shoulder and moving along the line of her collar bone until it was cradling her nape, four fingers lodged in her hair, his thumb stroking her jaw. He exerted slight pressure inching her closer. Their mouths nearer.

'*Bello*,' he murmured. He was past caring about restraint and all the reasons why kissing Nat, taking her clothes off and having her right here, right now, was a bad idea. All he knew was that in amongst all the bad things in his life at the moment this felt inextricably right.

That he suddenly felt more awake, more alive than he had in a long time. A very long time.

His hand drifted down to her neckline, coming to rest where the material scooped low on her breasts. She shut her eyes as her nipples responded to the blatant arousal. She watched fascinated as he dropped his head and kissed her not far from where the sauce had landed not even a week ago. His lips practically sizzled against her skin and she arched her back involuntarily.

'Nathalie…'

She barely had a chance to whimper before his mouth brushed against hers. Light. Gentle. A whisper of what was to come. 'Alessandro.' She wasn't sure if it was a warning or an invitation.

But it was definitely surrender.

Her hands snaked around his neck at the same time and their lips met again. Not gentle now. Not light. Deep. Deeper. Open mouths and questing tongues feasting on each other like starving beasts. She could hear his moan and felt its seductive stroke deep inside her before it travelled all the way to her toes.

Her head spun as the kiss spiralled out of control. She broke away for a second, dizzy and out of breath. Alessandro looked at her with a passion not even his hooded eyes could conceal. His lips were moist from her ministrations—full and beckoning.

She'd done that to him. Made this man look at her with eyes that devoured her, that branded her. She should be scared by this level of intensity but, God help her, she wanted more.

Alessandro rubbed his thumb across the soft swollen contours of her mouth. She had him on her lips. Them. And he wanted to be back there. Their mouths joined. To be joined even more intimately. To taste her more intimately. To be inside her. 'You're so sweet,' he whispered.

'So are you,' she murmured, before slamming her mouth back on to his.

He met her ardour, surpassed it. His hands tangled in her hair, holding her captive, making escape impossible. Not that she wanted it. She could feel he was hard for her, his cotton boxers and her position on his lap giving his impressive arousal nowhere to hide.

She squirmed against it, wanting to feel it pressed against her more intimately, not just the back of her thigh. She wanted to touch it, damn it. Without breaking the kiss, she manoeuvred herself until she was straddling his lap, her nightdress riding up her thighs.

Thank God for quality Italian furnishing.

The big leather chair accommodated her most adequately and she wasted no time grinding down against him, seeking the pleasure, the relief she knew he could give her.

He broke off the kiss on a groan, his breath outdrumming the rain. 'Nathalie.' She was beautiful, bits of her blonde hair wisped free from her ponytail and somehow, despite the experienced movements of her hips, she looked down at him with a wide-eyed wonder that could almost border on innocent. 'I want to see all of you.'

Without asking, his hands snagged the hem of her nightdress, lifted it up and dragged it off over her head. She was totally naked apart from a very inadequate scrap of lace. Her breasts fell free and he was mesmerised by them. They were as beautiful as he'd imagined, and God knew he'd imagined them often enough. Full and firm with nipples the colour of mocha.

He brought his hands up from her waist until they were full of her. They felt heavy in his palms and her peaked nipples dragged deliciously across the sensitive skin there. '*Inferno!* I want to taste you.'

And then, with one arm around her back, he swept her close, his mouth latching onto the nearest offering. He sucked hard on her nipple and Nat cried out, clutching his shoulders as her world tilted and spun.

His tongue rasped against her peaked flesh. It lapped and licked and sucked and rolled around the entire elongated peak. And just when he thought she could take it no longer he released her and she almost fell against him. But he steadied her with his arm and opened his mouth over the other one.

'Alessandro!' She wasn't sure if she was begging him to stop or egging him on further—all she knew was she was swirling like an autumn leaf in the wind and they hadn't even got to the main event.

Alessandro released her nipple, satisfied to see it wet and puckered from his ministrations. 'I want you.'

Three little words. Not the three words most women want to hear but Nat couldn't have cared less. She'd heard those words and they'd been an empty promise. Right now she needed this. Alessandro. A man who wanted her with an intensity she doubted she'd ever known.

But even so. There were some logistics that needed sorting. She battled with her breathing. 'Condoms?' she panted.

Alessandro shook his head. 'Are you on the Pill?'

She nodded. She could feel the ridge of his erection pressing against her and she was desperate to feel it inside. 'Of course. But it's about more than that, Alessandro.'

His arms tightened around her. Damn it. He knew that. 'I've had sex with one woman in the last five years.'

She looked into his eyes, warm like sable still, and saw the yearning and desperation that had got her into this chair in the first place. He wanted her. But he was telling her he was safe and, God help her, she'd die tonight if she had to leave this room unsatisfied. 'Same with me.'

'Good.' Alessandro returned his attention to her breasts and she grabbed his shoulders as lust slammed into her gut.

Barely thinking straight, she reached down for him, finding him bigger and harder and thicker than even she'd imagined. He moaned into her mouth and she felt a surge of warmth between her thighs as her body prepared to take him.

Alessandro pulled away as she manoeuvred him out of his material prison and her hand finally found bare skin.

'Nathalie…' he groaned, leaning his forehead against her chest. 'I don't think I'll last very long if you touch me like that.' He looked up into her face. 'It's been a long time.'

Nat squeezed his girth, her hand luxuriating in the

velvety glove sheathing the core of solid rock. He snatched in a breath and expelled it on another groan and she smiled down at him. 'Good. We can do slow later.'

And she lowered her head, opening her mouth over his, feeling him surge in her palm as his tongue thrust inside her mouth. She felt his hands squeezing her buttocks, dragging her closer, and she rubbed herself against his naked length, aroused beyond all rational thought.

There was no planning now. She was just moving to a rhythm as old as time. She needed to feel him inside her and without conscious control she was lifting over him, pushing the crutch of her knickers to one side, and then his head was nudging her entrance and she didn't even pause before her hips moved instinctively down as his moved instinctively up.

She cried out as he filled her more than she'd ever been filled before. She vaguely heard him calling her name but a pounding in her blood, like jungle drums, was taking over and she moved to their beat.

Alessandro groaned, hearing the drums too, and moved again, pulling her close, one arm still around her back. He kissed her lips, rained kisses down her neck, took a puckered nipple in his mouth, all the time obeying the throb in his blood, the rhythm in his head.

Nat held Alessandro's head to her breast, hanging on for dear life as the beat became a canter and then a gallop. 'Alessandro!' she cried.

Alessandro barely heard her above the tempo pulsing around him. It was inside, thickening his blood, and around them, pressing them closer with invisible hands. His loins moved to its beat, surging and thrusting into her hot, tight core.

Nat felt the drums rise to a crescendo and she knew she was going over the edge. 'Alessandro, I can't…Oh, God, I can't stop it.'

'Nathalie,' he roared, throwing his head back against the leather headrest, clutching her hips. He thrust one last time as the rhythm peaked and he along with it.

For a moment neither of them moved as the drums crashed to total silence and they both became airborne. And then Nat moaned and bucked, her nails digging into his shoulders as pleasure, so deep, so profound, rained down on her.

And Alessandro joined her, thrusting his hips, pumping up into her, riding the wave of his own orgasm, driven by the echo of the drums still spiking his blood and milked by her wild abandon as she bucked and rode him to completion.

And when it was over she collapsed against him and he gathered her close and he knew without a shadow of a doubt that having Nat Davies come to stay was the best thing he'd ever done.

CHAPTER SEVEN

AFTER not knowing the pleasures of a woman's body for a long time, Alessandro was insatiable. They'd made love another twice that night before Nat had slunk back to her own bedroom. And then every night since. Alessandro would put Julian to bed, read to him and then he would pounce again, no matter where she was. The kitchen, the shower, the laundry, the lounge. A week later there were very few places in the house they hadn't done it.

Thank goodness Julian slept like the dead.

It never crossed Nat's mind to refuse Alessandro. She'd been around long enough to know that the magic they'd made that first time didn't come along very often. And, anyway, her body betrayed her at every single turn. All he had to do was look at her and she practically self-combusted.

Why deny herself this little oasis of pleasure? As long as she took it at face value, remembered it was about two convenient bodies finding a little mutual gratification for a finite period of time, she'd be fine. She was an adult. There was nothing wrong with that.

For once in her life she was making a decision with her head and not her poor, easy heart.

And it felt liberating.

Plus there was something compelling about Alessandro's love-making that was addictive. He was so…driven. Intense, like the rest of him. Desperate, almost. When his body covered hers it felt like he was trying to absorb her into him. He wasn't satisfied with quick and easy and rolling over and going to sleep. They made love for hours each night until sheer exhaustion took over.

And his attention to detail was amazing.

Nat doubted she'd ever been so thoroughly bedded in her life. It was like by reaching for the maximum level of pleasure he was hoping to purge the grief. Not just sideline it. He was still hurting and it was if he'd found the perfect antidote for it—her body. And that was okay too. If her gratification helped him heal, who was she to argue?

And then there was the flow-on effect to Julian. The sex was making Alessandro more relaxed. He didn't seem so grim. He was more…laid-back. He smiled more. Laughed. And Julian was slowly becoming less serious, less wary in return.

They were careful, of course, to keep their relationship from Julian. Nat was always back in her bed by five a.m. It was hard and getting harder, especially when Alessandro was so warm and vital, his big arm tucked around her waist, his bigger body curled around hers.

And at that hour of the morning he was usually raring to go again with another treacherous seduction muddling her senses.

'Stay longer,' he'd whisper. His accent always seemed more pronounced when he was sleepy and it stroked seductive fingers along her pelvic floor.

Nat would smile as his lips nuzzled her neck, his hands

kneaded her breasts and his erection brushed her belly. The temptation to stay was great. 'Julian,' she'd murmur.

'He never wakes before seven, *bella*.'

Which was true, but Nat knew it was best not to be found together. Choosing to snatch these moments with Alessandro was fine—she was an adult. Julian was a boy who dearly needed a mother and who plainly adored her. And that wasn't fair. What did four-year-olds know of adult games? Adult relationships? It wasn't right to confuse him any more when his world had already been turned upside down.

So she dutifully dragged herself out of her lover's bed, out of his possessive male embrace, every morning. And even when he looked up at her with a sexy half-smile and smouldering sable eyes that told her more than words what he wanted to do to her, she still turned away.

But it was getting more and more difficult...

Alessandro had tried to not let their chemistry spill over into their work and for the most part it was successful. She only worked two day shifts a week in the department and usually it was on the triage desk so it was easier to avoid direct contact.

But today, on this crazy, crazy Friday, she'd been allocated to the cubicles and they seemed to have giant magnets attached to their butts. Today it was simply impossible to ignore her and their attraction. Impossible to not be utterly distracted by her.

'Twenty-year-old female, right lower quadrant pain, rebound tenderness, hypertensive, tachycardic, febrile.'

Nat pushed the chart at Alessandro, trying to be brisk and professional in her handover. Everywhere she'd moved today his incendiary gaze had been on her and she was about ready to combust.

Not to mention the fact that despite his dark trousers, dove-grey shirt and beautiful mauve tie, all she could see was the way he had looked last night on his way back from the bathroom gloriously naked, hands firmly on narrow hips, his arousal on proud display.

Alessandro smiled. He could see the simmer in her gaze and knew exactly where her brain was. 'Which cubicle?'

'Twelve,' she said automatically, a vague part of her still clinging to professionalism while his rough command from last night to 'Open your legs' squirmed through her grey matter.

Nat felt her internal muscles twist firmly in a knot. His broad shoulders bobbed in front of her and she followed blindly, trying to catch her breath.

Alessandro greeted his patient. 'Hi. Ellie? I'm Dr Lombardi.' He held out his hand and the harried young woman shook it briefly, grabbing her side with a grunt as she let go. 'Nat's been telling me you have some pain.'

'Yes,' Ellie agreed. 'The odd niggle the last day or two but worse this morning. And by the time I got to work it was unbearable.'

Nat watched as his attention turned solely to his patient. He questioned her closely before methodically examining her. Even in significant pain she could see how Ellie responded to Alessandro's calm professionalism. She was scared but somehow he managed to reassure her.

Alessandro returned his gaze to Nat. She was looking at him with admiration and respect and even that went straight to his groin. 'I'll call for a surgical consult. In the meantime I'll write up some morphine and let's draw some blood, Nurse Davies.' He handed back the chart and deliberately let his gaze fall to her mouth.

Nat's lips parted involuntarily as she took the chart. It felt as if he'd physically touched them. She reached for the bed rail and cleared her throat. 'Certainly, Dr Lombardi.'

And then he was gone from the cubicle and she was left staring after him, her lips tingling, her brain scrambled.

'Do you think I can get that morphine now?'

Nat dragged her attention back to her patient. Ellie was grimacing and clutching the sheet tight. 'Oh, sorry, of course. I'll be right back.'

Nat exited the cubicle determined to keep her mind on the job. 'Imogen,' she called seeing her boss. 'I need you to check some morphine with me.'

Imogen followed her into the room where the narcotics were stored. She inserted the key into the locked metal cupboard as Nat smothered a yawn.

'Are you not sleeping well?' Imogen asked as she reached for the boxes of morphine. 'You yawned all the way through handover this morning and you look like you haven't slept in a week.'

Nat busied herself with writing in the dangerous-drugs register to hide the sudden rise of heat to her cheeks. She was sleeping very well indeed. When she and Alessandro finally succumbed, they slept the deep sleep of the sexually sated. It just so happened that it only amounted to a few hours each night.

It had certainly been well after three last night before they'd worn themselves out. 'I'm fine,' she murmured.

Imogen removed a morphine ampoule and they counted the remainder. Nat drew up the injection as

Imogen signed the register then they left the room together and entered cubicle twelve.

Imogen smiled at the patient. 'Can I have your full name, date of birth and any allergies, please?' she asked.

Ellie prattled off the requested information as Imgoen and Nat checked it against her patient number in her chart and on the medication form. Satisfied they had the right patient, Imogen departed, leaving Nat to administer the needle.

'Thigh or bottom?' she asked.

'Oh, God, I don't care,' Ellie groaned. 'You can stick it in my eyeball as long as the damn pain goes away.'

Nat smothered a smile. 'I think your thigh will be easier,' she said, exposing her patient's leg. 'You don't have to move.' Nat prepped the area with an alcohol swab and delivered the morphine in a matter of seconds.

By the time she'd done another set of obs and drawn the blood Alessandro had requested, Ellie was already feeling relief. 'Better?' Nat asked.

'Oh, God, so much better. Thank you.'

The curtain flicked back and Alessandro poked his head in. 'Surgeon will be here in twenty minutes.'

Both the women nodded and Alessandro disappeared again, flicking the curtain back in place.

Ellie looked at Nat. 'That man is totally dreamy. He can park his Italian leather shoes under my bed any day.'

Nat laughed, understanding the sentiment totally. She felt a surge of female pride, like that of a lioness, that Alessandro's shoes were firmly parked under her bed. Or hers under his, anyway.

'Seriously, seriously gorgeous,' Ellie babbled. 'You could just eat him with a spoon, couldn't you? He doesn't have a ring—is he married?'

Nat suppressed the sudden urge to turn on her patient and growl *Back off, sister* as a sudden shard of jealousy sliced through her. Her patient was smiling like a goon and her voice was a little slurred. Nat reminded herself it was the morphine talking.

'Drugs have obviously kicked in, then,' Nat said, forcing lightness into her voice. 'I'll be back with the surgeon. Here's your bell if you need me for anything.'

Nat stepped out of the curtain and took a few deep breaths. Alessandro looked up from the desk at the same time her gaze fell on him and he blasted her with a dose of heavy-lidded heat. Every cell in her body leapt to attention.

'Nat, I've just put a Mrs Rothbury into cube ten,' Imogen said as she bustled by.

Nat dragged her eyes off Alessandro but not before she noticed a small smile touch his beautiful lips. 'Right. Cube ten. Check.' And she turned away without daring to look at him again.

It was like that for the rest of the shift. Wherever she was—he was.

Smiling at her with those private eyes as she handed over the twenty-six-year-old male who had accidentally ingested sterilising tablets instead of aspirin.

Brushing his fingers against hers as she handed him the chart of the forty-nine-year-old-woman who was having an allergic reaction to an unidentified substance.

Watching her intently as he moved his stethoscope around the chest of a twenty-year-old-male complaining of shortness of breath.

Grabbing her hips and lingering a little too long as he passed behind her in the cramped confines of a lift as they transported a thirty-six-year-old female who had suddenly gone blind in her right eye to CT scan.

And calling her Nathalie every chance he got.

By the time she was halfway through her shift, Nat's body was humming with desire like a damn tuning fork. He was everywhere and each hour cranked the anticipation up another notch. She doubted they'd get any sleep at all tonight.

Just after lunch Nat opened the curtains to cube nine and greeted her next patient. Seventy-two-year-old Mr Gregory, a five-year prostate cancer survivor, was complaining of hip pain. 'Hello, Mr Gregory, my name's Nat. Pleased to meet you.'

Her patient gave a loud hoot. 'Ron, please. Mr Gregory reminds me of my teaching days and as much as I loved it I'm damned pleased I'm not doing it any more.'

Nat laughed. He was a sprightly guy, tall and snowy-haired with crinkles around his eyes like he enjoyed a good laugh and clear blue eyes that contained a wicked sparkle.

'Ron it is.'

'Sorry to be such a damn nuisance. Bloody GP's making a fuss about nothing.'

Nat could hear a strained note in his voice and sensed that beneath all the sparkle and bravado Ron was a worried man. 'Better to be safe than sorry.'

'Hmph!'

Just then Alessandro pushed back the curtain and entered, and Nat felt the wild clenching of her stomach as his presence filled the cubicle. His gaze on her was brief but no less cataclysmic before turning his attention to his patient. 'Mr Gregory, what seems to be the problem today?'

Nat tried to listen to the examination but it was kind of hard to hear over the roar of her hormones. Even the way he doctored was sexy. He listened, he didn't assume or begin with preconceived opinions. He put his patients at ease. He let them talk and gently herded them back with a pertinent question if they wandered off track.

Alessandro put the stethoscope in his ears and Nat helped Ron get into a sitting position so Alessandro could listen to both back and front.

'I see you're not married, missy,' Ron said as he dutifully breathed in and out. 'Are young men blind these days or just plain stupid?'

Nat laughed. She was conscious that Alessandro needed Ron to be quiet and also that he could hear every word magnified through the bell of the stethoscope. 'Good question.'

'Or maybe you're just holding out for a more mature gent? Very wise. Take my generation, we know how to treat a lady.'

Nat laughed again. She was used to patients flirting with her, particularly men of Ron's age. She knew the drill. It was a bit of harmless banter to pass the time and take their minds off their problems. And if it helped distract Ron for a while then it would have served its purpose.

'What do you reckon, missy?'

'Well, now, that depends. What subject did you teach?'

'English.'

'Ah.' Nat sighed. 'I had the hugest crush on my high-school English teacher.'

'I see you're a woman of very good taste.'

Alessandro frowned as he finished listening to Ron's chest and eased the man back down. His patient was openly flirting with Nat and it was frankly annoying.

'He used to quote poetry all the time. I think I was a little in love with him.'

'Poetry? I can quote you poetry. Who's your favourite? Shakespeare? Shelley? Browning? Wordsworth?'

Nat tapped the man's wedding ring. 'Oh, and what would your darling wife say to that?' she teased.

'Ah, well as long as it was Shelley she'd probably forgive me. She's a sucker for Shelley.'

Alessandro blinked as Nat laughed and patted her patient's hand. A surge of undiluted jealousy spiked his bloodstream and he suppressed the urge to pick up Nat's hand and move it away from Ron's vicinity.

'We'll get an X-ray.'

Nat looked up, startled at the steely note in Alessandro's voice. Gone was the incendiary stare and the soft smile on his full lips. His mouth was a bleak slash and the planes of his face looked harsh and forbidding once again.

'I'll organise it.' He nodded at Ron. 'Excuse me.'

Nat frowned as they watched Alessandro leave. 'He's a bit of a grumpy old so-and-so, isn't he?' Ron dropped his voice an octave or two and gave her a sly wink.

Nat gave him a weak smile. 'I think he's just a little distracted.'

She did a set of obs on Ron, chatting with him a bit more about his heyday as an English department head. Then Nat excused herself, assuring Ron she'd be back shortly. Ellie was going to Theatre to have her appendix removed in half an hour and she needed to get her prepped and her pre-med given.

She headed to the small linen cupboard that was situated halfway down the main corridor that ran behind the cubicles for a theatre gown and hat. Alessandro strode towards her from the opposite direction. His powerful thighs made short work of the distance as he stalked closer.

His eyes commanded hers and held fast. She felt like he'd hypnotised her and she was powerless to resist as they moved inexorably closer. Even though his face was grim and his beautiful mouth, capable of such eroticism, looked almost savage.

They drew level and she frowned at him. 'Are you okay?'

Okay? He felt unaccountably not okay. A cold fist was lodged under his diaphragm as a primal emotion he couldn't put his finger on dripped icy poison into his bloodstream. He felt edgy and…tense. Like he needed to prowl. Or maybe go and hunt something…

Alessandro looked around the corridor. Satisfied no one was watching, he grabbed her arm and pulled her into the nearby linen closet, shutting the door.

Nat pulled her arm out of his grasp, jostling her even closer in the tiny room usually only meant for one person. She glared at him as the stuffy air, heavy with the smell of starch, tickled her nostrils.

'You like to flirt with other men?' he rasped.

Nat blinked. His accent sounded more pronounced and, glowering down at her, his gaze as glacial as black ice, he'd never looked more Italian.

'He's seventy-two, Alessandro,' she grouched, not quite believing she was having this conversation. 'He's worried, scared the cancer has come back. He needs someone to look at him as a person, not a chart number or a medical condition. It's harmless.'

Alessandro understood what she was saying. Hell, he even empathised. With any other nurse he would have applauded it. But not her. When she did it he felt the caveman deep inside roar to life. She was his. And he didn't care how crazy it was.

Without hesitation he backed her against the shelves, hands imprisoning her shoulders, and swooped his head down. Their lips met with a sizzle and his mouth opened wide, his tongue thrusting inside her already welcoming mouth. When she responded with a moan he pressed his body against hers harder so she was in no doubt that he desired her and she was his.

He pulled away as abruptly as he had pounced, taking a step back which was as far as the confines of the room would allow. His ragged breathing mingled with hers and filled the space as each stared at the other and caught their breath.

'Don't flirt with anyone, *bella*. I don't like it.' And then he turned, opened the door and left.

Nat reached for the shelf behind her as her knees wobbled and she practically swooned. She should be furious at such liberties. At such Neanderthal behaviour. But she didn't think she'd ever been on the other end of such a blazing kiss and frankly she was too turned on to do anything other than stare at the empty space and grin stupidly.

Nat was slightly preoccupied when she picked Julian up from the crèche that afternoon. Alessandro's kiss still blazed a tattoo on her lips and all she could think about was the coming night.

'I think he's coming down with something,' Trudy commented. 'He's been so much more interactive lately but today he was really quiet. He didn't eat much at lunch and he feels a little warm. We have had a couple of kids here coming down with flu.'

All thoughts of the night fled as concern rose to the fore. Nat placed her hand on Julian's forehead. He did feel a little on the warm side. She knelt beside him. 'Are you not feeling very well, matey?'

Juliano shook his head. 'I feel sore all over.'

His usually bright little eyes looked dull and his cheeks were flushed. 'Are your ears sore?'

Juliano shook his head. 'No.

'Your throat? Does it hurt to swallow? When you eat?'

He shook his head. 'No.'

It did sound like he was coming down with flu. She just hoped it wasn't the dreaded swamp flu that was all over the news. Not that they'd had any cases in Australia to date.

'Come on. We'll get you home and give you something for the fever. Papa can look at you when he gets home, okay?'

Julian brightened a little and Nat's heart did a little flip. It was gratifying to see that, even unwell, Julian was looking forward to seeing his father. They *were* making progress.

They arrived home half an hour later after stopping at the chemist to buy some medication for Julian's fever. Nat administered a dose and ensconced him in front of the television with Flo and strict instructions to stay settled.

Half an hour later Julian was in the kitchen, Flo in tow, seemingly back to his old self.

'I'm hungry.'

Nat quirked an eyebrow. 'You better now?'

Juliano grinned. 'Yep.'

Nat smiled. She hoped so but she wasn't convinced—it could just be the medication talking. Alessandro came home two hours later and she got him to check his son out. He looked in Julian's ears and down his throat and listened to his chest anyway.

'It all seems okay.'

Nat nodded. Alessandro's gaze bathed her in flame and it was hard to concentrate on anything other than him and what she was going to do to him when they were alone later.

By the time Julian was ready for bed a couple of hours later he was feeling warm again and looking a little subdued. She administered some more medicine which he took before Alessandro swept him up in his arms and carried him to bed.

Her heart gave a painful squeeze as Alessandro strode up the stairs with him. The way Julian's skinny little arms clung to his father's neck made her heart sing. They seemed like any other father and son and it was equal parts satisfying and, strangely, sexy.

Nat had a quick shower in her en suite, her thoughts bouncing from Julian's state of health to the thawing of relations between father and son to the smoulder in Alessandro's gaze that caused her skin to tingle everywhere as she scrubbed it.

She dressed in her pyjamas—a pointless exercise—and wandered out into her room at the same time Flo wandered out. Some kind of sixth sense alerted Nat to where her pet was heading. The cat didn't like to intrude on father/son time and seemed to have developed a fascination with Alessandro's bed—not that she could blame Flo.

'Flo,' she growled.

Flo ignored her, disappearing from sight. Maybe it was her mistress's scent, so ingrained in the sheets, that attracted her so strongly. Or maybe it was just some primal recognition of pure animal lust. Whatever the reason, Alessandro hadn't warmed as much to Flo as he had Julian.

She couldn't hear any of the usual giggles or excited interaction coming from Julian's room as she followed Flo's twitching tail down the hallway. Julian was obviously not his usual self.

'Flo,' she whispered at the cat as she crept into Alessandro's room to find her pet casually licking its leg in its favourite spot—the middle of Alessandro's huge bed.

At least the room was looking more lived-in now than the first night Flo had strutted her way in. They'd all gone through boxes marked *Master* last weekend and personalised Alessandro's room. Julian had been so excited when they'd come across a piece of pasta art he'd done for his father the previous year. When Alessandro had hung it in pride of place on the wall opposite his bed, his little chest had puffed out like a rooster's.

'Flo,' she said again, hands on hips, her low voice holding a note of warning as the cat continued to ignore her. 'You know you're not allowed in here, madam. Alessandro will not be impressed.'

A fine lifting of the hairs on the back of her neck alerted her to his presence a second or two before his arms encircled her waist and she was pulled back into the hard muscles of his front.

'Alessandro doesn't care as long as you're in here too,' he growled in her ear, applying pressure through his arms so she turned to face him.

Nat's breath caught in her throat as his gaze ate her up. There was wildness there, a level of desperation she'd not seen before, not even the first time.

'I've been thinking of you all day, thinking of doing this.'

He didn't give her time to process that. Time to even

suck in a breath as his mouth opened over hers and devoured every atom of oxygen in her lungs. He walked her backwards as she clung to him, dizzy from desire and hypoxia. And then his hands were plucking at the hem of her nightdress until somehow she was relieved of it and then his shirt was pulled out of his trousers and half his buttons were undone.

As they collapsed against the bed her hand had made short work of his zip and she could feel the heavy weight of his erection in her hand. His stubble scratched the soft flesh of her neck as he made his way down and she was parting her legs wider to cradle his hips, urging him closer.

'Alessandro!' She wasn't sure if she wanted him to slow down or go faster. Her mind was a blank. An empty space devoid of any thought, filled only with his scent and the sound of his out-of-control breath.

His mouth closed over a nipple and she cried out, almost convulsing with desire. His hands pushed at her knickers as hers plucked at his trousers. As soon as he had access he entered her and she dug her nails into his back, gasping as he slid home, stretching her, filling her, making her feel more female, more powerful, more helpless than she'd ever felt before.

He pounded into her with frenzied strokes, like a man possessed, and all she could do was cling to his shoulders as each jab built her to a crescendo of lust that contracted her muscles and energised every cell, innervating them to an excruciating awareness.

Alessandro felt the first jolt of his orgasm and crushed her close, burying his face in her neck. The sensation seemed to come from his very soul and he groaned and cried out her name.

Nat wasn't sure when it finished. It seemed to go for ever, suspending them on some plane that floated high even as it faded. It was almost as if she'd lost consciousness and wasn't aware of anything other than him until he grew heavy against her and her body moved involuntarily, protesting the weight.

He rolled off and somehow in the post-coital haze he managed to pull down the bed sheets and relieve them of their barely intact clothes. And then he was surrounding her again, spooning her, pulling her into him, pressing kisses into her neck, touching her breasts and between her legs. It was slower, lazier but Nat felt the heat building again quickly and gave herself up to the moment.

Several hours later, not long after they'd fallen into an exhausted sleep, Nat woke to a strange noise. Her eyelids flicked open and despite the pull of slumber she was suddenly instantly alert. Her heartbeat boomed in her ears as she strained into the apparent silence.

The she heard it again. A cry.

Julian!

Careful not to disturb Alessandro, she eased off the bed and groped around for her nightdress. Finding it discarded near the door, she threw it on and headed to Julian's room.

The muted glow from the illuminated fish tank by the window silhouetted Julian's tiny frame as he sat up in bed. 'What is it, matey?' she crooned.

'I've been sick,' he sobbed.

Nat, her brain still cloaked in slumber and her bones still heavy from sexual malaise, reached for the nightlight and snapped it on. Julian's hair was mussy from sleep, his face flushed. She could smell the acidic aroma of vomit and noticed the soiled bed linen.

She sat on the bed beside him and put her arms around his shoulders, noting immediately how warm he felt. 'It's okay, matey. Let's get you cleaned up and give you some more medicine.'

She helped him out of his soiled shirt and groped in his drawer for another. She picked him up and carried him into her en suite where she'd left his medicine just in case it was needed in the night. She administered the medication and then wet a washer and wiped his flushed face.

His fever now seemed to be accompanied by a runny nose and a slight cough. He denied a sore throat and ears and she resigned herself to shelving plans for a day at the beach and spending the weekend nursing him through flu. She carried him back towards his room but he clung to her neck and she didn't feel comfortable leaving him all alone in his bed when he was obviously miserable.

It didn't seem proper to take him into hers. She glanced at the open doorway at the end of the hallway. A memory from her childhood assailed her. She'd been seven and ill from something she couldn't remember now. But she could remember her mother bringing her into her parents' bed and how she had snuggled into her father. He had patted her back and curled his big arm around her and she had felt so safe and secure and loved. She'd felt like he'd held the cure for cancer in his palm.

It had been just before he'd left them and Nat cherished that memory like it was gold. Sure, her mum had always showered her with TLC when she was sick but without her dad and his big old arm there, she'd always felt a little less loved.

Nat didn't give it another thought. Everyone wanted to feel they were loved when they were sick. It was just…human. She crept into the room and onto the bed and laid Juliano next to his father.

Alessandro stirred and reached for her before he realised the situation. He half sat up and frowned. 'What's wrong?' he whispered.

'Julian's been sick. I think it's flu.'

Alessandro's first instinct was to refuse. Camilla hadn't believed in Juliano sleeping in their bed and her iron-clad opinions were ingrained.

Nat could see the indecision on his face. 'He's four years old. He needs you, Alessandro,' she said gently. 'There's no better place than Papa's bed when you're sick.'

Alessandro looked down at his son. Julian was looking up at him with dull eyes, a kind of hopeless despair giving them an added misery. He smiled down at him. *'Naturalmente il mio piccolo bambino, viene al Daddy.'*

Nat smiled. Her Italian may have been rusty but she knew enough to know Alessandro had consented, and by the look on Julian's face, he knew it too. Alessandro lay down on his side, wrapped an arm around Julian, pulling his little body close. He rested his chin on his son's head.

Alessandro's eyes drifted shut as did Julian's, but not before he'd tucked his hand in his father's. Nat sat and watched them for a few moments, her heart filling with an emotion she didn't want to investigate too closely.

They looked like father and son, like a family. Alessandro, the big protective patriarch, dwarfing Julian whose hand clung tight to his father's. Julian looked how she must have looked all those years ago safe in her father's embrace.

Content, secure, loved.

She sighed and eased herself off the bed, taking one long, last, lingering look before creeping out of the room. Even as she yearned to join them.

CHAPTER EIGHT

IT WAS amazing the difference a few weeks could make, Nat thought as she sat at a distance and watched Alessandro and Julian build a sand castle together down close to the shoreline. They'd spent the day at Noosa, swimming and playing beach cricket and eating fish and chips at one of the trendy little cafés that lined the board-walk.

There'd been a subtle shift ever since Julian had been laid up with flu for those two days. Whether Julian had been too sick to find the energy required to stay aloof or whether it'd had been Alessandro's complete attentive-ness, they'd come out of it much closer. It was like a bond had been forged—newer and stronger.

And they'd blossomed under it, opening to each other a little more each day. Chatter and laughter filled the house now instead of stilted conversation and the loud buzz of longing.

Julian smiled at his father. Sat next to him on the lounge. Sought him out to tell him things. He looked for hugs and went eagerly into his father's embrace. He'd lost that taut little set to his shoulders. The wary, defeated look that had haunted his features.

And Alessandro stopped looking a hundred years old.

It was heartening to witness and Nat just knew, as the sun beat down on her shoulders, that they were going to be okay. Sure, there would be moments when their grief and sadness would come upon them again, blindside them, but at least now they looked like they'd turn to each other for comfort and support.

At least they'd stopped looking to her for guidance.

'Nat! Nat!' Julian yelled, popping his head up from his all-fours position, waving an arm at her. 'Come and look at what Papa and I built!'

Nat smiled and rose. She'd deliberately taken a back seat over the weeks, pushing the two of them together at every opportunity. It did her heart glad to see father and son doing things together. To see Julian acting like a normal four-year-old. To see Alessandro looking less and less haggard.

But as she walked towards them, their dark, downcast heads together again, beavering away a bit more on their creation, she couldn't deny the tug at her heartstrings and the deep-seated yearning that rose in her chest. She knew it was good, as it should be, but she suddenly felt on the outside. Lonely.

'Isn't it great, Nat?' Julian enthused as she drew level with them.

Nat felt tears prick her eyes and was glad of her sun-glasses. It was great on many, many levels. 'It's totally awesome,' she agreed, ruffling his hair.

Alessandro smiled up at her and winked. He was in a sun-shirt that clung to his torso like a glove and boardies that hugged his butt and thighs like a second skin.

'Have I said that's a great bikini yet?' he asked.

Nat gave a half-laugh despite her heavy heart. 'Once or twice.'

His lusty eyes laughed at her and stole her breath. They looked like the smoothed, flattened black pebbles on the beach, warmed by the sun and utterly inviting. She wanted to push him back against the sand and have her way with him. He was easily the best-looking man on the beach.

'Papa and I are going to collect some shells. Can you make sure no one knocks the castle down?'

Nat dragged her shaded gaze away from temptation. She took a breath. Excluded again.

But it was good—so good they were doing stuff together. That Julian wanted to do spend time with his father now, looked to his father first. A few weeks ago he would have wanted her. So this was good.

She swallowed. 'Absolutely, I shall guard it with my life.'

'Come on, Papa,' Julian said as he picked up the bright blue bucket and marched towards the lapping ocean.

Alessandro vaulted upwards his gaze tracking his son's meandering path. 'You'd better wear that bikini to bed tonight,' he murmured, before moving off to follow Julian.

The next day they were all making popcorn in preparation for a movie afternoon. Alessandro and Julian had walked down to the video shop in the morning and chosen a couple of Disney classics.

'Ah, I think that's enough butter, don't you?' Nat laughed as Julian drenched the popcorn.

'Spoilsport,' Alessandro teased, and then gave his son a wink. 'Come on, matey, let's go watch the movie.'

They brushed past Nat, who was momentarily paralysed by the teasing note in Alessandro's voice and the way his sex appeal boosted into the stratosphere when the smile went all the way to his eyes. The fact that he seemed to have adopted the endearment 'matey' for his son was also rather…touching.

The doorbell rang, momentarily distracting her from her ponderings, and she absently called out, 'I'll get it.'

Quite who would be calling on a Sunday afternoon she wasn't sure. Maybe it was the little boy next door? He and Julian were the same age and she had told his mother that he was welcome any day for a play.

The entrance hall was warm and welcoming now with a large colourful rug breaking up the glare of the all-white tiles. Two large paintings decorated the walls on opposite sides and a hall mirror that had come from the ceramic ovens of the Amalfi coast hung by the door.

Last night Julian had helped his father hang a wind chime they'd bought in Noosa. He had passed tools to his father like a scrub nurse would to a surgeon and afterwards they'd stood, necks craned, Alessandro's hand on Julian's shoulder, admiring their handiwork.

The beautiful baby-pink mother-of-pearl discs, brittle and fragile, had cost a small fortune. But Julian had loved how they cascaded like a chandelier. And they certainly gave the entranceway a touch of mystique.

Nat opened the door. The person standing there was far removed from a little boy and very definitely Italian. He was tall and bronzed like Alessandro with an easy grin that emphasised killer dimples and a wicked glint to his brown eyes that would have put a pirate to shame.

So this is what Alessandro would have looked like had grief not hardened his features and permanently furrowed his forehead. The grin on the stranger's face quickly faded and Nat realised that not only was he staring at her rather fixedly but he was also frowning.

'Can I help you?'

As if he knew he'd been caught staring he recovered quite well and shot her a dazzling smile. 'Er…hi? I think I might have the wrong house. I'm looking for Alessandro Lombardi.'

The accent was like Alessandro's too and there was a similarity to this man that told Nat he was some sort of relation. She tried to ascertain his age. His face was smooth, unlined save for a few tiny crows' feet around his eyes, no doubt from laughter and, unlike Alessandro's, his hair was totally devoid of grey. A younger brother, maybe? Did Alessandro have brothers?

Bad time to realise she knew nothing about him. For crying out loud, she still didn't even know his wife's name.

Nat smiled back and held out her hand. 'No, you've got the right place. I'm Nat.'

The man shook it, smile firmly in place, his gaze studying her face intently. It wasn't creepy but it was dis-concerting. Maybe he was surprised to find Alessandro shacked up with a woman so soon after his wife's death?

She opened her mouth to explain, feeling unaccount-ably depressed as their hands disconnected. But what exactly could she say? She turned her head and called out, 'Alessandro!' He could explain. Maybe he knew what the hell they were doing.

Alessandro appeared in a few seconds, his face lighting up like she'd never seen before. 'Valentino! *Il mio cugino! Così buon vederlo!*'

Nat understood enough to know the stranger's name was Valentino and they were cousins. She watched as the men embraced and Alessandro kissed both of his cousin's cheeks. It was surprisingly sexy. She'd always loved that about Italian men. The way they so openly expressed their affection, no matter which gender.

That just didn't happen in Australian society. And she couldn't help but feel it was the poorer for it.

They laughed and clapped each other on the back and then embraced again. Nat was jealous of their easy affection and she looked away as if she was intruding on an intimate moment.

'Valentino, I'd like you to meet Nathalie.' Alessandro looked down at her. He could see the confusion in her gaze and he smiled at her. 'Nathalie, this is my cousin, Valentino Lombardi. All the way from London via Roma.'

He clapped Val on the back again. Considering they'd practically grown up together, it was wonderful to see him. Val had emailed last week to say he would be in town some time in the next month for an interview but he hadn't expected him so soon.

'Nathalie.' Valentino reached for her hand and kissed it. 'It's a pleasure to meet you.'

Nat blinked at the old-fashioned greeting. She got the feeling that Valentino Lombardi was an incurable flirt. Had she not been totally immersed in Alessandro, she might have even been charmed. But Valentino seemed like a boy in comparison. More like Julian than Alessandro. Too…carefree. Too…casual for her tastes.

'Come in, come in.' Alessandro ushered his cousin inside. 'Julian will be dying to see you.'

As if he'd been called, Julian suddenly appeared. 'Uncle Val?' He looked at the person in the doorway for a second, not quite believing who it was. 'Uncle Val!'

'Juliano!' Valentino held out his arms and the little boy ran straight into them. *'Il mio ragazzo caro, meraviglioso vederlo!'*

Julian hugged his uncle's neck tight. 'I missed you, Uncle Val.'

'And I you, *bello bambino*.'

'I'm not a bambino,' Julian denied hotly.

Valentino roared. 'Of course not. *Scicocco me!*'

Nat watched the family reunion, feeling even more on the outside than ever. 'I'll just go and put on a pot of coffee,' she murmured, pointing in the direction of the kitchen and taking her leave.

Alessandro and Valentino watched her go. Valentino turned shrewd eyes on his cousin. 'Alessandro, *che cosa state facendo?*'

Alessandro looked at Val's furrowed brow. *Good question.* What the hell was he doing? *'It' indennitia di s.'*

Val rocked Julian in his arms. 'Fine?' He raised his eyebrows. 'She's the spitting image of—'

'Conosco che l'fare di m,' Alessandro interrupted. He did. He did know what he was doing.

'Fate?'

Was he sure? Yes, he was. 'She's nothing like...' Alessandro couldn't say her name. Not in front of his son. *'You il ll vede,'* he explained.

And Val would see. Alessandro knew it would only take his cousin a few minutes in Nat's company to see she was nothing like Camilla. Not remotely. He didn't see the physical resemblance any more. He couldn't even remember the last time it had struck him.

They moved into the lounge and Val stayed for the afternoon, drinking coffee and beer and reminiscing. Alessandro felt a familiar spike of jealousy as Julian sat so eagerly, so naturally on Val's lap. He'd always adored his Uncle Val.

It had taken for ever to build up the same rapport with his son. But, then, he supposed Julian had always associated wild and carefree Uncle Val with fun and good times. And Julian, beneath everything that had happened, beneath the sadness and grief, was still a four-year-old boy.

And Uncle Val's lap was only temporary. Before too long his son switched places and had crawled onto his lap, content to listen to Val from the shelter of his father's arms. Alessandro looked over at Nathalie, his gaze triumphant, and she smiled back at him with understanding eyes.

He doubted they ever would have got where they were without her.

Nat left them to it as much as possible. It was another of those family-type events that were important to Julian. Important to them both to bond as a family, and she didn't want to intrude. Of course she caught snatches of conversation as she came and went, both in English and Italian, and it was obvious the cousins were close.

She remembered now that Alessandro had mentioned Val to Paige all those weeks ago. Was it Val's mother who was the deaf aunt he'd mentioned? The one he'd spent a lot of time with growing up? His second mother?

She guessed that explained their affection.

At one stage she caught the tail end of a conversation about women. Alessandro had obviously asked if there was anyone special in Val's life. Along with a hearty laugh, he got this response. 'The word is full of beautiful women, Alessandro. Why limit yourself to just one?'

It was pleasing to see Alessandro shake his head.

She asked Valentino to join them for tea but he excused himself citing jet-lag and the need to prepare for his interview in the morning. Alessandro and Val made plans to meet for lunch tomorrow.

As they stood to say their goodbyes Alessandro's pager beeped. He took it off his belt. 'Looks like we've just had our first confirmed case of swamp flu.'

Nat winged an eyebrow. 'Where?'

'Victoria.' He embraced Val again, doing the very European double-cheek peck. 'Do you mind if Nathalie sees you to the door? I really need to ring work.'

'It will be my pleasure.' Val grinned.

Alessandro glanced at him sharply as Nat headed for the door. Valentino, much like his name, was an incorrigible flirt. But this woman was off limits. Val was charming and despite there being only six months between them, used his younger years and baby face to his advantage. *'Recidi*, Valentino,' he growled low but steady.

Val looked at Alessandro's flinty obsidian eyes and nodded his head slightly. *'Naturalmente.'* And he followed Nat out of the room.

Valentino joined her by the door momentarily and she smiled at him, holding out her hand. 'It was nice meeting you,' she said.

Val took her hand and once again turned it over and kissed it. 'Thank you, *bella.*' He released her hand and looked at her for a long moment. 'Alessandro and Juliano are doing well. Much better than the last time I saw them. You're good for him, I think.'

Nat blushed at the speculation in his gaze. 'Oh, no, it's not like that. I'm just…helping out until my place is built.'

Val gave her a small smile and bowed. *'Arrivederci.'*

And then he was gone but she was left in no doubt that Valentino Lombardi hadn't believed her for one single moment.

Nat and Julian were sitting on the lounge, watching the television, when Alessandro rejoined them. 'Is it bad?' she asked.

'No.' Alessandro shook his head and sat beside them. Julian automatically crawled into his lap and he unconsciously opened his arms to accommodate his son. 'Fit, healthy forty-year-old male. But there'll be more.'

Nat watched the easy affection between them and her heart swelled. 'Had he been travelling?'

'Yes. He's just got back from South America. They're chasing down his fellow passengers and his other contacts now.'

Thanks to geography swamp flu, a mutant form of influenza A, had, until today, been kept from Australia's shores. But it had been declared a pandemic by the World Health Organization and there were protocols that had to be followed.

Julian's thumb had crept into his mouth and he giggled at something on the television. Alessandro rubbed his chin against his son's hair, his arms momentarily tightening around his little body. 'It was good seeing Uncle Val again, yes?'

Julian's thumb slipped out as he turned and looked at his father. 'Oh, yes. I love Uncle Val. I like being called Juliano.'

Nat watched Alessandro's smile slip a little and prayed he'd tread carefully. The first day they'd met he'd reprimanded her for using the Italian version of his son's name, citing his dead wife's preference for it to be anglicised. She could tell then it hadn't been his choice but he was just trying to stick with the wishes of the woman who had given his son life.

'You like that, *il mio piccolo bambino*?' Julian nodded enthusiastically. 'You know Mummy liked you to be called Julian.'

Nat held her breath. She'd rarely heard Alessandro talk about Julian's mother with him. Occasionally, as they'd emptied the boxes they'd come across something and Julian had mentioned his mother. Nat had encouraged it, had encouraged Alessandro to facilitate it. After all they should be able to talk about the woman they both loved so dearly. But neither seemed keen to talk openly.

Using the 'm' word now seemed like another good step forward in their relationship. Julian nodded. 'I know. But I like Juliano better.'

Alessandro raised his eyes to Nat. They looked like polished river stones—black and glassy with emotion. She could see the rush and tumble of feelings there as they swirled around. Would he insist on sticking to Camilla's dictates or would he follow his son's lead?

Alessandro looked down at his son, his heart stretching in his chest, growing bigger, like a balloon ready to burst. He'd expected tears, withdrawal, a return to the sadness at the mention of Camilla. Not a matter-of-fact reply.

'I can…' He hesitated and looked at Nat. She nodded at him and he continued. 'I can call you Juliano too, if you like.'

Both Alessandro and Nat held their breaths this time as they hung on Julian's reply. The boy simply nodded, said 'Okay', stuck his thumb back in his mouth and returned to watching the television.

Alessandro let out his breath. He looked at Nat who was blinking back tears. She smiled at him and he wanted to pull her close, put his arm around her and snuggle her in beside them, feel her head drop onto his shoulder. But Nat's very sensible insistence that they keep their relationship from Julian...*Juliano*...stopped him.

So he smiled back at her instead and mouthed, 'Thank you.'

Alessandro's elation didn't last long. By the time he'd finished reading to Julian—*Juliano!*—he was seething with frustration. It shouldn't be this hard to call his son by the name he had been christened with. It shouldn't feel so unnatural. He wanted to kick things, yell, shake his fist at God.

He wanted Nat. He wanted to tumble her into bed, pound into her, make all the thoughts that circled endlessly in his head, like vultures around prey, go away. She'd help him to forget, if only for a few hours. She always helped him forget.

Nat was coming out of her shower when Alessandro grabbed her, pulling her naked body hard against his, lowering his head to claim her mouth in a kiss bordering on savage. She responded instantly, twisting her head to give him all he needed, clutching at his shirt for purchase as the power of the kiss almost knocked her backwards. She gave way to his questing tongue, opening to him, and he growled triumphantly low in his throat.

He pulled back slightly, his breathing harsh, his hands kneading her bare buttocks. 'I need you. Now.' He was so close his lips brushed hers with every word.

Nat could feel his hardness even through the layers of his clothes and her eyes practically rolled back in her head as she fought the urge to rub herself against him like some half-crazed feline. He was so close and the smell of him, the taste of beer on his breath, his mere presence was intoxicating. She could barely think for the pheromones that were clogging her senses as their chests heaved in and out, loud in the quiet of the house.

But she knew something was wrong. He'd been so happy earlier, had gone into Juliano's room with a spring in his step. And now he was looking at her with trouble tainting the lust and desire.

She pushed against his chest. 'What's wrong, Alessandro?'

Alessandro's arms tightened around hers momentarily and then he sighed and stepped back. Damn her for being so shrewd. He raked a hand through his hair as his gaze raked her body. Despite his inner turmoil she was butt naked in front of him and he wanted her. 'Nothing,' he dismissed, reaching for her.

Nat stepped to the side, evading his touch. 'Alessandro.'

He heard the warning note in her voice despite the mesmerising sway of her breasts as she moved. Then she shook her head at him, rolled her eyes, reached for her nightdress at the end of her bed and threw it on over her head.

'Better?'

Alessandro shot her a grudging smile. 'No.' She sent him a reproving look and crossed her arms. He sighed and felt for the edge of her bed as he sat down. 'It feels so strange calling him Juliano. And it shouldn't. *Inferno!* He's half Italian, for goodness' sake. It should come naturally.'

He felt suddenly impotent, despite the raging hard-on in his pants. Pushing off the bed, he stalked around the room. Damn Camilla and their screwed-up relationship.

He turned to face Nat, rubbing at his forehead. 'He was christened Juliano.' He dropped his hand. 'Camilla insisted on it.'

Nat stayed very still. Camilla. So that was her name. She frowned. 'So why Julian?'

Alessandro snorted. Because it was just one of the ways Camilla had screwed with him, made him pay. But he couldn't say that to Nat because as far as she was concerned he was still in love with his wife and what kind of a man did it make him to admit he wasn't? Admit he'd never loved her in the first place?

He sighed. 'It's a long story.'

He looked sad and defeated and she felt dreadful that he'd gone from being so happy to deeply troubled. Had Valentino's arrival dredged up old, painful memories?

'Can we please just go to bed? I want you.'

Nat's stomach clenched at his blatantly sexual request. She'd hoped he'd take this opportunity to get some stuff off his chest but just because he finally uttered her name it didn't mean he was going to open up about Camilla.

A stronger woman would have pushed harder. A stronger woman would have insisted they have it out for once and for all. But the way he expressed his desire, the way he looked at her with those wounded eyes, she knew she'd give him anything. She pulled the nightdress up over her head and opened her arms to him.

Much later in his bed, Nat lay draped down his side, her head on his shoulder, his fingers absently running up and down her arm. Sleep hovered around them in a post-coital haze that was both energising and paralysing at the same time.

She rubbed her cheek against his shoulder, revelling in its warmth and their combined aroma. Her hand was resting on his belly and she trailed her fingers up his chest. 'Val looked at me very strangely this afternoon when I opened the door.'

'He was probably trying to work out how available you are,' Alessandro murmured. The mere thought punched him in the gut, even though he knew the real reason his cousin had given her such a strange look.

'You seem close.'

Alessandro smiled. 'We grew up in the same village. Our fathers were brothers. My parents, they were very…passionate people…they argued, a lot. They split up and got back together and split up and got back together. They were up and down like yo-yos. I would get shuffled to Aunty Rosa's when things were in upheaval. Which was often. It didn't matter that she was deaf or had six kids of her own, she always took good care of me. She and my uncle had this totally different relationship. Ben adored Aunty Rosa.'

'Did you have siblings?'

'No. Just me. Which was probably a good thing.' Even though as a kid he had yearned for siblings like Val. Someone to share the burden. 'My father finally left for good when I was fourteen and my mother really fell apart. We both moved in with Rosa after that.'

Nat heard the dull ache in his voice and felt it all the way down to her soul. She rolled on her stomach and propped her chin on Alessandro's chest. 'Did you miss your father?'

Alessandro dragged his gazed from the ceiling to mesh with the warm welcoming glow of hers. 'Not really. I barely knew him. He travelled with his work a lot. He wasn't exactly a hands-on father. He left it up to my mother mostly. And then when he was home they were usually arguing.'

Nat's heart broke for him. Her own memories of her father, before he'd walked out, couldn't be any more different. Maybe that explained Alessandro's clumsy fathering. No solid role model. Maybe he too had left it up to Camilla.

'I'm surprised you married at all with that kind of history.'

Alessandro looked away from her knowing eyes, his fingers stilling on her arm. If only she knew. It had never been his intention to marry. He'd been more than happy playing the field and having a damn fine time doing so. His childhood had cured him of the romantic notion of finding 'the one' and he'd been merrily working his way through the rest.

And then Camilla—clever, sexy, cool-as-ice Camilla— had fallen pregnant. Deliberately.

He looked back at the ceiling, his fingers resuming their feather-light strokes. 'You sound like you talk from experience. Are your parents divorced too? Is that why you haven't ever married?'

Nat shut her eyes as he firmly changed the subject. She'd obviously pushed him far enough for one night and he'd revealed all he was going to—which was a hell of a lot more than she'd known to date. They didn't do this— talk. They had sex until they fell into exhausted slumber. Talking had never been high on their list of priorities. But suddenly she wanted to know everything there was to know.

She sighed and turned on her side again, draping her

arm across his chest, her leg over his thigh as she pondered his question. She didn't want to talk about herself but maybe if she did, he might open up some more about himself.

'My father left when I was eight.' Her words fell into the silence and she felt Alessandro's finger falter temporarily before starting up again. 'No warning. He'd been having an affair for a year and the other woman, Roxanne, was pregnant. So he just…left.'

Alessandro heard the slight wobble in her voice and tightened his arm around her. 'I'm sorry.'

Nat shut her eyes. Why after all this time was the devastation still so potent sometimes? 'It was never the same after that. I spent time with him and Roxy and the kids over the years, Mum made sure of it. I have two wonderful half-brothers. But it was like he'd moved on from me. Sure, he still loved me, I knew that, but he just stopped being a father to me, like I stopped being his responsibility.'

Nat swallowed the lump that had lodged in her throat. It had been a long time since she'd thought about this stuff. 'He had his new wife and his boys and I was just always…an afterthought. The old love and affection we had was gone. He became withdrawn from me, emotionally distant, and I always felt like—still do, I guess—that I had to prove I was still worthy of his love.'

It didn't take Alessandro long to figure out why Nat had felt such an instant rapport with Juliano. When he looked back now at the distance between him and his son not that long ago he cringed. Thankfully she'd been here to show them the way.

'It must have been hard for you to watch Julian…' Alessandro shook his head. '*Juliano*. In the beginning.'

Nat nodded. 'I could see the way he looked at you with such longing and it reminded me of the way I used to look at my dad after he'd left. I know the situation was different with you two, that grief was involved, but…'

'It's okay,' Alessandro assured her. 'I knew we were in trouble, I just didn't know how to fix it.' He kissed her forehead. 'And then you came along.'

Nat smiled and snuggled closer. 'Super-Nat to the rescue.' Alessandro chuckled and her heart filled with the sound of it. 'Pity I wasn't so good at fixing my own problems.'

'Is this about the man you talked about in the lift that day? You said it had become untenable.'

Nat nodded. 'He was newly divorced when I met him and that was probably my first mistake. But he was so sad, so knocked around by life and so kind and caring and he was so happy to be happy again, with me, I fell in love with him. He was endearing.'

Which was exactly why being here with Alessandro was stupidity. Alessandro and Juliano were just history repeating itself. Except it was worse. Rob and his wife had chosen to separate. Alessandro hadn't chosen for his wife to be taken from him.

'So what happened?'

'His ex-wife was in his life, our lives, a lot.'

'You didn't like her?'

'I liked her fine. But I don't think either of them ever really let go. He spent more and more time with her, making excuses to see her. A leaky tap. A family wedding. A Valentine's Day meltdown. And after years of coming second to her I just couldn't do it any more.'

'That does sound untenable.'

Nat shut her eyes, the skin on her arms turning to goose-bumps as Alessandro drew circular patterns with his fingers. It had been awful. A long slow death, hanging on, hoping things would change.

'*C'est la vie.*' She shrugged. 'By the end there wasn't really any love left. Just hurt. I'm over it now.' She didn't want to talk about Rob any more. Or her father. It was his turn.

'What about your wife? Camilla? How did she die?'

Alessandro's fingers stopped abruptly. He couldn't talk about Camilla. Not to her. Not to anyone. He could barely utter her name without waves of guilt pinning him down. She had no idea how much it had cost him to say her name earlier.

He shifted, displacing her temporarily, and then moved over her, settling his pelvis against hers. 'I think we've talked enough for one night, don't you?' And he lowered his head, dropping a string of tiny kisses up her neck and across her jaw.

Nat should have protested. God knew, she wanted to know everything about him but she felt her body respond to his weight and his smell and the way his mouth found all her sensitive places. And did she really want to know about the perfect Camilla and their perfect love? Hadn't she had enough of that in her last relationship?

So she didn't push him away and insist on talking. She didn't get huffy. She didn't get up and leave his bed. Instead, she shut her eyes and let him sweep her away to the place she knew he could take her.

There'd be enough time for talking when she moved out and their relationship came to an end.

CHAPTER NINE

THE following Thursday afternoon Nat led Alessandro into cubicle fifteen to examine a thirty-eight-year-old woman complaining of a sore leg. She had her nine-month-old baby boy with her, who was crying and irritable.

Alessandro smiled at the rather harried-looking woman who apologised about the noise as she jiggled the babe on her hip. 'He's picked up a bit of a cold so he's not exactly a happy camper at the moment.'

'That's okay…' he searched for the patient's name on her chart label '…Nina. What seems to be the problem?'

'I've got this really sore leg,' Nina said.

'Why don't you give the baby to Nat and hop up here so I can have a look?'

Nat smiled at Nina and the baby and held out her arms. 'What's his name?' she asked.

'Benji.'

'Come on, Benji. Let's give Mummy a bit of a break.'

The baby went willingly enough, sneezing three times during the transfer. 'Bless you, bless you, bless you,' Nat cooed, stroking the baby's warm forehead as she settled him on her hip and began swaying.

Alessandro was momentarily distracted as he watched Nat with Benji. The baby had stopped crying and was looking at her curiously as Nat's ponytail swished with the rocking of her hips. Nat chose that moment to look up at him and he gave her a lazy smile.

She looked good in her uniform. She looked good in shorts. She looked good in her nightdress. And she looked absolutely sensational out of it. He should have guessed she'd look good with a baby on her hip.

Nina, oblivious to their undercurrent, climbed up onto the gurney, swung her legs up on the mattress and proceeded to roll up her jeans. 'That's a bit of a climb, isn't it?' she puffed.

Alessandro's wandering attention returned to his patient. 'So, have you injured yourself in any way?' he asked half his brain still engaged with other thoughts. Images of Nat last night straddling him, smiling down at him.

Nina shook her head. 'My calf's been sore ever since I got off the plane yesterday.'

Suddenly Alessandro's brain snapped into laser-like focus. 'Plane?' He frowned. Painful calf. Air travel. DVT? 'Where did you fly from?'

Nina's brows furrowed. 'Perth.'

Alessandro's gaze sought the area that Nina was rubbing. Perth was only a four-hour flight, which made it less likely for a blood clot to have formed in the deep veins of her leg but it wasn't unheard of. And Nina was a little overweight.

'But I guess that was only a day after our flight from London,' Nina continued. 'Boy was that an awful flight. I was stuck in my seat the whole time with Benji needing to be fed constantly because of the cold playing havoc with his ears. He drank practically all through the flight. It's times like those I wished I'd chosen the bottle over the breast all those months ago. At least his father could have helped out.'

Alessandro's antennae started twitching crazily. Firstly, without even laying hands on her, he could see the swollen red area of Nina's calf. That didn't bode well. But secondly, and perhaps the most importantly, as far as the big picture went, was Benji's cough. It may have seemed quite innocent when Nina had walked in—just another childhood cold. But teamed with the word 'London' it was potentially much more.

Swamp flu was prevalent now in the UK as well as the Americas. The cases they'd had in Victoria had all been carried into the country through international air travel, although not yet from the UK. It was certainly causing all kinds of consternation and hot on the heels of several deaths worldwide some schools with infected students in Melbourne had been shut down as a precaution.

There'd been nothing in Queensland yet but due to the worldwide level six pandemic status there were procedures he had to follow. He didn't think for a minute that Benji had swamp flu but he knew he couldn't let them leave without making sure.

But first things first. Alessandro gently examined Nina's calf, the concentrated area of heat obvious beneath his palm. He felt for a pulse at the back of her knee and also felt for her foot pulses. 'Can you draw you toes back towards your knee?' he asked.

Nina complied, wincing as a hot arrow streaked straight to the centre of her sore calf. 'Ouch.'

'Hmm.' Alessandro urged her back against the pillow. 'I'm just going to feel for a pulse in your groin,' he said. He located the full bound easily. 'Any chest pain?' he asked, taking his stethoscope out of his ears and placing the bell on her chest.

'Nope.'

Satisfied her lung fields sounded clear, he helped Nina up into a sitting position. 'I think you may have something called DVT. Have you heard of it?'

Nina screwed up her face. 'That clot thingy? The one they do the talk about on planes?'

Alessandro nodded. 'Yes. You have the classic symptoms and your forced immobility on the long-haul flight definitely put you at a higher risk. We'll get an ultrasound to confirm the diagnosis.'

Nina looked at him, a worry line between her brows. 'I'm not going to die, am I?'

'They are potentially very dangerous but we've caught this in time and we can treat it.'

Nina looked relieved. 'So…what happens now? Do I have to go into hospital? I have three other kids as well as Benji.'

'I'm afraid it will mean a short hospital stay. We need to start you on a special intravenous drug that helps to thin your blood. And once you have therapeutic levels you go onto an oral form of the drug and you'll need to be on it for several months.'

Nina looked at Nat. 'Holy cow.'

'Can your husband get time off work?' Nat asked. 'Or do you have family to look after the kids?'

Nina nodded. 'My husband is still on holidays till next week. Luckily I have plenty of expressed breast milk in the freezer.'

Nat smiled. 'I'll refer you to our welfare worker as well. She can help with any of the logistics.'

Nina shot her a grateful smile. 'Thanks.'

'There's another thing,' Alessandro added.

Nina raised an eyebrow. 'Oh.'

'I'm going to have to test Benji for swamp flu, I'm afraid.'

Nina's eyebrows practically hit her hairline. 'Swamp flu? You think my Benji's got swamp flu?' She held her arms out for her baby and Nat handed him over.

'No. I don't think he has it. I think in all likelihood he has a common cold but I'm afraid there are certain protocols I'm governed by now because of his symptoms and the fact that he's just come from another country where the infection is prevalent.'

Benji, who was squirming and protesting his mother's tight hold, stopped as soon as Nina relaxed. 'Oh.' She kissed her son's head. 'But what if he does have it?'

'We'll start him on some special antiviral medication, which will help lessen the duration and vigour of the symptoms. We'll have to get the infectious disease team involved who'll track all contacts. The rest of your family will need to go into home quarantine immediately—just in case.'

'For how long?'

'Seven days. But we should have the test results back by tomorrow afternoon so hopefully only a day until they come back negative. You'll have to be nursed in isolation too until we know the results.'

'Hell. What a mess.'

'Yes.' Alessandro nodded. That was putting it mildly. 'But, as I say, I really don't think you've got anything to worry about. Okay?' He patted her hand and smiled. 'Let's just take this one step at a time.'

Nina's worried expression dissipated beneath Alessandro's comforting gesture and calm authority. She nodded. 'One step at a time.'

Nat and Alessandro left the cubicle a few minutes later. 'I'll call ID and X-Ray. We'll have to get a mobile ultrasound,' he said. 'Get an urgent NPA on both of them and move them to an iso cube. Limit numbers in there and make sure anyone going in wears a gown and mask.'

Nat nodded as she prioritised his rapid requests, feeling the thrill of medicine in action. She loved working with him almost as much as she loved sleeping with him.

The next afternoon Nat was smiling to herself as she opened one of the few remaining boxes stacked in Alessandro's formal lounge area. She could hear father and son chattering away as they cooked tea together and she was looking forward to the weekend.

This time with Alessandro and Juliano had been satisfying on levels she hadn't thought possible as she'd watched their journey back to each other. And she was going to miss them when she left.

But, in the meantime, there were still boxes to get through. The progress had been slow as Nat had given priority to activities that kept Juliano and Alessandro together and focused on the future. Going to the beach, heading to the movies, taking a ferry trip on the river, playing soccer in the park.

Sure, going through the boxes was also something they did together and helped them connect. They talked about the things inside and it was interesting learning about their lives before they'd entered hers. But she was more than aware that it wasn't a task Alessandro relished—the memories, she guessed—so she found it was better in small doses.

Still, as she looked around the house she couldn't deny the sense of accomplishment. Emptying the boxes, decorating Alessandro's house, seeing it turn from an igloo into a warm, welcoming home, also helped by the flowering of the father/son relationship, had been immensely satisfying.

Something that had started out as a way to help, a thank-you to Alessandro for his generosity, had become much more. And seeing the dividends it was paying in every aspect of their lives was very special.

She settled on her haunches next to the nearest box and opened a lid, finding yet another stash of linen. Whoever the mysterious Camilla had been, she'd had impeccable taste. Egyptian cotton sheets and the very best quality hundred per cent duck-down quilts—a bit unnecessary in Brisbane but too beautiful to shove in a cupboard and ignore.

As she reached in to pull out the next sheet her hand knocked against something hard and she peered in. Something was wrapped in the sheet. She felt it—it was about the size of a large book but not as bulky. Was it the elusive photos Alessandro had assured her were in one of the boxes? She'd almost forgotten about them over the intervening weeks and all their distractions.

Nat's heart tripped in her chest as she gingerly unfolded the fabric to find the back of a photo frame staring at her. She felt nervous as her fingers advanced tentatively towards the object. Was she ready to come face to face with Camilla? Her hand shook a little as she turned it over.

She needn't have worried. It was a photo of Juliano as

a baby. He was sitting like a little chubby Buddha in a sailor suit with a little sailor hat plonked artfully on his head. He was grinning at the camera, one hand stroking a sleek black cat.

She smiled. She couldn't help it. Juliano looked so happy. Loved, content, secure. Not a worry in the world—as it should be. So different to the boy she'd first met. How unfair was it that in only a few short years after this candid snap his whole world would be turned upside down?

The resemblance to his father also struck her. Looking at Juliano, she had a glimpse at what a young Alessandro must have looked like. Dark hair, dark eyes, olive skin and cherubic lips. She traced Juliano's mouth with her finger, so like his father's. And that sparkle in his eyes. One that she was seeing more and more of in Alessandro's gaze these days.

He must have been a beautiful baby.

She dipped into the box, eager to see more, her hands finding the tell-tale signs of more frames wrapped in sheets. She pulled them out one by one, unwrapping them like Christmas presents, each one a moment captured in time, a window, an insight into Alessandro's life.

Most of the frames held pictures of a solo Juliano at various stages of his life, chronicling his four years. Crawling. Walking. His first birthday party. But there were two with other people. One with an older Italian-looking woman holding Juliano in what appeared to be a christening gown. Alessandro's mother? Or maybe his aunt? Valentino's mother?

And the other with Alessandro on the London Eye, the magnificent Houses of Parliament forming an imposing backdrop. Juliano looked about two and both he and

Alessandro were pointing at something outside the glass bubble and beyond the view of the camera. It was obviously a candid shot. Father and son had been caught in fierce concentration, not smiling, their brows wrinkled, their faces frozen in serious contemplation.

It was strikingly similar to how they'd both looked when she'd first met them. Unsmiling, serious. But there was an ease in the older photograph that hadn't been evident then. Their heads were almost touching, Alessandro's hold was loose and comfortable and Juliano's little arm around his father's neck spoke volumes about his innate trust.

Nat dragged her gaze away from the photo and put it aside, delving for more. The next several frames were academic qualifications of Alessandro's. She spent a few moments trying to decipher the formal Italian, practise her rusty command of the language. But it was too academic for her and she put them aside with a mental note to make sure this weekend they tackled Alessandro's office.

The box was almost empty now, with just two folded sheets sitting on top of some plump cushions. Without even having to look further, Nat knew these were the frames she'd been looking for. Finally she'd get to see the woman who had won Alessandro's heart and for whom he still grieved.

Oddly, she hesitated. After weeks of internal speculation about Alessandro's wife she wasn't sure she wanted to know. What if she was simply the most gorgeous creature she'd ever seen? Could her ego stand that? And yet there was a part of her that needed to know and she cursed it. Cursed her innate female curiosity. Her vanity.

What had Camilla Lombardi looked like? Beautiful, no doubt. Glamorous too, she'd bet. She couldn't see Alessandro, a breathtakingly handsome man who must have had his pick of women, marrying anyone less than stunning. Had she been dark and exotic like Alessandro or maybe a glamorous redhead with milky skin and green eyes?

She stared down at the sheets. Was she ready to come face to face with Alessandro's dead wife? The woman who'd claimed his heart. She drew in a ragged breath at how much it hurt to think of him being loved by another woman. How much it hurt to acknowledge that even when he was buried deep inside her, pounding away, his heart belonged to someone else.

Goose-bumps marched across her skin and she rubbed her arms. This was stupid! They were no more than convenient lovers and she had no right to such thoughts. And his wife was dead. Did it matter what she looked like?

She reached for the sheets and pulled them out of the box, unwrapping the first one and refusing to pay any heed to the knot in her gut. She flipped the frame over briskly, businesslike, mentally chastising her hesitancy. Her eyes instantly connected with an eerily familiar pair of blue ones.

And everything in that moment crashed to a halt. Her heart stopped in her chest. Her breath stilled in her lungs. The synapses in her brain ceased to function. The frame fell from suddenly nerveless fingers and slid off her lap. A loud rushing noise echoed in her head and she couldn't hear anything above the roar. It sounded like she was in a wind tunnel or in the centre of a tornado.

A terrible dreadful sense of déjà vu swept through her, paralysing her with its ferociousness.

It wasn't until her lungs were burning, bursting for

breath, and her vision started to blacken at the edges that her body kicked into survival mode and took over. Her jaw fell open, her lips, completely independent of her will, pursed into a tight pucker, sucking in a desperate breath.

Nat coughed and spluttered as it rushed in, abrading her oxygen-starved membranes. She fell forward, extending her arms to stop herself collapsing altogether. She hung her head, eyes squeezed tightly shut as the coarse white carpet pricked at her palms. She gripped it hard as she gasped for breath, for sanity.

She didn't know how long she sat there, fighting for stability in a world that had suddenly tilted on its axis. She panted and rocked on her haunches like a woman in labour waiting for the contractions to stop, for the pain to ease.

It felt like hours could have passed when she finally opened her eyes and the world slowly came back into focus. Camilla's clear blue eyes looked calmly back at her from the frame on the floor. A small smile hovered on the other woman's perfectly made-up lips, like she'd gotten everything she'd ever wanted in life and she knew it.

A splash of moisture fell on the frame and Nat blinked. She felt her cheeks, surprised to find tears running down her face. The same sort of face that looked back at her from the glass. Same blue wide-set eyes, same blonde ponytail, same high cheekbones, generous mouth and pointed chin with the cutesy-pie cleft.

Nat shook her head as her earlier thoughts came back to haunt her. *Did it matter what she looked like?* She couldn't believe it had only been mere minutes ago that she'd been that innocent. That she'd ever been that innocent.

She picked up the frame and stared at the familiar

contours of the other woman's face. *They could have been sisters.* Her and Alessandro's dead wife. Their resemblance was uncanny.

The knowledge punched her in the gut.

Nat climbed awkwardly to her feet, clutching the photo, her legs rubbery, numb from sitting too long in her cramped position. She stood motionless staring at the dead woman's face, feeling like her heart had been ripped out of her chest and stomped on. Feeling rage and impotence and desperation in equal measure as the awful, awful truth sank in.

She was in love with Alessandro.

In love with a man who was still so in love with his dead wife he'd chosen a look-alike replacement with no thought to the consequences.

Her sense of loss was so profound not even the sobs that were choking her chest, threatening to strangle her, could find an outlet. She could hear a low kind of keening and knew it was coming from her, but didn't seem to be able to stop.

It was like Rob and her father all over again. Worse. Way worse. She'd had to compete with two women in her life for the affections of men she'd loved deeply. But at least those women had been alive. Tangible. How did she compete with a perfect memory? A ghost?

And, *goddamn it,* why was she always the bridesmaid and never the bride with the men in her life? Why was she always second choice? Wasn't she good enough? Lovable enough? Her father had left her for a new family. Rob had left her for an old one. And Alessandro?

Nat heard a little voice inside her ask the question she'd never allowed herself to ask. Had always felt selfish even thinking it. *What about me?*

'Nat! Nat!'

Nat jerked as Juliano came haring into the room, jumping up and down. She hugged the frame to her chest automatically as Juliano babbled on.

'Daddy and I have cooked the tea. It's his nonna's recipe from Roma and it's so delicious.' He paused, bunched his fingertips together and kissed them for dramatic effect, like Nat had seen Alessandro do the other night in the kitchen. Normally she would have laughed but she was barely taking any of it in.

'He says as long as it's okay by you I can go and play with Flo in the back yard but I have to make sure I wash my hands afterwards before I eat dinner because that just good hygiene.'

Nat blinked, her sluggish brain catching up with Juliano's rapid chatter several seconds later. She noticed some movement in her peripheral vision and glanced up to see Alessandro lounging in the doorway in the half-light like a big lazy cat. She looked at him helplessly. Even now, even knowing what she did, even mad as hell, her body still responded to the blatant sexuality of his.

'Nat!'

Her attention returned to the excited little boy in front of her hopping from one foot to the other. 'That's fine.' She nodded.

'Yippee-ee!' Juliano took off, heading for the lounge room and calling for Flo.

Alessandro pushed off the doorframe and prowled towards her. With Juliano occupied outside he had a hankering to kiss her. Last night seemed forever ago. 'How many boxes to go now?'

Nat's heart boomed in her chest as she read the intent in

his black eyes. A part of her wept inside as she realised she'd never kiss him again. She took a step back as he advanced.

Alessandro frowned as he entered the arc of light spilling across her. She looked pale and shocked, her blue eyes red-rimmed and flashing with pain. 'Nathalie!' He took two quick steps towards her. 'What's wrong?'

Nat took another step back, moving her arm out of the way as he reached for it. He stopped and looked at her, his frown deepening.

Nat released the frame she was holding and turned it around. 'When were you going to tell me about this?'

Alessandro's gaze flicked down to the object he hadn't even noticed she'd been holding in his haste to touch her. Camilla's face stared back at him, her Mona Lisa smile taunting him. So like the woman in front of him. And yet so not.

He shuttered his gaze as the painful memories assaulted him. Their loveless marriage, the argument, the knock on the door. He stuffed his hands into his pockets. 'Ah.'

Nat felt the casual comment right down to her toes. *Ah*? He knew. No what-the-hell-are-you-talking-about? frown. No immediate this-isn't-what-it-looks-like explanation. He knew.

Oh, God—it all made so much sense now. The way Juliano had looked at her that first day like he'd seen a ghost. Followed by Alessandro's own, more subtle but definitely, looking back at it now, stunned reaction later that same day. And more recently, Valentino's double-take.

She shoved the frame at him, pushing it hard into his abdominal muscles and releasing it as his fingers closed around it. 'Is that all you've got?' she demanded. His face was the grim mask of old. She couldn't tell whether he was desperately searching for an explanation to give her or whether he just didn't give a damn.

She scrubbed at her face. 'You know, Alessandro I knew you had an ulterior motive when you asked me to stay. I knew you wanted me to be some kind of substitute mother. But I had no idea what you really wanted was a substitute wife!'

'No!' His denial was swift and certain. Yes, the evidence was damning but how could he explain to her that the physical resemblance was where the similarity between her and Camilla ended? Without going into all the sordid details? Without exposing his guilt and shame? He didn't talk about that. Not with anyone. 'You are nothing like her.'

Nat couldn't tell whether it was an affirmation or an insult. She stabbed her finger at Camilla's frozen face. 'That's not what I see.'

'Trust me,' Alessandro intoned. 'The resemblance is only skin deep.'

Nat snorted. 'Trust you?' She stared at him incredulously. 'Why should I do that? When you haven't trusted me? Hell, Alessandro, you had the perfect opportunity to tell me the night Val visited. I asked you why Val had looked at me so strangely. And you dismissed it.'

Nat shook her head, feeling an edge of hysteria building. 'No wonder you weren't keen for me to find these pictures. Why weren't you just up front with me from the beginning? Why didn't you say, "Gee, Nat, you look freakily like my beloved dead wife"?'

Beloved. She thought he was still in love with his wife. Well, of course, he castigated himself, why wouldn't she? Marriage did imply love and it hadn't even been a year yet.

Alessandro watched as tears splashed down her

cheeks. He took a step towards her, the urge to pull her into his arms, to comfort her, overwhelming. But she took another step back from him and it was like a blow to his solar plexus.

He opened his mouth to deny it, her tears clawing at his gut. But how could he say the words aloud? *I didn't love her. I didn't love my wife.* What kind of a man did that make him?

Alessandro shook his head helplessly, wanting to wipe away her despair but shying from the words he knew he'd have to use. 'It's not like that.'

His generic reply cut deep. 'God,' she wailed. 'This is just like Rob all over again. Like my father. Playing second fiddle to another woman.'

She'd bounced back from her father. She'd had the love, understanding and support of her mother and other family. And her sunny personality. And she'd come through the Rob nightmare too—a little more bloodied and battered but still with belief in herself and in others.

But she knew without requiring any deep thought or analysis that her love for Alessandro far outweighed anything she'd ever felt for Rob. The slow gentle realisation of her feelings that she'd experienced with Rob was chicken feed compared to this all-encompassing, bubbling cauldron of desire and emotion Alessandro had hurled her into and been marinating her in for these last magical weeks.

She looked at Alessandro's emotionless face. The only sign that any of this was affecting him was the clench of his jaw. 'Did you ever just want me for me?'

It was a startling thing to admit to herself. But she knew she was right. While she'd been falling in love he'd just been using her body to try and erase the memory of his wife.

Loving the one he was with.

It certainly explained his insatiability. The almost desperate way he reached for her every night. Pounding away deeper, faster, harder, like he was afraid she'd evaporate in his arms if he wasn't constantly touching her.

Alessandro flinched at her accusation. 'I think I've more than adequately shown you how much I desire you.'

She looked at him like he'd just grown a second head. Desire? He might as well have reached into her chest and ripped out her haemorrhaging heart. When you loved someone, desire was just an empty vessel. It meant nothing without love.

'Really, Alessandro? Can you honestly stand here and tell me that every night with me, every insatiable moment, it was about me and not some kind of sick reconnection with Camilla?'

Alessandro felt a rage building inside. He knew she'd been played by men but he'd never use a woman in the way she was accusing. Surely she could see that his desire for her was one hundred percent genuine? 'That I can guarantee,' he ground out. 'When I've been in bed with you there's been no one else. I'd have thought you'd know me well enough by now to know that deep in here.' He tapped her chest.

Nat's heart beat frantically beneath his fingers as if it was trying to touch them. Traitorous organ! She knocked his hand away. 'This isn't about sex, Alessandro. It's about love.'

Alessandro blanched. What the hell did love have to do with it? 'Love?'

Nat flushed. Her chest had swollen with a mix of emotions that threatened to crush her and the truth had tumbled out. She hadn't meant to blurt it like that but she was damned if she was going to back away from it now.

'Yes, Alessandro, love,' she threw at him. 'I'm sorry, I know that this wasn't about love but it happened anyway. I guess I'm not quite as callous as you.'

Alessandro raked his hand through his hair, feeling more and more out of his depth. 'Nathalie…'

Nat shut her eyes and shook her head vigorously. 'No. Don't say anything.' She couldn't bear to hear any platitudes. 'I'll be out of your hair before you know it.'

Alessandro reeled a little more. She was leaving? The thought was shocking. 'But…your place won't be ready for weeks yet. What about Juliano? You can't just up and leave with no notice. He adores you.'

Nat felt a sob rise in her throat. His son did. But he didn't. Not quite the impassioned plea she'd hoped for, even though somewhere inside she felt a surge of pride that he was at last thinking like a father. Thinking about his child even before himself.

And he was right—leaving Juliano would be heart wrenching too. She loved the boy as much as the father. But at least she knew they now had each other.

She shrugged. 'I'll tell him something has come up and a friend needs me.'

'Where are you going to go?'

Nat didn't have a clue. All she knew was she couldn't stay here another minute. She felt like she was bleeding and it was sure as hell going to make a mess on Alessandro's perfect white carpet.

'I don't know. Paige's maybe. A hotel.' She shook her head. 'Frankly, I don't care. Just away.' She backed up as she spoke. 'Far away from here.'

Alessandro reached out and snagged her arm before she could run away. He couldn't bear the idea of her gone. 'Please don't go. We need you.'

Once it would have been enough. But she was tired of men needing her too much and not loving her enough. Now she knew the true depths of love—its power, its breadth—she knew she couldn't settle for anything less.

Nat shook her head. 'No, you don't. Not any more. You two are going to be just fine.' She pulled out of his grasp, her heart breaking, her soul aching.

The phone rang and they both looked at it, suddenly becoming aware of the surroundings outside their immediate circle of misery.

'You'd better get that,' she murmured, backing away.

Alessandro ignored it. 'Nathalie,' he called after her.

Nat turned away, the desire to run from him crippled by overwhelming misery and the weight of her heart in her chest. The stairs before her suddenly seemed like Mt Everest, her room way beyond at the summit.

Alessandro watched her go. He couldn't remember ever feeling so impotent. But she was asking too much. Love? Didn't she know that he wasn't worthy of her love?

The phone's insistent peeling nagged at him and four angry strides brought him level with the infernal contraption. He snatched it off its cradle.

'Yes?' he snapped.

Nat had almost packed her bag when Alessandro strode into her room. She was crying, tears blinding her progress. Her hands were shaking and her breath occasionally caught on a sob.

'Stop packing.'

Nat gave a harsh laugh. 'Go to hell.'

'That was the ID director from St Auburn's. The baby yesterday we screened for the swamp flu tested positive. As of now we're both on seven days' home quarantine. I'm afraid you're going nowhere.'

CHAPTER TEN

THE only person remotely pleased about their enforced confinement was Juliano. Having never had his father's absolute attention for an extended period, he thought all his Christmases had come at once. He even suffered the daily nasal swabs that were couriered to and from the house with a cheerful disposition.

He was completely ignorant to the suddenly stilted atmosphere between Alessandro and Nat. He didn't notice the strained politeness or the wary avoidance of any kind of physical contact. Not even the absence of laughter or easy conversation penetrated his happy little bubble.

But Nat was excruciatingly aware of it. It was a double loss. Not just the loss of what could have been but what they'd already had. It had been a surprise for her to realise the feelings for Alessandro that had stealthily invaded her every cell were love and a particularly cruel blow to discover it at the very second it was ripped out of reach. It had become crystal clear to her in that moment they'd never be able to return to what they'd had before.

Alessandro had tried to broach the subject again that next morning but she'd cut him off at the pass with a frosty 'Don't'.

She didn't want to hear any platitudes. She didn't want to watch him tie himself into a verbal pretzel with pretty euphemisms. She didn't want to know his justifications. The truth was he had hurt her way more than Rob's or her father's rejections ever had. At least they'd declared their outside interests from the beginning.

Alessandro had been utterly disingenuous.

After three days in home quarantine, or house arrest as Nat had come to think of it, she was at screaming point. If she hadn't been young fit and healthy she might have begun to worry about the constant pain in her chest and the heaviness in her limbs. Her jaw ached from the continuous fake smile she wore and her eyes felt gritty from three nights of crying herself to sleep.

She despised the nightly ritual more than anything. But no amount of internal dialogue castigating Alessandro and his deception derailed the tears. Her mother would say they were healthy, that she was grieving and they were a painful and necessary part of the healing process, but Nat would have done anything to stop them.

She wished she could be more like Paige whose opinion of men since her husband's desertion had always made her wince. Paige wouldn't have fallen for Alessandro. Paige's heart was guarded by barbed wire and thorny bushes a mile thick. Why hadn't she done that to hers? After her father? After Rob? Wrapped it up, protected it? Why had she been lumbered with this damn eternal optimism?

Because even now, despite everything, she wanted him. Every time he looked at her with his black eyes, she felt her pelvic floor muscles shift. Every time he walked by, her nipples pebbled as if he'd brushed his hand across them. Every time he opened his mouth, she wanted to kiss it.

Despite his soul-ravaging betrayal. Despite knowing he didn't feel the same way about her. Despite knowing that every time he looked at her all he saw was his dear, darling Camilla.

She was helpless against his pull. Oh, she hated herself for it but that didn't seem to matter either. Why? Why did love have no pride?

But mostly she was worried. About her willpower. If her belly lurched just at his nearness, how was she ever going to steal herself against him? How was she going to walk out the door? How strong would her resistance be by the end of seven days? Lord knew, it had been three days now since they'd shared a bed and despite how mad she was, she wanted him on top of her and inside her with an almost crazy desperation.

What if he asked her to stay again? Would she sacrifice her integrity and stay? Like she'd stayed with Rob, hoping it would be different? Like she'd held out hope that her father would, one day, remember that he also had a daughter?

No, seven days couldn't come around soon enough. Putting on an act for Juliano was a bigger strain than she'd ever thought it would be. And it felt wrong to lie to him. She knew how it felt to find out you'd been lied to. Only too well.

On the evening of the third day she excused herself after tea. She had a headache and was feeling weary. The sleepless, teary nights were catching up with her.

'You haven't eaten much,' Alessandro commented as he inspected her almost full plate.

She stared at him, absently rubbing her bare arms that had suddenly become covered in goose-bumps. 'I'm not very hungry these days.' It was said pleasantly enough for Juliano's ears but her gaze left him in no doubt as to the cause of her poor appetite. She couldn't afford to soften her stand or let her guard down. 'Excuse me.'

Alessandro watched her go, his hands fisting in his lap. He wasn't sure whether he wanted to shake her or kiss her. It had certainly been a long time since he'd tasted her lips and her flushed cheeks and red mouth had drawn his gaze tonight like a moth to flame.

He knew he deserved her contempt. Looking at it from her perspective, his actions must have seemed extraordinarily callous. But he wasn't sure he could stand four more days of the cold shoulder.

It was like his marriage all over again. Constantly pretending everything was all right for Juliano's sake and for those outside their marriage. The stress of projecting the illusion of marital bliss had been a constant drain when it had all been a sham.

'What's wrong with Nat?'

Juliano's question broke into his reverie. He smiled down at his son. 'She's fine.' He smiled. 'Why?'

Juliano shrugged. 'She's really quiet. And she looks sad.'

Alessandro was surprised by his son's insight. They'd both been trying to carry on as normal, to protect Juliano, but he was obviously a lot shrewder than they'd given him credit for. This wouldn't do at all. Surely for four more days they could make more of an effort?

By the time Nat was halfway up the stairs waves of goosebumps were marching across her skin and every footfall jarred through aching hips and knees. She shivered and rubbed her arms, her shoulders protesting the movement. Great! Marvellous. Just what she needed—swamp flu.

Her chagrin with Alessandro vanished as fantasies of a

steaming-hot shower took over. If only her room didn't seem so far away. She held onto the rail and gritted her teeth as she hauled herself closer. After a shower she was going to bed. With a little luck she'd sleep for three days and then this whole quarantine thing would be over and she could get as far away from Alessandro Lombardi as was possible.

She entered her room, walking straight past her bed, and started pulling at her clothes, tearing them off, uncaring where they fell. Her teeth chattered as more and more of her body was exposed to the air. She stepped into the shower cubicle and flicked on the taps, shivering as she waited for it to heat up and then gratefully stepping into its fiery embrace.

But still she felt cold, so cold, beneath the spray and she reached for the taps, reducing the amount of cold water till it was practically scalding. She sighed when it finally seemed hot enough, leaning her forehead against the tiles as it seeped into her tissues, her bones, her marrow.

It had been years since she'd had flu and Nat had forgotten how truly horrible it could be. She felt dreadful. Her head ached, her joints felt like they were on fire, her throat was scratchy and she didn't need a thermometer to know she had a high fever.

As if a broken heart hadn't been enough to contend with.

Alessandro left Juliano sitting on the lounge with Flo, watching a DVD, ten minutes later. He needed to talk to Nat, whether she wanted to or not, and he didn't want little ears listening in. He heard the shower as he entered her room and his gaze tracked her path to it from her discarded clothes.

He hesitated for a moment but, hell, he had seen her

naked before. They'd showered together numerous times. Had even had hot, wet, soapy sex on more than one occasion. He was damned if he was going to tiptoe around in his own house!

He strode into her en suite, stopping in the doorway to lean his shoulder casually against the jamb. The bathroom was full of steam and even if he'd wanted to catch a glimpse of her wet naked body, the fogged glass made it impossible. 'Maybe I should have installed a sauna in here for you,' he said dryly.

Nat's head shot up and she winced as her neck objected to the sudden movement. 'Get the hell out of here, Alessandro.' She was hoping for assertive but her voice had developed a croak and it sounded more desperate than definite.

'Nothing I haven't seen before,' he drawled.

Satisfied he couldn't see her through the fog, she placed her forehead back against the tiles. 'Nothing you're ever seeing again,' she grouched.

'I want to talk to you.'

Nat shut her eyes as her head thumped. 'Yeah, well, I don't want to talk to you.'

Alessandro's jaw tightened. 'It's about Juliano. It's important. Now, we can do it out here or I can come in there but we *are* having this talk, Nathalie. Now.'

Nat heard the menace in his voice and believed him. She felt so wretched all she wanted to do was burst into tears but she'd done that too much lately as it was. She was sick of feeling weak and helpless around him. Surely she could stand it as long as they focused on Juliano? And then maybe she could go to bed and sleep for a week.

'Fine,' she muttered, flicking off the taps. 'Pass me a towel, please.' She waited a moment or two and one appeared over the top of the shower stall. She grabbed it and gave herself a brisk once—over, every joint groaning but thankful that the shivering seemed to have been remedied by the hot water.

The fogged screen didn't allow her much of a view but she could see a dark figure looming in the doorway. Nat wished she had the gumption to waltz from the shower completely naked and sail past him with utter indifference. Just to show him what he was missing out on. But she knew she didn't have the guts to pull it off.

'My nightdress is hanging on the rail.'

It too came over and she quickly pulled it on. Her knickers were outside in a drawer—she could worry about them after Alessandro had had his say.

She took a moment to gather herself and then pulled the door open, walking gingerly from the stall. A blast of cool air hit her heated skin and the hairs on her arms stood to attention. Her stomach lurched as she took in his casual stance. His tie was long gone and his top button was undone. His sleeves were rolled up to his elbows, baring strong forearms covered in dark hair. Her already wobbly knees weakened further. The overhead light glinted off his hair like moonbeams off a dark sea.

'If you're going to try and justify what you did, you're wasting your breath,' she warned as she pushed past him.

Alessandro counted to ten before he turned to face her. *No, he wasn't.* It was better this way. Let her think what she wanted. It couldn't be worse than names he'd called himself. If this was his punishment for entering into a loveless marriage, for the argument with Camilla and its subsequent domino effect, so be it.

He didn't want neither did he deserve her feelings. He'd squandered love once already and now he was paying. He didn't expect happiness.

His gaze roved over her face. Her cheeks were flushed from the hot shower. She looked all pink and fresh. He could smell soap and he wanted to pull her close and bury his nose in the place where her neck met her shoulder. He shoved his hands in his pockets.

'I told you, it's about Juliano,' he said gravely. 'He knows something is up. He's worried about you.'

The thought that Alessandro's precious little boy was worrying about her was touching. She pictured his uptight little face when she'd first met him and knew she couldn't bear to see him so solemn again.

'I was thinking today we should float the idea of me moving out at the end of the week so it's not sprung on him,' she said. 'We'll tell him the unit's finished earlier than expected.'

Alessandro nodded with difficulty. She'd made such a difference in their lives it was hard to believe she'd been in it for such a brief time. Like Mary Poppins. Juliano, who'd already been through a major loss, was going to miss her. So would he. He already missed the smell of her and her warmth plastered to his side as he lay in bed at night.

'Perhaps in the meantime you could act like we haven't been quarantined for ebola?'

Nat glanced at him sharply, each neck vertebrae groaning in protest. 'I beg your pardon?'

'Well, you haven't exactly been your usual touchy-feely, happy-go-lucky self,' Alessandro pointed out. He missed that the most. The little smiles she'd give him, the brush of her hand on his arm or his back as she went by, the quick automatic ruffle of Juliano's hair.

Nat felt another shiver quake through her abdominal muscles as her ire rose. She wrapped her arms around her middle and glared at him. 'Gee, sorry bout that. I don't know what on earth could have come over me.'

Alessandro watched a spark of anger glitter in her eyes and her cheeks redden further. 'I never meant to hurt you, Nathalie.'

'Yeah, well, you did, Alessandro,' she snapped. 'So you'll have to forgive me if I can't just shake that off and act like nothing happened.'

Her bitterness was tangible and Alessandro felt lower than snake's belly. The last thing he'd wanted to do was hurt another woman. Especially one who had come to mean so much in such a short space of time.

But, damn it, he'd never promised her anything. Certainly not love or any kind of happy ever after. Same with Camilla. She'd known the deal when they'd married. But she'd never tired of turning the screws ever tighter. The weight of his guilt was like a boulder on his chest and sometimes he felt like he could barely breathe.

He was sick of carrying around all that extra weight. He'd let Camilla pile it on him but standing in front of Nathalie he was suddenly utterly over being the guilty party. 'I never asked you to fall in love with me,' he snapped.

Nat's head was throbbing again and her body felt like one giant bruise. It hurt to talk, it hurt to think, but something goaded her on. Maybe it was the flu—she'd never been this bitchy with Rob. After years of sharing she'd just accepted that she couldn't compete with his ex and let him go. But this was like a festering wound and deep inside she knew it needed lancing.

'No, you didn't. It was just about the sex, wasn't it? And what a bonus you got in me, huh?'

Alessandro ignored the edge of hysteria. He'd never seen her so riled. But her assertion that he had just been using her body was way off base. It may not have been love but it had been more than a superficial physical liaison—of that he was certain.

'I think you know I feel more deeply than that,' he said lightly. 'How many times have I shown you these last weeks?'

Nat wasn't sure if it was the fever or his simplistic statement that caused her hysterical laugh. 'Sex?' Her eyebrows practically hit her hairline as her voice rose an octave to almost a squeak. She felt her blood surging through her neck veins and pounding around her head, flushing her cheeks further. Her head felt like it was about to blow off her shoulders.

He had to be joking! 'Sex isn't love, Alessandro. No matter how many times you do it.'

The fervour in her eyes was compelling. '*Inferno,*' Alessandro roared. She was being impossible. 'I only meant—'

'Stop it, stop it, stop it!'

Alessandro and Nat looked down as Juliano hurled himself between them. He had tears streaming down his face and was clutching Flo in his arms.

'Juliano!' Alessandro crouched down and hugged the distressed little boy in his arms. How long had he been watching them?

Nat was speechless. What an awful thing for him to

have witnessed. The poor darling had probably never witnessed a man and a woman arguing like this. She felt a rush of light-headedness as she stroked Juliano's head.

Alessandro glanced up at Nat in time to see her sway dangerously. 'Nathalie?'

She heard his voice coming from far away as her vision blackened at the edges, becoming narrower and narrower. 'Alessandro?' she whispered as she stumbled forward.

He reacted quickly, catching her before he was even fully upright. She slumped against him as if her bones had dissolved and he frowned as her heated skin scorched his. *Inferno!* She was burning up. He swept her up into his arms. 'Nathalie?' He shook her gently, her limbs swinging limply rag-doll fashion.

'Papa?'

Alessandro could hear the fear and worry wobble Juliano's voice. Nat stirred and murmured something unintelligible. 'It's okay, matey. She's just fainted.'

Alessandro gave her another shake. 'Nathalie? Are you okay?'

Nat could vaguely hear him. She sighed. It was bliss to have the burden of keeping upright taken from her. 'Damn flu,' she muttered.

'Is she sick, Papa?'

Alessandro looked down at Juliano. 'I think she may have flu.'

Juliano's eyes grew saucer-like. 'Swamp flu?'

'I'd say so.' Alessandro looked at the bits and pieces of paper, the three books and two magazines littering the surface of her bed. 'Come on, Juliano, help me get her into bed.'

Juliano also looked at the bed and then shook his head. 'No. Your bed. When I was sick you let me sleep in your bed. And Nat said there's no better place when you're sick then Papa's bed.'

Alessandro gave him a wry smile. Somehow he didn't think she'd meant it to apply to her. But he looked down into her flushed face. She looked so…still. He couldn't bear the thought of her sick and alone. Plus, given the flu's severity it would help him keep a closer eye on her. She may well hate him for it in a couple of days but Juliano was right.

He grinned down at his son. 'Good thinking, Juliano.' And he strode out of her room with Juliano and Flo trotting behind.

Juliano stayed with Nat while Alessandro went downstairs to get her some of the antiviral medication they'd been given in case one of them did come down with flu. It wasn't going to cure it but hopefully it would reduce the severity and duration. He also grabbed a couple of cold-and-flu tablets he had with his other medicines.

When he returned, Juliano was stroking Flo with one hand and Nat's hair with the other. 'She's still sleeping, Papa,' he said earnestly as Alessandro sat on the side of the bed.

He smiled at his son. 'I imagine she'll be sleepy for a couple of days.' He reached out his hand and shook Nat's shoulder gently. 'Nathalie, wake up. I have some tablets for you.' She didn't move so he shook her a little firmer.

Nat prised her eyes open even as sleep fought to tug them closed. The room was dim and her surroundings were blurry but somehow though she knew she was in Alessandro's bed. His smell surrounded her.

Their smell surrounded her.

She half sat, displacing Flo. 'I shouldn't be in here. I don't want you to catch it.' And for about a million other reasons.

'The best place when you're sick is Papa's bed,' Juliano repeated gravely.

Alessandro smiled. 'Juliano's recent flu will probably be more than sufficient immunity and I got flu in January so don't worry, I reckon we'll be fine. Anyway, it's too late now. If we're going to get it, it's already incubating.'

He opened his palms to offer her the pills and was grateful when she didn't argue any more. He passed her a glass of water to swallow them with. 'The results from your nose swab today should be in tomorrow so we'll know for sure whether it's swamp flu.'

Nat nodded wearily as she sank back into the pillows, her eyes already shut. 'Hmm,' she muttered as she drifted towards a dark abyss.

Alessandro put Juliano to bed a couple of hours later and checked on Nat again. She'd kicked her coverings off and was lying in a fairly good likeness of the recovery position, her back to the door. Her nightdress had ridden up and he could just see a glimpse of bare cheek. He'd forgotten she wasn't wearing any underwear. He strode across the room, pulled the sheet up and got the hell out.

A few hours later he came up again with some more tablets. The sheets were kicked off again but she was much more decent this time, having rolled onto her back, her clothes covering her completely.

He woke her and she roused only enough to swallow the pills and slurp down some water before collapsing back against the sheets again. He pulled the covers up and headed back to his office.

It was well after midnight when he returned to his room for the night. He was tired and couldn't avoid it any longer

The sheets were off again when he entered and he smiled to himself. She was worse than Juliano. He left her as she was for the moment, knowing he'd pull them up when he joined her after his shower.

He lingered under the spray, his mind wandering to the peek of bare flesh he'd had earlier. It seemed like months since he'd touched her intimately. Run his hand over the curve of her bottom, had it snuggled into his groin.

Knowing she was back in his bed and had nothing on beneath her nightdress was having a predictable effect and he quickly turned the hot water off, bracing himself against the cold spray. *Inferno!* She was sick, for God's sake. Feverish and fluey. How dared he let his libido take control?

He towelled himself off briskly and threw on some cotton boxers and a T-shirt then gently eased into bed, careful not to disturb her. She was on her side again, her back facing him. He lifted the sheet over her, his hand touching her arm to gauge her temperature, pleased to find her skin was cool to touch.

Maybe she'd be spared a severe infection and recover quickly? After spending half the night scaring himself senseless by reading swamp flu stats, he hoped so. The thought was comforting anyway and despite doubting he'd be able to sleep at all he actually drifted off with surprising ease.

He woke half an hour later to Nat's shaky voice and groping hands trailing fire down his abdomen.

'I'm s-so c-cold,' she stuttered, her teeth chattering as her body, like a biological homing device, instinctively sought the nearest source of heat.

Alessandro automatically bundled her closer, pulling her into his side, his hand rubbing up and down her arm.

Despite her shivering, she felt very hot and he knew she was having rigor.

Nat felt some relief from the cold that bit at her arms and legs and nipped at her fingers and toes as she absorbed the warmth from Alessandro's body. Her teeth chattered and she whimpered as her whole body trembled violently, shaking through already inflamed joints and her thumping head.

'Shh,' Alessandro murmured as he rhythmically rubbed her back and arm. 'Shh.'

She tried to snuggle closer. Tried to press as much of herself against him as possible, tried to become absorbed into him, into his heat, into his vitality. 'So c-cold.'

'Roll onto your other side,' Alessandro murmured.

Nat protested but he was moving and turning her gently, his hand on her hip, and with his help she rolled over. And then he was wrapping himself around her, spooning her, pulling her into his big warm chest, covering her limbs with his and plastering himself to every square inch of exposed skin.

It felt heavenly and she almost groaned out loud. She felt him kiss her hair and she nestled closer. Somewhere beneath the fever and the chills and the aches and pains she knew it was wrong but frankly she was too sick to care and as the rigor held her in its grip she'd never been more thankful to be held.

Nat wasn't sure of time and place when she woke alone the next morning. The curtains were drawn, only a few rays of sunlight finding the gaps. It took a few seconds to realise she was in Alessandro's bed and the memory of him holding her, spooning with her, in the middle of the night returned in a rush.

She looked over her shoulder to see the bedside clock. Her neck was stiff and her head felt all fuzzy, like she'd been given a lobotomy in the middle of the night and her skull stuffed with cotton wool.

Ten a.m.

'Ah, you're awake.'

Nat rolled on her back. He was standing in the doorway in shorts and T-shirt, his hair ruffled, his jaw dark with stubble.

'How are you feeling?'

'Like I've been run over by a truck.' Her mouth was dry and she licked her lips.

'Fancy some breakfast?'

Her stomach revolted at the very thought. 'Just some water.' She ran her tongue across her teeth. 'And a tooth-brush.'

Alessandro grinned as he entered the room. 'Here are your next lot of pills. Why don't you take them, get up, have a shower and come back to bed?'

A shower sounded like bliss but just stretching her legs was a challenge. They felt like someone had been punching them repeatedly all night. She looked in the direction of her bedroom and doubted she could walk that far. 'I'm not sure I'm up to the trek.'

'Use my en suite. I'll get you some fresh clothes.'

He'd gone before she could answer and she was too weary to argue. It was, after all, the most sensible sugges-tion. And it wasn't like it was uncharted territory for her.

She shuffled to the side of the bed and slowly sat upright. A wave of light-headedness assaulted her and she shut her eyes until the dizziness passed. She downed the tablets and then stood gingerly on rubber legs, walking slowly to the shower.

Nat felt as weak as a newborn foal standing beneath the water and knew despite the luxury of the spray needling her skin she wouldn't be able to stay there for long. She leaned against the tiles, made a paltry attempt at throwing soap in all the right places and then shut off the taps.

She poked her head out of the screen and found a towel and clean pyjamas, even a pair of knickers hanging over the rail. She leaned against the vanity as she dried and dressed, her gaze falling on her toothbrush sitting next to Alessandro's.

She reached for it, catching a glimpse of herself in the mirror. She looked exactly like she felt, like a wrung-out dish mop. Pale, drawn, dark circles under her dull eyes, hair hanging limply around her face.

Her body was starting to ache again as she exited the bathroom, holding onto the walls for support. The freshly made-up bed was close but seemed light years away suddenly. She practically crawled to it and sank gratefully into its cool depths, utterly exhausted.

The aroma of clean linen filled her nostrils and on an empty stomach it was quite dizzying. She vaguely marvelled at the domesticity of it all. Toothbrushes side by side, clean sheets, her water glass topped up. If she hadn't been so weary it might have depressed the hell out of her, but it was nothing more than a fleeting thought before sleep once again sucked her under.

A few hours later Alessandro climbed the stairs to check on his patient. He'd just come off the phone from S

Auburn's, who had confirmed that Nat had indeed contracted swamp flu. Thankfully both his and Juliano's swabs were so far negative.

She was due some more tablets and he thought she might like to know. He pulled up short in the doorway when he realised Juliano, Flo in tow, was propped up on the pillow next to Nat, chatting away. Her eyes were closed but that didn't seem to be bothering him.

He opened his mouth to motion for Juliano to come away but then his son said something that rendered him totally powerless.

'Please get better, Nat. I want you to be my mummy.' Juliano stroked Nat's forehead gently. 'We love you Nat.'

Alessandro's heart thundered in his chest as his son's innocent comments. Nat stirred at that point and murmured, 'Love you too, matey,' before settling back to sleep.

Alessandro held his breath. Was she lucid? Had she heard Juliano? He wasn't sure. A roaring in his ears threatened to deafen him as his chest filled with a feeling he was becoming all too used to. Except now he knew what it was.

All that he cared about in the world was right in front of him and he'd been so blind.

He was in love with Nathalie.

He'd been so busy punishing himself for past mistakes he hadn't been paying attention to what was happening in the here and now. When Nat had mentioned the 'l' word he'd run a mile because he'd still been looking back. But looking at his son and the woman in his bed—pale and ill and the best thing that had ever happened to him—he knew they were the way forward. He knew they were his future.

If it wasn't too late.

CHAPTER ELEVEN

NAT slept for the rest of the day, waking only for water, medication and the odd rest stop. She took the news of the confirmed diagnosis with a sleepy shrug and a 'Nice to know I'm a World Health Organization statistic now'.

Alessandro was pleased for the time. It gave him time to think, to strategise. He knew he had his work cut out for him. He knew that she'd been betrayed by two men in her past over another woman and that this time round she wouldn't be so forgiving. He knew she wouldn't take any platitudes or settle for any slick proclamations.

He was going to have to tell her the truth. The whole truth. Something he'd never told anyone. What was that old saying? The truth will set you free. Maybe it would. He hoped so. Maybe it was time to get it all out in the open instead of keeping it inside and beating himself up about it.

Surely he deserved love too? Juliano certainly did. He knew he couldn't let her walk out of his life without trying. Hiding in the past hadn't done either of them any good. Maybe it was time to start looking forward, to start living for the future?

* * *

Alessandro came to bed late again that night, having gone over and over in his head what he was going to say to her once she was well enough. He was nervous, a sick kind of feeling sitting heavily in his stomach, like a layer of grease, sludgy and stagnant.

She didn't stir when he joined her and he turned on his side and just looked at her. He wanted to reach out for her, pull her into him as he had last night, but resisted. He wouldn't take advantage of her. Not when her defences had been knocked flat.

But he hoped she'd allow him to share her bed every night of his life. If he played his cards right maybe she would.

On that positive note he drifted to sleep

Nat woke with a start early next morning. Again it took a while to orientate herself as a pale finger of daylight peeked through the gap in the curtains. *Alessandro's room.* She became aware of him behind her, wrapped around her again, his strong forearm so close to her cheek she could have turned her face and pressed a kiss to it.

Had she sought him out like the previous night or had it just been a natural position for their bodies to assume? The lovers within finding a way to be together if only subconsciously?

She realised suddenly she actually felt quite good. She wriggled slightly. No aches or pains. Her headache had gone and her thought processes didn't seem sluggish. She didn't feel feverish and her throat no longer hurt. She certainly couldn't run a marathon but it seemed as if the worse had passed.

She wriggled again for the sheer joy of being able to do

so without pain and suddenly became aware of a hardness pressing into her from behind. And she knew instantly it was what had woken her, as surely as she knew her own heartbeat. The lover inside had subconsciously responded to the signal from her beloved.

'Alessandro?' she whispered.

Alessandro, who had been awake for fifteen minutes trying to quell his hard-on without waking her up, groaned behind her. He placed his forehead against her shoulder blade. 'I'm sorry, *il mio amore*. My body betrays me.'

A rush of desire slammed down low and she squeezed her legs together as a burst of heat tingled between them. He sounded in agony and she could definitely relate.

Alessandro took a deep steadying breath. 'If you let go of my arm, I'll get up.'

Nat realised his lower arm was trapped against her body. But suddenly she didn't want to release him. They'd forged a new kind of intimacy the last couple of days and she didn't want to let it go—not yet. She wanted to feel him around her, in her. Like before. Like old times.

Maybe her illness had weakened her but suddenly her blood was boiling with lust. His aroma filled her senses and the lust surged around her body, filling up every cell, every heartbeat, every breath. It was crazy, she knew, but was it so wrong to want one last moment with him to cherish for ever?

She reached behind her and slid her hand between them, seeking and finding his taut erection straining against his underwear.

Alessandro shut his eyes, pressing his forehead hard against her. 'Nathalie!' he groaned.

She gave him a fierce squeeze before burrowing past his

waistband and touching his naked length, revelling in his guttural moan that echoed around the room. He sounded like a bull elephant in rut and she could barely see she was so inflamed with need.

She grabbed his lower hand and brought it to her breast, crying out herself as he squeezed it. 'Yes!'

'Nat…' Alessandro dragged in a breath as her hand slid up and down his length, sliding it enticingly against the cheek of her bottom. 'I don't think we should be doing this now. You're not well.'

Nat shook her head as his hand rubbed against the tortured peak of her nipple. 'I'm fine. I need this, Alessandro.' She moved her hand off him to push up her nightdress and shimmy her knickers down over her hips. She pressed her bare bottom back into him, rotating it against his erection.

'Nathalie!'

She reached for him again, wrapping her hand around his girth. 'Please.'

Alessandro was seeing stars in his efforts to hold back his desire while his body betrayed him. There was so much he wanted to tell her but he couldn't now. Not in the middle of all this. She would think it was just pillow talk. Things people who didn't love each other said in bed that weren't necessarily true. And he didn't want to diminish what he had to say.

But he could show her. He could make love to her. Show her with his body, his touch, that she was more than sex, more than a substitute.

His hand left her nipple and she whimpered. 'Shh,' he said, kissing her neck. 'Just for a moment.' His fingers dragged up her nightdress so he could touch her warm vital flesh. The nipple was hard against his palm and as his other hand slid between her legs her arched back told him he'd definitely hit the sweet spot.

'Now, Alessandro. I need you in me now.'

Alessandro's hand stroked in unison. 'Slow down,' he whispered.

Nat shook her head. 'No.' She knew she was ready for him and she rubbed her hot slickness against his rampant hardness. She stretched her arm over her head, slinging it around his neck. 'Now,' she demanded.

Alessandro removed his hand reluctantly from between her legs and guided himself to where she was wet and hot for him. He nudged his head in, angling his hips at the same time she pushed back, and he slid in to the hilt.

Nat cried out at his decisive invasion, revelling in his thickness, his power. He pulled out and thrust in again as he squeezed her breast and she cried out, 'More.'

Alessandro's other hand returned to the wet cleft between her legs, her corresponding whimper travelling straight to his groin. Her hand tightened on his nape as he stroked between her legs and he dropped his head and bit gently along the length of her neck.

Her whimpers grew more frantic as he thrust deeper and stroked harder. Every frenzied noise drove him towards his own release. As she built he built too until she was trembling and clinging to him, crying out. When she shattered around him his own climax was tingling in his loins and surging through his abdominal muscles, rushing up to meet hers seconds later.

'I love you,' he called as the world fell apart around him.

Alessandro's unexpected declaration floated up to her in the surreal surroundings into which she had been flung.

Maybe he hadn't even said it? Maybe her post-feverish brain had just conjured it up in her strangely inert yet somehow gliding state. She let it pass her by, not wanting to interfere with the slow burn of ecstasy fizzing in her blood.

It seemed to take for ever to bump gently back to earth, like feathers on a gentle breeze.

'Nathalie.' Alessandro nuzzled her neck, his hand resting possessively on her hip. 'We need to talk.'

No, she didn't want to hear him trying to backpedal or justify his orgasmic slip. She just wanted to stay cocooned here for a bit longer, his arm around her, his body jammed tight against hers.

'Shh,' she whispered, tucking his arm snugly around her waist. 'Later.'

Then post-coital malaise and post-illness lethargy combined in a potent double whammy and sleep dragged her under.

It was full daylight when Nat next woke. The clock said six-thirty and her bladder was making itself known so she gently moved out of Alessandro's embrace. It was good to feel her legs strong beneath her as she padded to the en suite. Her stomach growled and she actually felt hungry for the first time in two days.

Alessandro's *I love you* played through her head as she used the toilet and then washed her hands. How could it not? She looked at her rather wan reflection, admitting to herself now how much it had hurt. Another pretty lie. Something he'd thought she wanted to hear.

Which she did, of course. But not if he didn't mean it. Not if he didn't feel it.

She steeled herself to go back out. To face him. To

excuse what had happened with a cheery smile and get through the next few days with it firmly plastered on her face. Being ill had sapped her energy. And being angry required more energy than she possessed. She just wanted it to be over now so she could leave and lick her wounds far away from the man who had inflicted them.

He was sitting on the side of the bed, waiting for her when she stepped out of the en suite. Her gaze hungrily ate up his broad shoulders and his long, bare, powerful thighs.

'We need to talk.'

Nat faltered. Wanting to prolong their nearness, to hear his voice but not wanting it at the same time. 'It's okay. You don't have to explain, Alessandro.' She looked at the floor then at the bed then at the bedside clock. 'I'm not going to hold you to anything you might have said in a moment of passion.'

Alessandro caught her wandering gaze and held it. 'I love you.'

Nat shook her head, rejecting his words, the sincerity in his gaze. 'It was a nice thing for you to say but you really didn't have to and I understand where it came from.'

Alessandro prayed for patience. 'I love you,' he said again.

Nat refused to let his words affect her. Rob had said he loved her. So had her father. Neither of them had stuck around. 'No. You're still in love and grieving for your wife. And I remind you of her. I think they call it transference, don't they?'

Alessandro pushed off the bed and stalked two paces to the window, yanking back the curtain. This was the moment of truth. He placed his fists against the window ledge, the persuasive words he'd practised yesterday completely deserting him.

All he had now was the bald truth. 'I didn't love her.'

The silence stretched as Nat tried to figure out what he was talking about. She frowned. Who the hell were they talking about now? 'Who?'

'Camilla. My wife. I didn't love her.' The words he'd kept locked inside for so long were finally out and damn if it didn't feel good. He turned to face her, leaning against the window sill. 'I never loved her.'

Nat blinked. 'What?' But the man she'd first met had been deeply mired in grief.

'You're right,' he admitted. 'You and she are very similar. I was shocked when I first met you. But it took me about two seconds in your company to realise that your physical similarities are where it ends. When I told you that you and she were nothing alike, I was deadly serious.'

Nat wasn't sure if her brain was still sluggish from her illness but she just couldn't take in what he was saying. 'I don't understand.'

'Camilla was my lover. Before we met I was having a fantastic time playing the field. I never planned to marry. You grow up with parents who fought and spent more time apart than together, you don't really see the point…'

Alessandro couldn't believe he'd ever been so stupid. 'She was beautiful and sophisticated, from aristocratic stock. Witty and charming and looked fantastic naked. All the things I looked for in a date. And then she fell pregnant. So I did the honourable thing.'

He paused waiting for the burn of bitter memories. For his internal censor to step in. But neither came.

A first.

'It was a huge society wedding and I was determined to make a real go of it. So, my life hadn't gone exactly ac-

cording to plan but I knew if we worked at it, we coul‹
succeed.'

He shook his head at his naivety. 'Valentino, who, I hav‹
to say, never really liked her anyway, overheard her at th‹
wedding talking to her best friend about how she'd trapped
me. Deliberately fallen pregnant because she'd wanted t‹
marry me. I told him he was mistaken and confronted he‹
about it later, in the honeymoon suite.'

His lips twisted into an ironic smile. 'She admitted it.
She looked straight at me and said, "*But, darling, you
wouldn't have married me otherwise*." It was like the
blinkers had been ripped away from my eyes and I could
finally see the person Val had always seen. The cold, calculating socialite out to marry a doctor.'

Nat watched him closely as Alessandro fell silent, his
matter-of-fact retelling betrayed by the turmoil in his sable
gaze. To say she was horrified was an understatement. 'I
didn't know,' she murmured.

He nodded. 'So I told her it was going to be a marriage
in name only. Which apparently suited her down to the
ground. Initially anyway. So we entered into this strange
existence where we smiled publicly but slept in separate
beds. And then Juliano was born and I was crazily busy at
the hospital, working long hours, and she suddenly realised
being married to a doctor wasn't so glamorous after all.'

He gave a stiff laugh. 'I think she thought I'd give up
the emergency lark and become a Harley St specialist.'

Nat shook her head. She'd known Alessandro for only
a matter of days when she'd realised he was a gifted emergency physician.

'She wanted a divorce. But she wanted me to file.
Couldn't have that stain on her family's reputation. I knew

I'd never see Juliano again if I agreed. As it was, she was already using him to get to me. Don't get me wrong, she was a great mother and they had a close bond but she deliberately alienated him from me. Rationing our already scant time together. Insisting I only speak English with him. And…I let her. I felt guilty about our relationship and it was easier to give in and play by her rules. Juliano was happy and healthy and loved. And work demanded so much of me. It was easier that way. I guess I turned into my father…'

He trailed off and Nat waited for him to start again. She sensed this was something he needed to get off his chest.

'By the time she died, Juliano and I were relative strangers.'

Nat nodded. 'I noticed.' She sat down on the edge of the bed. 'How did she die?'

'A car accident. We'd argued and she'd squealed off in the flash BMW she insisted I buy for her—another guilt gift.'

Nat shut her eyes. No wonder Alessandro had looked so wretched when she'd first met him. He obviously blamed himself for Camilla's death. Guilt and remorse were powerful emotions. 'What did you argue about?'

'The divorce. What else? We didn't argue often, I didn't want that for Juliano. I didn't want him to experience the type of childhood I'd known. It was easier just to give in to her. And Camilla was much too passive-aggressive for it anyway.'

He swallowed, parched from talking and the burn of memories. 'But we rowed that day. I couldn't believe I was in a marriage like my parents'. But Camilla had a way of picking a fight.'

The ugly words taunted him to this day. 'She said she'd

taken a lover and wanted to be free to marry again. I told her over my cold dead body and that I would fight her every inch of the way. Fight her for Juliano. That she'd made her bed and she was just going to have to lie in it.'

He went silent and Nat finished the story for him. 'So she hared off in the car and crashed it?'

Alessandro nodded and her heart went out to him. She rose from the bed and went to his side, leaning her body in to him, pressing a kiss to his shoulder. 'It wasn't your fault, Alessandro.'

'I know that. Rationally, I know that. But…'

Nat nodded, dropping another kiss in the same spot. 'You've been beating yourself up about it anyway?'

Alessandro felt the warmth of her seep into him and he began to hope. 'I looked on it as my punishment. For insisting on a marriage on paper only and then for keeping her in the marriage. A marriage neither of us wanted. If I'd only forgiven her and gone on from there. Tried to make a real go of it instead of drawing the battle lines right from the start. But I was proud and angry.'

'It must have been hard.'

Yes, it had. But, then, a lot of it had been his doing.

'So you see,' he said, looking down at her, 'I don't deserve to have love, to find love. That's why I fought these feelings for you for so long. Because this isn't supposed to be my lot. And then I saw Juliano in bed with you yesterday. You were asleep and he was stroking your head and telling you he wanted you to be his mummy and he loved you and you murmured, "I love you too," and I realised that right in front of me was my whole world. You and him.'

Nat didn't remember Juliano being in bed with her but

smiled at the picture Alessandro painted. Her heart started to beat crazily as his words sank in. She wanted to believe him. But she was burned and wary.

She looked up and captured his gaze. 'I just can't get her picture out of my head.'

'I know. I should have told you earlier but I honestly didn't notice the resemblance after being in your company for just a few seconds. You were obviously like chalk and cheese.'

He lifted a finger and stroked it down her face. 'It's you I want. And not because you look like Camilla. Because you're Nat. Nathalie. Our Nat. Funny and down to earth and kind and generous and sexy, and you gave me back my son, you gave me back Juliano, and you opened my heart enough to see that maybe I do deserve a chance at love. Real love for the first time in my life.'

Nat's chest bloomed with an outpouring of the love that she'd kept firmly in check since she'd blurted it out. 'Of course you do, Alessandro. We all do.'

Alessandro saw the compassion in her gaze and dared to hope. 'Does this mean I haven't destroyed everything you felt for me?' he asked.

She smiled up at him, her heart skipping in her chest. She slipped her palm up to cradle his cheek. 'Of course not. I love you, Alessandro. I can't turn that off and on. It's a fact of life. It's who I am.'

She raised herself up on tiptoe and pressed her mouth to his. 'I will always love you.'

Alessandro grinned for the first time since he'd started talking. Then he picked her up, ignoring her squeal, and threw her in the centre of the mattress. 'So you'll stay,' he said, climbing on the bed and lying beside her on his stomach, propped up on his elbows. 'For ever and ever.

And you'll marry me and have brothers and sisters for Juliano?'

She put her arms around his neck. 'Yes, I'll stay. Yes, I'll marry you. And, yes, I'll have brothers and sisters for Juliano.' She pulled him down to seal it with a kiss. 'You want to start now?'

Alessandro grinned. 'I thought we did that already.'

A noise at the door had them both breaking apart as Juliano eyed them. 'Is Nat better now?'

Alessandro grinned at his son. 'She sure is. And guess what?' he said, gesturing Juliano over. He grabbed his son's hand and pulled him onto the bed with them. 'Nat's staying. For ever.'

Juliano's eyes grew large in his head as he looked from his father to Nat and back to his father. 'Really? Are you going to be my mummy?'

Nat beamed at him. 'Would you like that?'

'Oh, yeah! That'd be the best thing ever,' he said enthusiastically, bouncing up and down on his haunches.

Alessandro couldn't have agreed more. 'Well said, matey.' He grinned as he grabbed Juliano and lifted him in the air above his head, tickling him with his fingers, boyish laughter filling the room.

Nat laughed too as Juliano giggled and begged his father to stop. She pinched herself. She was really a part of all this. She couldn't remember every being this deliriously happy.

It couldn't get any better than this.

But it did.